THE TREE

A NOVEL

*Tragic and Triumphant Tales
of the Human Soul*

R.D.K. MARJORAM

First published in the United Kingdom in 2026 by

The Choir Press

ISBN 978-1-78963-571-3

THE TREE

A NOVEL

DISCLAIMER

This is a work of fiction. Names, characters, places, events, and incidents are either products of the author's imagination or are used in a fictitious manner.

Any resemblance to actual persons, living or dead, or actual events is purely coincidental.

The narrative explores emotional and psychological themes that are universal and representative of human experience but should not be interpreted as referencing any specific individual or real-life situation, but may be inspired by the author's own personal experiences.

DEDICATION

For the lost, the lonely, the despairing and the frightened: you are stronger than you know, your shadow and your light can co-exist, you are not alone ... and I for one am glad that you are in the world!

I hope this story strengthens your roots to keep you from falling; reminds you to decorate your branches in whatever way makes you happy, and is a reminder for you to face the inevitable storms of life knowing that spring always follows winter, such is the cycle of life.

And to my husband Teddy, my cats, my family and my friends – thank you for everything that you do, and all that you are ... the world is wonderful place simply because you are in it.

CHAPTERS

PROLOGUE:
Aftermath

H eavy rain enveloped the valley like a fog. A torrential downpour cleansed and purified the terror that had befallen The Tree and the valley on that fateful Halloween night, at the end of the first quarter of the twenty-first century. Five lives had been claimed that night.

The large continuous drops of water quenched the unforgiving flames that had torn through The Tree's branches and trunk – extinguishing the fierce rage and vengeance that had erupted from within its soul.

The rain created a beautiful fresh and crisp aroma, which emanated from the grass and surrounding forests. It was mixed with the powerful scent of burnt wood … and blood. The last remnants of smoke could be seen swirling into the sky from the top of the hill, where an enormous tree – most of which was now charred from the fire – towered above the valley. Its vein-like and leafless branches reached upwards like blackened lightning – a monstrous silhouette against the deep grey and purple sky.

All evidence of the tragedy and bloodshed that had befallen the hilltop and valley was washed away by the fresh rain. But the poisonous remnants of the horror seeped deep into the earth where no beauty would flourish for several years thereafter. Some of the broken bodies remained and were not so easily removed by the purifying rain. But this was not the first time that this particular site of natural beauty had witnessed – or indeed participated – in death.

1

The Tree's lower branches had warped and created a domed mesh of hardened vines that resembled a cage. And inside this cage was a beaten, lifeless body. The Tree feared that the man had not survived his injuries from the previous night ... but lovingly cradled him in its arms, as the dawn greeted that first morning in November before the rain came. It would not give up on him! But The Tree's soul ached and was shattered. It had no more tears left to weep. The Tree's soul was sick and dying – its inner torment and regret giving way to apathy ... and ultimately a desire for death.

In a final desperate act, The Tree willed the blackened branches that protected its charge to spread wide one last time, as tiny white flowers grew in seconds on its fragile limbs. With a shudder and a swish, a cascade of jasmine petals fell like snow on to the body in an act of love and lamentation. But this gift of compassion and generosity expended too much of The Tree's already depleted essence.

Filled with shame and guilt, The Tree's soul shut down. And as it did so, a dark wave emanated from its heart. It shimmered through its branches and its roots – permeating the mountainous hill which held it aloft, and the heavy air that now surrounded it.

The once beautiful colours that painted the valley and the myriad sounds of wildlife that had once been carried on the wind (enchanting so many visitors over the years) began to fade and disappear.

The valley fell silent.

The Tree's soul collapsed.

And without entirely knowing why, the world became a much darker and sorrowful place because of it.

***

This is a story about the life of a tree. Not just any tree, but a magical tree – an ancient being with a wise and kind soul. A tree with consciousness. This is a tree who bears witness to the miracle of the human soul with its suffering and despair but also its joys, triumphs, healing and growth. The Tree would be touched by the stories that people shared as they came to visit it over the years, and would impart wisdom and meaning to guide us all through the darkness.

This is a tree that possesses amongst its branches twelve powerful silver limbs, hidden amongst its canopy of leaves. And in different ways, these sacred parts of The Tree would come to save the lives of a select few who shared their stories within the stone circle – a select few who came to rely on The Tree for its kindness, its love, its understanding ... and its protection.

The Tree feels love ... it experiences joy ... it experiences excitement. And it has faith. Faith that healing is possible ... even from the most harrowing of experiences. But it also shares in the shadow and losses. And grieves with the people that it comes to love over the years.

But like anything with a soul, when we see the truth and feel powerless to change it, we too can fall into fear, desperation, rage, and despair. We can lose sight of that which is good and succumb to darkness ... a shadow that we all carry within. The Tree came to know that for life to be in balance, there must be good and evil. Joy and sorrow ... and everything in between. But like all of us, The Tree was not immune to the impact that these stories would have on its own soul.

The Tree would be profoundly moved but also haunted by all that it bore witness to ... and this is its story! The Tree would discover that for it to have branches that could reach up to heaven, it would need to cultivate roots that clawed down into hell. There could be no light without the dark. No healing without sacrifice. And no vengeance without redemption.

So, what happened to The Tree on that fateful night in the October? What events led to such tragedy and ultimately its fall from grace? And how did this particular tree come to have a soul?

Well, this last question is still a mystery. But it may have something to do with where it was first planted and the circumstances of its birth.

To understand The Tree and its journey, we must first go back to the beginning and watch its life unfold ...

PART ONE

CHAPTER ONE
January: Life

I

It was a cold and bleak day in January – New Year's Day. The year is not important but suffice to say it was many years ago. As one would expect from an early January day, the sky was heavy with thick grey cloud. A light misty rain was sweeping across the landscape – threatening to become heavier. A mountainous hill could be seen rising in the distance – a rather imposing mound, upon which was a circle of stones. This was a place of spiritual power, and one frequently visited by those who held true to the religions that revere nature. It was a place of both beauty and serenity, a place of comfort and soothing for so many in the past ... and would come to be so for so many more in the future.

The mood of the day was sombre, as were the events that were just about to unfold. A huddle of people emerged from the nearby forest and braced themselves against the elements. The figures were dressed in dark clothes and the sound of weeping could be heard amidst the wailing wind. The figure leading this group was holding a small wooden box. A tiny coffin big enough to hold a child who had not long entered this world ... and had departed it as quickly as they had entered. Sadly, such tragedies were not uncommon during the time when this scene took place but the enormity of such losses are universal and transcend time. Loss is loss and the pain caused by such tragedy endures. However, no one knew – certainly not the small child – just how important their role would be in the events that would unfold.

Towards the back of the procession another robed (but much smaller figure) held the early beginnings of a tree. Its roots wrapped in fresh earth – contained in a small cloth sack that had been tightly wound around the damp earth and roots to protect it on its journey. Its trunk was no more than an inch thick. Its tiny leafless branches reached up and outwards, hoping to catch any glimmer of light and nourishment that the world could offer. But at this moment in time, The Tree was just a tree. It didn't know where it belonged or what its future held. All it wanted for now was to survive. It could feel the droplets of water in the atmosphere. It could sense the river and its power. And it heard the creaking of its fellow trees as the wind and rain lashed them on this cold January morning.

The funeral procession walked slowly through the elements, crossed the river at the foot of the hill, and made their way carefully across the stepping stones. Once safely on the other side of the river they began their ascent of the hill, journeying towards the sacred circle of stones.

The view from the top of the hill was breath-taking. Even amongst the mourners, their awe could not be hidden. The dark clouds extended across vast landscapes of mountains and hills, and the river below snaked through the base of the hill and into the forest where the mourners had emerged. One side of the hill was characterised by a sheer and treacherous drop – much less accommodating than the gentle incline that the mourners had traversed. From their new vantage point, they could see their village in the distance … a reminder of how far they had come but how far they still must go. This latter journey would be one of grief and healing, and one not so easily traversed as simply crossing fields in the rain.

Once all of the mourners had safely gathered at the top of the hill, they spread out around the circle. The leader of this particular clan walked slowly around the circle and touched each of the stones whilst whispering some words of prayer and blessings. The mourners echoed these whisperings just as quietly.

The head of the clan positioned themselves in the centre of the circle of stones and mourners, and raised both of their hands above their head towards the sky. The mourners fell silent, as did the wind and the rain. For a moment it was as though time had stopped. All that could be heard was the sound of the river below and the gentle hum of the earth.

The elder of the clan began to sing. His low voice matching the hum of the earth and its energy. The mourners joined in – their chants rising up into the sky. As the singing became louder, the elder lit a fire in the centre of the circle. A strange blend of ingredients were cast into the flames, creating strange and beautiful scents, as well as seeming to fuel the fire despite its damp surroundings.

As the fire eventually burned low – its embers emitting a comforting orange glow – so did the chants and singing of the mourners. Members of the group came forward and where the fire had been, they began to dig. The ashes and upturned earth blended together as the mourners, using both rocks and their own hands, dug down into the hill – the richness of the damp soil and its scent filling their nostrils.

At last, there was a hole deep enough to contain the precious cargo that they had carried from the village. The mother and the father now emerged from the group, holding the tiny coffin. With tenderness and a heavy heart, the mother bent down and gently lay the box containing her child into the earth. The howl that emerged from her mouth came from the deepest wound within her soul. A wound that no words or kindness could ever soothe. It is the wound of a mother who has lost a child, the pain of which can never truly find peace. The echoes of her sobs rippled through the mourners, and indeed across the land itself.

The father placed his arms around his wife as he silently wept. She felt his strong arms around her and for a moment felt safe – believing that someone would have the strength to prevent her from falling into the abyss of her despair and grief. She turned and embraced him … they wept together for everything that was and for everything that would never be.

As they pulled back from the grave, the remaining mourners came forwards. Fruit that they had grown, herbs and flowers that they had cultivated, and stones carved with various symbols were just as lovingly and gently lowered on to the coffin. As the earth was piled back into the grave and covered its precious contents, a small girl – the child's sister – came forth with the small tree and lastly removed the sack covering its roots before planting it on her brother's grave.

As she did so, the sweetness of her voice began to sing, accompanied by her parents and the mourners. And as they did so the dawn broke through the clouds. Light and colour seeping through the grey – the first glimpse of hope on a sad winter's day.

Led by the village elder, the mother, the father, the sister, and the mourners departed this sacred place. The ritual was complete. Now their journey of grief and healing could begin. They made their way down the slopes of the hill, back across the river, and into the forest as they returned to their village. Whilst the villagers would return to this place many times, their story ends here.

As the villagers faded from sight, something strange began to happen. Something that has never happened to a tree before. Not only was this tree alive, as all trees are, this particular tree upon the hill, in the centre of the sacred circle, began to stir ...

The small tree felt a tingling in its roots. It was as though an electrical current was pulsating through its entire being. It could feel its trunk and branches stretching and thickening – reaching higher and wider, grasping for air and light. And that was another thing ... light!

Darkness gave way to light and colour, shape and form. The Tree knew that it didn't have eyes, but it could still see. The Tree could see everything. It could feel everything. As it tuned into these sensations, The Tree felt deep down into its roots and the precious box that they had wrapped themselves round. But it also felt the tunnelling of its roots deep down into the earth of the hill upon which it stood. Not only could The Tree hear the sound of rushing water from the river below, it could actually feel the river, as though they too were connected. The Tree could hear the sound of the gentle wind, the rustle of trees, the birds in the sky, and the myriad animals that lived in the surrounding grasslands and forests. The aliveness of the valley mirrored the aliveness of The Tree's emerging soul.

The Tree had knowledge of things that it could not possibly know. The Tree had a soul, consciousness ... it was alive. It could feel its fellow trees, plants, and flowers nearby ... but it could also sense that it was not like them. Whilst they too were teeming with life, they did not have a soul. The Tree knew what a soul was because one had been buried beneath it – one that had not had chance to fully live his life and impact the world. The Tree had flashes of memories of being placed in the ground. Of the beautiful singing. Of the heartbreak and sorrow. The Tree knew that life was a gift but that such a gift and the cost of loving a human life can feel like a terrible price when that life is then stolen.

Throughout these moments of reflection, The Tree continued to grow. It realised that it wasn't like other trees because it could grow so fast. The Tree also knew that it could change. Change its appearance, change its shape, change its smell, and even the flowers and blossoms that would bloom amongst its leaves. The Tree realised that the seasons (yes, it knew about the seasons) would not change it. It could learn from other trees but could also choose what it wanted to be. The Tree knew that people are unique. That their souls were as unique as The Tree was. And sometimes to be able to care and support others in the deepest and darkest hours of need, The Tree would need to change and become what people needed in that moment. It knew this because this was how its life had begun. It was a reminder to the villagers that life is precious and does not last forever but from death can spring new life.

Amongst The Tree's branches, twelve silver limbs had started to grow. These branches hummed with power ... a power that The Tree would not come to understand until much later on in its life when these branches would change the life trajectory of a select group of individuals who came to have a profound impact on the very soul of The Tree.

The Tree now beheld the circle of stones that surrounded it. It was curious what power these smooth and sometimes jagged but imposing rocks might have ... and indeed the influence this would have on those who stepped into the circle and leaned against the hard body of The Tree. It could feel the shimmer of energy that was contained within the circle ... the gentle hum and vibration of the earth's very soul. The Tree knew that if it tried hard enough, it could connect to this soul and know life beyond its home on top of the hill and surrounding valley. But this didn't feel important just yet. Instead, it simply enjoyed the feel of its branches as they continued to unfurl into the sky. It enjoyed swaying in the breeze and the rustling of its leaves as it did so. Leaves which it could shake off or regrow on a whim.

And the animals. How curious The Tree was about the animals. And equally their curiosity towards The Tree. The Tree loved these strange yet beautiful creatures that would explore the stone circle and gingerly approach The Tree over the years. Some finding sanctuary in its branches, or the shade that it provided. Or protection from the rain and wind. Some even found home deep within its roots through tunnels and holes that gave a refuge from predators but also the safety for creating new life. This miracle of love and birth both astonished and overjoyed The Tree.

It found its soul weeping with joy at the birth of rabbits and fox cubs, the hatching of birds from their eggs, the swarms of bees on their journeys of pollination and the giving of life, despite their small size. But equally The Tree knew heartbreak as the creatures that it came to love would also experience loss. Being hunted by other animals, hunted by humans, or sometimes simply dying because of the conditions for life not being right. The Tree knew the inevitability of impermanence but with each birth, each life, each triumph that it witnessed, it allowed itself to know the sorrow of pain and loss because one cannot exist without the other. The Tree knew that to be truly alive it would witness and experience countless emotions. It would bear witness to a world of new experiences and where possible, hold and nurture those who needed it the most.

Time did not seem to impact The Tree. Having come to full maturity so quickly it was able to remain and appear like that of a fully grown ancient tree. Equally it knew that it could alter its appearance at will depending on what the occasion – or indeed the person – needed. But The Tree was conscious of the passing of time by the months and accompanying seasons. With each year that passed it felt its soul and wisdom grow. It could learn and adapt to the everchanging world that it was part of. With each January that came and went, The Tree gave thanks for its existence. It knew that in the world of humans they celebrated this as a birthday. The Tree was glad to be in the world and would speak to the wind, the rain, the sun, and the earth and give thanks for whatever miracle had brought it into consciousness and into the existence.

The Tree liked that it had been born in January. As the month that starts the year, The Tree felt that this was symbolic. It also knew that this could a difficult month for many because of the long cold and somewhat gloomy days. The Tree did not find such days gloomy or hopeless though. In fact, it reminded itself that during this darker month that there was opportunity for reflection. To take stock of the learning that had come from the months before, as well as giving thanks for the darkness, the frost, the snow, and the rain – all the ways that the elements nourished the earth.

The Tree also knew that after every January, life continued. Light would return as would life that can seem so absent in nature during this month. The animals would hibernate. Very few people would visit. But the solitude during this time felt necessary and kind for The Tree. It reflected on the wisdom that it acquired with every passing year, and the triumph of the human soul in the face of tragedy and adversity.

The Tree would sometimes mirror the other trees and shake loose all of its leaves in the heart of winter. It would marvel at the weird and wonderful shapes that its branches could make and their silhouette against the sky. The Tree felt dazzled as the morning dew clung to the intricate spider webs that hung in the most magnificent and curious patterns between its branches. And the even more striking beauty as the temperature dropped to freezing thus creating an enchanting spectacle of nature's magic. On days where the wind howled, the rain thrashed, and the sky was a deep and heavy grey, The Tree was reminded of the day that it was born and would allow its branches to once more be covered by leaves. It would sway dramatically in time with the wind, and shake loose a flurry of blossom within the circle of stones, creating the illusion of a snow-like blanket, infused with scents of lavender and rose.

During other years, The Tree would simply be still. On those rare January days where the sky was blue and the weather crisp, The Tree would simply gaze into the horizon marvelling at the mountains, hills, forests, and lakes ... all with the sparkle of frost that painted the landscape like a fairytale. At other times, the hill upon which The Tree stood would be covered in a thick blanket of snow – the clouds softly releasing a flurry of ice that once settled gave the valley an even deeper silence as the remaining sound was absorbed. The Tree basked in these quiet and unspoilt days. Nature simply being nature and The Tree enjoying these moments of solitude and beauty, calm, and peace. The Tree was a patient observer, not seeking itself nor the valley to be anything other than it was. It embraced change rather than resisting it, and in doing so felt its soul settle.

The Tree knew its past and could feel the present ... but it could not know the future. It did, however, have faith. Faith that its very existence would bring some kind of joy and healing to whomever braved the climbing of the hill to cross the stone circle, to take refuge under the safety of The Tree's branches and leafy canopy and feel the sturdiness of its trunk against their back during moments of fragility and vulnerability, unable to support themselves.

As one of the many Januarys in The Tree's life came to an end, it gazed up into the clear winter night sky. A waxing crescent moon hung amidst the myriad constellations and the far-off glow of the planets that the naked human-eye could barely see. The Tree felt grateful for this nightly spectacle – a privilege to behold and feel part of nature's beauty. There was a comforting chill in the air but The Tree's soul burned with warmth and love. Without knowing it, The Tree was about to embark on an adventure that would allow it to glimpse into the minds, hearts, and souls of humanity ... a journey that would leave The Tree forever changed, and not always in the ways that it expected.

II

As one particular month of January neared its end, The Tree found itself contemplating the echoes of its past. Not just its own birth, but also the history of the hill that its body, branches, and roots now occupied. Having marvelled at the splendour and brilliance of nature, and growing to love all the creatures that had blessed it with their presence over the years, The Tree felt a sense of foreboding. A shadow that lurked within the heart of the earth where its own roots buried into. It not only witnessed and felt the pain and sorrow of loss ... it also glimpsed cruelty. And not the instinctive cruelty that could be observed amongst the beasts and insects, the birds, or the creatures of the sea as they fight for their survival. No, this was a darker force that lurked in the hearts of humanity.

The Tree allowed itself to attune to the energies of the hilltop upon which it stood, hoping to procure a vision of the world that it had been born into. As it did so, an unfamiliar sensation overcame The Tree. A fog enveloped The Tree's mind, and the valley and hilltop seemed to dissolve as The Tree found its consciousness being transported back through time, allowing it to bear witness to a scene that unbeknownst to The Tree would shape its perception of life on this planet, and all those who inhabited it.

As the fog cleared, The Tree heard the raucous screams of the blood-thirsty mob. Their taunts and jeers unsettled The Tree, so unaccustomed was it to the screams for violence against ones fellow human being. It felt chilled to its soul as four people – two men, and two women – dressed in torn and muddied clothes, were dragged through the crowd, their limbs bound and their mouths gagged with rags as filthy as the garments they wore. Toothless and snarling villagers hurled rotten fruit and vegetables in their direction whilst hissing obscenities through their snarling, salivating mouths. Men, women and children all participated in this vile spectacle, the parents sometimes goading their children, and other times the children simply mirroring what they observed. A feeling of uncontained abhorrence, disgust and pure animosity swelled within the crowd. It was visceral.

Compassion and a desire to intervene filled The Tree as it watched the scene unfold … but The Tree – much like the paralysed and fearful members of the crowd – could do nothing to save these four poor wretched souls. Souls who had been condemned to death for crimes that as yet remained an unknown to The Tree. It saw the terror frozen on their tear-streaked faces, and the unmistakeable sorrow in their eyes as they knew their fate … but also the fate of the people that they loved.

The Tree gleaned from their hearts that these four people were kind souls. Souls who loved and worshipped nature. That they shared a love for each other that was without restriction, that defied convention … and was forbidden during these times. The possibility that four people could experience such love and physical affection for each other outside of the sanctity of marriage, and that man could love man, woman could love woman, and all four could love each other, was simply unthinkable. But it was not their love and expressions of intimacy that they were explicitly on trial for, although The Tree suspected that this may be at the root of their persecution. No, the charges announced by the self-proclaimed 'witchfinder' were of witchcraft and making pacts with the devil. The Tree saw that the witchfinder was a pale and gaunt man with robes as black as obsidian, a dark wide-brimmed hat, and a face etched with decades of persecution and hatred. He seemed possessed of power beyond measure as he clutched an ancient-looking tome – thick with the pages that brought accusations of witchcraft, devil worship, and wrongdoing. And this powerful book, held by a powerful man, incited a mixture of fear, envy, and disdain towards the four tragic captives.

With a deep and bold voice, the pale man who resembled an angel of death cast his dark and bitter judgement upon the four – two of whom now had been bound to long wooden stakes planted firmly in the centre of the very stone circle that had once been so delicately placed on the top of the stunning hill in harmony with the elements of the breath-taking valley. As the witchfinder preached on ... and on ... and on ... various villagers scuttled around the imprisoned, laying wood at their feet in preparation for the next wave of suffering and torture that would be induced. The victims were known to the villagers – and were once friends to many of those who dwelt there. Mari and Eleanor, Davyd and Krayg were condemned to death for their 'crimes against nature'. For their heresy and pacts with the spirits of the dead. For their alleged frolicking with the devil himself, and for their use of unnatural means to both heal and harm the other villagers through their magic and trickery – all clear violations of the natural laws under God.

As part of their punishment, the wicked man announced triumphantly that they would be forced to watch their respective partner's execution ... though it was not entirely clear to the crowd which partner belonged to whom. Nevertheless, their hunger for bloodshed grew – so eager were they for the witches to be burned ... for their own abominable sins to be denied and projected on to the doomed foursome, thus absolving them of the most hidden and hated parts of themselves.

The Tree looked on in horror but came to know a truth. That human beings will turn on each other if it means saving their own lives. That they will watch whilst atrocities occur because they do not see themselves as having the power to change things ... or even the desire to. That they are afraid that to stand up for the other, if it means death and persecution being drawn to themselves instead.

The Tree came to know that they could be capable of the most heinous atrocities in the name of a hallowed deity, or their own fanatical beliefs, or simply because of their denial and hatred for the otherness of the other – for the freedom of mind, of thought, of love that people have the capability of experiencing and sharing ... but only if the powerful deem it not to be a threat.

The Tree observed the onlookers as they cheered and goaded for the fellow men and women – once friends to them all – to be humiliated, punished ... and burned alive. How quickly they forgot the help they had received from their friends in the past, the herbs and elixirs that had eased their childbirths and had remedied their illnesses. The rituals that had brought an abundance of healthy crops to the village, thanks to the perfect blend of weather that was summoned, which gave rise to new life.

Yes, how quickly they were to forget the times that they had begged these four gentle and kind souls for help. For comfort. For advice. For their knowledge and wisdom of the stars and rhythms of nature. For spells to bring them love and luck, and prosperity. For medicinal potions and concoctions that brought about good health. How they had secretly yearned to be part of the sacred rites that took place under the soft glow of the moon, as the four witches danced naked around the flames, chanting and calling forth the elements and spirits, and making love to each other in a final explosive release of power and energy into the cosmos.

The Tree was sad in its heart because it knew that the mob was afraid. Afraid of themselves and afraid of what they did not understand. But also afraid of difference ... of those who had the courage to defy convention, as perhaps they themselves longed to do. And they were afraid of the witchfinder and others like him who sought to control and deceive, and exert their power through force and violence ... and ultimately fear.

As the last words of condemnation were uttered, Mari and Davyd were forced to their knees a few metres in front of their beloved Elenor and Krayg. Their eyes locked and a silent prayer passed between them. The Tree could feel their love for each other but also the resignation to their fate. And in doing so, The Tree felt something awaken within itself as it saw the souls of the coven connect. A strange calm befell the four of them, as though they had slipped into a deep trance. The hungry mob of course had not noticed, so consumed were they for the sin and danger to be destroyed and cast from their village – not knowing that their own souls would be forever contaminated by their actions, and in some case inaction, to save the very people who had enabled their lives to thrive.

The two pyres were lit and burst into flames as the crowd erupted in sickening cheers. A fiery inferno licked at the feet and clothes of the condemned, but their faces remained passive and calm. Their counterparts returned from their trance-like state and roared through their gags. Tears stung their eyes and adrenaline surged as they desperately tried to free themselves from their binds and captors, only to be kicked to the ground and forced back onto their knees once more to bear witness to the atrocious injustice before them.

Through the black smoke that encircled the now burning bodies and the grotesque smell of sizzling flesh, the witchfinder smiled triumphantly. The crowd continued their jeers and roars of approval until their frenzied excitement turned to primitive and savage rage. They wanted more … and like a vicious pack of wolves they set upon the two remaining prisoners, beating and tearing at them with anything their wicked hands could procure.

The Tree felt pain for its fallen comrades. It roared with rage at the cruelty and cowardice of the villagers. And a part of it sought vengeance and justice upon all those who stood by and did nothing on the hilltop. But The Tree also knew that it was a peaceful soul … that it was different from the hateful mob and the cruel, dangerous witchfinder.

However, when a final scream and curse echoed from the mouths of the four dying witches, something remarkable happened. As their souls left their bodies, their blood, burned flesh, and ashes seeped into the heart of the hilltop, and another wail joined The Tree's … the wail of a ferocious wind. A wind that brought with it a violent and terrible storm that lashed the hilltop, quelling the flames and embers, and washed the remains of the condemned deeper into the earth of the stone circle … earth that The Tree's roots now took nourishment from.

As the storm raged, particles of ice formed in the chilled January air and further assaulted the fleeing and screaming villagers. The flash of lightning and accompanying growling rumbles of thunder forced people to their knees as they prayed to their own God for forgiveness … forgiveness that would never come, so cursed would their souls forever be. Rocks and debris from the hilltop swirled within a monstrous cloud that further assaulted the fleeing villagers who scattered from the hilltop seeking refuge in the valley below.

The Tree witnessed the intriguing spectacle with awe.

As the storm eased, it left behind a scattering of trampled and wounded bodies – the cruel witchfinder being one of them. His precious book – a book that had brought persecution and death to so many kind and misunderstood souls on this hilltop – now lay torn and trampled. The pages were stained the blood of his head wound, the consequence of a single small but powerful rock hurled mercilessly by the wind of the conjured storm. A rock that brought death.

As the remaining villagers scattered from the scene of unspeakable crime and injustice, The Tree noticed its compassion retuning for those who had been slain as it surveyed the bleak scene. It knew the desire to deny and hide the part of it that had felt relief … relief that even in their dying moments the four victims had rallied in their strength to bring about some form of destruction and retribution to those who had betrayed and sacrificed them. The Tree was not proud of this part of itself and vowed to keep this part hidden.

The storm finally abated, giving way to a soft and crisp powder blue sky, and so too did The Tree's conflict, shame, and self-doubt. It had witnessed the courage of the four captives and made a promise to itself that it would empower and inspire the same courage in all those who visited the hilltop in the future. That it too would not watch and do nothing, but instead would inspire, guide, and ultimately bestow love on its visitors. And teach them how to forgive. How to heal. And how to grow.

It was this very glimpse into the origins of its own existence that stirred something powerful within The Tree as the echoes of the ghastly scene dissolved and its consciousness returned to the hilltop and valley, where it was very firmly in existence. The Tree felt desire – a desire to change … a desire to influence … a desire to protect … and a powerful need to provide safety to all those who were vulnerable. The Tree vowed to itself that this hilltop would be reclaimed. That it would no longer be a place of punishment and pain, betrayal and death, but instead a place of sanctuary and compassion for all those who were lost, lonely, frightened, and abused.

And so came the first necessary sacrifice of one of The Tree's silver limbs.

The Tree could sense its own power but did not yet understand or know its extent. It did, however, know in its heart that this was to become a sacred space. A wonderous space that would give rise to the innermost thoughts, fantasies, and hopes and fears of all those who visited. That the stone circle would become enchanted by the silver branch, and thus become a place of safety and containment that would facilitate trust and openness, and allow The Tree to support and guide. That animals and humans alike would find sanctuary in this place of spiritual power.

And so, The Tree drew upon the essence of its first silver branch – after all, what did it mean to lose one when eleven still remained?

The branch hummed and glowed, and eventually dissolved … its power and spirit being drawn into the body of The Tree, and deep down into its roots. A golden shimmer rippled through the earth, blessing the hilltop, the stone circle … and all who would brave the journey to speak with The Tree.

And so, without knowing why, all those who entered the stone circle and met The Tree would become enchanted by the ancient magic that now possessed this unusual place of natural beauty, and would willingly share their stories.

III

Over the years, The Tree bore witness to numerous curious fables and memories, and both weird and wonderful, strange and enchanting people over its many years of life. The Tree's stories follow the months of the year and span several years of its life.

The Tree was humbled as it shared some of the most secret and precious moments of its visitors lives. It was also deeply saddened as it bore witness to human atrocities throughout the world. It saw the rise and fall of empires, told through the stories of survivors. It heard from grieving widows of the genocides committed throughout the planet – genocides that claimed entire families and loved ones, with the storytellers only narrowly escaping themselves.

It heard the confessions of the those who witness wars and crimes against humanity and did nothing, much like its observations of the villagers on the hilltop. But The Tree also felt their fear, their powerlessness, and their need to deny the truth … because sometimes the truth is just too intolerable, and to know the truth means to fight. But sometimes to fight means the risk of dying.

The Tree sympathised with their bind, whilst holding contempt for those who lied and murdered without care or conscience. And given that it was a tree with consciousness, conscience, and indeed a soul, how could it not become deeply impacted by what it heard and saw? Unlike its passive cousins across the valley, The Tree found itself becoming more deeply involved and connected to the people who shared their tales. Some of whom it came to love … and some whom it came to despise. The Tree experienced love, faith, courage, and compassion, but by opening its soul to the beauty of human experience, it was just as open to feeling as lost, hopeless, and despairing as the people who shared their stories.

What follows are some of the most significant stories of tragedy and triumph that The Tree came to experience throughout its precious life. Stories that facilitated its rise … but also its inevitable fall from grace. From the moment of its birth, The Tree knew it had a calling … but it did not yet know the cost of caring so profoundly.

CHAPTER TWO
February: Courage

I

S everal years had passed since the birth of The Tree. It had seen the landscape change, the villages become towns, and the growth of the communities within. From its high place upon the hill, The Tree surveyed the beauty of the valley that it was blessed to be part of. It welcomed the numerous visitors who came to admire its size, its sturdiness, and both the comfort and shelter that it provided. And in doing so, it felt its soul sing and grow. The Tree came to love the people who leaned against its trunk and spoke to it about their lives, their hopes, their dreams, but also their fears.

Over the years, The Tree continued to marvel at curious phenomenon that when people entered the stone circle and leaned against the sturdiness of its wide and comforting trunk, they could not help but speak their truth, even when this truth may have felt confusing, frightening, and even forbidden to the person. Thanks to the magic of its first silver branch, there was something about The Tree that the people could not help but trust and feel held and contained by. Visitors beheld its presence and calmness with reverence, and unburdened themselves with their stories. And in doing so, something shifted within their own soul, allowing them to move forward with their lives with greater wisdom, clarity, and self-compassion. The Tree suspected that this may have something to do with the sacrifice of its first silver branch all those years ago and the aura of safety that this gave to the stone circle, and indeed, The Tree itself.

Over the years, The Tree had come to associate this particular month with the emotion of love. In this part of the world, The Tree had observed all sorts of rituals that the gatherers engaged in as they expressed their feelings of love and affection for one another. Despite its fellow trees still hibernating because of the tail-end of winter, The Tree drew upon its immense power to decorate itself with blossom of the most beautiful shades of red and pink. It also called upon the roses – a particularly favourite flower for these kinds of expressions of love – to burst forth and surround the stone circle. The scent was enchanting and even the presence of the thorny vines, whilst sufficiently tamed and close to the ground so as to not cause harm, seemed to give the circle and The Tree a sense of protection as well as beauty.

The Tree knew that love, beauty, and also pain cannot be disentangled and that those who are naïve to this truth feel the affliction of loss with even greater severity, as they cannot hold on to both the good, the bad, and everything that manifests in between. The Tree tried to teach people about the presence of both the good and the bad, that neither has to cancel the other out – that both can exist in harmony if we are able to accept these seemingly opposing concepts. Within this can be a sense of peace where all encounters with other sentient beings can be a precious gift because of the teachings they provide, and of course the moments of love that are shared.

Sometimes The Tree would take great pleasure in releasing a flurry of petals onto the gatherers below or simply shake off and observe the petals as they were lifted by the wind and carried by the breeze down the side of the hill in swirls and arcs, gently settling in the river below. The carpet of petals rippling in the water combined with the sparkle of the sun created a most hypnotic display. In this part of the world, the weather was so changeable that no February was the same. The Tree revelled in this and would enjoy being thrashed by the elements, whether these be fierce rainstorms, the chill of heavy snow, or a still and mild day where The Tree would gently dance and sway in silence, and bask in the warm rays of golden sunshine. Sometimes it branches were bare like its fellow trees, other times lush and green with leaves, and other times decorated with an assortment of coloured blossoms to suit the mood of The Tree, and the desires of the gatherers below.

II

One mild February morning, The Tree woke to the sound of two giggling children – The Tree assumed to be late primary school age – who were playing within the stone circle. Their parents were no doubt close by on another part of the hill. The Tree knew about schools as places where children go to learn and grow, and hopefully become kind and well-educated human beings. The Tree often felt befuddled when it heard about the subjects that were taught ... The Tree wondered why lessons on kindness, compassion, empathy, and love towards one's fellow human beings were not deemed to be important. The Tree also wondered why these small human beings were being made to feel like they only had worth because of how well they did in these buildings where such lessons were being taught. From what The Tree had experienced already in its life, it had come to marvel at the uniqueness of each human being, celebrating their joy and creativity but also their depth of soul. Why were children not being celebrated for this, The Tree wondered.

As a reward for the creativity of the two children giggling in its presence, The Tree spoke to the roses and asked two of them to grow to an unusual size for such flowers, and to change their colour from red to violet. The children of course noticed such an absurd contrast in the flowers as they ran around the circle and squealed with delight as they approached them. Instinctively they both turned to The Tree and asked if they could take the flowers.

How curious, thought The Tree. So many people take what they want without thinking to ask. The Tree basked in the children's respect for nature and released the flowers from their thorny vines, tossing them into the air so that neither child would be pricked by the thorns. The Tree gave itself an additional shake and unfurled its branches ready to greet the two newcomers to the circle.

The laughter and conversation between the little dark-haired boy and little red-haired girl were infectious. The Tree could feel their excitement and innocence. It could feel their creativity but also the unwavering kindness and love that seemed to be exchanged between them both. The friendship between the two seemed strong.

As the two children played, The Tree noticed that the little boy was very pale and thin, and at times he struggled to keep up with his little friend. Despite chasing each other and playing all sorts of fun imaginary games, the little boy would tire more quickly and was prone to falling down. He seemed thinner than the little girl, not by much, but The Tree could tell that there was something that afflicted the little boy. Something perhaps which the little boy was not so aware of. His friend, however, did seem very aware of this. The Tree noticed that whenever the little boy was struggling, she would sometimes slow down so that he could catch her in the game. She would also sometimes fall down herself … but she would do so on purpose. During moments where the little boy was resting, The Tree, without words, asked the little girl why she did this. Over the years of its existence, The Tree had learnt that it need only to think a question for it to be heard by whomever was in the circle and willing to listen.

The little girl responded simply with a shrug and told The Tree that sometimes people can feel sad when they can't do things that other people can. It can make them feel as though there is something wrong with them, and that this feeling can make their heart break and feel in pain.

The Tree sensed that the little girl cared deeply for her friend and wanted him to be happy. The Tree also knew that when the little girl saw her friend struggling, she too felt sad because of what she could do but knew that her friend could not. It saw her wanting to make her friend's life better but not draw attention to little boy's struggles in case he felt ashamed.

When The Tree saw the little boy fall, it longed to scoop him up in its branches and tell him that everything was okay. However, this was not necessary. The Tree admired the little boy as he fell, saw his lips tremble, his eyes become glassy, but just as quickly as he had fallen, he would pull himself up and continue to run, albeit with a slight limp and watery eyes. The Tree would ask him if he was okay, to which the little boy always replied with a big smile and the words:

'I'm fine!'

The Tree's soul ached in these moments because it knew that the little boy did not feel 'fine' but The Tree also knew that sometimes people can't always be honest with themselves, let alone other people. To acknowledge the truth within oneself means having to admit to hidden truths that can often be painful. The Tree did not want the little boy to feel in pain or to feel sadness. So, The Tree would respond with silent words of encouragement and hoped that the little boy would hear them.

There was a tenderness between the two children as they played. A kindness exuded from the little red-haired girl and a staunch façade of courage from the little dark-haired boy, despite his evident struggles. As the two shared their little lunches together, they took comfort in the shade of The Tree's enormous branches as the unusually warm sun beat down on them.

The little boy asked The Tree where he might find the prettiest flower. He wanted to give his friend a gift, something that would match the beauty that he saw in her soul. At first The Tree guided the little boy towards the many roses that surrounded the stone circle but the little boy sighed and admitted that whilst pretty, they all looked the same. He wanted something unique for his friend because she was unique and beautiful.

The Tree loved moments like this – it gave it the opportunity to dazzle and defy the expectations of how other trees normally behave. The Tree silently nodded at the little boy's request and sent a shiver of energy from its roots to the tips of its branches. In doing so a most unusual flower began to grow on one of The Tree's branches. A curious specimen that the little boy remarked would not look out of place on some distant planet. Not only did its colour shift between different hews of red, orange, gold, and yellow, it looked as though it was on fire. Its many tiny petals shimmered and moved as though they were alive, and it gave off the most beautiful scent that made the little boy's mind feel fuzzy and warm. Once the flower had grown to the size of a melon, The Tree flicked its branch, letting the fiery flower spin in the air before gently floating down into the little boy's open hands. He then walked back to where the little girl was still enjoying her sandwiches and timidly presented her with the gift.

'For you,' the little boy said tenderly and with a smile. 'It matches the colour of your hair,' he said boldly but then blushed, fearing that he had said something wrong.

The little girl looked up from her sandwich to the boy and then to the flower that he held. She was mesmerised by its unusual colour … but then blushed herself, mirroring the pinkness of the little boy's cheeks. She felt great love for her friend but knew that he felt something deeper for her that she could not return. She felt sad that she could not be what her friend wanted. She smiled and thanked the boy for his kindness and put the flower quite hurriedly into her little shoulder bag.

The little boy's smile faltered, as did his friend's. Something passed between them without a word being said. Whilst there was a special kind of love that the two friends shared, it was clear to The Tree that one person felt this more keenly than the other. And for this, The Tree felt sad. It desperately wanted the little girl to love her friend back in the same way that he loved her. But The Tree also knew that people cannot make themselves feel something that is not true, and to try to do so, even for the sake of the other, is not kind for either person. People can only feel what is true in their heart, and sometimes this has to be enough.

The Tree could see tears starting to form in the little boy's eyes.

'Are you okay?' The Tree asked silently so only the boy could hear.

'Yes … I'm fine!' replied the boy in his characteristic tone of feigned indifference.

And with that he forced a smile and playfully tapped his friend on the shoulder and yelled, 'TAG! You're it!'

And with that he turned and ran. Relieved by her friend's playful interlude, she flung her half-eaten sandwich and the bag on the ground, collected a handful of nearby petals that had been shaken loose from The Tree, and began to pursue her friend with the same laughter and joy as The Tree first beheld upon their arrival.

As The Tree watched the scene, the throwing of flowers, the falling down of the little boy, and the girl always stopping to help him up, it noticed that it couldn't share in the fun and laughter between the pair. Every interaction felt tinged with a slight feeling of sadness and disappointment. The Tree didn't know if this belonged with The Tree itself, or if it was feeling something of the little boy's sadness. But it knew something was forever changed between the pair. And so did the little boy.

III

A handful of years would pass before The Tree would meet the little dark-haired boy and the red-haired girl again. And when it did, both children had grown up into teenagers.

It was a particularly cold and frosty morning in the middle of February. The sky was cloudless, except for a few faint wisps, and was a beautiful shade of blue. The Tree had been enjoying the company of the foxes and rabbits that seemed to enjoy gathering at the base of its enormous trunk, as well as the dance of the dragonflies, butterflies, and even some bees, all of which were quite unusual for this time of year. Curiously, the animals seemed to exist in harmony when they were within the stone circle – there was almost an unspoken pact between all the animals and birds that this was a place of sanctuary and safety for all.

The Tree's focus was suddenly pulled away from the playfulness of the animals who disappeared out of sight as the sound of familiar, but somewhat deeper, laughter could be heard. Climbing up the hill were the little boy and little girl, neither of whom were so little anymore. Their voices and appearances had of course changed with time but The Tree recognised their souls.

'Come on Luke ... hurry up! Do you need a hand?' The Tree heard the red-haired girl yell.

'Don't be stupid ... I'm fine!' came Luke's reply, his voice having deepened and broken over the years.

As if there was any confusion in The Tree's mind about who was soon to emerge into view, such doubts were thwarted by the familiar phrase of 'I'm fine'. The Tree chuckled to itself but quickly stopped as the pair emerged into view. The girl had blossomed and looked both happy and healthy. Luke, however, looked even more frail. He remained extremely thin and with very little muscle. But his eyes and his soul still radiated courage and determination, and a strength of character that is very rare.

As they came into view, Luke fell down, exhausted from the climb up the hill. The Tree hadn't realised that with the help of his friend, Luke had needed to crawl up the hill, so determined was he to reach the top. The Tree noticed that his legs were weak and could barely support him. It didn't know how the boy had gotten here but assumed it must be thanks to a wheeled mechanical device from the modern world that aids people who struggle to walk. Despite this, Luke's eyes widened in wonder and triumph as he surveyed the familiar space where he and his friend and played when they were children.

'You're nearly there!' the red-haired girl said encouragingly. 'I could carry you if you wanted?' she added hesitantly.

For a moment The Tree saw a flash of colour rise in the boy's cheek, which was quickly replaced with a look of determination and the familiar words, said more forcefully this time.

'I ... AM ... FINE!'

The red-haired girl held up her hands defensively and backed away, knowing that to push any further would cause her friend to feel ashamed and angry. She knew that he hated to feel powerless and vulnerable, and did whatever she could to avoid making him feel this way. The Tree knew that the red-haired girl's kindness hadn't diminished with age. Nor had the courage and pride of the dark-haired boy. However, The Tree could feel his pain and the suffering he endured by trying to convince others (and, indeed, himself) that he was 'fine'.

There were moments when Luke rested against The Tree's sturdy trunk – taking a sip of water or eating the fruit that he had brought with him – that The Tree glimpsed aspects of the boy's life away from the hill. It felt warmth and relief when it saw the compassion and tenderness of his family. A household of love and care, support and encouragement. A sanctuary for the boy no matter what happened in the world outside. But The Tree also saw that teenagers can be cruel. It saw the spiteful gestures and hushed mocking giggles of other teenagers towards the boy, and heard their hateful words when Luke was out of sight, but also sometimes still within listening distance.

The Tree saw Luke's frustrations when he couldn't play certain games and sports like his other friends ... or when they had romantic relationships that he himself longed for. The Tree silently wept at these memories but saw that Luke did not. Instead, he told himself firmly 'I AM FINE!' and that the people who were unkind did not deserve his time, his care, or his tears. The Tree witnessed Luke's gratitude for the people who did show him care and kindness, and also marvelled in the compassion that he generously offered others who were struggling in various ways in their own life. The Tree felt a swell of love for this courageous and loving young man and held hope for how his life could be.

The Tree was an observer but sometimes it allowed itself to be more than that. It knew that it could not change a person's past or even take away their afflictions, but it could be with people during times of their greatest sadness and struggle so that they would feel less alone. For the time that people visited the stone circle and The Tree, the gift that it gave was being able to hold some of the weight of what its visitors held, in the hopes that they could find some peace ... albeit temporarily. Today The Tree wanted to do more ... it felt a deep and precious love for Luke and his red-haired friend and wanted to do something kind. The Tree had marvellous powers of regeneration and decided that today it would split one of its silver branches into two and give these to Luke in the hope that it could ease his struggles.

And so, it sent a shimmer of energy into the silver branch, causing it to split, change and distort. The Tree willed the split branches to become the shape of a tall letter 'T'. Both lost any leaves that were attached – their edges now becoming smooth, whilst remaining robust and strong. Once formed, The Tree allowed these silver wooden objects to fall from amongst its existing branches and to land softly on the grass that surrounded the base of its trunk.

However, a familiar burning sensation ripped through The Tree's soul as the silver branches fell from its body. It winced in pain but did not let this show … The Tree sought to emulate the same courage and strength of its young fragile friend. But the impact was profound, although The Tree did not yet fully understand the extent, or indeed the cost, of each sacrifice that it had made … and would continue to make to enrich the lives of the people it came to care for and love.

Luke was also an observer. He often saw much more than people realised. In this instance, his eyes did not let him down and he saw the curious phenomenon of The Tree moulding and releasing the two branches at its base. Being a person of faith, he was open to miracles and knew that there was more to this world than what we immediately see. He was a person who held a hope and stubbornness that made him courageous and determined to never give up. As he saw the strange behaviour of The Tree his mind was cast back to a pilgrimage that he himself had undertaken in the hopes of experiencing a miracle.

The Tree's curiosity was ignited by the boy's memory, and it beckoned Luke to come to the foot of The Tree so that he might share his story.

Seeing that her companion was still exhausted from the climb, the red-haired girl put her friend's arm around her shoulder and hoisted him up and together they crossed the stone circle and found their way to the base of The Tree, where its gift for Luke lay nestled in the soft grass.

The gift that The Tree had created brought tears to both Luke and his best friend, although he turned his head away and did his best to hide these both from his friend and The Tree. He held the long T-shaped branches in his arms and knew that they would support him like crutches. But there was something strange about them … they felt light in weight but also strong and robust. When Luke placed them under his arms, he felt like he could do anything. It was as though any feelings of shame or self-doubt, fragility or vulnerability disappeared. He marvelled at the speed in which he was able to manoeuvre himself with the help of the once silver branches, and laughed at the stunned expression on his friend's face. Again, his mind went back to his pilgrimage and his quest for a miracle.

The Tree asked the animals and surrounding elements to be silent so that the dark-haired boy could share his memories of faith and hope.

Luke spoke of a family pilgrimage to a place in France known to have waters that could heal the afflicted. The boy and his parents held a strong faith in one of the religions that The Tree had become familiar with over its existence, thanks to the stories and prayers shared by those who visited The Tree. According to Luke's recollection, the mother of Christ was said to have appeared to a young peasant girl named Bernadette in the year 1858. She was instructed to dig the spot where the apparition had appeared, and upon doing so there burst forth a spring which was said to have healing properties. Luke described the excitement and humility that he felt upon entering the grotto in France, and the calm serenity he experienced when bathing in the waters. His mother procured water for him to drink as they all sent prayers of hope and faith for the boy's health, surrounded by others who too had journeyed from all around the world in the hopes of being healed.

As The Tree listened intently, it could feel the love that the dark-haired boy had for his parents. It could feel their tenderness, the compassion, and their hope for his recovery. Luke smiled, and tears filled his eyes as he recounted the prayers that they offered on his behalf, the candles that they lit, and the look of anticipation in their eyes with every mouthful of holy water that he swallowed. But The Tree could also sense something else. Despite Luke's love and gratitude towards his parents, beneath the smile was a deep sense of sorrow and disappointment. The water had not healed him. His body continued to waste away. He continued to get sick.

As Luke told his story, he could feel that something had changed within his audience, it was as though they had read his mind and heart in this moment.

'Of course it didn't work … but maybe it has given me a few extra years. And I'm fine with that … I AM FINE!' Luke added, hastily.

The final sentence was accompanied by a weak smile which again betrayed his true feelings. He was losing faith. Losing faith in his God and losing optimism for a different life. His anger and resentment were faint and well hidden … but The Tree knew that they were there, forbidden emotions that were eroding Luke's belief as well as his body.

As they all sat in silence, a sombre atmosphere enveloped Luke, his friend, and The Tree. It was at moments like this that The Tree had learnt that people can reclaim a sense of joy when they are met with the beauty and innocence of nature. Nature helps people to connect to their soul whilst also feeling part of a much bigger picture, even if that picture isn't always clear. As such, The Tree communed with the elements and nearby animals, asking them for a sign. Something that might at least give the boy some semblance of joy and faith that all is not lost.

The two teenagers looked up as they heard the slight tinkle of a bell, accompanied by a bleat. Trotting up the hill and into the stone circle was a small goat. It almost skipped towards the two friends whilst continuing to make the most excited noises between its bleats and the tinkling bell around its neck. The two friends exchanged befuddled glances and then fell into peals of laughter. The small goat approached them both without hesitation or fear and nuzzled itself into Luke, who proceeded to gaze adoringly at the sweet animal, and tenderly stroked its head and back, caressing its coarse white fur. The Tree momentarily felt something lift in the boy. For those few moments he wasn't sick or in pain. He was simply a teenager stroking a small goat and was filled with an overwhelming sense of love and care for the animal.

'What shall we name him?' the red-haired girl asked, as she too fussed and tickled the goat under his chin.

'Aussie,' said the boy without hesitation. 'I've always wanted to go to Australia, and this little guy is now – and forever more – my good luck charm. So yes, I thus crown him Aussie!'

And with this proclamation in an imitation of an Australian accent, he touched each of the goat's shoulders with his branch-crutch, holding it like a sword as though he were knighting the creature amidst its constant but joyous bleating.

The red-haired girl placed a garland of flowers that she had made whilst listening to her friend's story around its neck.

The little goat seemed to bow its head in acceptance before strutting off and trotting around the stone circle.

Luke with his new crutches and the red-haired girl spent the rest of their afternoon chasing and playing with the little goat, its carefree nature and innocence being as infectious as its cheerful bleats. Any sense of pain, resentment, sadness, or suffering that The Tree had observed in the boy seemed to melt away as the day continued. The sound of laughter and of course the bleating of Aussie echoed through the valley until the sun began to set and the warmth of the day gave way to the chill of the emerging dusk.

Before the pair left the stone circle, they both approached The Tree and from opposite sides of the trunk spread their arms around it, embracing it in a warm hug. Neither of them said a word. And nor did The Tree. Love, compassion, and gratitude don't always require words or explanation. Sometimes they just are what they are and just need to be felt. Not wanting to feel left out, Aussie joined the hug and rubbed his body affectionately against the trunk of The Tree, and then against Luke and red-haired girl.

With a final bleat and tinkle of his bell, Aussie trotted out of the stone circle and down the hill until he was out of sight. As the two friends left the circle, they too turned to wave goodbye to The Tree, who reciprocated with a swish of its branches and a flurry of pink and red petals, which cascaded into the boundaries of the stone circle, a symbol of love and the celebration of such that continued during this month, every year.

Using his new crutches, Luke made his way down the side of the hill, accompanied by the distant and familiar echo of the impatient phrase in response to his friend asking if he needed help …

'I AM FINE!!!'

IV

Ten years passed. On a particularly cold morning in the middle of February, The Tree awoke to find a blanket of snow covering the ground surrounding its trunk and clinging to the leaves of its branches. In the distance it heard the crunching sound of someone making their way up the hill. The Tree wondered what would make anyone brave such a climb in this weather but was grateful for the company and anticipation of what such an encounter would bring. As the crunching sound drew closer, The Tree sensed something familiar. It could feel its past discarded branches continuing to support the dark-haired boy – now a young man in his mid-twenties – up the hill and into the stone circle.

The Tree rejoiced at the sight of Luke as it had been so long since their last meeting. The strength of its severed branches seemed to have remained constant but sadly the young man's condition had continued to deteriorate. He of course looked older but remained thin and frail in his appearance, a dark stubble covering the young man's jaw and chin, his eyes still wide and still determined, as was the resilience and courage that emanated from his soul.

The Tree bowed as the young man approached. Luke bowed back. The Tree noticed that the young man, despite his frail appearance, had colour to the once pale skin that he remembered from his past meetings with him.

As if sensing The Tree's observation and curiosity, Luke beamed back at The Tree.

'I finally made it to Australia! It wasn't easy but I did it,' he stated triumphantly.

And then he told The Tree all about his adventures there: the people he met and new friends that he had made, and the memories that he had created which were now emblazoned in his heart. The Tree swayed with joy to match the young man's triumph and in doing so sent a shower of snow from its branches, exposing the luscious green leaves beneath.

The young man entered the circle but as he neared the base of The Tree's trunk, his arms shook, and despite the sturdiness of his crutches, his legs gave way beneath him. As the young man lay crumpled on the ground, he let out guttural scream of frustration, his now even deeper voice booming through the valley. The Tree silently echoed the young man's scream, the vibration of which caused the birds nestling in its branches to hurriedly soar into the sky.

'How are you my young friend?' The Tree asked, radiating compassion in the hope that Luke could feel its concern for him.

The young man sighed deeply, and said in a tone that was much less convincing than what The Tree had heard in the past, said, 'I'm fine.'

The Tree felt a heaviness in the Luke's soul and an even deeper sense of loneliness.

'Where is your friend?' asked The Tree.

'Oh, she moved away. She went away to study ... acting, or something like that ... she has a different life now. I sometimes see her ... but not as often as I would like. She seems happy. And I'm happy for her. But I don't get to see her very much anymore.'

His eyes were downcast and starting to fill with tears. He quickly wiped them away and added, 'But it's fine. And I'm fine. I'm happy for her ... I really am!'

The Tree tried to imbue the young man with the courage to be able to speak his truth, without holding back.

'I've noticed that you often say the opposite of what you feel,' said The Tree tenderly. 'Why is that?'

The young man looked startled and then thoughtful for a moment. His eyes began to fill with tears again but this time he did not wipe them away. He cleared his throat.

'I suppose it is because I'm too afraid to say what I really mean ... or feel how I really feel. If I can tell myself that I'm fine often enough, maybe I'll start to believe it. I've been trying to do that for years.'

The Tree gently bowed and rustled its leaves to show that it understood.

'What do you really want to say?' The Tree asked gently, and then corrected itself. 'Or perhaps more accurately, what do you NEED to say?'

Luke paused for a moment, and then looked downwards, an expression of sadness across his face.

'It's not fair ...' he whispered. And then more loudly, 'IT'S NOT FAIR!' startling both himself and The Tree, such was the rawness of his honesty and anger.

Luke took another deep breath and leaned himself up against the trunk of The Tree, its sturdiness supporting his frail back. In a softer tone, he said, 'I also see the sadness in other people's eyes when they see me struggle. It feels like pity ... and its unbearable. Sometimes I tell them that I'm fine because in some ways perhaps they need to believe it. Because to sit with the truth is too painful for them, and for me too. I can't bear their pity!'

'Is pity all that you see in their eyes ... or might there be something else?' asked The Tree.

'I guess I hadn't really thought of that,' the young man replied and then leaned back even harder against The Tree, feeling its support. Feeling its love.

'I guess they might also be feeling compassion. Perhaps even love?' Luke pondered.

The Tree spread its branches even wider so that a light flurry of blossom rained down on to the young man to demonstrate its agreement. The Tree then asked, 'And what if you were to allow yourself not to be fine, to have the courage to speak your truth from your heart right now? What do you feel?'

The young man was quiet. He looked at the ground, then away to the horizon, and then finally to his thin and painful arms and legs. He took another deep breath and said quietly, 'I don't think I'm fine. I think … I'm getting worse. I think …' The young man paused and took a deep breath.

'I think … that I'm going to die. And I fear that I don't have much longer on this earth.'

And for the first time that The Tree could remember since knowing the young man, Luke began to cry. A cry that shook the valley, and indeed The Tree, to its very core. A cry so deep and full of sorrow that even the river, the birds and all the animals of the valley felt their souls weep in sympathy for all that the young man had endured – and all that he had held inside.

A heaviness weighed on The Tree's soul. It ached as it felt the courage of the young man's honesty but also the despair of his reality.

'Go on,' implored The Tree.

'I don't feel I have done enough. I don't feel that I loved enough. I don't know what will happen next. Everyone moves on and leaves me behind. And I hate the world for doing this to me. I hate that I feel that this isn't fair when I know fairness has nothing to do with it. This is who I am and this is how I was born. I know that I am loved … but I'm also frightened. I sometimes feel alone. And I feel like I've got to be fine because everyone needs me to be fine. But I know that I'm not. I can feel that someday soon I will die … But I'm not ready.'

The young man placed his face in his hands and wept. He wept for everything he knew, everything he would never do, and everything he couldn't bring himself to say. The Tree wept too and brought its branches down to hold the young man as he finally let go of the weight he'd been carrying. The young man cursed the sky and the God that he believed in. The Tree cursed too.

But as they did so, there was a familiar tinkle of a bell and loud and absurd sounding bleat. Luke looked up and began to both laugh and cry though his tears as the familiar trot of Aussie's hooves could be heard crunching through the snow towards the young man.

'How on earth …?' the young man exclaimed and then opened his arms wide to embrace his old friend.

Aussie reciprocated by nuzzling into the young man, licking his face and bleating cheerfully as he too was reunited with his old friend.

Hours passed where no further words were exchanged. There was something comforting and soothing for Luke as he sat in silence with The Tree and Aussie. Something within the young man had shifted since allowing himself to speak his truth.

As night fell, the snowy clouds from the day melted away giving way to the blackness of the sky, peppered with the myriad stars and constellations. Aussie was dozing in the young man's arms but opened his eyes lazily as the young man began to reach for his crutches and pulled himself back up to standing. As he did so, he mustered all of his strength, leaned the crutches against The Tree's trunk and gave it a long embrace. An embrace so powerful that a warm glow could be felt within The Tree's soul.

'Thank you,' whispered Luke. 'I'll not leave it so long. Same time next year?' he said with a smile and a laugh.

And with that, both Luke and Aussie made their away across the stone circle and back down the side of the hill – the sound of the young man's crutches crunching in the remaining snow, and the tinkle of Aussie's bell fading into the night.

V

The following year, The Tree eagerly waited for Luke to appear. It surrounded the stone circle with roses, and coloured its branches with the curious fiery flower that the young man had first given his friend when they were children. The Tree waited … and waited … but as the day wore on, The Tree began to lose hope that the young man would be able to make the climb.

Deep down, The Tree feared that it would not see Luke again. The climb up the hill had become too much and it knew that the young man's health was continuing to deteriorate. The Tree told itself that it was time for the young man to rest ... and that was okay, even though the pain in its heart told The Tree otherwise. The fiery flowers illuminating The Tree began to fade until they were only a dim glow amongst its leafy branches. It was a beautiful but unusual spectacle that could be observed throughout the valley.

Just as The Tree had given up hope, it heard a sound coming from the valley below. The most heavenly sound The Tree had ever heard seemed to be coming from the river below. As The Tree looked down from high upon its hill, it saw a small wooden fishing boat carrying a woman and a young man, who appeared to be sleeping in her arms. And from her mouth came the most beautiful but heartbreaking song that The Tree had ever beheld. A song that would haunt its heart forever but also give it peace. Behind the boat were many small candlelit lanterns creating an enchanting sparkling trail that followed the mother and her son as they glided upon the river's gentle waters, as though they were riding a comet in the sky.

The Tree recognised Luke at once and could see that he was at peace as he slept in the arms of his beloved mother. Her glorious song serenaded the valley – a valley that was now utterly silent but for the melody of love and sorrow that come from his mother's heart and soul. In the distance, The Tree could have sworn that it heard a faint and mournful bleat, accompanied by the sound of a tinkling bell. And for a fleeting moment, The Tree thought that it saw the young man open his eyes ever so slightly and smile before his face became passive once more, and his eyes closed. It was an expression of such simplicity that it could easily have been missed. But in return The Tree sent a flurry of the reignited fiery petals from the blossom on its branches, adding to the glow of candlelight as they settled on the rippling water and followed behind the small wooden boat in its procession of love.

Deep within its soul, The Tree wept. It wept for the joy of having known the little boy. It wept for his bravery. It wept for the young man's pain and anguish. And his courage to speak and know his own truth and fears. It wept for his friends and family. But ultimately The Tree wept for itself – for its own loss, whilst rejoicing in the young man's courage, and his silent teaching about compassion, love, and vulnerability.

The Tree felt its limbs sag, and the remaining blossoms on its branches began to fall … a cascade of soft pastel fiery tears, until the grass beneath The Tree was no longer visible, just a ring of flaming orange, red, and gold within the stone circle.

'Fear not,' said a soft gentle voice from the valley below, interrupting The Tree's silent lament.

'Our little boy was a gift from God … but now God wants him back. And who are we to argue with God? The little boy, and the young man that he became has given us the best years of our life … and his next journey is only just beginning. Let us be grateful for what he has given us and for the hope and courage he will continue to give others when they remember him. And for the love that we feel when we remember him.'

The Tree didn't know if it believed in God. But The Tree knew that faith gives comfort to those who love, who lose, and need hope to carry on. And so, because of this, The Tree allowed itself to trust the words of the young man's mother in the hope that these words would bring it some semblance of comfort.

As it gazed down into the valley from high upon the hill, The Tree felt the air surrounding it change, becoming cooler and crisper. It saw the small boat with Luke and his mother gliding along the shimmering river, the procession of lanterns behind it, each containing a single glowing candle.

The young man's boat inched further and further away from The Tree's hill, along the serpentine river, until their image faded into the horizon. The last thing The Tree saw was the silhouette of the boat, a mother and son bathed in the warm and comforting glow of the setting sun, and the procession of candlelight and fiery petals that followed.

The Tree knew that Luke was at peace. And as such, it too could find peace in its soul. It thanked the young man's mother, the sky, the river, the mountains, and the sun for bringing the little dark-haired boy into its life. The Tree was grateful for the love that it felt towards him, and knew that it would be forever changed in its heart for having known him … even if his time on this earth was short.

The Tree sat with the truth that whilst life is not permanent, the impact of one person on another can last for eternity… and The Tree vowed that it would carry some of Luke's courage in its own heart. Unbeknownst to The Tree … it would certainly need it!

CHAPTER THREE
March: Loneliness

I

It was the beginning of spring in the valley, which was now decorated with sumptuous blossoms all the colours of the rainbow. High upon its hill, The Tree stood alone. It enjoyed its own company and the myriad reflections and wonderings that it thought of each day. However, the more stories that it heard, and the more experiences it had of being with human beings, The Tree began to long for their company and miss their presence when they were absent. Of course, it would continue to commune with the elements and the wildlife that sought comfort and refuge amidst its branches and under its canopy of leaves. But there was a growing yearning in The Tree for more.

At times it could feel its soul ache when months would pass by and no visitors braved the stepping stones, the hill, or crossed into the sacred circle of stones. The Tree knew that this feeling had a name. It was loneliness. It had heard tales of this from many of the people who had visited over the years. The Tree knew that human beings seek relationships with others in order to thrive. And in the absence of this, their minds and souls can atrophy. They are left with a hunger that cannot be satiated with food or any other substances that may be used to fill the void. It is when someone feels cared for, important to another person, and held both in heart and mind that the human soul can flourish. And The Tree longed for these connections itself.

As seasons can do, the changing landscape, colours, and scents that had burst forth in the valley evoked strong and powerful memories within The Tree. Memories of similar spring days in the late part of the twentieth century, and the associated stories that accompanied them, came flooding back to The Tree. And in this instance, it was the tale of two lonely teenage boys, Christoph and Sergio. Their unlikely friendship formed and blossomed, despite their differences, during a time in nature when new life bursts forth.

The Tree understood that what bound these two lost souls together was the need to be understood. The need to be accepted for who they were without fear or shame. And a desire to connect to another living soul – to know that they were not alone in the world. These were valuable lessons that profoundly impacted The Tree, causing it to recognise and reflect on its own loneliness and yearnings.

II

Christoph frequently visited The Tree when he was supposed to be at college, a place that he felt was dull, unstimulating, and tediously slow. For someone whose mind worked quickly, creatively, and jumped from one topic to another, a lacklustre place such as this could not possibly hold him prisoner. And so, he came to The Tree and would bring with him his latest hobby – of which there were many. But The Tree delighted in the young man's visits. It loved to hear the excited and rapid narrative of Christoph's hopes and plans for the future, and the next project that he would be undertaking. The more excited he became, the more he would slip back into speaking Swiss German, which was not a problem for The Tree, who discovered that it could understand all languages because it listened to the hearts and souls of all those who visited it. Even when speaking in his second language, Christoph's accent was soft but ever present, giving him an additional charm.

The Tree knew that other people had not always been kind to Christoph – it caught glimpses of this in the memories of the young man but also in his stories. When Christoph's family moved from Switzerland, the young man had difficulty fitting in. People would make fun of his accent. They would make obscure references to wars in the distant past and would purposefully exclude him from their group

The Tree was saddened to hear of the times when Christoph would deliberately change his voice in an attempt to sound more like the people who excluded him – a desperate attempt to form friendships. And thus, The Tree delighted when the young man was able to fully be himself and speak in his native tongue when he climbed the hill and sat beneath The Tree. Whenever the young man spoke, The Tree felt itself become alive and matched the energy of Christoph. It fantasised about where his projects and interests would take him, and the creative ways that he seemed to perceive the world and all of the opportunities that life presented him with. This was a young man of drive and ambition but also of distractibility, as not all of the projects that he spoke of were completed – often something new and more exciting coming along, which grasped Christoph's attention. But The Tree delighted in this for him, and the enthusiasm and detail that Christoph would share on those spring days.

Whilst sharing impassioned stories about his latest projects, Christoph would become distracted … a beautiful bird, the scampering of rabbits, a change in the temperature, the roar of the river below. He loved being with The Tree and gazing out over the valley – it reminded him of home. He described a mystical sounding village in Switzerland famous for its seventy-two waterfalls, majestic peaks, and towering cliffs. A place of such beauty that it had served as inspiration for a famous but now deceased author who went on to write an epic series of fantasy novels about hobbits, dwarves, rings, and elves who dwelt in a land similar to the luscious green valley that the young man had called home.

Christoph recounted days where he would ramble through the valley, following the clear glacial waters as they weaved through the valley, often bathed in glorious sunshine. And the shadows cast through the valley by the majestic peaks of the Eiger, Mönch, and Jungfrau mountains as the setting sun melted behind them.

Christoph recounted times where he and his friends would play in the rivers, would hike into the mountains, or catch a train to the small nearby towns and villages where they would drink hot chocolate,

42

eat delicious food, and plan their next adventures – he missed these friends deeply. They would write letters to each other but over the years since Christoph moved away, the letters became less frequent, as did the desire to share his stories. It was hard to share his adventures with his old friends when he knew they were continuing to have them whilst he was alone, desperately trying to adjust to a new country, a new culture, and an environment that could in no way match the beauty of the home that he longed to return to. But Christoph had come to love this valley and had found solace and comfort in the rare tree that he had discovered on top of the hill.

When Christoph was with The Tree, feelings of loneliness disappeared. He was able to marvel at the beautiful valley and – at least for a short while – reconnect with a sense of peace that reminded him of home.

The Tree listened to his stories and ideas, and was interested in all that he had to say – much like his friends had on their many hikes. They were not preoccupied with technology or computerised devices – such things were few and far between where he had come from – and were an unwelcome distraction from the beauty of nature. Instead, he and his friends would share and listen intently to each other's hopes, dreams, and interests, and would celebrate these without criticism or judgement.

Christoph longed for these friendships again. And to admire the beautiful Staubbach Falls gushing over the steep valley walls into the U-shaped valley below – to both feel and run through its cold mist, basking in the tender and refreshing touch against his face on those glorious springtime days. But Christoph was grateful to The Tree, whose valley offered him a different beauty. And for The Tree itself, who seemed to delight and enquire into all that he was interested in, even when he didn't complete a project or moved on to the next exciting hobby.

And The Tree did delight in Christoph because it knew that in order for someone to know and truly feel their worth and inherent goodness, they need to have others delight in their presence simply for who they are, not as a measurement against the needs or expectations of others. The Tree's love and interest in Christoph was unconditional, and Christoph knew this, hence why he returned to The Tree over and over again.

Sadly, the other people in Christoph's life were not so kind or interested. His parents were critical. Being an only child, they pushed all of their hopes and expectations on him. They failed to see his uniqueness, creativity, and talents, and instead only saw what they felt was absent. In essence, they did not see their son. And Christoph felt invisible and inadequate. The Tree could feel his sadness when he visited but could also feel his energy. It could feel the young man's creativity, his joy and excitement, and felt enlivened within itself after every meeting.

Sometimes Christoph would bring the newly built and painted miniatures that he had created – figurines for a fantasy game that he would sometimes play with strangers. Other times he would bring sketches for homes and gardens that he planned to design one day. Other times he would bring cooked and baked goods that had taken his fancy. And on other days he would bring an array of musical instruments that he would make music from to serenade The Tree.

The Tree delighted in the sharing of these hobbies and would swish its branches to the beat of the newly composed music, cascades of blossom raining down on the young man. It would be still and silent as Christoph sang and listened intently to the plans that he had for the future – his latest desire being to help people who were sick. To The Tree, Christoph was a delight, and would no doubt achieve anything that he put his mind to … if he could stay focused for long enough, that is.

One day, Christoph climbed the hill and sat beneath The Tree, muttering in Italian to himself. This was a language spoken in his home country but one that he had never learnt. He had decided since his last visit that this would be the language for him. And perhaps Japanese at a later date. But something seemed different about Christoph, thought The Tree to itself. The light and energy that burned so bright within him seemed to have been extinguished. His voice was flat and his eyes were downcast. He confided in The Tree that there was nothing else to do. He'd run out of things to focus on and was being told by his parents and tutors that he had to pick one thing, and one thing only, to focus on. And that nothing else mattered.

The Tree felt it's heart sink, no doubt an echo of what Christoph felt – but dare not express. When implored to share his thoughts,

Christoph recounted his recent desire to move to the countryside instead of going to university, and to become a farmer where he could tend to his own crops and look after animals. This had been met with befuddlement, ridicule, and criticism, by his parents, his peers, and tutors – and as such, this dream had died, along with a part of Christoph's soul.

The Tree was incensed. It had grown fiercely protective of its young friend and hated the idea of his dreams dying on the wind. The Tree knew that it could not impact the words or behaviours of those outside of the stone circle but it could return some hope to Christoph. The Tree knew that sometimes all it takes is an act of kindness and an apparent sign from something outside of consciousness that can both inspire and motivate life and joy in human beings. Determined to lift this young man out of the growing sense of depression that was suffocating his spark, The Tree called upon the elements and all the creatures of the valley to give Christoph a sign that would inspire joy and excitement in his heart once more.

In the distance, far off in the valley, a faint humming could be heard. It got louder and louder until both The Tree and Christoph saw a dark amorphous cloud weaving through the sky – the loud hum reaching a rather frightening crescendo. Terrified, Christoph pulled his jumper over his head, and The Tree instinctively brought its branches down into a protective embrace, to shield its friend from the approaching swarm. The buzzing insects that revealed themselves surrounded The Tree in a strange hurricane-like cocoon until the hum of their wings began to quieten, creating a soothing and hypnotic buzz that evoked an unusual sense of calm and wonderment in both The Tree and Christoph.

Peeking out from underneath his jumper, and through The Tree's protective branches, Christoph saw the most enchanting honey bees dancing around them. They weaved in exquisite patterns in the air around them, communicating to each other in ways that Christoph could not fathom but was deeply allured by. Their tiny brown and orange bodies could be seen settling on the flowers that had burst forth on The Tree's branches, and the assortment of flowers that The Tree now willed to the surface around the stone circle, further enticing the bees to settle.

The Tree unfurled its branches so that Christoph could now eagerly approach the settled swarm with awe – a rapid narrative of German being muttered under his breath as he did so. The Tree didn't think it had ever met someone so curious about the wonders of the world and its natural inhabitants. No one else, except its night-time friend – the young man who would climb its branches and gaze at the stars all night long without saying very much. That particular young man would simply mutter a few Spanish words of delight when a shooting star was seen burning across the sky, or when the constellations became crystal clear as the clouds parted.

Perhaps this could be a friend for Christoph, The Tree thought to itself, as both young men seemed lonely but equally fascinated by the world.

When Christoph visited The Tree again a few days later, he was delighted to see the bees continuing their dance around The Tree, clearly determined to find pollen and nectar for their hive. In the short time that Christoph had been away, he had of course thoroughly researched the lives and patterns of the bees, and was now further determined that his life's trajectory would involve the bees, and keeping them both safe and alive so that they could 'save this wretched planet', a phrase that he would continually repeat.

The Tree would watch Christoph with delight as he fearlessly approached the bees, the flowers they were on, and studied them intently – making various notes in his notebook and taking photos with an old camera that he had procured. He would then spend hours chatting away to The Tree, his voice becoming more animated and slipping into his native Swiss German as he did so. He recounted his wisdom about how the queen was made, how the hive survives, and indeed the consequences for the planet if the bees were to become extinct. He spoke emphatically of the impact on the ecosystem, agriculture, the security of humans being able to procure food, and the inevitable destruction that would manifest as people would fight for scarce resources and would end up tearing themselves apart. In essence, Christoph concluded, without the bees, life on this planet would be catastrophic, and it was therefore his mission to support the bees and help them to thrive.

The Tree asked Christoph how he would do this … it asked from a genuine place of curiosity and encouragement so that the young man's dreams could be fuelled rather than ridiculed. In an act of support, The Tree manifested a colourful assortment of flowers to erupt within the stone circle and on its branches, further drawing the attention of the buzzing bees.

Christoph, without knowing why, felt a deep warmth and sense of excitement – electricity running through his entire body. He was not used to people being excited with him and for him. He half expected The Tree to simply dismiss what he was saying, to ridicule him, or even worse, remain passive and indifferent as so many of the people in his life appeared to be.

The Tree knew that everyone deserves to have their dreams celebrated and to be met with the same energy and vitality that each person brings with them. And The Tree knew that if anyone could make a difference in the world, and indeed have some meaningful impact on it, it would be Christoph. And so, The Tree listened. It encouraged. And it celebrated the ideas that Christoph had for his emerging bee farm and life as a beekeeper. And for once, Christoph did not feel shame or self-doubt. He did not feel alone. He believed in himself because he could feel that for once, someone else believed in him. And this fed his soul, his imagination, and his drive to turn his fantasy into a reality.

III

It was 21 March, also known as the spring equinox, where the hours of light and dark were equal to each other. The Tree had been listening to Christoph's latest plans, who was describing them with such enthusiasm that he did not notice the dusk as the sun slipped behind the surrounding hills. He also recounted the flippant comments made by people at college when he announced his new plan, but rather than feeling defeated he was all the more determined to prove to them (and himself) that this was something he could really do.

As Christoph was doing so, The Tree was momentarily distracted by the familiar panting of another young man emerging on the side of the hill, breathing heavily from carrying the weight of his rather cumbersome telescope, and a heavy backpack no doubt filled with a heavy blanket and the same snacks that he always brought to satiate him through the night. The young man liked his routine and rarely, if ever, deviated from this. He arrived at the same time, left at the same time, enjoyed eating the same food, and was completely immersed in the mysteries of the skies above.

Sergio was a young man roughly the same age as Christoph. His parents had moved from Mexico City, seeking better opportunities than they were able to procure in the poor area of the city where they had lived. This change was deeply distressing for Sergio – not just because change was difficult, but because of what he was leaving behind. Unlike, Christoph, Sergio was not sad to leave his friends behind. This was because Sergio didn't have any friends.

The children at his previous schools would laugh at him. They would call him names, such as 'Chico loco del espacio', which The Tree had come to learn meant 'crazy space boy'. They ridiculed his theories about UFOs, aliens, and the origin of the pyramids. They would hide his books and bag and school, and often followed him down the corridors between classes, hurling insults and objects at him.

Sergio learnt to run fast and always be on alert. He was almost never beaten by the other children, despite their efforts, because he learnt to anticipate their cruelty, and escape where he could. And that was how he found the solace and safety at the pyramids of Teotihuacan. He learnt the bus routes and travelled twenty or so miles north of the city where he would spend hours walking around the enormous site, marvelling at the hulking majesty of the Pyramid of the Sun, eating his lunch in the shadow cast by the smaller but no less enigmatic Pyramid of the Moon, before traversing the two mile stretch of the Avenue of the Dead to the lesser visited but equally intriguing Pyramid of Quetzalcoatl. Here he would read his books and wonder about the origins of this glorious archaeological wonder, and all the secrets and mysteries that it held. He had learnt when to come and go so that he could avoid the tourists and the ferocious intensity of the sun as it beat down on the golden sand and volcanic red coloured structures of limestone. When Sergio was there, he felt safe. He felt at peace. No one could hurt him. And ultimately, no one would laugh at him.

When he and his family moved away, Sergio was heartbroken. The schools here were no better. The other teenagers were even more cruel. They burned his books. They found ways to surprise him and kick him after they knocked him down. They mocked his broken English and tried to mimic his accent.

But Sergio's parents were kind people. They helped him to feel pride for his country and for who he is … and what he believed in. They did not have much money but hoped that their new life would give Sergio the opportunities that he longed for. They home schooled him instead, and did whatever they could to facilitate his passion for archaeology, history, space, and astronomy.

Even though Sergio hated large groups, and was generally mistrustful of others, he felt pangs of loneliness – feelings that were assuaged when he found The Tree, and the unspoilt views starlit sky that the valley and hill gave him. It wasn't the pyramids of Teotihuacan, but it was a sanctuary where he could be himself and not be hurt or made to feel ashamed for who he was and what he liked.

And The Tree was kind. The Tree listened. The Tree would deliberately lose its leaves every night that the young man visited so that its branches became easier to grasp and climb. It twisted and distorted its branches so that a platform could be created for Sergio, giving him an ideal lookout point with views that stretched way beyond the valley and up into the night sky without obscurement.

As Sergio entered the stone circle towards The Tree, he stopped abruptly and eyed suspiciously the young man with his neat blonde hair and pale skin. The young man was almost the opposite to Sergio with his ruffled black hair, golden brown skin and dark eyes. He did not like change. And he did not like strangers. But he did notice that the other young man's eyes were blue … and also very kind, as was the smile that he beamed towards Sergio. Looking downwards, he continued his awkward walk towards The Tree and did not look up again. He struggled with eye contact generally, even more so with strangers. He made a slight nod towards The Tree in acknowledgement of its presence, and on cue The Tree withdrew its leaves and blossoms from its branches, now that the bees had departed back to their respective hives to deposit the nectar and pollen they had gathered.

Sergio began his ascent of The Tree, carefully choosing where to place his feet and hands to maximise his grip.

'Hallo, I'm Christoph,' came a strange accent and voice from below.

Feeling both confused and awkward, Sergio said nothing and continued his climb, so determined was he to reach his favourite spot on The Tree to set up his telescope in a timely fashion, and not be robbed of valuable stargazing time.

'Hola!' came the same strange accented voice again. 'Me llamo Christoph ... como estas?'

This caused Sergio to stop and finally look down. This person knew Spanish. He had yet to meet anyone since moving here who either could or would speak his native tongue – other than The Tree, of course. So he replied in a quiet and uncertain voice.

'Hola, Christoph, soy Sergio.' And in an awkwardly formal manner continued in English, 'I am very well thank you very much,' before turning his head back towards his desired branches and continued the climb.

Christoph's excited and eager voice came again, bellowing up towards Sergio as he continued his climb.

'Hey! Wait for me ... what are you doing? Can I come up there, Sergio? I've never stayed here this late before. Can I look through your telescope? What food do you have? I'm a bit hungry myself but I've only got these brownies. They're homemade. I made them but there's too many just for me. They are delicious. Do you want one? What are the stars like form here? I'm saving the bees ... do you know much about the bees?'

Somewhat befuddled by the barrage of questions and at times struggling to understand what was even being asked, Sergio took a deep breath, and looked back down at the eager expression in Christoph's face and said quietly, 'Si ... ven aqui y sientarte conmigo.' And with a gesture of invitation, he said again, 'Yes ... come here and sit with me!'

Without hesitation Christoph scrambled up The Tree's sturdy trunk and up to the newly formed platform that The Tree had created. Both young men looked at each other and smiled, and simultaneously held out their hands, which they both shook as they formally greeted one another. They both then turned their attention towards the horizon and sat in silence as the valley darkened and indigo sky gave way to the deep engulfing vacuum of space, scattered with thousands upon thousands of twinkling stars and constellations, and a waxing crescent moon.

As The Tree held these two unlikely friends aloft in its branches, something within it glowed, a glow that was warm and joyful ... and full of anticipation. The Tree suspected that these feelings were not just its own, but also belonged to Sergio and Christoph as the sparks of a budding friendship ignited.

As the night wore on, and the young men took turns gazing at far-off planets and galaxies through the powerful telescope – the surrounding air becoming cooler. Sergio noticed a slight but distinct shiver in his new companion. And without a second thought rifled through his large backpack to produce the heavy woollen blanket that he had been carrying. He tenderly draped it around Christoph's shoulders. It was an act of such simplicity and kindness but one that was not lost on The Tree – nor was it lost on Christoph. And in response to hearing the faint but distinguishable rumble of a hungry tummy, Christoph gave Sergio the last of his own homemade brownies.

The Tree rejoiced silently. And somewhere deep inside both of the young men something wonderful rejoiced within them too.

V

Over the next ten days, both Christoph and Sergio came to visit The Tree ... but The Tree knew that they were really coming to see each other. The Tree found itself blending into the background, a silent observer to the beautiful friendship that was unfolding. Even the changeable weather did not deter the two young men who would perform their respective daytime and evening tasks – Christoph observing the curious behaviour of the bees whilst drawing up plans for a small hive that he planned to construct at home, symbolic of the beginning of his beekeeping empire. And Sergio continuing to observe the night sky and track the planets and constellations as they silently glided across the night sky. The Tree noticed that Christoph tended to stay much later than he used to. And Sergio arrived much earlier than he used to.

During the crossover, both young men would speak enthusiastically about their passions, feeding each other with excited smiles and questions. Christoph spoke of valleys and waterfalls, the life cycle of bees and their necessity for human survival. He would speak of his plans to create a farm back in Switzerland where he would sell honey and candles, and grow crops to feed his family, and care for the plethora of farm animals that would no doubt inhabit the small holding that he would create.

Sergio would gush about the ancient pyramids of Mexico and their similarities to those found all over the world. He drew comparisons between his beloved pyramids of Teotihuacan to those found in Egypt, and the fascinating earthbound mirroring that both complexes served to the constellation of Orion, as well as providing maps of our solar system when viewed from above, and being encoded with mathematical and astronomical information far beyond what the history books taught was possible during the times of their construction.

Both young men took it in turns to speak ... but often their excitement overcame them, meaning they often spoke over one another and lapsed into their respective native languages. But as is the case with true friendship, this did not matter. And at times they even lapsed in to speaking each other's language, such was the depth of the connection, and their desire to listen and learn from one another.

The Tree saw how despite their differences, the connection between the two young men was true, and deepened the evident attunement, interest, and understanding that they demonstrated towards each other. The Tree learnt that whilst people long to find similarities between themselves in order to feel accepted, the desire for relationship can override perceived differences, especially when two people are lonely and are simply longing to connect.

The Tree saw that each young man didn't always understand the depth of fascination that held the focus of their friend, but they continued to delight in the passion that they respectively expressed to each other. Both Sergio and Christoph saw what was important to their friend, and – knowing how it felt to be judged, laughed at, criticised, and rejected – gave each other something that was deeply craved within their own hearts. Kindness. And in turn they gratefully received this.

A parliament of owls could be heard screeching across the valley as the sky began to fill with stars – the air still sweet with the scent of the spring flowers that The Tree had been creating to further entice the bees to it, much to Christoph's delight. The two young men would share their food with each other and laugh as they tried to avoid the colony of tiny bats that had also come to swoop and swarm around The Tree.

'Why don't you go to school or college?' Christoph asked tenderly, as Sergio routinely set up his telescope.

Sergio stopped for a moment and replied without looking at his friend.

'Children back in Mexico were not kind to me,' he said softly.

'When I was at primary school the other children would call me names as I walked down the corridor. One boy took a particular dislike to me and punched me in the face for no reason … that's how I got this …'

Sergio looked at his friend and revealed the broken bottom tooth as he forced a smile.

Christoph hadn't noticed this as Sergio's smile was rare but when he did, his whole face lit up.

'And a bloody nose,' Sergio added. 'One time they took the pyramid I had made and stomped on it before setting it on fire in the field … they said it was stupid and that I was muy loco because I had also made a UFO hover above it using some wires.'

Sergio's voice was flat as he recounted these memories to Christoph, who listened intently with sadness and without interruption.

'We thought it would be better when we over moved here but the children at high school were even worse. They wouldn't speak to me because they said they couldn't understand me. They would also tell me that my skin looked dirty and that I needed to wash. I like to be by myself so I can read but they would find me at lunchtime and steal my books and sometimes tear them apart. They would mock me in lessons when my sentences sounded muddled. They would wait for me after school and throw stones at me. Once they followed me home and took turns to kick me in an alley. When I was lying on the ground, the main boy actually pissed on me. Another one threatened me with a knife. He said it was because I had "eyes on his girl". I'm not sure what that meant exactly but his girlfriend often smiled at me in lessons and was one of the few people who ever spoke to me kindly.'

As he said this, Sergio's voice cracked and Christoph could see tears in his eyes.

'So that's why my parents took me out of school. They tutored me at home and found a way for me to study all the things that I enjoy. They are very kind people and have always wanted the best for me. And now I get to read what I want, study what I am fascinated by, and come to this beautiful place to observe the universe ... and I met you,' he then added quietly.

The Tree listened in the background in silence. Its heart broke when it heard of the cruelty that Sergio had been subjected to. It felt waves of fury that even children can act so despicably towards their fellow human beings. The Tree felt a pang of despair ... the world was changing, and so it seemed were the people who inhabited it. But not changing in a way that was kind or peaceful. There was a growing sense of malevolence that was starting to manifest in people, and this concerned The Tree.

However, the momentary sense of hopelessness was interrupted as The Tree observed Christoph instinctively lean forward and put his arms around his friend. Sergio looked both surprised and awkward at first – touch not being something that he was particularly comfortable with. But in that moment, the love and care from his friend warmed his heart and as such, he allowed himself to melt into the embrace.

'Do you miss your friends?' he asked, still holding tightly to Christoph.

Christoph slowly pulled away from the hug and looked out across the valley, his mind drifting back to the carefree days that he and his friends had spent in their own valley in Switzerland. His eyes began to glisten with unshed tears as he quietly replied.

'Yes ... but I am glad that I've met you!'

'The people here are different,' he continued. 'Everyone wants to be the same. They act the same. They look the same. They even force themselves to like the same things because it's fashionable to do so. I loved my friends back home because we were all different. We all had different family experiences, different interests, different styles.

And we celebrated that. Here, people attack you for it. Sometimes my friends would find me annoying because I know I speak a lot, and I am impatient when people don't speak as quickly or think as creatively as I do. You sometimes speak slowly, which was frustrating... at first,' he chuckled.

'But now I know it's because you're thinking ... you're trying to process lots of different things, and you're also trying not to say the "wrong thing" because people have been unkind to you in the past. My friends and I back home accepted and celebrated all of our many quirks. Our difference and willingness to accept difference is what made our bond so strong. And that is why I miss them ... but also why I like you so much. You are yourself. Even though people have been cruel to you, you continue to be who you are, and unapologetically like what you like. And that is why I am so glad that you're my friend! I wish I'd known you back then too. The people I formed some kind of friendship with here are fickle. They get annoyed and impatient when I share my ideas and interests. They think I don't see the faces they make when I tell them about my hopes for the future ....it hurts to see that they don't care.'

Christoph lowered his and a sadness emanated from him.

'They make plans but don't always include me. Sometimes I feel that I'm the only one who makes an effort. I would sometimes skip classes so I could be with them because they didn't have lessons, but when I had time off they were nowhere to be found. I would always invite people to my house ... but they never came. And when I asked them why, they would tell me that sometimes I am "too much" and that they needed space from me.'

Sergio was moved by his friend's disclosure and leaning forward, mirroring the hug that his friend had offered him. The attempt was somewhat clumsy and awkward, and seemed to catch Christoph a little off-guard ... but the sentiment and embrace was welcomed.

'I don't think you're too much,' Sergio said tenderly. 'For the first time in my life I don't feel that I am alone. The stars have been my friends, and so have my books. But until I met you, I didn't know what it truly meant to not feel alone.'

He then added, 'And I would come to your house,' with a hint of embarrassment and uncertainty in his voice.

Christoph smiled warmly and replied to his friend. 'I would like that very much!'

VI

It was the last day of March. The Tree and Christoph were bathed in a soft orange light as the sun set behind the hills of the valley – the trees in the valley below casting long shadows, and the gentle churn and rush of the river below providing a comforting accompaniment to the final bird songs being carried by a gentle wind.

The Tree could feel Christoph leaning against its trunk as he read his latest book about beekeeping and gardening. The Tree noticed that something was different about Christoph ... there was both a sorrow and anticipation that it could sense.

When Christoph heard the familiar panting of his friend dragging the telescope and bag up the hill, he ran to aid Sergio and welcomed him to their favourite place together. As they began to set up the telescope on The Tree's carefully crafted lookout, Sergio turned to his friend.

'Something is wrong ... you don't seem yourself!' he said matter-of-factly.

Christoph's blue eyes looked sad as he replied, 'My college tutor called my parents ... they know I've not been going in for my lessons. They've said I'm not allowed to keep coming back here.'

His tone then changed slightly to one of excitement. 'But I told my parents about you and all my plans, and they actually said that they would love to meet you. And they actually want to hear all about the pyramids ... not necessarily the alien stuff though,' he laughed. 'And they said they would support me with my dreams. They even started researching places where I can study back home if I want to ... which is wonderful. But ... it also means that I will leave this country in the autumn ...'

Christoph stopped and looked hesitantly at his friend. Sergio was looking away, making it hard to gauge what he was feeling.

'Are you okay?' Christoph asked gently.

'I will miss you,' came the response. It was simple. Short and heavy with grief.

'But it's not the end,' Christoph said eagerly. 'You can come and see me before I go. And you can come and see me in Lauterbrunnen. And Grindelwald. And I can show you all the other amazing valleys ... just think of the stars you'll be able to see!' he added, desperately trying to lift his friend out of the sadness that he could feel emanating from him.

'My parents even said that they will pay for you. And I can come back and visit you too. I'll bring you the honey that I'll harvest and we can then come back here and watch the bees and stars together!'

Sergio appreciated his friend's kindness and enthusiasm. But it did not soften the heartbreak that he felt at the impending loss.

The Tree could sense the young man was trying to muster the same energy and enthusiasm that his friend was bringing but knew the fear and loneliness that Sergio had felt – and feared that he would feel again.

'That sounds nice ... I would like that' replied Sergio quietly, attempting to smile. He then added thoughtfully, 'Maybe I need to spend less time looking up ... and perhaps see what is here on the ground. Maybe I could return to Mexico and study there. I love archaeology. And I love astronomy. Maybe I could do both. AND work at the pyramids. I know there is so much more to discover!'

As Sergio said this, The Tree saw a light came back to his eyes, as well as a sense of hope.

'And then you could perhaps come and see me?' he added hesitantly to his friend.

A surge of relief washed through The Tree and indeed through Christoph.

'OH YES!' he cried excitedly. 'I would love that. You can show me your world and I can show you mine.' And then he said, 'It is strange, I didn't think I would ever say this, but I will miss coming here. This valley, this tree, meeting you ... for the first time in a long time I actually feel like I belong!'

'Me too,' came the succinct and simple response of Sergio.

The young men both spent the rest of their evening eating the honey cakes that Christoph had brought and gazing up at the stars. The constellation of Orion was high in the sky, bringing much excitement to Sergio as he spoke of how his beloved pyramids of Teotihuacan and the pyramids of Egypt were aligned to the three stars of Orion's belt.

He was convinced that this was linked to extraterrestrial involvement, whereas Christoph laughed playfully and tried to convince him of the slightly more grounded theory of ancient civilisations that predated those of which we know – who may have had more advanced technology which has been lost in time. The two went back and forth for hours in their debates before finally settling into silence for the evening and absorbing the nigh time symphony of animals and insects in the valley, and the celestial spectacular that was the night sky.

'Whenever I taste honey, or notice the bees on their flowers during the day, I will think of you,' said Sergio, breaking the silence.

'And whenever I look up at the stars at night, I will remember you,' replied Christoph.

The Tree's heart broke. It could not bear the thought of these two friends being separated. Not just by circumstances, but by entire oceans. The Tree felt compelled to act, to do something that would ensure the bond of their friendship would never be broken. And so, The Tree made a choice. It had once split one of its many branches to aid a little boy who could not walk. Could it not give another piece of itself that would keep these two young men connected, no matter what distance was forced between them?

Drawing upon its strength, it focused its energy and will on to one of its concealed silver limbs and fed it with the same love and devotion that it could feel between the two friends gazing out into the universe. The branch began to glow. The white-hot limb shimmered and melted, until two metallic spheres now hovered between Sergio and Christoph. As the spectral orbs landed in the open palms – much to their wide-eyed amazement – something curious happened. The two young men became connected, their minds able to read each other's without a word needing to be spoken.

Both teenagers rejoiced at this newfound gift of communication … one that would ensure that they were never separated. But in their delight they did not notice the change in The Tree as a jarring sensation echoed in its soul. It was only slight, but The Tree could feel it, even more so than when it had generously given before. Again, The Tree did not understand this sensation – it rationalised that a pain in its heart was inevitable when a precious piece of itself was given. But it felt neither regret nor resentment, so invested as it was in the preservation of this beautiful friendship. It did, however, feel a distant echo of disdain, disdain for the people who had been cruel to these young men. But it did not dwell upon this, and instead reconnected to the valley, the night sky … and of course the two young men now communicating telepathically about their future plans, with the precious silver orbs held firmly in their hands.

After several hours passed – with the warm heavy blanket wrapped around their shoulders – the two young men sat quietly, looking out onto the horizon. Both feeling grateful for their friendship, but also an unspoken sadness and uncertainty about what their futures held.

VII

Since that final evening in March, The Tree did not see either of the young men again, but it found itself often wondering what had become of them and their friendship, and whether or not the silver orbs had indeed kept them connected.

It felt a surge of joy that they had found each other. That despite their differences, something powerful and been exchanged between them, creating (The Tree hoped) an everlasting bond. And as such, they no longer needed The Tree for company. They would have each other, and would no doubt go forth into the world and make waves that would impact their friendship and others in profound and wonderful ways.

So why did The Tree feel so sad? It was curious about these conflicting emotions. As the bees came to visit The Tree, and danced around its blossom, seeking the necessary pollen to return to their hive, wherever that may be, The Tree felt a strange sense of longing in its heart. And when the stars shone brightly in the sky, unobscured by cloud or light, The Tree would find itself marvelling and wondering about the universe, but then lapsing into a deep aching yearning.

The Tree realised that it missed its two friends – they had come to play a significant role in its life. They had made the days of March become filled with curiosity and wonderment – instilling an energy where anything and everything was possible. The Tree held the lessons taught to it by the two young men. It clung to the fascination and intrigue that nature and the universe had to offer. And The Tree accepted that it had played a supporting role in the lives of the two young men ... but their story was now with each other and the uncertain trajectory that their lives would take.

They had no need for The Tree anymore because they had each other. And this was 'fine' The Tree told itself ... but it desperately hoped that it would see both Christoph and Sergio again.

The Tree realised something, and its soul sank. The Tree felt lonely.

In the early years of life, The Tree had simply enjoyed its relationship with nature. But over time, it had come to enjoy the company of the strange and wonderful folk who braved the hill. It was excited to hear their stories and their adventures. And of course, it also came to share in their pain. The Tree knew that it did not always say the right thing, but it also knew the value of simply being with another soul who is in pain so that even for a short while, they can feel less alone in their suffering. And maybe ... just maybe, that pain would be eased simply by being in the presence of someone – or something – that cared.

As the night drew to a close and the stars faded, The Tree could not help but gaze at the other trees clustered together in the surrounding forests like a family, and silently wept into the stillness of the breaking dawn – the uncertainty of another day stretching out before it. And the possibility of an endless lonely solitude without the excited voices of its two friends to keep it company.

CHAPTER FOUR
April: Worth

I

'You are an abomination of Christ ... do you hear me?! YOU ARE AN ABOMINATION OF CHRIIIIST! May the good sweet lord forgive yuh!'

The young American man made his voice high-pitched and shrill as he recounted the words of his mother, elongating the vowels in an exaggerated and thick American country accent.

And then in a slower, much deeper and husky drawl he mimicked his father's voice.

'You're goin' to hell son, you're goin' to hell ... and we don't want nothun' more to do with yuh ... yuh hear me boy? NOTHUN'!'

'And so, I packed my bags and I left last night. I took the few birthday cards that I had. I stole some cash from my pa's bedside drawer and one of Momma's precious rings. And then I headed downtown. The cities here are nothun' like New Orleans ... Not that I really remember much of it ... we left when I was seven years old. Did I tell you that?'

His accent was less pronounced than his father's and had faded over time but still contained the elongated vowels – the sleepy, smoky way that turned 'New Orleans' into 'Naaww 'luhns' – which The Tree found enormously endearing. It wondered to itself if the young American had deliberately tried to change his accent – no doubt an effort to fit in with a different country, and ward off unwanted attention and mockery from others who could be cruel when they perceived difference. Or perhaps he did so to sound and be less like the father that he despised. But when he was deep in his emotions, the American 'country' twang would always find its way back into his impassioned speeches.

'But anyway, Momma said they'd never go back. Too dangerous. They said that's why they took me away from there when I was just boy. But I don't believe them ... there is something else they've never told me. I don't know what but there is a secret. I can tell! They clam up whenever we used to talk about it, especially if I mention Oklahoma, y'know? That's where they lived before they had me and moved to New Orleans.'

'No place to raise a little boy, Momma used to say. But I ain't a little boy no more. I'm eighteen years old. And I don't care where I end up ... as long as it's far away from them!'

'Happy fuckun' birthday to me,' the young man then muttered under his breath, his eyes downcast.

'I'm not surprised,' he added. 'But I think a part of me hoped that they would favour their own son over Jesus Christ and that fuckun' church they haunt ... but I guess not, I guess I was wrong – as they kept tellun' me over and over again.'

The Tree was overcome with the swirling images from the young man's memories. He saw his father's large rough hands. Hands that had been carved through working the land – from the ranch they had back in Oklahoma and the farm that he cultivated in his new homeland. The Tree saw these same rough hands striking his son repeatedly. And the bawled-up fist that met his father's jaw in return, as the young American fought back. The Tree saw the broken furniture. The pictures ripped from the young man's bedroom walls. The clothes carelessly torn from the wardrobe and thrown into a gym bag, which his father then hurled at him before bellowing for him to leave. His father's final words echoing in the night ...

'YOU AIN'T NO SON OF MINE!!!'

'And then I waited in the barn for the sun to rise and caught the first bus here ... I had to tell yuh ... 'cuz I promised that I would didn't I? I said I'd tell yuh when I'd told them. And so, I have, and this is where I'm at. Alone. A fag. And talkun' to a fuckun' tree ... no offence.'

He laughed bitterly and then the laugh gave way to tears. The sadness and disappointment was deep in his heart and permeated The Tree's tough bark. It felt the young American's pain.

The Tree listened to Austin's story. What had started as a mixture of anticipation and excitement within The Tree as the young American was heard climbing the hill towards the stone circle, had been replaced with a sense of sadness and anger as the tragic coming-out story of the night before was told. Through the rustle of its leaves, and the soft warm breeze winding through the valley, The Tree whispered to Austin.

'You are so brave. You have not done anything wrong, nor are you wrong in any way. You have the courage to be yourself and have chosen to live a life of truth rather than being ruled by fear. You are perfect as you are, and I couldn't be prouder of you!' And then it added tenderly, 'But I'm sorry for what they said. And what for what they did. You are an amazing young man, and you deserved better than how they have treated you ... both now, and in the past.'

Despite the compassion and concern that it felt for the young American, The Tree knew that its words felt brittle and hollow. How could they truly comfort this young man who had been disowned by those whom he trusted and relied on for survival? How could a few well-chosen words of kindness truly heal the depth of the wounds that had been inflicted?

Despite its doubts, The Tree sensed something shift in the young man. The words, when said with truth and from the heart, seemed to touch something in Austin, whose eyes now filled with tears. The Tree realised that these words had never been spoken before, and perhaps they would not sound as brittle as glass or shatter once spoken. In fact, the essence and care conveyed by The Tree touched the young man deeply. In this moment, he needed to hear that was he good – that he was not the abomination that his mother had described. That something older and wiser than himself could see the goodness within him, and remind him that he was not going to be cast into hell.

'You know what else he said?' the young man said through his tears. 'After he called me a filthy faggot, he called me a "worthless piece of shiiiit!"' he elongated vowels in his father's drawling voice again.

'I mean ... who says that? What kind of a man calls their son a worthless piece of shit?! I bared my fuckun' soul, and my own momma and poppa kicked me outta home.' He gritted his teeth and his breathing quickened.

'He's the worthless piece of shit … not me. Not fuckun' me!' Austin's hands clenched by his side. He jumped up suddenly and ran to the side of the hill where the drop was sheer, the river winding below. And then he bellowed into the valley, 'YOU HEAR ME, BOY? YOU'RE THE FUCKUN' PIECE OF SHIT … YOU HEAR ME, PA? I HATE YOU! I – FUCKUN' – HATE – YOU – BOTH!'

And then he sobbed. He retreated from the rocky edge and back to The Tree where he slumped against the sturdiness of the thick trunk and cried even harder.

The Tree too wept silently in sympathy for the young man, its heart breaking for Austin's disappointment, for his courage, for the betrayal by his parents, and for his loneliness.

'I'm goin' to the city,' the young American announced stoically through his tears – a strength and power being reclaimed in his voice.

'I ain't gonna let them win. I'm gonna make something of myself … they'll see … I don't fuckun' need them … I don't need nobody!'

The Tree knew that this was not true. That everyone needs someone to care for them. To show them kindness. To validate their existence, and let them know in so many different ways that they are okay. That they have value. That they have worth simply for being who they are. The Tree also knew that to have needs and for these not to be met can feel intolerable to human beings. And what he saw in the young American was a desperate attempt to protect himself from the wounds inflicted by disappointment and betrayal, by those whom he needed to love him the most.

The Tree longed to share this truth with its companion but knew that such words would fall upon deaf ears. He was not ready to hear such wisdom – what he needed now was to survive and believe that he could without the support of others. Austin was trying to convince himself that he didn't need anyone, and therefore told himself that he didn't need to get close to others and get hurt because 'everyone' would eventually disappointed and betrayed him. In that moment, Austin vowed to harden his heart and not let anyone get close. And for now, The Tree had to accept this and wait patiently to see what would unfold.

II

It was a mild and tranquil day in April when the young American returned to The Tree. Five years had passed. Life and colour rippled through the valley as springtime brought with it a sense of hope and the promise of new life and beauty. The Tree silently sang in unison with the chirping of the birds and swayed its luscious green branches to mirror the dance of the butterflies that fluttered around The Tree. They eventually settled on the rocks of the stone circle, slowly opening and closing their wings hypnotically, and absorbed the warm and energising rays of golden sunlight.

The valley scenery was a sharp contrast to the appearance of the young American as he crossed the stone circle – walking like something resurrected from the grave. Austin made his approach towards The Tree. His once bright eyes and youthful face appeared aged and haunted. His eyes dull and hollow, bloodshot and struggling to focus. The Tree observed that his physique had changed. He looked muscular, stronger – but his soul screamed of fragility and vulnerability. It was as though a flame had been snuffed out leaving a feeble glow that failed to reignite.

Austin's face was unshaven and his clothes – dishevelled but fashionable – were representative of the era in the latter part of the twentieth century. As the young American edged closer to The Tree, he paused, a look of unease and discomfort spreading across his face followed by a lurch, and the expulsion of the what The Tree assumed was the previous evening's 'adventures'. The smell of the thick liquid was sour and rancid, only briefly eclipsing the sweet and fruity scents of the emerging flowers and honeysuckle that surrounded The Tree. The butterflies alighted into the sky, and in a colourful smoke-like plume they took their leave from the sorry sight that now occupied the beautiful space.

Now on his hands and knees, wheezing and spitting the remainder of vile tasting liquid from his mouth, the young American crawled towards The Tree, and in a sound all too familiar to The Tree, began to cry.

'My dear boy ...' said The Tree sorrowfully. 'You have been on my mind since you left here five years ago. I have been so worried about you.'

The Tree's care and concern for the Austin was palpable. Its warmth and compassion emanated like a blanket of love enveloping the shadow-like form that was nestled against its trunk. It brought its branches lower to embrace the young man, surrounding him with the beautiful scent of spring, and the feeling of being safe, held, and contained. The young American melted into the embrace and closed his eyes, his breathing slowing down, and an ease beginning to calm his body and mind.

'I don't know what I've done to myself,' he began to say quietly. 'I hate myself for what I've let them do to me … for what I've done to myself.' And then echoing the haunting words of his father he added in a whisper, 'I'm just a worthless piece of shit.'

The Tree's soul broke. Hearing the words of the young man's father repeated back – not as an echo, but as a deeply ingrained belief that the young man had come to hold about himself – was devastating. The Tree could feel that something had changed within its friend. Austin's spirit had been crushed. His mind had been polluted by the words of his parents. And his body too seemed to have been subjected to similar contaminations, the strange smell of drugs and alcohol seeping from the young man's pores. The Tree also sensed that the young man had stopped caring for his body, and sadly others had seemed to demonstrate the same disregard and disrespect to this young man's body and soul, using him for their own pleasure but also as an object to attack and spoil for their own unsavoury needs and envy.

Austin looked exhausted. He hadn't slept for days but had been determined to reach the sanctuary of The Tree. A place of safety where he could rest, feel safe, and know that for a brief moment, his body and mind would be his own – and not the possession of others. His eyelids were heavy. The still air and the soft scents of springtime enveloped him. And so, he allowed himself to sleep – and as he did so, his mind began to recount the events of the last three of the five years, processing them in his dreams which he shared with The Tree in a kaleidoscope of images and scenes crashing into each other and telling the young man's story.

The sweeping valley disappeared from The Tree's view and was instead replaced by the loud and vibrant sounds and colours of the London club scene in the year 1990.

The Tree beheld a sea of shirtless men dancing amidst the smoke and coloured lights. The curious and unfamiliar sound of electro dance music pumping through the club speakers and echoing the rhythm and euphoria of the people for whom it entranced. The Tree saw Austin in the crowd – equally animated by the music and the intoxicating scent of the men that surrounded him. Everyone felt like an opportunity for him, his wide eyes darting from person to person, body to body, seeking out connection, no matter how briefly.

The Tree saw him amongst his people – the tribe that he had sought to be a part of. The scene was a far cry from the fear and threat of loneliness that his parents had said would be his fate. The young American laughed and smiled, and moved his body to the electronic beats his group of friends emerging through the crowd to join him. The Tree too felt the euphoria from the scene, and a sense of being truly alive rippling through its soul – the lights, music and cocktail of scents elevating The Tree to a new level of consciousness.

The next scene had a different edge. This time the club was less well lit. It had the feel of being darker, not just because of the lights, which were now an erotic glow of scarlet, but the energy too of this place felt dark … Hungry … Seductive! But also, dangerous. The building that The Tree found itself witnessing felt less open and inviting than before and instead felt secret and maze-like … underground corridors leading into smaller darker rooms inhabited by entwined bodies, writhing and sliding over each other like eels in pit. The sound of moaning could be heard echoing through the tunnels of the labyrinth … a seductive mixture of pleasure and pain.

There was a search for euphoria, but not through the music this time – instead through the sensual pleasures of the body. Austin was wandering the labyrinth. His eyes were wide, and his pupils dilated, giving them a strange hollow and deadened appearance. He silently watched the other men as they explored each other's bodies, aroused, a mixture of fear and excitement coursing through his body. But something else too … The Tree could sense that the young man's body and mind were heightened. Not just from the scenes that he found himself so seductively enticed by … but by something synthetic … a deluge of strange and manufactured chemicals shared with him by his friends, a curious bond that chained them together on these familiar nights until the dawn broke, along with their spirits. And when the chemical euphoria finally abated, they were left only with a sense of hopelessness, despair, and loneliness.

As the scene melted away, The Tree's mood dramatically changed. A sensation like being punched in the chest and struggling to breathe overcame it. It felt afraid for Austin and the path that he appeared to be on. The Tree felt a desperate desire for someone to take care of its vulnerable friend and keep him safe.

The Tree saw the faces of different men: men of different ages, different body shapes, different colours. All smiling at the young American. Telling him how handsome he is ... How they could help him go far in this world ... How they would help him ... How they would love him and take care of him. How they would pleasure him in ways he could not even dare to imagine! And The Tree felt the young American's heart leap in these moments, so hungry was he for acceptance, for love and validation. Austin believed that he had worth in the eyes of these men. Through his handsome face. Through his muscular body. Through his 'country' accent, which others found so appealing. All of this was a sharp contrast to what he knew from his parents and from the beliefs about himself that his parents' religion had told him.

And so, Austin consumed their praise like a baby bird longing for its first feed ... but never fully feeling satiated. He hungered for their adoration, for their love. For their acceptance. And so, he did what they asked, he accepted the compliments they gave him. The gifts that they promised him. And in exchange he offered his body to them, the only currency that he believed he had.

At first, he enjoyed their bodies, the pleasure, the exploration. But The Tree saw how people lied. How they used him. It saw the subtle ways they would manipulate the Austin, pushing him to go further into a darker drug-fuelled sexual abyss, even when it hurt, even when deep down both they (and the young American) knew that he no longer wanted it. But they kept going. And so Austin found ways to disappear into the corners of his own mind until they had finished ... and eventually discarded him.

A terrible grief swept through The Tree as the scene changed, and it witnessed Austin by the hospital beds of some of his friends. An unusual disease had overcome them, causing their bodies to lose the ability to fight off illness and infection. The Tree felt the heartbreak of witnessing the young American's friends deteriorate in their health … becoming thin, pale, and ghost-like wraiths in their appearance. Strange blemishes appeared on their skin, and a confusion and terror descended on their minds. And sadly, for many of them, death came quickly, unexpectedly and without dignity.

The Tree saw the mixture of care and persecution these men were subjected to. There was compassion from the medical staff who tried to help them and make them comfortable, desperately trying to understand and fight this mysterious illness. Whilst others took to the streets spreading messages of hate and blame, often echoing the words that Austin had heard throughout his life from his parents and religious leaders. Now, it was also being spoken from people in government, people in power who controlled the country. And instead of keeping people safe, or giving hope to the population, or compassion to those who were sick, they embarked upon a campaign of hate and negligence.

The Tree was confused. It could not understand how or why those in power could ignore the plight of these sick people. People who had done nothing wrong. Nothing to deserve the savagery of this mysterious illness as it tore through an entire community of men. The Tree could not understand why they would not unite to care and love these people who were sick but instead chose to demonise them.

Sadly, Austin did not feel confused or question this. The Tree sensed that he had come to expect this. The messages of hate simply reinforced what he already believed about himself. That he was worthless.

Another scene … The Tree saw the young American, cold and huddled under a grim-looking blanket. His face gaunt, eyes hollow, his face dirty. Asking passers-by in the street for change. Anything so that he could get something to eat and drink. The Tree silently wept as the people ignored him. Some looked at him with disdain and judgement. Others would look embarrassed and attempted to continue their conversations, as if the young man's presence was an afront on their happy existence and threatened their denial about the reality and horrors of the world.

The Tree silently implored Austin to stop and to be kind to himself as it witnessed him offering his body to people for money. It watched helplessly as the young American did what he needed to do to survive ... an exchange of his body for their money, so let down was he by the society that he perceived to hate him so much. He no longer cared what they did to him. He saw his only worth as being intrinsically linked with his capacity for sex – that exchanging this for food, shelter, and warmth for the night felt like a small price to pay. But The Tree could see the impact on Austin's spirit – a spirit that once full of hope was now brutally and absolutely shattered.

The Tree's consciousness came back to the valley and the sleeping young man under its canopy of leafy green branches. The Tree felt in shock ... the young American's life had taken such a sad turn. It was not the life that The Tree had hoped for him when they had first met. A life that seemed so full of hope and promise had taken a dark turn, leaving Austin broken and all alone in the world ... and without a sense of worth.

The Tree knew that people needed to feel cherished and loved for who they are, and for the love they receive to be unconditional and not based on who or what others need them to be. It also knew that when a child is made to feel worthless, they carry a deep sense of shame that tells them that they are wrong. Not that they have done something wrong, but that they are wrong to their very core. And if this harmful belief is reinforced through their encounters in the world, then their soul begins to wither. They come to believe that the cruel and careless ways that people speak or behave towards them are justified. That they are deserving of unkindness. That they are nothing more than a toy to be played with, used, and eventually discarded.

The Tree saw this in the story of the young American. It longed to hold Austin and tell him that everything would be okay. That he was good. That he was loved. That he would survive. But how could The Tree know this or even promise this? How could it give the young man asleep against its trunk a message of hope that would eradicate years of harmful messages that told him that he was 'no good'? The Tree saw glimpses of the world that Austin was part of, and it felt powerless to change it. And similarly to the young man's soul, The Tree felt its own soul begin to falter.

III

Several hours passed. The young American slowly opened his eyes. He was aware of feeling nauseous but having expelled the previous night's contents from his stomach and having slept, he felt much better than he had. Until he remembered why he had consumed the drink and cocktail of drugs the night before.

Austin remembered the cold and sterile hospital room. The expressionless face of the doctor before him. The words that seemed to be uttered in slow motion, words that he couldn't quite comprehend, other than the accompanying feeling of doom. A sentence of death had been given to him. He, like his friends, would face a similar fate of hospitals, of sickness, judgement ... and eventually death. He had the mysterious disease that his friends and community had succumbed to. And he was terrified.

No words of comfort had been offered by the doctor. Just a matter-of-fact statement of 'you have it!' That they would do their best to help him but that treatment was in the early stages. There were no guarantees. There was no 'I'm sorry'. There was no 'Is there anyone we can call for you?' There were no warm words of comfort or a caring embrace. Just a flat statement of fact. A look of both judgement and disdain. And then silence.

Austin remembered the dread and loneliness that overcame him as the doctor left the room, proclaiming that they would simply give him a few moments to contemplate what this means, to gather himself, and then leave. Which the young American did. He left the hospital in a daze. Time had slowed down. Everything felt hazy as though he were walking through a thick treacle-like fog. He 'had it'! He had what had killed all of his friends ... and deep down he thought to himself, I always knew something would get me ... this is my punishment. I am a worthless piece of shit!

The Tree felt Austin's anguish in that moment, their combined sorrow sweeping through the valley. The birds and animals fell silent. The trees of the valley were still. All that could be heard was the gentle rush of water from the river below and the light rustling of The Tree's leaves as its branches slowly swept downwards and embraced the young American.

71

'DON'T TOUCH ME!' Austin screamed. 'Everything I touch gets fucked up ... gets destroyed. Please ... I don't wanna hurt you too!'

The Tree paused out of respect for the young American's wishes, so frequently had others not respected his body. And then spoke softly and calmly. 'I am not afraid. You are worth more than you know. And I care about you very much. You don't have to be afraid ... nor do you have to protect me from anything.'

And with that, The Tree opened its branches once more before tentatively moving back into the embrace. An embrace that was without force, without agenda, and without malice or desire – an underrated gift of offering love and attuned contact that did not expect anything in return. And this time, Austin leaned into it and wept. He could feel the love and care from The Tree. He felt relieved that something would care enough to hold him. That they were not afraid of being 'contaminated' as he feared they would be. That something had uttered the words that he had longed to hear from his parents. From his doctor. From the people who had told him that they cared for him but carelessly used his body and discarded him.

For a moment – feeling the love and compassion from The Tree – Austin experienced a glimmer of something unfamiliar ... he felt that he might not be so worthless after all.

As he continued to lean into the embrace, The Tree felt the urge to offer words of reassurance but instead it paused. The Tree knew from experience that sometimes reassurance may feel hollow or suggest that pain and uncertainty can't be tolerated. The Tree didn't want the young man to feel alone anymore. So instead, it asked, 'What are you afraid of? You can tell me.'

Austin looked up, his face thoughtful and streaked with tears, and his eyes looking up to the sky as if hoping for an answer to be beamed down by the warm sun. And then looking downwards at his grubby clothes and dirty hands, he said ...

'I'm afraid that no one will love me now. I'm afraid that no one will ever touch me again ... and I don't just mean for sex, I mean at all. People are so afraid to even hug someone like me in case they catch "it". I'd never really thought about it before but I'm afraid that I'll never be able to have children, not without passing "this" on to them. I'd kill myself before I let that happen ... before I gave this thing to anyone. I'm a dirty pig. I'm fuckun' vile. And I fuckun' hate myself!'

The tears came again. And not just from the young American's eyes. But also from within the soul of The Tree. Its silent sobs echoing those of its young friend. And then it said tenderly …

'Those things that you believe about yourself are lies – the lies of people who are ignorant and spew hate about things they don't understand. People have not treated you kindly. They have not given you the love, or care, or acceptance that you deserved. People have not shown you or your body respect or tenderness. Their actions do not make you wrong … but maybe they have to make you feel these emotions, so they themselves don't have to feel them within themselves.'

The Tree continued. 'And I can tell you from the depths of my soul that I don't believe that you are vile. Or bad. Or wrong. I know you to be wonderful. Kind. And generous with your love. You have a soul that is bright and vibrant … but you have taken a dark path. But all paths can be changed, and new roads can be forged, if only we have the courage to try. Sometimes we forget that we have the power to change the trajectory of our own lives, so powerless others can make us feel. But you are not powerless, my friend. And you do have the strength to fight this.'

The Tree's impassioned words stirred something within Austin's heart. A light that had been extinguished so long ago by the seduction of the new world he had found himself in was ignited once more. It was a tiny flame of faith and belief that he had forgotten existed within his heart. The Tree knew that sometimes it takes the kindness and honesty of another to reflect back what people already know about themselves – what they had sadly forgotten because of the cruelty and lies spoken by others.

The Tree knew that Austin didn't need reassurance. He needed someone to reflect back his goodness and remind him of his worth, but to also remind him that there are some aspects of life that one cannot have control over – that learning and growth can come in the aftermath, once the experience has been understood. And it was the light of this realisation that The Tree felt was beginning to glow within the young American. The seeds of knowing were beginning to embed

– that he does not have to succumb to a fate that others had decided for him, and instead he could find a way to fight. To fight for himself, his future, and – if he was able to muster the strength – maybe to fight for his community too.

IV

Some years later, the young American returned to The Tree. It was not uncommon during the month of April for The Tree to wonder about the young man and his journey – so deeply impacted it had been by his story. The Tree knew from other people who had visited it over the years of the widespread impact that the virus that afflicted Austin had had on so many others.

So many lives had tragically been lost. But The Tree also knew that times were changing as the new millennium approached. That there was help available that could slow down the impact of the virus so that it did not have to be the 'death sentence' that the young American had believed. But as the years passed, The Tree found itself ruminating on Austin's fate, hoping that he was safe ... that he was happy ... that he was loved. So, when one day in April a familiar and husky 'HOWDY!!!' was yelled across the hilltop, The Tree's soul soared with joy.

A very healthy-looking man swaggered up the hill and crossed the stone circle towards The Tree. In his jeans, plaid shirt, and cowboy hat, the young American looked vibrant, as though he had found himself once more. The confident man walking towards The Tree on this particular day was a stark contrast to the fragile and broken version that The Tree had witnessed during their last encounter.

With a wide grin on his clean-shaven face, the young American yelled again ...

'Howdy ... did yuh miss me? It's been one helluva ride ... you got some time to hear about it, bud? You ain't never gonna believe it!'

The Tree spread its branches wide and welcomed the return of its friend. It felt a surge of joy and relief, the fears that it had dared not allow itself to ponder concerning the young man's fate evaporated like morning dew in the sunlight. If The Tree could smile, its grin would have matched that of its American friend. Instead, it sent a surge of energy and love through its branches, creating a curious change to occur in The Tree's appearance.

Amidst the varying shades of green leaves, there grew flowers of pink and white. And amongst the flourishing blossoms grew fruit from a curious silver branch. Tiny green orbs began to swell and grow, and morphed into large heart-shaped apples of deep pinks and reds in colour ... but the essence contained within reflected the mercury-like silver of the branch from which it came.

The hum of small honeybees and the soft fluttering of butterflies joined the spectacle, enjoying the colours and scent now emanating from The Tree. A shiny silver apple – the unusual size of a small melon – drew life from the rare silver branch until it disintegrated. The apple was tossed towards Austin playfully, who expertly caught it and laughed.

But in this moment, something curious occurred that Austin did not perceive, and that The Tree recognised. A strange and familiar sensation of pain ricocheted through its soul as the silver branch dissolved and released the strange apple. Without entirely understanding – or even consciously willing this to be the case – The Tree had given something more to Austin than a simple piece of fruit. It had given him a piece of its soul. The Tree felt no regret, after all, this was not the first time that it had given something of itself to ease the suffering of those whom it had come to love.

Staring at the apple with wonderment, Austin raised it to his lips and bit through its soft skin – the flow of delicious, sweet juices filling his mouth. But it wasn't just the juice that was delicious. It was the very essence of the apple itself, which caused a warm glow to tingle and spread throughout the man's entire body, leaving him feeling energised and alive.

Feeling nourished by these curious sensations, and the apple having been devoured so that it was no more than just its core, an even stranger thing happened. The flesh of the apple began to swell and grow, until the tiny core and pips were engulfed, and its smooth and shiny silver peel had also grown back so that the apple was whole once more. Not to the size that it was previously, however. But it had grown back into an ordinary-sized (but nonetheless beautiful) metallic-looking apple, leaving Austin laughing in astonishment at the strange fruit.

'Easy now, partner … enough of the theatrics,' he laughed. And then added, 'And thank you … I'll save this for later. But for now, can I tell you where I've been?'

The creatures of nature occupying the hilltop had now grown tired and retreated back to their places of rest. The sun was now high in the azure sky and sparkled off of the gently flowing river below. And so, The Tree settled and opened itself to listen intently to the rest of the young man's story.

'Please,' implored The Tree. 'Tell me everything.'

The young man continued with his story, and as he did so, The Tree's surroundings began to fade and disappear, giving way to a collection of scenes that The Tree knew to be the young man's memories. But this time, they were accompanied by his now confident 'country' voice, as he narrated the past five years of his life.

'Something strange happened after I left you. It was as if all the words and feelings of comfort that I felt disappeared. I left them here with you, at least I thought I did. But maybe they were just locked away somewhere deep in my mind. I think I needed to forget what I had just been told by the doctors. But when I did, I also erased what we spoke about … and your kindness. Because If I had held on to it, then it would mean that what I was actually facing was real. I didn't want it to be, so anything associated with it had to be forgotten – even if it was only for a short time.'

The Tree understood this. It knew that sometimes the truth can be too painful to bear, and that people need to make themselves forget so that they can tolerate the intolerable. The Tree also knew that in doing so, the young man had separated himself from all of the memories that surrounded the painful one, even though what he had received from The Tree in that moment was necessary and reparative. It understood that in that moment Austin had been terrified, in shock, and needed to protect himself in the only way that he could. If he couldn't use substances to block out the feelings and memories, he would instead order his mind to creatively lock away the difficult feelings and images until they stayed out of awareness – without him even having to consciously will them to be so. The Tree felt sad that the young man had needed to do this but it could understand why, especially when it knew that the young American had witnessed many of his friends die from the very illness that he had just been diagnosed with.

'So I went out. I kept doing what I had been doing. I went to bath houses. I hooked up with guys, sometimes several in one night. I still had to hustle ... a boy's gotta eat and I had no money. I'm not proud of myself but I did what I had to do. Survival, y'know? But, a part of me must have still known what I was doing. Because I always played safe. I didn't always in the past ... I mean, we didn't know what was causing this thing to spread. And before then, we didn't even know we could get hurt. No one taught us about this stuff. The stupid laws in this country meant that even teachers at school couldn't talk about this stuff, otherwise they would be fired for "promoting a lifestyle", as they called it, "that threatened the true family" – whatever the fuck that meant!'

'But despite all that, I listened to what I heard the doctors and nurses say when my friends got sick. And even though I didn't want to believe that I could follow a similar fate, a part of me still knew that I had to keep other people safe. People didn't always show me the same courtesy though. Some guys outright refused and said they didn't care. I was able to stop but I know other friends of mine who haven't been so lucky. Or haven't felt able to say no. It's so sad, but when you're constantly told that you're bad, or wrong, and worthless ... eventually you start to believe it. Hell, I did believe it.'

The young American paused. He looked sad as he recalled the memory of his own self-loathing and despair. The Tree felt the ache in Austin's heart and the desperate sorrow that he felt his existence would be ... but it also felt the change in him. That something had shifted. That the young man had recovered a sense of worth and was perhaps even allowing himself to dispel the lies about himself that he had been told, but the memories being shared highlighted that this had been a long journey for him.

'And another strange thing that I noticed ... I found myself becoming cruel on the inside. I felt anger and hatred to those guys who looked healthy. Who were younger than me and seemed so carefree. I know this is going to sound terrible but there were moments where I fantasised that they would get used in the same way that people had used me. That their friends would get sick. That they would know what it was like to watch people that they cared about die. Sometimes, I wanted them to get sick and die. But also, I wanted to die myself. Again, I didn't know why. It was like I had completely forced the truth from my memories. But what I did know is that I wanted the handsome, young, and healthy guys to suffer. To be spoilt in some way.'

The Tree could feel the young man's anguish. The conflict that he had felt back then. And the shame for having such fantasies. But The Tree knew that sometimes people cannot bear the parts of themselves that they hate and need to put these parts of themselves into others, as though cleansing themselves of what they believe to be bad or impure parts, locating them within the soul of another person instead. The Tree had, after all, witnessed this many years ago when it saw the villagers burning their fellow men and women on the hilltop in the name of religion ... but secretly because of their own envy and self-loathing.

The Tree knew that people also feel angry towards others who are perceived to have something that they themselves lack. And as such, they find ways in fantasy and reality to take from and destroy the source of goodness in others. And in doing so, they would feel (albeit temporarily) less bad about themselves. But that kind of envy comes at a cost. Because The Tree had heard and seen over the years that these attacks don't bring comfort but further fuel the internal sense of lack and self-hatred. The guilt makes them feel ashamed and worthless, and thus they seek to find a new target to 'spoil' but the cycle begins again, and is often out of the person's awareness.

As if hearing The Tree's thoughts, Austin confirmed this and continued his story.

'I think you're right ... I envied these guys. I wanted to be them. But I also hated them. I wanted to be with them but I also wanted to hurt them. I didn't do it, but I felt the urge to do so. And that's not me. It has never been me, and it made me hate myself even more!'

As Austin paused, The Tree was once more engulfed in his memories. It saw his conflicting sexual encounters. The lonely nights in a cold damp studio apartment. A single light bulb providing an insubstantial glow which barely lit the gloom of the dismal space. The cheap processed food that was all he could afford. And the echo of sirens and screams from the city below that gave him some semblance of company in a world that he felt had fundamentally rejected him.

The Tree saw the grubby mattress on the exposed wooden floors, and the young American curled up like a child – sobbing into the unwashed covers. With sorrow, The Tree heard the voice in the young man's head at the time. A vicious voice of self-contempt willing him towards his next sexual encounter in the hopes of a warm and inviting place to stay, even if for just one night. Or a potential client from whom he could extract some form of financial recompense for the sexual acts he would inevitably have to perform in order to survive.

The Tree sensed his desperation in these times and tried to reconcile these images and feelings with the healthy young man who presently sought comfort and refuge under its branches. The Tree longed for the story to be complete – Austin's anguish during these past moments feeling intolerable. The Tree's soul twisted in agony as it continued to share in its friend's tragic tale.

V

The bleak and dismal apartment scene finally dissolved and gave way to the unforgivingly bright fluorescent lights and clinical scent of a hospital ward. The rectangular metal-framed beds were covered with neat, clean and crisp sheets, and there was a hum of activity from the staff as the nurses bustled around the bays tending to the patients occupying each bed – one of whom was Austin. His eyes were closed and his skin was clammy. He looked like a haunted shadow of the eighteen-year-old that The Tree had first met. His skin was now ghostly pale, and his once muscular body from the hours spent with his friends in the gym looked frail and skeletal, the hospital sheets enveloping his shrunken body like a death shroud.

The Tree could sense the growing concern from the staff as the young man's health continued to deteriorate, his body struggling to fight off one new infection after the other – several had now taken hold. It saw the sad exchange of looks between the staff when the young man would ask between his rasping breaths and rattling cough if he would get better. They would reassure him that new treatments

were being developed and that they would do everything they could …
but they were insistent about him contacting his 'loved ones', the
unspoken message being that he may not have much time left. Austin
refused their invitation.

The Tree observed a particularly difficult night where a fellow
patient was stealthily removed from the ward, accompanied only by
the sound of the squeaking wheels of the metal bed and the hushed
whispers of the staff. He had lost his battle with the virus and the
collection of infections that had overwhelmed his body. Austin didn't
know his name … another nameless and faceless victim who would be
forgotten. But as the patient was taken away in the early hours of the
morning, a deep fear gripped the young American. Will I be next? It
was at that moment that he conceded – not to the illness, but for the
staff to call his parents. A part of him didn't believe that they would
come, but if he was going to die he wanted to see them. It was time.

'And so they came. I woke up one day … who knows what
day it was, they all seemed to blend into one. I was in and out of
consciousness. But I woke to see Momma's face gazing down at me. She
looked so frightened. Her face was streaked with tears. Pa was there
too … but he wouldn't look at me. I could tell he was furious. His jaw
was tense, as it often was when he spoke to me as a boy. I could tell he
didn't want to be here … that nothun' had changed 'tween us. When
he did finally speak, the contempt in his voice and the resentful way
that he looked at me was crippling.'

The Tree then heard the low drawl and snarl of his father's
cruel words.

'What have you done to yourself, boy? You should be damned
ashamed … look at what you're doing to your momma. You think
she needs this shit? You think I do? We already lost one child … that
poor sweet girl was taken from us by God. She did nothun' wrong. But
you … you live this … this lifestyle! This dirty sinful lifestyle. And this
is God's punishment for you. For all you fags!'

Austin's father's eyes were filled with hate and tears, his body
remaining tense and his hands trembling as they clenched and
formed fists.

Austin stared aghast at his father. It was as though he'd been
slapped. He was confused. The wickedness of his father's words aside,

the only thing he could focus on was the revelation of a long-held secret – a secret that Austin had always sensed. I had a sister?

'Our sweet little girl deserved a life. But you've thrown yours away and now you're being punished. I ain't got no sympathy for you, boy. And I won't let your momma be put through this again … she ain't gonna watch another one of her kids die. Especially not when one has chosen death! Your sister … she didn't get chance to choose nuthun'! I would trade your sickening life for hers … if only God would let me!'

The Tree had no memory of the young man sharing this detail with him but as it gauged the shocked expression that was frozen on his face, neither did Austin. He looked tired and gaunt, his strength dwindling as his illness continued to take hold. But he pulled himself up in his bed using the little strength that he had left. And asked simply in a whisper …

'What are you talkun' about, Pa?'

Austin's father swung his head back towards his dying son and glared at him. 'Your momma made we swear we'd never talk of it with yuh but this is the last chance we're gonna get …'

Austin's mother said nothing and looked away.

'Our daughter died when she was just seven. It's why we left Oklahoma and moved to Naw'luhns. It's why we had you … to try and erase the memory of that what happened that day. We wanted another daughter. We were told that you'd be a little girl, but all you were was a disappointment. Back then, and even now, with this lifestyle you've chosen to live! But the lord God claimed our sweet little girl.

'It was during the storms of '72 that hit Oklahoma. We thought it was going to be a beautiful day. But it wasn't, it was anything but. The tornado hit at dusk. The sirens went. We hid in the storm shelter in the yard. But she ran from it … back into the house to save her favourite stupid toy.'

The Tree saw the man's face reddened as his jaw clenched even tighter. He couldn't look his son in the eye. His wife reached out and touched his arm tenderly, but still refused to look at her son.

'I couldn't get to her in time. I tried … I swear, I ran after her. We'd had storms before but nothun' like this. The wind was so strong. The animals were scared and ran to the barn. Your sister couldn't hear me over the wind. But she saw me, she was in her bedroom staring out at me through the window. Poor little girl … she looked so scared. And then something hit me, some kinda debris. I fell to the ground and that's when I saw it. The tornado that killed your sister!'

In that moment, The Tree saw the monstrous funnel snaking out of the clouds like a hungry beast … the cone as black as the night sky as it wreaked havoc through the surrounding corn fields.

'There was stuff swirling all around it and it was tearing up the ground, the trees, and heading right for our house. The roar of that wind was like nothun' I'd ever heard before – sounded like a plane engine crashing into the earth. I felt sick and dizzy from whatever hit me. And then everything went dark and muffled. I don't know what happened next cuz I must've blacked out. When I came to, the barn was still standing but the house was gone … and so was your sister.'

The Tree's shock mirrored Austin's – his mouth agape and his dark eyes now wide with disbelief. The Tree couldn't speak. And neither could the young American. After a few moments he reached his hand out to touch his father's …

His father sharply pulled his own hand out of reach – a look of disgust spreading across his face. Ashamed, Austin pulled his pale and skeletal hand back too, and then glanced at his mother, who was silently sobbing. Instinctively he reached his hand out to her, but was met with the same rejection as from his father. His mother's look was less contemptuous and more one of fear. And then she spoke for the first time, wide-eyed and frantic.

'That day, I made a promise to God that we would do better. That we would be better. That we knew this was a sign from Him to leave Oklahoma and start again, and devote ourselves to Him and only Him. Soon after we arrived in New Orleans I fell pregnant. We joined the church and tried to put the past behind us. Nothun' good comes from dwellun' on the past. We had God's love and we would have you. But you weren't like the other little boys. You didn't like what they liked. You only played with little girls, like some kinda sissy – you liked their toys and not the ones we got you. It just ain't natural for a boy to like those kinda things. To like to sing and dance, even at that age. Even the preacher said so. He said, "That boy ain't right." He said, "That boy's got the aura of sin around him. Your boy is gonna go bad." And lord help us, you did. And now this is God's punishment. We thought that by taking you away from that sinful city you'd get better. You wouldn't be corrupted, you would be saved – and your sister didn't die for nothun'! But you're not saved. You're damned … and we can't be here no more. We've done our part, and the rest you're gonna have to face on your own.'

No tears fell from his mother's eyes now. There was no apology amidst her monologue. Just this final statement delivered in a cold, detached, matter-of-fact way. And then she took her husband's hand, and without another word stood up and turned her back on her son. As did her husband.

The last thing Austin saw was both parents – now strangers to him – nodding politely at the nurse before turning back to survey the ward and its patients. They shook their heads from side to side in unison, and tutted – an expression of their disgust and contempt for the patients on the ward, one of whom was their son. Without looking at him, they turned their heads forwards once more and left the hospital ward.

Austin knew in that moment that this would be the last time he ever saw them. He was dying … and he was all alone.

The Tree felt a sensation in its soul like it had been shot with both barrels of a shotgun. An excruciating pain penetrated its trunk, accompanied by what felt like an inability to breathe. It felt shocked. Confused. And then numb. What had it just beheld? Was this real? Could this young man's parents really be so cold? So callous? So hateful? Could they not see that their son was dying? That he needed them? That he needed their love, their compassion?

The Tree felt such pity for the dying man in the hospital bed. And then it felt hate. A hatred that burned in its own heart towards Austin's parents. It wished harm on them. On their precious church. It wanted them to know the pain that they had caused their son. It wanted them to feel the pain of their first loss, and could not understand how they could speak of death in such a strange way. What was wrong with these people?

But The Tree knew that its anger and hatred was pointless. That its hate needed to be quenched with love … love and kindness for the young American, and for its energy not to be wasted on his heartless fanatical parents.

VI

Austin's memories faded away and The Tree was brough back to the familiar sounds and smells of the valley – a sharp and welcome contrast to the sterile hospital ward where it had beheld the young man looking so vulnerable.

'I am so very sorry for what they said to you. And I'm deeply sorry your loss. For the loss of your sister, and for not having the parents that you needed and deserved. You are a remarkable young man, and I would have been proud if you were my son.'

There was such kindness in The Tree's voice. Such tenderness. This was not lost on Austin, who in response reached his arms around The Tree's wide trunk and hugged it – finally hearing the words that he had longed to hear all through his life.

The Tree reciprocated the embrace with the same warmth and love, gently bringing its branches downwards and around its friend's body.

There was a moment of silence that seemed to last forever. No words were spoken but a simple exchange of love and gratitude passed between The Tree and the young American.

With tears of gratitude in his eyes, Austin eventually released his hold on The Tree, turned, and walked to the edge of the hilltop. He took several slow, deep breaths, inhaling the sweet perfume of the valley on this gloriously still spring day. He surveyed the beauty of the hills and the river below, the gentle sound of wildlife that could be heard all around him, and the firmness of the ground beneath him. He smiled contentedly and then walked back towards The Tree.

Sitting down on the ground beneath its enormous canopy he looked up and The Tree's outstretched limbs and the subtle shades of green that he beheld as the sunlight flickered through the leaves, creating a hypnotic and comforting emerald aura to surround them both.

'So of course I felt like shit when they left,' he said honestly. 'But, in some ways it was a relief too. I finally knew exactly where I stood. I finally knew the truth about somethun' that had never been spoken before but that I had felt all through my life. That there was something missing. That I could never live up to something, and until then I never knew what or who that somethun' was. I always thought that I was the problem 'cuz that's how they made me feel. But in that moment when they left me dying in that hospital bed, it wasn't their words that echoed in my mind … it was yours. The words that you said to me all those years ago.

'As I said before, I think I had buried them because to know them meant to know something that I wasn't ready to hear. But in that moment when they left me, I thought of you. I heard your words. And I could finally allow myself to feel your love, your kindness, and ultimately the truth. The truth is that I do have worth and just because other people have treated me bad, that doesn't mean that I am bad. Sure, I've made some mistakes, but I am and always have been a good guy. I have value. I have worth. And I don't deserve to be treated like a piece of shit. And you helped me to see that and finally to believe in myself.'

As Austin looked up at The Tree, his eyes wide with appreciation and a sweet smile spreading across his face, The Tree felt its soul swell with the familiar feeling of love and joy towards the young man, and shook a light flurry of sweet apple-blossom petals down on to him. The action caused the kaleidoscope of butterflies that frequently resided in the sanctuary of The Tree's branches to awaken and join the curious display of free-falling petals as they too took to the air around The Tree in an entrancing dance of colour.

The young American laughed heartly, enjoying the theatrics of The Tree, catching the petals as they landed in his open palms, and marvelling at the few tame butterflies that trusted him sufficiently to land in the soft nest of petals that he cupped in his hands.

The Tree beamed and reflected back what it saw in the soul of its young friend.

'Something has changed. I can see it, but I can also feel it. You seem healthy, you seem happy, despite what you have experienced. And you have a confidence and optimism that I have not seen in your eyes since the first time we met.'

'It's true,' Austin replied simply. 'Somethun' happened that day in the hospital. I knew that I couldn't rely on them. That I was on my own. Well, sort of …' He paused and then smiled, reflecting on a passing memory that clearly had impacted him deeply.

'The nurses and doctors on my ward were so kind, and very different to what I saw when my friends were sick. These guys were gentle. Empathic. And really seemed to care about me. They told me about a new medication that had come out, that I was eligible to for it. That it would slow down the impact of the virus that I have and actually improve my immune system again. Before, I wouldn't have cared. I wouldn't have believed that it was possible ... and I definitely wouldn't have believed that I was worthy of it. But this time I felt different. I believed I was worth saving.'

'I saw another guy, a really cute guy, who had already started taking it.' He grinned and then blushed. The Tree sensed that there was something of this other person that had a larger role in Austin's story but it did not probe further, and allowed the rest of the young man's story to be told.

'He was doing well. And he told me how the drugs were changing his life. The side effects were bad at first and you have to keep to a really strict regime. It's been a long a difficult road so far, and I know I'm not outta the woods yet. But it works. People have stopped dying from this thing. Who knows how it will develop as time goes on, maybe one day we'll not need to take so many of the pills. Maybe even one day they'll be a cure, or at least the virus won't be detectable in our blood no more. But either way, it is working now. I feel like I can live my life again but I've still gotta be careful ... and that's what I've been doing since I started taking the pills.' He paused and then looked downwards, clearly feeling a lot but not quite knowing how to express it in a way that did justice to his feelings.

'But it was your words, and the words of those nurses who saw and heard what my momma and poppa said to me,' he finally said. 'It was you, and eventually them who hugged me and let me now that I was safe. They weren't afraid to hold my hand or just be kind. And these are people who don't even know me. But they cared, and I felt it. And I was determined to get better. And so here I am. I'm getting healthy, I'm being safe and ...' He paused for dramatic effect with a large smile spreading across his face again.

'And ...?' echoed The Tree, leaning into the young man's final words with a mixture of excitement and anticipation.

'And,' Austin continued, 'Me and that guy – y'know, the one from the ward? So me and him are gonna go to school. We're gonna train together to be nurses, like the ones who specialise in sexual health, like the ones who helped me and made me not want to give up. We wanna be able to help people in the same way they helped us, and we can go to school together to do it. A part of me wanted to go back home to Naw'luhns or maybe even Oklahoma, maybe visit my sister's grave. I think that's a part of my story that I still need to process ... but maybe not just yet. But I will, when the time is right. But I can't go back there yet. I gotta disclose my illness if I go back home and they make it pretty clear they don't want people with my disease coming into the country. Can you believe that? They check your meds and everything so I can't even lie, because if they find my tablets then I'd be sent away!'

Austin looked angry as he said this but then a look of calm resumed.

'It's their loss. Maybe one day it'll be okay for me to go back but until then me and this guy are gonna help people like us. We don't care how long it takes but we're gonna make a difference so no one has to feel like I did. Or how he did. Or how any of us have been made to feel. Laws are changing, and so are people's attitudes towards us ... and towards this virus. But there is still a long way to go – I'm gonna be part of that change!'

There was a look of clear determination and resolution in his expression.

The Tree swelled with pride towards the young American and the journey he had been on, but also the one he was about to embark on. And in that moment, The Tree knew that it would be some time before they would meet again. It hoped that the young American would be safe. That he would remain healthy. That his life would not be cut short like the lives of so many people in his community that had come before him. The Tree hoped that he would continue to hold his sense of worth and be open to the possibility of love from others. It also hoped that the world would change and show acceptance and compassion towards people who had suffered like Austin and his friends.

Austin knew that it was time to leave The Tree. Still clutching the curious silver apple that The Tree had gifted to him, he slowly rose and gave The Tree one final embrace, to which The Tree reciprocated immediately.

'Thank you for everything,' the young American whispered, tears forming in his eyes.

'You have no idea the impact your kindness has had on me. Because of you I feel I deserve to live. That I have worth. And that I can be happy. I will never forget your words, and I will cherish the love that you've helped me to feel towards myself.'

With that, and one final squeeze, The Tree and the young man released each other, Austin's silhouette disappearing as he walked through the stone circle. The sun was low and orange as it began its descent, and so too the young man began his own journey down the side of the hill until he was out of sight.

'Goodbye, my friend. Be kind to yourself always. And please, never forget your worth!' whispered The Tree into the dusk.

The sun finally set in the west causing the sky over the valley to transform from azure to a mixture of golds, oranges, reds, and violet until the valley was plunged into the hazy dusk. And once more The Tree stood alone on the hill, wondering about the fate of the young, and sitting with the uncomfortable uncertainty that this brought.

The Tree was deeply moved by the many layers of Austin's story and felt hope that it has given him something that he would be able to hold onto – a sense of his own worth and goodness, despite how his parents, society, and even members of his own community had treated him. The Tree knew that its words and love for the young man had made an impact. It just hoped that these would last.

A sadness lingered with The Tree as it recalled the words of Austin's parents, and the laws and beliefs held by people from the young man's past. The anger that it felt towards Austin's parents also glowed like hot embers in its roots. But there were glimmers of optimism that changes were beginning to occur, and so these embers of fury were quenched … for now!

CHAPTER FIVE
May: Gratitude

I

A strange and eerie quiet had descended upon the valley. It was a cold day for May and a curtain of drizzle swept over the surrounding hills soaking everything that it came in to contact with. The Tree was enjoying this immensely and felt quenched by the tiny droplets of water that clung to its branches and leaves. Even the pale grey sky gave it a sense of comfort, like a weighted blanket silencing the manufactured din of the world – leaving space for the sounds of nature only. On days such as these The Tree did not expect to see a single human soul, so adverse they seemed to be to the nourishing deluge of water that so often fell from the sky. The Tree used these moments of solitude for reflection on what it knew, what it had heard, as well as simply allowing itself to just be.

The Tree's vantage point upon the hill allowed it to see and sense for miles, much like a watchtower. On certain days when the wind was just right, it never failed to feel amazed by all the distant noises it absorbed from the world, and the learning that came with this. But this May felt different. Something had changed in the world. A silence had befallen it ... and so had a virus. A new virus that the world had no name for yet, and had not experienced before. It was a different type of virus that it had once heard of from a young American who had come to visit it several years ago in the month of April. This new virus seemed to affect everyone, especially those who were elderly or already unwell. And the fear that was spreading as a result of this was palpable. Even without people visiting The Tree or its stone circle, the wave of terror amid the uncertainty vibrated through the air and was felt deeply within the soul of The Tree.

Gratitude was not lost on The Tree. It knew, and was thankful, that it could not be harmed by such things, that nature would continue and perhaps even thrive. It reflected on its years of existence so far: the people who had come into and left this world, the stories they had shared, and the memories that The Tree had felt. Lifetimes had passed and still The Tree and the valley, the mountains, the rivers, the skies, the sun, the moon, and the stars all remained constant. They absorbed the energy and vibrations of all those whom they encountered and continued to endure – silent observers to an ever changing and evolving world.

The Tree knew that human beings often took such wonders for granted. That they didn't always consider or care for the planet, or the impact that they had on it. They didn't always appreciate how their own lives were inextricably linked to the cycles of nature and if nature was destroyed, so too would they be. But if the humans disappeared, the opposite would be true. Nature would live on, and if anything, it would thrive without the harmful interference of those whom it shared its existence with.

However, The Tree didn't want human beings to disappear. Its many encounters with them over the years had meant it had come to love them. For all their trials and suffering, for their fallibility and triumphs, but also for their capacity to love and to show kindness, often in the most unexpected ways.

What The Tree did not know or foresee was just how important the notion of gratitude would come to play in regard to its own life. That its own healing following a crisis would be dependent on the kindness and gratitude from others. But that day would not come for some time yet, and right now The Tree was too busy to even consider such things. Instead, it basked in the halcyon rhythms of nature and the elements that nourished its sturdy trunk and leafy branches, its soul, and of course the surrounding valley.

After several hours, the torrential downpour that the light drizzle had become finally abated, giving way to blue skies interspersed with large fluffy white clouds which drifted by without struggle or care. Something that The Tree had noticed over the past few months since the unknown virus had spread across the globe was just how clean the skies and indeed the air in general had become. Rarely was the sky streaked with wispy serpentine trails that followed the flying vehicles that humans seemed to enjoy. Nor did it sense the presence of the more earthbound vehicles which too contributed to the air becoming thick and heavy with fumes. Instead, there was both a crispness and a freshness that appeared to be felt and enjoyed not just by The Tree but by all of the plants and animal life that it could feel. The river had taken on an even more crystalline appearance, not too dissimilar to the rich and beautiful glacial rivers and lakes that it had viewed in the memories of a young man from Switzerland – a young man who had once found friendship underneath The Tree's protective watch during the early springtime months of the past.

Lost in memories, The Tree did not at first notice that two curious kittens had scampered across the stone circle and were now playfully squabbling and rolling around at the base of The Tree's trunk, and meowing loudly. The cats were clearly related, one completely ginger and resembling a small and rather cute but gentle tiger with lively green eyes. The other one was similarly ginger but was distinguishable from his brother by his white paws, a white fur waistcoat chest, and white cheeks. Instead of green eyes, his eyes were flecked with hazel, giving him a somewhat fiercer appearance. Despite their small size, both were handsome and somewhat regal in their appearance.

Within a few short moments, two figures ascended the hill and similarly crossed the circle towards The Tree. It was here that The Tree came back into the present and out of the cascade of memories. And to its delight, The Tree's favourite couple, Jonathan and Mary, were stood before it once again.

This couple had been visiting The Tree since they were in their late teens and twenties. Despite both now being in their late sixties, The Tree could not help but marvel at their energy, their agility, and their youthful appearance. As a couple, The Tree knew them to be both kind and loving – simple souls who loved each other fiercely without greed or preoccupation with material wealth or status. As much as one ever can be, The Tree experienced them as both happy and content, and astonishingly able to find the silver lining no matter what crises ailed them over the years.

Both of them hugged The Tree warmly when they arrived and preceded to share their latest tales. They both spoke rapidly, often completing each other's sentences, and shared both a knowing look and then a laugh every time they did so. They shared how they were now grandparents, something that they had craved for so long but feared would never happen. They also laughed when they shared that they were also grandparents to cats and explained how they had been charged with looking after their other son's kittens for the next few days – he and his partner had taken this opportunity to fly to a different county now that the country's lockdown had lifted. This explained the presence of the two spirited beasts that continued to tumble and play, their sights now turned towards any other moving creature that foolishly dared to draw their attention.

The Tree listened, intrigued, as the couple spoke about the pandemic that The Tree had come to be aware of. About the terrible toll it had taken on people's health and mental wellbeing, and the small ways that the couple had maintained their sense of hope, love, and ever-flowing gratitude for their own health and safety during such a confusing and frightening moment in history for them.

The Tree listened intently and felt its soul swell with sadness and compassion as Jonathan recounted the day that he had been hospitalised, unable to breathe and experiencing severe pains in his chest. The Tree wept when it saw the memories of Mary alone by her husband's bedside, her face covered by a surgical mask, and silently weeping as she feared the worst – their sons were forbidden to visit in case they brought contamination into the hospital from the outside.

Jonathan's heart had been left fragile but with time and care he had recovered, and both he and Mary had been able to return home and be reunited with their children and their partners, their two grandchildren, and of course the two ginger kittens. Despite their heartfelt expressions of gratitude for their circumstances, The Tree could feel the unspoken fear that still remained for both of them … but neither felt able to share this. They would both still wear masks when in public but were no strangers to going for long walks in the countryside where the air was fresh, and there were very few people – so carefully were these locations chosen. But, as both of them kept saying (perhaps trying to ward off the fear of believing something more frightening), they were very grateful for their health and for everyone they felt blessed to have in their lives.

The Tree expanded its focus to see both Jonathan and Mary, and the kittens. There was something delightful about the way kittens playfully tumbled around the grass together, and the clear love and affection that Jonathan and Mary felt for their son's pets. They treated them with the same protectiveness and adoration as they gave to their eldest son's children and regarded all – no matter whether they were human or animal – as being their grandchildren. The Tree loved to hear the sound of Mary's laughter and the unchanging adoration in her eyes as her husband chased the cats but quickly and instinctively scooped them up if they got too close to the hill's steeper and unforgiving edges.

Despite being a man in his sixties, Jonathan remained agile and energetic. His years of physical work meant that he enjoyed staying active but the years of stress from trying to make ends meet, especially when his jobs had changed suddenly, or money was scarce for the couple when raising their children, had indeed taken their toll. True to form, he always remained grateful for the opportunities that he had, and for the way his small business had grown to give him and Mary a modest but happy life. There were of course times where he felt worried, angry, and resentful, but these feelings were quickly pushed aside and the familiar mantra of gratitude would instead be drawn upon.

The Tree could remember the many experiences that Jonathan and Mary had shared with it over the years, and how their love for each other had helped them to overcome even the most difficult and sometimes traumatic of obstacles. The Tree had come to love them both ... and the family that they had raised and then sent forth into the world.

The Tree observed the kittens moving further away from its trunk as the hazel-eyed waistcoat-wearing kitten set its sights on a small bird with shades of blue, yellow, and white in its feathers. His body now flat and outstretched on the grass, The Tree could see how the kitten had silently stalked the small bird and was now waiting for an opportune moment to pounce. His brother, Aslan (a name given to him based on a favourite character from a childhood series of books), however, seemed blissfully unaware of their prey and was trotting smugly by the edge of the hilltop – clearly proud of the large grey feather that it had somehow managed to procure, and much less inclined was he than his brother to stalk an actual bird.

Seizing his moment, Falkor (The Tree learnt that this was the hazel-eyed kitten's name – again, named after a favourite childhood character from a film) pounced towards the bird who instinctively flew out of reach, and towards the safety of The Tree's highest branches. The movement of Falkor was so quick that it startled his brother who froze but lost his footing on the steep edge of the hill and tumbled out of sight. Falkor seemed to freeze also and then propelled himself towards where Aslan had stood, and ignoring the large feather now laying on the grass jumped out of sight and after his brother.

With lightning reflexes, Jonathan leapt to his feet and ran towards the edge of the hill where both kittens had been and bellowed both of their names with the same concern The Tree knew that he would no doubt show towards his grandchildren. The triumphant bird chirped gaily from the safety of its branches, seemingly ignorant to the scene now playing out beneath it. Jonathan sped towards the spot where both kittens had been and then after a pause at the edge of the hill, he too disappeared from sight.

The sound of a dull thud could be heard.

Within seconds Jonathan's head appeared, much to the relief of Mary and The Tree. He was clearly on a part of the hill that mercifully was not a sheer drop but a rather sharp slope downwards. Out of breath but smiling, the rest of his body became visible as he climbed over the ledge, with the two yowling kittens clutched in his strong hands.

A wide-eyed Mary, seeing that her husband was safe – and the kittens – heaved a sigh of relief and broke free of her paralysed standing posture, placed her hand over her thumping heart, and returned her husband's smile. Another thing to be grateful for, she thought to herself. Her breathing was still rather rapid but she returned her focus to the picnic hamper and blanket she had laid down. The Tree couldn't help but smile to itself … so familiar was it to this scene. The carefully soft and woven blanket for them to sit on. The old-fashioned but charming straw picnic hamper. And of course, the selection of food which had no doubt been baked with love by Mary. This was something that The Tree had come to witness and love about her over the years.

Jonathan – holding both kittens in his hands and close to his body retreated from the edge of the hill – began a careful walk back towards his wife, who had settled under The Tree on the picnic blanket, with the assortment of homemade food spread out ready for them to enjoy. As he approached, his own heart still racing, the huge grin on his face began to fade. A curious expression emerged and his eyes widened, like those of a vigilant owl. His grip on the two writhing kittens slackened, who leapt free from his hands and scampered towards Mary.

As if mirroring her husband's face, Mary's expression also changed from one of joy and laughter to confusion … and then concern.

Jonathan's free hand slowly rose towards his chest, a look of bewilderment and fear now on his face. And then his face became ashen in colour and went blank. He seemed to move eerily in slow motion as he dropped to his knees, remained motionless for what seemed like minutes, and then collapsed forwards onto the soft grass.

In that moment, Mary's husband, the man whom she cherished, the father to her children, and the man she had come to love throughout all of her adult life, lay disturbingly still and stopped breathing.

Jonathan's heart gave its final beats before stopping completely. And in that moment, on a beautiful and seemingly ordinary day in May, Jonathan died.

II

The Tree stood frozen, shocked and horrified at the scene unfolding before it. The Tree had come to love Jonathan ever since he and Mary first climbed the hill and walked through the stone circle hand in hand just a few weeks after they had first met.

As their entire history flashed before Mary's eyes, so too did these memories flash through The Tree's soul as the story of this beautiful couple was remembered …

The giddy couple appeared on the hilltop. He was aged twenty, with long brown hair, a full beard, and a sweet but dopey grin. He was sporting the signature corduroy flares that were the fashion of the time, and leather sandals. She was aged twenty-three, with similarly long brown wavey hair decorated with flowers, a kind and pretty face, and she too sported the fashionable flares of the era, except hers were denim and accompanied by a pair of platform shoes that were totally inappropriate for a hilltop climb. Nevertheless, their charm and innocence awoke The Tree to their presence.

'I love you, my darling wife!' were the first words The Tree heard come out of the young man's mouth.

'I love you too, my darling husband!' was the reply that came from her, and was accompanied by a passionate kiss.

The Tree noticed the shiny gold band on one of his fingers, and the humble but beautiful diamond that twinkled from the wedding ring on hers. Never before had The Tree beheld two people who were so enthralled and in love with each other. Their energy could be felt in waves that emanated from their bodies, evoking in The Tree a giddy excitement and feeling of sublime intoxication.

As the happy couple settled on one of the larger and flatter rocks of the stone circle, he produced a bottle of fizzy liquid whilst she produced two plastic vessels in the shape of champagne flutes. He popped the cork, and the fizzy contents burst from the bottle, spraying them both … no doubt the contents having been disturbed from the vigorous climb up the hill. But the happy couple just laughed and continued to pour the fizzy liquid into their plastic glasses and proceeded to raise them into the air.

'CHEERS!' they said in unison, before both taking a large gulp of the drink.

'I know it's not the most expensive stuff … but it's all I could afford,' Jonathan said softly, his eyes downcast. 'One day I'll be able to buy us the real good stuff … I promise!'

He seemed so earnest as he delivered his promise. The Tree felt a swell of love for him but also felt a sense of sadness … The Tree could feel the young man's shame, as though a part of him felt that he didn't deserve his bride. That he was not good enough. He didn't dare to look up at his wife … just in case she reflected back what he feared.

Tenderly, his new bride shook her head and placed her finger on his lips to silence him. 'As long as I have you, I have everything I need.

No matter what happens in our lives together, I am thankful that we met because we make each other strong. Whatever struggles we face, we will do so together!'

The Tree was moved by her kindness and felt the love and honesty in this remark. She was not just trying to make him feel better, she genuinely wanted nothing more than his love. And The Tree could tell that all he wanted was the same ... and how lucky they both were to have found this.

A feeling of longing was stirred within The Tree ... so often did it sway majestically in the breeze, alone and contemplative, and satisfied. But sometimes it recognised that it felt lonely. That the company of the beautiful souls who paid visit to the hill did something wonderful for The Tree. They enriched its own soul, and helped it to feel less alone in the world. Sometimes it was necessary to be in denial about loneliness ... because what would it really mean to spend an eternity on this planet all alone?

'But what about our honeymoon?' the young man said to his wife. 'I really wanted to take you away somewhere beautiful.'

'And you did ...' she replied kindly. 'We spent two nights on that lovely boat!'

'But we never actually left the docks ...' And then in the same downcast tone as before, 'Because I couldn't afford petrol for the boat ... and I got sick.'

'But we were with each other,' came her reply. 'And the stars still looked beautiful, as did the lights of the quayside as they sparkled on the water.'

He smiled lovingly at her and then laughed. 'And what about all those ships that honked their foghorns at us because of that silly "JUST MARRIED" flag that your friends painted and stuck on the roof of the boat? And all those kind people who brought us food from their restaurants on the quayside ... that last one making me sick though.' He rolled his eyes and laughed, as if to suggest that this was typical of their lives.

'Oh gosh ... and the fire!' he then added, more seriously. 'The fire that happened in the same docks the night that we left. All those boats destroyed, including the one we stayed on. Thank God I did get sick ... we could've still been inside the boat when it caught fire!'

'But we're grateful,' she said. 'Everything worked out because it was meant to be what it was. People were just kind to us. We're good people and yes, we may not have as much as other people, and maybe we never will. But that won't make us any less happy. Or any less in love. And as for the fire ... we were lucky. Very lucky! And thankfully we were safe and grateful for every day of life that we have!'

He put his arm around her, and she closed her eyes and nuzzled into him, a look of peace and contentment settling over both of their young faces.

III

The next memory was sad. The Tree saw a tearful young Jonathan, his arms wrapped around his silently sobbing wife. Their clothing was black and matched the mood of the day. No parent should have to bury a child. Especially one so young. The tiny coffin delicately held the newborn baby girl and was lowered into to the freshly dug earth. Religious words were offered by the priest but offered very little comfort to the grieving couple as the harsh wind whipped leaves from the surrounding trees in the bleak cemetery and carelessly discarded them into the open grave.

The scene did not last long and was replaced with a tearful Jonathan holding his silently sobbing wife. But this time the tears that flowed were ones of happiness. An additional cry echoed around the sterile hospital room. A little boy, red-faced and shrieking was brought into the clinical and sanitised hospital room, and away from the warm, watery bubble of suspension that had contained him only a few moments earlier. Relief, joy, and love emanated from the couple accompanied by the phrase that they said in unison.

'We are so grateful ... we have our baby!'

Mary and Jonathan exchanged quizzical looks in the next memory that followed. How unexpected, they both thought. Is this right? They both looked a little older but not by much. A smiling nurse looked down at them in the hospital bed and presented their second child after a long and painful labour. The three-year-old at their side looked equally confused. 'I don't like him,' he said petulantly. 'I want a sister. Send him back!'

'All those clothes that people gave to us …' Jonathan said with a playful laugh. But he didn't care what colours or style of clothes that his child wore. Or what sex it was. He only cared that he had another child.

'I'm so grateful that he is healthy. That he is here. And that he is loved!' said Mary. And both she and Jonathan gazed lovingly at their new son. His older brother, however, continued to pout, his back turned to the baby, arms folded, and his bottom lip sticking out. He still wanted a baby sister, as was promised. Both Mary, Jonathan, and the nurse giggled and tried to suppress their mirth at their son's blatant indignation.

IV

The Tree remembered both Jonathan and Mary introducing their sons. Frequent visitors to the valley and hilltop, The Tree met the two boys once they were old enough to make the climb. The eldest would happily kick a football around the standing stones, whistling to himself, so focused was he on the art of his skill. Or he would sit and draw … fantasies of incredible buildings that he would one day come to design.

The youngest had his head buried in a book, as always. Both children were content and lost in their own worlds. Neither asked for much from their parents, so grateful were they for the small blessings that they had. Two loving parents, their love of sports and drawing, and a passion for escaping into other worlds through the magic of books. They had grown up without much money but what Jonathan and Mary lacked in financial comfort, they more than made up for in kindness. Both boys felt loved and well cared for.

Jonathan would sometimes join them at The Tree, only when the sun was setting, or at the weekends. His long working hours exhausted him but time with his family was precious. Mary would bake fresh goods that her family would devour hungrily before resuming their respective hobbies of football and reading. Mary would simply gaze at her children lovingly and out over the valley, admiring the tranquil beauty that had become a safe haven for them all. And as a family, they would share their stories and their feelings. Rarely were they consumed by the technological advancements that can so often cause families to cease all communication. Instead, they appreciated their strong relationship with each other, the ability to be present in the moment, and to never take for granted the beauty and magnificence of nature.

The Tree overheard their conversations, even the ones in hushed tones shared between Jonathan and Mary. Whisperings about money and how they could make ends meet. Jonathan spoke of selling his old car so that they could buy new clothes and beds for the boys. Mary spoke of selling some of the more fancy clothes and jewellery from her youth to pay for small treats for the family, and a bicycle for her husband.

The Tree listened with admiration and sadness as they forged plans together to build their own furniture in the evenings when their sons were sound asleep ... beds, wardrobes, tables, and chairs. And the nearby places where they could picnic and have days out in nature for free, rather than the expensive holiday cottages that their friends would often frequent in other countries.

Longing to do something kind for this humble little family, The Tree would produce an assortment of fruits for the family to pick from its branches and enjoy upon each visit. The Tree was delighted by their astonishment as they grasped for the bananas that grew one day, the oranges the next, the grapes and berries on other days, and the huge juicy apples that seemed to magically fall at their feet on other days.

The children, whilst enchanted, accepted the gifts without question. Jonathan and Mary sensed that something curious was afoot, but despite this would mouth the words 'THANK YOU' at The Tree as they shared silent moments of relief and gratitude at their good fortune, and the generosity and kindness from The Tree.

V

'They called again,' Mary said, her voice trembling. 'It wasn't just silence and heavy breathing this time – they ended the call with a horrible laugh. Why? Why are they doing this to us?'

'I'll sort it, darling, I promise. They won't get away with it!' came Jonathan's serious reply, as he unconvincingly tried to conceal his anger.

'Please don't do anything stupid darling,' she implored. 'We need this job ... mine isn't enough to support us and also the boys through university. Can't your manager do anything?'

'His hands are tied, honey, but we've got a plan. Well, I've got a plan. My boss sort of knows but said he would prefer to be "kept in the dark" but he will have my back.'

Mary looked fearful. 'Well, what on earth does that mean?'

'It means that no one fucks with my family! Tonight, I need you to come with me to the office. You don't have to do anything. Just wait in the car and let me know if anyone comes by … the less you know, the better!' he said seriously, and then winked.

'JONATHAN! This isn't a joke. You can wipe that silly smirk off your face. This is serious! Tell me now! What you are planning to do! I won't have you going to prison for those idiots! And I will not be a part of this lunacy that you're planning!'

He couldn't help but laugh at his wife's response. 'Oh gosh, darling, its nothing like that. Please calm down. They are going to be fired from the company. There is enough evidence to suggest they've been embezzling money, but they have also made threats against all of us. Something to do with having "evidence" that will land us all in trouble, and potentially shut the whole firm down.'

'What evidence?' Mary's voice became louder and more shrill.

'It's nothing … we haven't done anything wrong. Well, I can honestly say that from my perspective. But apparently they've got something, possibly on my boss … and I THINK I know where it's hidden. All I need is some time to get it before the meeting tomorrow morning. And then this will hopefully all go away.'

'Oh gosh. I don't want to know,' Mary said, covering her face with her hands and slowly shaking her head. 'Please … please don't do anything stupid. We can find another way. We always do!' And then she added in a desperate whisper, 'I can't lose you.'

Seeing the fear in his wife's face, and the desperation in her pleas, Jonathan abandoned his plan and hugged Mary. She leaned into his hug and breathed a sigh of relief.

Upstairs, there was a soft click as one of the bedroom doors closed, followed by the hushed exchange of whispers.

The following morning, Jonathan sat at the dining table for breakfast with his two sons … a rarity for them both to be back home from university at the same time. They both looked tired. Jonathan knew they'd been out last night and heard them creeping in, suppressing giggles – no doubt drunk – during the early hours of the morning. This was not uncommon when the boys were together, and Jonathan delighted in their closeness, and the somewhat mischievous nature of both of his sons.

Mary entered the room, the smell of a fresh cafetiere of coffee accompanying her. She set down the steaming coffee in the centre of the table. And with a slap, she slammed down a folder ... a folder bursting with documents and photographs!

'WHAT ... IS ... THIS?!' she demanded furiously. It was rare for Mary to raise her voice. And when she did, the whole family knew that there was trouble. Both boys stopped eating, their hands frozen in mid-air – mid-bite of their toast.

Jonathan looked down at the folder. Then up at his wife, and then back down at the folder. He was as surprised as Mary to see this document. He certainly recognised it. But how in the hell did it get here? Jonathan thought to himself, baffled.

The Tree then caught a subtle glimpse of the sons driving to their father's office. Carefully using his keys to enter the premises, and hunting in the darkness until their flashlights found what they'd been looking for.

The Tree then saw both sons gathered around a large metal bucket. The sound of water could be heard lapping on the sand. Orange flames and black billowing smoke rose up into the night sky as one folder of documents after another was reduced to ash as the brothers took it in turns throwing their contents in the fire.

As the eldest went to drop the penultimate folder into the flames, the youngest brother who had been scanning their surroundings in case they were caught, returned his focus to the fire and suddenly shouted, 'NOOOOOOO!'

'What ... WHAT?' he cried, wide-eyed and clearly startled by his younger brother.

'NOT THAT ONE ... that one we need! I have no idea what was in those OTHER folders ... but this one, this one I do. This one proves that those dickheads have been stealing from the company. And that they've been the ones making those phone calls. And they've been watching us! There are photos of our home. Of Mum and Dad ... even one of us! We need to do whatever it takes to protect our family! Those tossers are going down!' His serious expression hardened even more.

The eldest brother's expression similarly darkened to match his brother's. A pale orange glow now bathed both of their faces. Their eyes burning. He kept hold of the precious folder of evidence and dropped the last of the other folders into the fire. Both brothers looked at each other and nodded. A sign of mutual respect was shared between them. They stayed still and didn't utter another word until the flames finally died down, and nothing remained in the metal bucked but a pile of ash.

Back at the breakfast table, Jonathan and Mary continued to exchange confused looks. He opened the folder and anxiously removed the contents. Both he and Mary held the same documents that their sons had seen, and had nearly accidently destroyed the night before. They both appeared perplexed.

Mary knew that her husband had not left her side the night before, especially after her heartfelt request for him to reconsider his plan. She knew that he would never betray her trust. But the contents of the folder would help them. And with a clear conscience, she allowed Jonathan to take these into the office with him and do what he felt was right. With a gentle smile returning to her face before he left, Mary kissed her husband tenderly on the cheek, a silent expression of gratitude for her husband's love and protective nature.

Later that morning, a meeting of the managers and employees was called. Within an hour, one woman, and one man were found to be responsible for the harassing and abusive phone calls to Jonathan and Mary ... and the long-standing theft from the company. The police were called, and the pair were promptly arrested and remanded in custody.

That same evening Jonathan and Mary heaved a huge sigh of relief but both were still confused about what had actually happened. Where had the evidence against the firm gone? thought Mary to herself.

And how the hell did the folder exposing the thieves get into their house? thought Jonathan.

Two days later, a bottle of champagne arrived for them at their home. The card displayed the company's familiar logo and just three simple words ...

'With Sincere Thanks!'

Still befuddled but equally relieved, they popped the cork and began to pour a glass for themselves. Hearing the sound of celebrations, the two brothers bounded down the stairs to join them.

'I think you need another couple for us,' said the youngest with a wink.

'And why would we do that?' said Jonathan playfully.

'Let's just say,' said the eldest son, 'I think the card that came with this is for us!'

He and his brother smirked. Jonathan and Mary, however, looked at each other quizzically. Then at their sons, and the truth dawned on them.

'Boys ...?' said Mary, her tone one of trepidation, knowing that she wasn't going to like the answer to her next question. 'What exactly did you do?'

In unison, the brothers mimed pulling a zip across their mouths, clinked their glasses of champagne, and downed their contents in one.

VI

Another memory. A middle-aged Jonathan with tears in his eyes, holding hands with his wife, who was also tearful. The Tree saw a modern glass-fronted hall filled with graduates and students, celebrating their accomplishments accompanied by roaring cheers and the sound of the nearby ocean as their first son graduated.

The Tree also witnessed the gothic church-like hall where the second son accepted his university degree, and the raucous partying that followed afterwards in the nearby park.

The Tree could feel how proud both parents felt about their sons' respective achievements, but also reflected on the secret costs that they had hidden from their children to give them a better start in life than they themselves had had. In the blended memory, both sons could be seen in their caps and gowns from different universities, as they grinned into the audience, mirroring the pride that they could see in the faces of their loving parents.

But The Tree also saw the hardship that Jonathan and Mary had endured, the long and sometimes additional working hours they had completed to pay for their children's rent and tuition fees, or to buy them new books ... or bail them out when – in particular the youngest son – had overspent on silly frivolities.

The Tree also sensed their worry when their two sons regaled stories of drunken nights out in dangerous parts of their respective cities. Of the heartbreak their sons felt when they broke up with their respective girlfriends and boyfriends. And the hidden losses that Jonathan and Mary felt as they invested in their sons' numerous relationships, only for them to come to an end. But they remained grateful that their sons were true to themselves, and trusted their parents enough to share their stories of love and loss ... and sometimes outright debauchery, much to the despair but also vicarious enjoyment of Jonathan and Mary.

VII

Another memory came as the others dissolved. Time seemed frozen for Jonathan and Mary as the doctor solemnly shook his head. Mary's situation had worsened. As suspected, it was cancer. They squeezed each other's hands as the options for treatment were shared in a cold and clinical manner. Both of them just nodded, too stunned were they to form words.

Jonathan – a deep concern showing in his wide and sleep-deprived eyes as he held Mary's hand – stroked the fine whisps of hair that remained after her first round of treatment. As she recovered from the surgery that had also been advised as a safety precaution, the rich scent of flowers were experienced by The Tree in the private hospital room as the once bleak room was transformed into an oasis of colour and fragrance.

'We'll get through this, darling!' Jonathan said resolutely. 'The worst of it is over ... you beat it!'

Mary smiled weakly at her husband. She felt fatigued from the procedure but also relief. She had indeed beaten it! Her own mother had not been so fortunate several years ago. But Mary was grateful. And she silently thanked whatever powers existed in the universe that had given her a second chance at life – a life with her husband. With her children. And indeed, the grandchildren and son and daughter in law that she loved as much as her own children.

Mary accepted that her life, and indeed her body was forever changed, but that her life was still good ... her husband still looked at her with the same doe-eyed expression of love as he did on their first date. That he was an ever-present anchor and source of strength that they would both draw upon in the coming months. And no matter what, she and her husband would always find something to be grateful for, no matter what life threw at them.

VIII

And then came a memory that The Tree could recall first-hand. The infectious laughter of their two blonde-haired grandchildren. The little girl dancing and singing as she performed for the crowd that gathered in the stone circle, whilst the slightly older boy looked embarrassed, but was secretly enjoying the show. His sister, he knew, would grow up to become a little star.

His own speech before the hilltop feast was admirable for one so young. He spoke of his love for his uncle and the man that he was marrying ... and even his nervous stammer at times was endearing and melted the hearts of the crowd. In essence, it was the perfect speech and one which his uncles would cherish forever.

The autumnal shades that blanketed The Tree's canopy of leaves gave an enchanting feel to the wedding. Guests had been informed to dress in similar colours. The whole valley, and now the hilltop, was filled with happy people in shades of orange, green, browns, and reds against the unusually blue sky for the time of year. Whilst crisp, the light chill in the air did not deter the celebrations, which were no doubt helped along by the ever-flowing wine and frivolity being enjoyed by the guests.

Even the lost bunting had become a distant memory. When hearing that the beautifully woven bunting had somehow disappeared (or, as The Tree suspected, had been forgotten), and sensing the disappointment and annoyance from the grooms, Mary of course set to work and made her own, much to the delight and gratitude of her son in law.

The Tree too played its part and decorated the stone circle with an array of flowers, and called upon the various creatures of the valley to sing their bird-song choruses, and for the insects of the evening to provide a fairylike array of glowing lights to accompany the man-made sparklers that fizzed and crackled like fiery magical wands.

The Tree looked on adoringly as Mary danced with her newlywed son to the delicate classical music of the harp, violins, and cello. Her beautiful hair had fully grown back and framed her pretty face like a dark cloud. Jonathan was laughing as he slow-danced with his new son in law, as they shared a private joke, but both kept slyly sneaking a loving glance at their respective life partners whom they could see dancing in the centre of the stone circle. The eldest son and his own stunning wife with her long hay coloured hair took full advantage of the day's festivities and could be seen laughing and dancing with their children, as well as the other drunken guests.

The day was perfect, and The Tree felt honoured and grateful to have been a part of it. And indeed, to have been invited to be a part of this beautiful family, and celebrate in their triumphs as well as witnessing their sorrows.

IX

In the final memory, The Tree welcomed Jonathan and Mary as they leaned against its trunk.

'What are we to do with all this money?' Mary said.

It wasn't a huge amount but certainly more than they had ever had. The Tree could feel Mary's grief. Her uncle had been like a father to her. Jonathan wrapped the blanket he'd brought with him around his wife's shoulders. It had finally stopped snowing but the air remained freezing, not completely atypical for a January day. He sneezed loudly, startling his wife.

'I hope you're not coming down with something, darling,' she said with concern. 'There's been something in the news about people on the other side of the world getting very unwell ... some kind of respiratory disorder. It's really quite worrying.'

'I'm alright,' he said. 'You don't have to worry about me, and it's not like whatever is happening over there is going to affect us here. I've just got a cold, that's all, and more importantly, it's you I'm worried about.' He pulled Mary close, keeping her warm as they both looked out over the snow-dusted valley, and pale grey sky. Everything seemed so quiet. Eerily so.

'I'm all right,' Mary said, echoing her husband. 'You know me. I'm just so grateful. Not for the money, but for the childhood he gave me. Those weekends and holidays away from home were such a relief. He was so kind to me. So loving. He never spoke badly of my father … but I knew he was trying to be the father to me that his brother never was. I know so many people have had it worse, and the time I had with him was so precious. Whatever we decide to do with the money, I want it to mean something.'

'Maybe we'll set up that donkey sanctuary we've always talked about. You know how we could never resist a poor sad unloved donkey!' Jonathan said and smiled. 'The kids would certainly love it,' he added. 'But that's for tomorrow. Now, let's get you home before we catch our death up here.'

The Tree watched as the grateful couple carefully made their way through the snow and down the side of the hill, holdings hands, and as always providing each other with support – not knowing just how quickly their lives, and indeed the lives of so many people, would change as the mysterious overseas virus took hold and made its way across the oceans.

The Tree found itself swimming in an ocean of love for Mary and Jonathan. They had taught The Tree over the years the power of gratitude. That life will be what it will be, and that people cannot always control the outcome. But what they can do is learn and grow from every experience. To find some semblance of light even in the darkness, and to be appreciative of every lesson and blessing that life is able to give.

The Tree also knew that sometimes it can be difficult to access gratitude, especially when aspects of life and loss can feel so cruel. And in these moments, it is important to not just seek appreciation for what one has but to also be open to experiencing all of the emotions – even the more painful and disturbing ones – that are evoked by these experiences.

The Tree knew that it is only when people face their true emotions head on that they are able to work through these and eventually – even if over a long period of time – reach a place of enjoyment and gratitude for what one has, rather than losing oneself in regret and longing for what one does not, or cannot, have.

X

The Tree was brought back to the present with a sharp jolt as Mary leapt to her feet.

'Jonathan?' she whispered tentatively, and then more frantically screamed her husband's name again. 'JONATHAN!'

Instinct took over and Mary ran from the picnic blanket towards her husband. Kneeling down, she pulled Jonathan onto his back and placed her ear to his mouth to listen and feel for his breathing whilst simultaneously reaching for his wrist with one of her free hands and checking for his pulse. There was nothing.

'JONATHAN?!' she screamed again – the heart-wrenching desperation in her voice echoing through the valley as tears began to roll down her cheeks.

Determined not to lose her husband she began a series of actions that The Tree knew to be techniques learnt by humans to try and initiate life when someone's heart has stopped.

'Come on, come back ... please, darling, please don't leave me!' The pleading in her voice broke The Tree's heart as it stood helplessly watching the tragic scene unfold. It desperately wanted to help but felt useless in its size and strength. What could it do?

As The Tree found itself drowning in its own feelings of inadequacy, the harrowing scene of Mary attempting to revive her husband continued in the background – her sobs now sounding muffled as The Tree searched its soul for some way in which it could help. As it did so, it felt the familiar tingling in its branches, the branches that unusually appeared silver in their appearance.

One of these silver branches had once been given by The Tree to a young man as a means of helping him to walk. And yet another had been given to two lonely boys as a symbol of their beautiful friendship to solidify this forever. And yet another to its dear young American friend. It did not know how this would work, but it knew that its essence, a part of its own powerful life force resided in these branches. And perhaps sacrificing another one could somehow save its favourite couple from having to endure the tragedy of loss.

With all of its might, The Tree willed its energy into one of the silver branches. As it did so, the familiar shimmer and tingling of energy coursed through the bulk of The Tree and became concentrated in a single branch. A soft glow emanated from the branch as the silver essence seemed to be pulled into the wide trunk of The Tree, causing the now blackened branch to become ash-like and disintegrate. The silver essence churned in The Tree until a substance akin to the appearance of liquid mercury began to seep through The Tree's bark like large shining metallic tears.

Mary, sensing that something strange was happening, turned quickly from her husband and towards The Tree. She stared wide-eyed at the strange spectacle of the silver sap seeping from the bark of The Tree and heard a soft and tender voice carried on the breeze that simply said, 'Drink!'

Without question or hesitation that it is what she did. Mary hurried to The Tree and collected as much of the silver sap that she could contain in her own mouth and then returned to her husband's side. She carefully opened Jonathan's mouth and allowed the thick silver liquid to pass from her own mouth into his, a thin trickle of silver missing his mouth and gathering in his neat grey beard.

The liquid disappeared into Jonathan's throat.

Mary ran back to The Tree and repeated the same actions but this time she had help. The two kittens which had stood immobilised now seemed to be helping her. They too licked at the silver sap now gathering at the base of The Tree and carried the tiny contents of their mouths to Jonathan's lifeless body, which they deposited on his chest so that two silver pools formed on his semi-open shirt. As they did so, the liquid seemed to vanish as it permeated the cotton of his shirt and was absorbed by his skin.

How peculiar this scene was, yet one which was engaged in without question, just sheer desperation and hope.

'Live!' The Tree whispered and pleaded in its soul. And then more forcefully, 'PLEASE LIVE!'

Mary had resumed her attempts to revive her husband. She breathed into his mouth whilst attempting to stimulate the electricity of his heart.

The Tree observed with wonder the forceful compressions on his chest with her small but strong arms – the pure adrenalin coursing through them as she too willed her husband to live amidst her anguished sobs.

Jonathan's eyes opened! A loud gasp erupted from his mouth as his lungs breathed in the air, followed by another gasp.

Mary fell backwards in shock as Jonathan's body jolted upright, his hand on his chest and the small trickle of silver liquid still clinging to his beard. He looked confused and bewildered until his head turned to face his wife. As their eyes locked, the truth of what had happened was known between them. No words needed to be spoken.

Jonathan knew in that moment that he had died. And that somehow, he was alive once more.

And Mary knew that for a moment that felt like an eternity, she had lost her husband. But now he was back. She didn't know how. She didn't care why. But what she did know was that she was grateful. As grateful as she had ever been for anything in her life. And with tears still rolling down her cheeks, she embraced her husband whilst silently mouthing to The Tree those two very powerful words ...'Thank you.'

The Tree bowed discretely in response, so relieved was it that Jonathan lived. The couple had been through so much in their lifetime, and The Tree had genuinely come to regard both Jonathan and Mary and their family as a family of its own. It felt touched and inspired by their kindness, their courage, and the ever-flowing appreciation that they felt for what they had, rather than becoming consumed by longing and envy for what they didn't.

The Tree knew that there was so much in the world that it could not change ... even though at times it wished it could. But it did know that it had the power to impact the lives of some of the people who visited it. And it hoped that in doing so, a ripple-effect would occur and cause change and transformation in the lives of those who did not know of The Tree's existence, but were parts of the lives of the people whom The Tree could help.

The Tree knew that it had not saved the world … but it had saved Jonathan, and hopefully spared their growing family from any more unnecessary pain. At least for now. Jonathan and Mary safely cradled the two kittens, and enjoyed the picnic that Mary had so lovingly prepared. After much many embraces and continued expressions of gratitude for their health and good fortune, and the magnificence of The Tree, they packed up their belongings and prepared to leave.

The Tree felt tears forming in its soul. It would miss them both and hoped that they would continue to live long and happy lives. Jonathan and Mary looked so happy … the brush with death having evoked an even stronger state of gratitude and enjoyment for all they had, and all that they would create.

They both hugged The Tree before leaving, and repeated over and over again their gratitude for the life-changing gift that they had received. But The Tree somehow knew that this was the last time that it would ever see Jonathan and Mary.

As Jonathan and Mary, and the kittens, left the hilltop and disappeared from sight, The Tree looked out over the valley. The beauty of the setting sun casting long shadows across the grassy hillsides and surrounding mountains. The sound of the river and chorus of nature filled its ears and made its soul sing.

There was indeed so much to be thankful for in its life.

CHAPTER SIX
June: Escape

I

The first thing The Tree noticed when Shaun came to visit the stone circle was how his age did not reflect his appearance. For a young man who was in his mid-twenties, there seemed to be an invisible weight that he carried on his shoulders. A burden that was unspoken. The Tree observed a haunted look in his eyes – a haunting that would eventually come to possess the young man's entire being over the coming months.

At first, Shaun was a silent visitor to The Tree. A young man steeped in ruminations and memories ... but these were heavily guarded. The Tree was not unused to such defences. Whilst many of its visitors would openly share through words or images the story of their lives, Shaun's past remained hidden, thanks to the carefully constructed shield that he had cultivated over time.

The Tree knew that sometimes the only way people can protect themselves from the painful truths of their reality is to create an internal fortress that contains the memories and forbidden desires and fears associated with their past, that to survive in the present moment requires a skilful process of locking such memories away in the hopes that they will be forgotten. The Tree had also learnt over the years not to try to penetrate such a fortress and instead learnt that with time and care, the walls of such a place may gradually lower – but only when the conditions in the present are sufficiently safe enough for someone to do so.

The Tree did not know what Shaun had witnessed or experienced, but it knew that his defences needed to be respected and that if this young man could trust The Tree, he may one day feel safe enough to invite it into the fortress to know him better – even if ever so briefly. But for now, it was the young man's present that seemed to overwhelm him, and this is what The Tree allowed itself to attune to.

The Tree awoke one morning in June to discover the young man leaning against its trunk. A handsome and well-built young man wearing sunglasses and a pensive expression. Occasionally he would run his hands through his thick mop of curly black hair but would quickly resume his stillness, interrupted only occasionally by a heavy sigh. The day itself wasn't particularly remarkable. It was a bright and clear day on the hilltop and a peaceful aura emanated from the valley. The Tree's experiences of these early summer months were that the weather could be temperamental, but today there was a warm and calm stillness, as though nature were holding its breath in anticipation of what truths would be spoken.

The only disruption to the silence were the sighs that Shaun would occasionally release, and the sound of breaking twigs as the young man would pace around The Tree, walk towards the edge of the hill and gaze out across the valley, and then returned to his pensive seated position under The Tree's branches, using its sturdy trunk to support and ground him.

When the young man removed his glasses, The Tree noticed his bruised and swollen eye. As the temperature of the day started to increase, he also removed his jacket, revealing the crisp white shirt with the words 'Her Majesty's Prison' and a location The Tree did not know (but assumed must be close by) embroidered into the breast pocket. The shirt was specked with blood. The bright red colour suggested to The Tree that the blood was fresh as it had not yet had time to dry. The young man tenderly touched the area around his eyes and winced with pain. He looked down at his bloodied shirt, sighed deeply, and then placed his head in his hands and silently cried.

The Tree felt his sadness but remained as still and silent as the young man had been. It quietly observed the subtle shaking of Shaun's shoulders as he released the pain that he was holding from the event that had just taken place. Shaun continued to guard this carefully in his mind – the heaviness of the experience, however, was felt by them both.

After several minutes, Shaun wiped his eyes, wincing again as he touched the bruise, and returned to his position on the edge of the hilltop, overlooking the valley. For the first time, The Tree heard the young man speak.

'What am I doing?' came his husky voice. And then again more desperately in a whisper, 'What the fuck am I doing?'

The Tree could see the tears forming in the young man's eyes again but rather than reaching for something to wipe them, The Tree watched him take something out of his pocket, place it to his lips, and light the end of it instead. The Tree had seen people soothing themselves in this way before, and was familiar with the scent of tobacco that would be omitted when burned. But there was something different about what Shaun was smoking on the edge of the hilltop. There was a sweet, tangy and somewhat alluring scent that the light breeze carried from Shaun's exhalations of smoke.

The Tree found itself absorbing the sweet smoke with an unashamed enthusiasm. And the more the young man smoked, the more eager The Tree was to also inhale the intoxicating light grey cloud that seemed to swirl about the young man. The Tree willed him to come closer.

As if reading The Tree's mind, Shaun did just that, a look of dopey serenity starting to spread across his face. The more that the young man smoked beneath its branches, the more curiously strange The Tree began to feel. It was as though a warm and fuzzy fog was enveloping its branches and reaching into its soul. It even had the urge to giggle to itself, and curiously so did Shaun. Time seemed to slow down and sounds became muffled as though it was listening underwater.

An unusual stillness grew in The Tree's core as well as a sublime sense of calm, like drifting on the ocean without a care in the world. It felt its limbs gently swaying to a slow and hypnotic rhythm but also tension melting away from its trunk and limbs, allowing its branches to comfortably droop. The Tree was uncertain if what it was feeling belonged to Shaun, or was a result of the unusual smoke ... but it found itself without a care in the world, and a simple sense of acceptance of the hazy numbness that it was sharing (and enjoying) with its new friend.

Shaun lay on his back, mesmerised by the sway of The Tree's branches and the way the sunlight danced through the leaves, accompanied by its earthy perfume. The haunted look that he first appeared with seemed to have dissolved, giving way to a look of blissful peace. Something within the psyche of the young man must have shifted in this moment as very briefly the door to his inner fortress opened and released a succession of moving images, not particularly coherent, but enough for The Tree to acquire its first glimpse into Shaun's world, through its own drug-induced fog. And in doing so, the door to The Tree's own memory palace of sorrow receded further and further into a hazy and satisfyingly unreachable distance.

II

As the moving images of Shaun's memories came, The Tree allowed itself to gently glide into the gloomy and dismal aura that they conveyed. The Tree felt itself dwarfed by the huge concrete walls that surrounded the prison, all topped with metal fencing and spirals of barbed wire, the barred windows, and the unnerving silence that engulfed it. It was a curiously located structure surrounded by roads and places of public residence. The Tree found itself surprised that such a place would be located here and not somewhere more remote … but as it peered through Shaun's eyes, The Tree felt strangely comforted, knowing that the robust fortress-like walls kept its inhabitants safely locked away. The outside world was safe … but within the walls of the prison, it was a very different story.

What struck The Tree as it wandered through the strange juxtaposition of modern and Victorian prison wings was the curiously haunted and dismally bleak atmosphere the buildings had. Through its somewhat compromised capacity to think clearly, The Tree struggled to acquire a narrative for what it was feeling but it could sense the power of the emotions that saturated the prison walls, the echoing hallways, and all the spaces in between. It glimpsed moments of silence in Shaun's fragmented memories – usually when the prison was locked down at night and all the respective inmates had been returned to their cells. It was then that he would feel the heaviness of all that was unspoken in this citadel of rage.

The air felt thick and oppressive, especially in the derelict Victorian wing, which The Tree saw would later be torn down. The prison cells may have been physically empty but the ghosts of those who once inhabited lingered on. The Tree shuddered – the building was cold, dark, and unnervingly foreboding with its deafening stillness. The Tree could not help but hold its breath, such was the heaviness that it felt in Shaun's soul, and indeed its own.

There was a palpable sense of fear as The Tree's imagination wondered with a morbid curiosity about the time when this block would have been occupied by the men who had had committed all manner of crimes that had led to their incarceration, not knowing what had befallen them whilst in residence here. Both Shaun and The Tree sensed the essence of what they had left behind though. Fear … fury … oppression … hate … violence … envy. These emotions seeped through the doors of both the empty cells of the old wing but even more intensely through the doors of the now occupied cells in the newer parts of the prison. The Tree feared for Shaun and the power of these emotions to seep into all those who came to occupy the prison, both staff and prisoners alike … and perhaps even The Tree itself.

As quickly as these images came, a door was quickly closed on them, giving way to a more dramatic scene. The frantic yell of someone screaming for Shaun to 'SOUND THE ALARM!' accompanied by the deafening and repetitive wail of the prison alarm being initiated, the sound of heavy footsteps running and getting closer to the scene. It glimpsed the thrashing limbs of a beast-like man, scarred face and snarling like a rabid dog, his arms and legs striking out at whomever he could hurt the most. A string of hateful and vile insults were hurled at the attending officers as they prised the small homemade weapon from his fiercely clutched hands. And then came the succession of well-aimed spit that he directed towards their faces.

The Tree heard the thud of soft flesh against a hard cold floor as the supernaturally strong man was brought to the ground, his face slamming into the floor, and a spatter of blood spraying the shirt of one of the young male officers – the same officer who moments later received a painful kick to his face. It was this strike that inevitably led to the swollen eye that The Tree recognised behind Shaun's sunglasses.

A look of smug triumph spread across the bloodied face of the inmate as he saw the young officer reeling backwards clutching his face. The triumph was fleeting as he himself winced in pain at the force of the wooden baton that struck between his shoulder blades. He was dragged into a dark and solitary cell, the heavy metal door being slammed and locked behind him, leaving him alone with his hate ... and a thirst for vengeance.

III

The Tree's consciousness was pulled sharply back into the valley and hilltop with the same speed as the slamming of the inmate's cell door. It found itself gasping for air, bewildered and bemused. And terrified! Its gaze fell upon Shaun, who seemed blissfully unaware of his own memories, and indeed that these had been briefly witnessed by The Tree. The temporary fog that had shrouded its mind had now lifted. Shaun, however, seemed happy to remain in his self-induced state of disconnect from the ordeal that he had clearly just escaped from. And The Tree could understand why.

The Tree felt a strange and unfamiliar queasiness. It was struggling to orientate itself – its mind still swirling from the assault on its senses as it briefly glimpsed Shaun's world. A part of it felt as though it were both falling and drowning at the same time and a sense of panic began to ignite in its soul. Instinctively it turned its focus away from the confusing sensations coursing through its trunk and limbs and instead focused on what it could see. The unremarkable day that it first beheld had become quite beautiful, such was the contrast of the luscious green trees populating the valley slopes and the sparkle of sunlight from the gently flowing river below.

As The Tree connected to these sights, it expanded its vision to take in the cloudless blue sky, and the warmth of the sun as its leaves soaked in the sun's light and nourishment. It connected to the distant sounds of singing birds, to the quiet but perceptible rustling of leaves, and the symphony of perfumes emitted by the myriad flowers that carpeted the valley.

The Tree felt its soul begin to settle and a wave of relief wash over it. It was safe. You are not planted on the grounds of that hateful place, The Tree reminded itself. Nor was it the victim or perpetrator of the violence that it just witnessed. It was merely an observer. It is The Tree ... and is safely contained and protected within its circle of stones. And for that, it felt both grateful and safe once more.

IV

A few days later, The Tree awoke to the familiar scent of Shaun's special tobacco. Still somewhat confused and unnerved by its previous experience, The Tree willed itself to be immune to the seductive and dream-like effects of the intoxicating smoke in the hopes that it would be receptive to whatever Shaun needed to say, if indeed he would actually speak to The Tree. On this occasion he did not and remained silent.

Shaun continued to wear a look of deep contemplation on his face. His swollen eye still looked painful, and a swell of compassion emanated from The Tree towards him. As if sensing something, Shaun approached The Tree from his familiar standing point overlooking the valley, and gently placed his hand on The Tree's rough bark, took a deep inhalation of his special cigarette, and exhaled a plume of thick smoke which danced through its branches like a swarm of mystical fairies. Despite The Tree's efforts, it could feel itself being lured into the delightful aroma – toying with the feeling of peace that it could induce. But The Tree resisted ... in as much as it could.

Shaun unfurled the blanket that he had brought with him and set it down a few metres from The Tree, carefully choosing a spot that would maximise his contact with the sun's golden rays. He looked tired and haunted still. The Tree assumed he had just finished working as he was still in uniform. His shirt was clean this time – all evidence of the events a few days ago having been washed away. But only from his clothes.

It was still morning so Shaun must have been working overnight. As if to satisfy The Tree's curiosity, Shaun's face relaxed, and the familiar spell weaved by his burning joint took hold, and lulled him into a dreamless foggy sleep. Whilst Shaun was spared reliving the events of the previous evening, The Tree was hit full force by the cascade of memories that permeated its own mind …

V

The prison ward smelled damp and rank. A combination of bodily fluids and poor hygiene. Night had fallen on the prison and so The Tree shared Shaun's memories. They walked towards the entrance of the dark and depressing prison ward where Shaun was to be stationed for the evening. A clear plastic shield, the height and width of a person, was left in the doorway with a note that simply said …

'USE THIS!'

The Tree watched Shaun apprehensively pick up the shield and brace himself for whatever was to come. Nights on the psychiatric ward were always the worst. They were unpredictable, they were strange, and they were always disturbing. They left Shaun feeling befuddled and haunted, not feeling quite sure what belonged to the prison patients, and what belonged to him.

Shaun entered the shadowy and hollow ward containing twelve cells, the nurse's office, and an open area with a few ordinary tables and some chairs. He waved to the on-duty psychiatric nurse. The Tree felt Shaun's relief when he saw the nurse … a young man of similar age to him with whom he had fostered a good relationship. He smiled and waved towards him, to which the nurse responded with a look of warning and pointed to Shaun's right whilst silently mouthing the words …

'BE CAREFUL!'

The Tree watched as Shaun instinctively raised and positioned the shield to his right-hand side, as instructed, and with a deep breath stepped onto the ward. As he did so, what The Tree assumed to be flying excrement was launched and splattered on the shield, accompanied by a rampage of incoherent rantings and vaguely decipherable threats. Further yells then erupted from one of the cells on the opposite side of the small ward. Again, a tirade of threats … but this time towards the other patient. Threats of violence in the most graphic form were screamed as well as the heavy and aggressive pounding on their own side of the metal cell door – begging to be let out so they could 'Slash the fucking lunatic's throat.'

Seemingly unperturbed by this, Shaun continued walking toward the nurse's office, gratefully accepted the freshly brewed mug of coffee that was handed to him and muttered a familiar phrase to his colleague ...

'This is going to be a very long night.'

As The Tree witnessed, this was indeed the case. Whilst only catching fleeting images and scenes, the undertone of these was enough for The Tree. It saw how patiently and protectively Shaun stood guard next to his colleague when one of the prisoners' cells had to be opened. This was not common practice during the lockdowns that took place every night, but was permissible during an emergency. One of that night's particular crises involved a patient requiring medical attention after he slashed both sides of his own face in responses to the voices that he reported were tormenting him.

The Tree heard the inmate's sobs as the nurse spoke to him softly whilst cleaning his wounds and offered care and support to ease his distress. It observed Shaun leap forward to restrain the man when between sobs the same inmate lunged at the nurse, now being accused of trying to put 'bugs in his veins so he could be controlled', followed by the tirade of tears and apologies that were delivered by the tragic confused soul. Throughout the night the man's cell would be opened and closed as medication was given to calm his rantings, and to prevent the re-opening of his painful wounds, which the man continued to do by punching and clawing the side of his face where the bandages had been so tenderly applied.

The Tree heard Shaun frantically calling for the nurse during the early hours of the morning upon discovering a patient attempting to strangle himself with torn up bed sheets. Once again, another cell door was opened, revealing the patient hiding under his own bed having successfully knotted the sheets – his eyes now bloodshot, bulging, and his face turning an ugly shade of blue.

But again, the two members of staff worked together to remove the makeshift rope and safely resuscitate the man back to consciousness. Through his coughs and splutters, the man pleaded with Shaun and the nurse to 'Just let me die!' as well as accusations, such as 'Neither of you bastards care anyway!'

The same man made three more attempts that same night ... and each time his plans were thwarted. But with every disruption, the energy on the ward became more and more saturated with agitation and fury. As the other inmates were woken with every disturbance, the crueller their threats of violence became, as did their own extreme acting out behaviours. Attempts to set fire to their cells. Head-banging and nonsensical screaming. Threats of violence towards the other inmates, but also towards Shaun and his colleague.

The night wore on, as did the madness. But Shaun and his colleague remained calm and continued to do their job with care, with compassion, but also with a hidden detachment.

The Tree was bemused and troubled by what it was seeing. It had not beheld this level of disturbance before. And it felt amazed at how calm both Shaun and the psychiatric nurse had remained throughout. They seemed to bounce off each other's energy but acted in a somewhat robotic way, almost as though they were being controlled by an external force, thus not needing to think or feel – just act quickly and in the moment, without fear or panic.

The Tree, however, could sense within Shaun the terror and apprehension but also the cleverly cultivated defences that enabled him to minimise what he was seeing and hearing, and simply just do his job. And there was always the reward of his own special cigarettes, once the working day (or night) was done.

The Tree felt both curious and sad for the wretched souls incarcerated in the prison, but also understood the necessity of their absence of liberty because of the unspeakable crimes that they had committed. But mostly it felt pity for its new friend. The young man with the swollen eye lying in the sunshine and vacantly staring up into the sky with no thoughts ... no feelings ... and for the time being no memories of where he had just been.

The Tree's mind swarmed with the fractured and horrifying images expelled from Shaun's own mind, and it found itself experiencing a similar feeling to its new friend – a desire to somehow block out these images. To not feel the disturbance, or the fear, or the pity. In fact, The Tree longed to feel nothing!

Again, as though reading its mind, Shaun in an almost trance-like state relit his cigarette, took a deep inhale, and then exhaled a comforting billow of smoke towards the sky. A gentle breeze caught it and generously wafted it towards The Tree, who, with a sigh of relief (and also a flicker of shame), welcomed the familiar warm and fuzzy haze that meant its mind and soul could temporarily feel unburdened and at peace.

VI

Over the next few days, the June weather continued to be generous. The sun shone and provided a seemingly endless cloudless beauty and sustenance to the hilltop and valley. Everything seemed vibrant and humming with life, a stark contrast to the flashes of memory that Shaun unknowingly shared with The Tree amidst his drug-induced haze.

The Tree came to both dread and look forward to Shaun's visits. It felt disturbed by the grim and desolate scenes conveyed by Shaun's flashes of memory as he worked with mentally disordered offenders. But it did come to welcome and embrace the strange sensation of detachment that he shared with Shaun every time he sparked up a joint. The Tree even found itself longing for the sweet sensation of numbness in between Shaun's visits as it was plagued by images and feelings – the echoes of the traumas that Shaun carried within him but was desperate to forget.

As The Tree fell into the fragmented memories projected outwards by Shaun, it lurched between a sea of faces, each telling their own stories to the prison guard as he wandered the prison wings and the harrowing psychiatric ward. The Tree could feel the toxicity of the environment, so saturated was it with the stories and emotions of the cruel, the vengeful, the violent, and the disturbed – a disturbance that The Tree could sense was infecting its own soul the more it saw and heard. It observed the same process taking hold of Shaun as his need to escape through dissociation increased, as did his smoking.

The Tree hovered between clarity and fog, memories and fear, as it glimpsed Shaun and his colleagues attending to fights breaking out in the exercise yard – an uninviting concrete slab surrounded by a high metal fence, populated by the prison's inmates. They walked in circles, some like lifeless zombies, whilst others gathered in groups, whispering and planning their next move. Splashes of blood streaked the concrete, as well as other bodily fluids … a horrifying reminder to everyone in the cage of what could befall them. Nowhere and no one was safe.

Fear and paranoia rippled through the staff, as well as the inmates. The Tree saw moments of Shaun's reflection in the mirror taking deep breaths – psyching himself up before re-entering the maelstrom. The Tree felt Shaun's suspicion of his colleagues, of the inmates whom he thought were pretending to behave whilst all the while suspecting that they were plotting his own demise.

The Tree heard the sound of wailing sirens and witnessed Shaun running to various scenes … adrenaline coursing through his body – breathless and terrified of what he would find. Would someone be hurt? Would someone be dead?

The Tree saw cells covered in human filth, a desperate and grim protest against the authority that detained them. It saw bodies in states of undress and violation. It felt the terror and shame for those who had been dominated and used sexually as a cruel exertion of dominance and power.

It recoiled in horror as Shaun arrived in the shower block to prevent a gang assault, and the subsequent clean-up of makeshift weapons and bloody clothes. The Tree saw a wet, naked, and beaten body being taken to the hospital wing, and the subsequent restraint of the other larger men as they were dragged to an even darker place within the bowels of the prison to be segregated from the rest of the population.

The more Shaun visited the hilltop, the less able he became at concealing his thoughts and his feelings. The Tree felt assaulted by the torrent of stories – whispers of the histories that the inmates confided in Shaun as he became more and more enmeshed in the harrowing lives of the people he both feared but also came to care for. Shaun came to know stories of abandonment and neglect, of parental betrayal and cruelty. Of despicable acts of physical and sexual violence against one's fellow human beings.

The Tree was sickened by the absence of conscience in the people who perpetrated harm and felt confused by the desire of others to destroy and triumph over the innocent. It came to know the envy and hate that emanated from these men, as well as glimpsing the abhorrence that they themselves had been subjected to when they too were only children.

Like Shaun, The Tree felt conflicted by its pity for the children that they were but also scorn and disgust towards the men that they had become. And as such, it continued to welcome the blissful moments of sharing that The Tree and Shaun created as they drifted into the glorious colours of the valley and momentarily left the despairing catacombs of human misery and suffering behind in a cloud of intoxicating fog.

VII

As the summer solstice approached, The Tree became aware that it had not seen Shaun for several days. In his absence The Tree felt both a sense of longing for contact with the young man and concern for his wellbeing. It also found itself missing the moments that they would share together as they disconnected from the troubles of the world. But equally, The Tree found itself experiencing a sense of relief at not having to witness the memories and disturbing emotions associated with the men whom Shaun guarded.

In these moments of peace and solitude, The Tree found itself relishing in the bright and warm days, and was once again able to feel connected to the valley below, the sky above, and all the woodland animals who once again visited The Tree thanks to the absence of the smoky vapour that had come to envelop the hilltop in recent days.

As The Tree swayed cheerfully in the mild breeze, its attention was drawn to masses of white flower heads as elderflowers came into bloom, their sweet and succulent scent attracting a host of curious insects. Red admiral butterflies with their crimson wings decorated with eye-like patterns had returned to dance through the air around The Tree's branches, thus enchanting its soul, and reminding it of the beauty of the world, so forgotten when lost in the chasm of despair that was the prison.

At one point The Tree could have sworn that it both saw and heard the delighted splashes of small otters playing joyfully in the river below, undisturbed by any of the threats that The Tree knew the world to behold. For these glorious moments, The Tree felt its soul settle and a sense of hope returning.

Dusk settled over the valley, and a contented Tree found itself dozing in and out of consciousness – remaining sporadically awake for short periods of time to welcome the first stars of the evening, as the warm golds, pinks, and violet of the sky gave way to a deepening shade of indigo. As evening became night, the perfectly clear sky showcased the dazzling constellations, many of which The Tree could now recognise thanks to the guidance and stories of a past friend who had taken refuge in its branches as a beautiful friendship developed between him and another young man.

Before The Tree could slip too deeply into its memories, it heard the sound of footsteps thumping on the earth as they made their way up the hillside, and eventually emerged into the stone circle. A figure in a hooded jacket could be seen. As they reached the stone circle, the figure lowered his hood revealing a shaved head and what appeared to be a slight pink discoloration to the left-side of his clean-shaven face. But The Tree could not be sure as the figure's face was lost in the shadow of the night.

As he edged closer and made his way towards The Tree, it could sense a familiar energy about the young man and finally recognised him. It was Shaun.

But there was something different about him. It was not just the wound on his face that The Tree could now recognise as being a burn mark. It was also the severe alteration to his appearance through the shaving of his head. And the seeming muscle mass that he had been accumulating since beginning to visit The Tree. What did remain the same, however, was the haunted look in his eyes.

As Shaun approached The Tree, he did something unfamiliar. He looked straight at The Tree and spoke.

'He nearly killed me … I think that place is going to kill me. If I don't find a way to escape, I know I am going to die in there.'

Surprised and concerned, The Tree gestured with its outstretched branches towards a pile of wood in the centre of the stone circle and invited the young man to light a fire to keep warm and to share his story in words, which he did.

'Tell me my dear friend, what has happened to you? Who tried to kill you?'

Shaun settled close to the fire, holding his hands outwards towards the flames in an attempt to feel something other than fear. The Tree could see that he was visibly overwhelmed and remembered the calmness it had felt earlier in the day when it reconnected to the beauty of its surroundings. Seeing that Shaun was physically agitated and struggling to form his words, The Tree invited him to just pause for a moment, to slow his breathing so that it matched the gentle movement of The Tree's branches as it swayed without a breeze. It invited him to focus on the colour of the fire's beautiful flames as they danced before him, on the sweet and pungent smoke billowing into the dark sky, and to listen to the soft crackle of the wood as it burned and glowed, emanating a safe and comforting warmth.

Shaun's body began to settle, and so too did The Tree's in response.

Feeling back in the present moment, Shaun took a deep breath and shared the events of the previous day.

'I should've known this was going to happen. This guy has been gunning for me ever since he came inside. He is the guy that we had to restrain at the start of this month. I came up here the morning after it happened. Do you remember?'

The Tree nodded. It did indeed.

'The fucker had kicked me in the face and spat at me. I don't remember much afterwards but I do remember coming up here. I remember feeling safe when I was with you, which is strange because you're just a tree. But the more I came up here, I knew that there was something different about you. Something strange. But also, something comforting. That is why I kept coming back.'

And with a laugh, he added, 'And I remember getting stoned … with you!'

Shaun's laugh felt hollow as he acknowledged the silent relationship that he had been establishing with The Tree, and the tragic circumstances that gave it context.

'I'd do anything for a smoke right now … but I've got nothing,' he continued.

The Tree felt relieved that this was the case. Even though Shaun had not yet shared his story, the mark on his face and his altered appearance suggested to The Tree that something extreme had happened. Something that Shaun needed to speak of and process. The Tree also knew that when faced with painful memories and experiences people will seek to escape from these through whatever means they can. The Tree had seen that when people did this, the relief from their horror was only short-lived. The experience became buried somewhere deep in their minds, locked in a cellar never to be seen again … until they experienced something similar again, causing the metaphorical cellar door to smash open.

Not only would they become lost in a wave of confusing and nightmarish feelings associated with the present – all of the unprocessed emotion from the past would also erupt and push the person into a sea of overwhelm and terror. The Tree had seen Shaun desperately trying to do this … and had itself felt the relief when they had both been able to disconnect by getting high. But The Tree knew that this was not what Shaun needed right now. He needed compassion and support. He needed someone wise and grounded to help support and make meaning of his story.

Shaun continued his story.

'So, this guy – the one we had to take to segregation unit – he did this to me!' He pointed to the side of his face where small patches of the skin were raw and clearly burned.

'It could've been worse,' he continued. 'I've been watching him for days on the Seg. He's been eyeballing me and doing the usual bullshit of trying to intimidate me. He stares at me unblinking like a mad dog. Or he stands in the doorway of his cell with this creepy maniacal grin and then drags his finger across his throat as if to say he's going to slit my throat. Pretty standard stuff,' he then added nonchalantly with a dismissive shrug and wave of his hand.

'But over the last few days his behaviour became even stranger. I could hear him whispering incoherently to himself at night. And then the giggling came. Weird high-pitched giggling and always in the middle of the night. I heard him chatting to one of the nurses, saying something about hearing voices. Voices telling him to do stuff, hurt us, hurt himself and telling him that we are all after him. That there's a plot to kill him. To be honest, I've heard it all so many times that you sort of get complacent. They can be manipulative fuckers at times – sometimes it's for real and we take them on down to the prison ward. But not this guy. He's just bad guy. I mean, you should hear the things has done – kids, adults, and even animals. Honestly, this guy is a monster. He's a proper sicko.'

Shaun's voice trailed off and he looked deep in thought as though swimming back into the memories of the convict's past, as well as the events that he was beginning to describe.

Conscious of wanting to help Shaun stay grounded with The Tree, it reminded Shaun to come back to where he was now, in this moment. To smell and feel the fire, to observe The Tree itself and its leafy branches reaching into the starlit sky, to feel the solid earth beneath him, and just to remind himself where he was in the valley and not inside the prison.

Gratefully, Shaun did as he was invited and noticed a feeling of calm returning to his body, which had up until that point stiffened and become tense. Slowing his breathing down as instructed by The Tree before, Shaun continued, but a slight tremble remained in his hushed voice.

'So, he finally got me. I could sense something was going to happen right from the start of the day. You know when you just have that feeling? That something really bad is gonna happen but you can't really explain it?'

The Tree nodded. Over the years it too had a cultivated a heightened sense of awareness. It could sense changes in the atmosphere and its surroundings but had also learnt the language of human beings. Their tone of voice, their body language ... but most strongly, a sense of attunement and connectedness that allowed it to feel that which was not spoken but also that which the person did not even know within themselves. The Tree's intuition had served it well. And it empathised with Shaun, a young man who had clearly learnt how to read these signs in others too – a skill which no doubt had helped him to survive in the prison but perhaps, also more sadly, a skill which had been learnt at a much younger age when anticipating and escaping from threat.

'So I came on shift and went straight down to the Seg. As I was coming through the gates, I felt unnerved. There was silence. Like literally no sound at all was coming from the Seg, which was unusual because normally at that time of the morning there is some movement taking place. But the silence felt weird. I could even feel the hairs rising on my arms and neck.'

Shaun shuddered as he said this and then continued.

'Finally there was the familiar metallic creaking and a clanging sound as one of the gates ahead of me opened and I saw my mate, that nice psych nurse who I sometimes work with on the ward. He looked pretty rough though, he had bags under his eyes and looked tired. So, I knew it had obviously been a heavy night down here. We greeted each other as we normally do but he gave me a warning.'

'"Be careful mate" he said, "He's on one today. He's slashed up his arms and legs all through the night and keeps tearing open his sutures … for fuck sake!"

'He also told me that every time he goes into this guy's cell, he just stands still like a statue, unblinking with this weird smile on his face, like he's waiting to pounce or something.'

The Tree felt uneasy, it couldn't help but visualise the scene and felt a sense of fear and anticipation building within its trunk.

'So, when I finally got down there, I didn't go to our office as I normally do first. Instead, I went to the railings in the middle of the Seg and looked down. We've got eight cells on the level where our office is. But then another eight one level below us. The Seg is sort of hollow in the centre but there is a net … y'know, in case someone tries to jump. The cells are on the outside so four on one side and four on the other. It's just like a mini version of the main prison wings, which are massive.'

'I could look down and see some of the cell doors in the level below us, some of which have a sort of reinforced clear plastic front so we can observe the more dangerous inmates. Especially if they are a risk of doing stuff to themselves. Of course, my guy was in one of these. He looked up and saw me. He was still pulling that stupid maniacal grin. But when he locked eyes on me, the smile faded and his eyes hardened.'

Shaun shuddered as he spoke.

'Honestly, mate, I have never felt so freaked out. There was something so cold and dead behind his eyes but also a real wave of hate coming from this guy towards me. I have no idea why.'

The Tree shuddered too. It could feel the malice that the prisoner felt towards Shaun … it was visceral. The Tree had always been able to show others compassion and even in their darkest moments find some kind of love and understanding for them. But as Shaun spoke about this particular prisoner, it felt a chill trickle through its trunk and branches. This man did not possess goodness but seemed to be filled with a cold rage that emanated from him like a malevolent spectre in a horror story.

'So, he's staring at me, not blinking, not moving … honestly, it was so fucking creepy. I gave him a courteous nod – I didn't know what else to do – and then I backed away from the edge of the railings and went to the office to get the handover from the night staff.

'Nothing out of the ordinary happened for the rest of that morning. Me and the other officers spoke about how strange the vibe was down there on that day. It was so quiet, even the other guys on the Seg were silent. I just did my normal checks – a few pleasant and oddly courteous conversations with the guys who were locked up down there, but they too seemed unnerved. It was just odd … there's no other words for it.'

He paused and then sighed. His body was tensing again and The Tree noticed that his breathing was starting to quicken, and the physical trembling that The Tree had noticed before was back.

'You're okay,' said The Tree, softly and kindly. 'Whatever happened, it's over now. You are safe. You have survived it. He cannot hurt you now because you are here, with me, on this hilltop. You are in front of the fire, with the earth beneath you and the stars above you. You aren't in the prison now. You are safe and you are with me.'

Shaun's body once again began to settle as he absorbed The Tree's words and looked around him, connecting with his senses that did indeed remind him that he was safe and not in the prison. But his face had a grave expression as the light of the fire danced across it.

'He started whispering my name. At first, I thought I was imagining it but the whisper became this unsettling hiss which the other officers started to notice too. The guys know that if they want us, they need to press their cell buzzer, so I just ignored him and waited for him to press his buzzer if he actually needed something. But the whisper got louder and turned into a strange low taunt one minute and then a high-pitched screech the next.'

'There's something about that fucker's voice that just goes right through me. And through the other officers too. One of them was clearly getting pissed off and shouted for him to "SHUT THE FUCK UP!" He did ... for about an hour. And then the buzzing began.'

The Tree could hear the piercing electronic buzzer – shrill and violating as the inmate went from intermittent bursts of sound that assaulted the senses and echoed around the segregation unit, growing to a constant wail. The Tree saw from Shaun's memory him throwing down the newspaper that he was reading. It saw the smirks and sniggers of his colleagues as he stormed from the office and down the clanking metal stairs to the cells on the lower level.

The Tree could sense Shaun's fear but also his need to prove himself.

The Tree knew that sometimes when people have been made to feel afraid in the past, they may, without knowing always knowing why, gravitate towards similar situations of threat in the present. Not because they like it, but because it is all that they know. The Tree wondered if a part of Shaun was desperate to prove himself, to perhaps prove his courage and his strength in a way that he couldn't do when he was a child. Or to perhaps even bring threat to himself, so that he was not left in a constant state of anticipation and waiting. Whilst these memories were locked away and not accessible to The Tree, it sensed a familiar process in Shaun which it feared would result in future harm befalling its new friend.

The Tree continued to watch the scene now unfold as though it were witnessing it from above ... and it was afraid.

'WHAT?!!! WHAT THE FUCK DO YOU WANT?' exploded Shaun, clearly agitated and losing control from the endless taunting and anticipation that he had been feeling since walking on to the small and isolated prison wing.

'I want you ...' came the rasping whisper of the triumphant inmate. 'And I have something for you ... something special. Just for you!'

The sickening grin returned as he said this from behind his cell door. Thrusting his arms forward, the inmate proceeded to rip open the wounds that he had carved into his arms the night before.

Shocked by the sudden attack on his own body, Shaun yelled for him to stop and firmly shouted at the inmate to get back and sit down on his cell bed so he could help. He instinctively unlocked the inmate's cell.

Whilst The Tree saw the inmate obediently do as he was told, blood dripped from his open lacerations and he grinned insanely back at Shaun.

Shaun surveyed the cell quickly and noticed a faint mist caused from the steam of a recently boiled kettle and looked down at the man's bleeding arms to assess what to do next.

Wide-eyed, and without warning, the inmate leapt up from the bed and screamed.

'BEHIND YOU!!!' he said, pointing directly behind Shaun, a terrified look frozen on his face.

Shaun whirled around instinctively to face the attacker behind him.

There was nothing. The space behind him was empty. No one was there.

His heart was pounding. His breathing quickened. Before he could turn back towards the cell, a searing pain blazed across the side of his face as boiling water laced with sugar splashed off the door behind him and caught his face.

Shaun winced in pain as a fist made contact with the back of his head, causing him to stumble forwards.

He felt disorientated … confused. Before he could act, a strong, bloodied and snakelike arm wrapped itself around his neck, crushing his windpipe. Shaun was dragged backwards into the inmate's cell.

'Man … it was the strangest sensation. Everything became slow and woozy. It was like I was watching the scene unfold but I was a ghost looking down on it all. I remember screaming in my head to fight back. To do something. But I just remember that I couldn't. My body went numb and I sort of just flopped. That has never happened to me before. I've always been able to get myself out of trouble but there was something about this time. About this guy. He really frightened me, and in that moment, I remember thinking to myself … This is how I die!'

'There was a sort of weird calm acceptance as I swam in this weird foggy state. But then something must've kicked in, a survival instinct or something. I remembered something from my training about how to protect my neck if I were to be strangled. This kind of thing is expected,' he laughed ironically.

'And so I used my hands to pull down on his forearm. It was just long enough to gasp for air. And panicking, I shouted the only thing that I could …

'What the fuck are you doing? WHAT THE FUCK ARE YOU DOING?!'

'He dragged me on to his bed and tightened his grip again. He was whispering something vile in my ears but I can't remember exactly what it was … but it was something sexual. Something he was going to do to me. It must've been something pretty grim, and given what the sick fuck was inside for, I believed him too.'

'A surge of strength returned to me. I knew had to get away no matter what it took. Things still seemed in slow motion, but I remember twisting my body and jerking it until we both rolled off the bed and onto the floor. I think he hit his head on the bed frame because I heard a THUNK, followed by a moan, and his arm loosened its grip again.'

'All I could think to do was jerk my head backwards … so I did. He yelled in pain. I could feel the blood from his mouth drip down my neck and the sharpness of his teeth as my head bashed his mouth. I sort of then propelled myself forward out of the cell and heard the wet slap of more boiling sugar water narrowly missing me and landing on the floor next to me.'

The Tree heard a loud siren echoing through the Seg and what sounded like an army of soldiers running down the metal stairs.

'All I could see at first were their boots running past me and the sound of them piling into that fucker's cell. Through the siren I could hear grunts and thuds. There was clearly a fight going on. But I couldn't see as I was still face down on the ground. I remember someone putting their hand on my back and saying "It's okay, buddy, we've got you. We've got you! You're safe!"

'The next thing I knew I was back in the office. I had my hands in my pockets. My hands were shaking so badly but I didn't want the other guys to see. I was still in a bit of a daze. I could hear one of the officers – a really nice guy – talking to me. He sounded calm and kind. I don't know what he was saying though, but I could feel his care.

'One of the other officers walked in and looked at me. I remember his smug face and him saying with a smirk, "HA … that'll teach you won't it!"'

Insensitive prick, The Tree thought angrily to itself, surprised at its own change in tone.

'I felt anger, and shame. This officer was always a prick to me. I don't know what his problem was but he always seemed to take joy in other people's misfortunes. Thankfully, the kind officer bellowed at him to "GET OUT!", which he did very quickly.'

'Eventually the sirens stopped, the extra guards left the wing, and that guy was safely locked in his cell again. I heard one of the nurses being called to deal with some of his injuries but a few of the officers remained with shields to make sure they could tend to his wounds safely. The last thing I heard when I left Seg after my shift was his hateful giggle and that sick taunting whisper of his...

"Shauny ... OFFICER SHAUNY. C'mon you little pussy. You faggoty little cunt ... fucking talk to me. Filthy little punk. TALK TO ME!"

'And then in flat, hollow and matter-of-fact voice for everyone to hear, I heard him simply say, "I'm going to kill you!"

'The metal door to the Seg clanked shut. I walked out of that God forsaken place and staggered home like a zombie. My face was stinging where the boiling water and sugar had congealed. When I fell asleep, my dreams were haunted by his stupid grin and the final words he said.'

Shaun fell silent. He was as still as The Tree as he stared into nothingness. Light and shadows continued to flicker across his face from the glow of the fire. The night and the valley echoed his stillness. It was as though everything and everyone, including The Tree, held its breath. Noticing this and the tension in its dissonantly still branches, it let out a sigh and deliberately swished its arms. The sound of the creaking Tree and the rustle of its branches awoke something in Shaun. The movement of The Tree sent a wave of air towards him, causing the fire to flare and the smoke to waft, a necessary assault on Shaun's senses to bring him, and indeed The Tree, out of the memory and back to the safety of the hilltop as the night air began to cool.

Breaking the silence, The Tree spoke.

'I'm so sorry that happened to you. I can feel and see how frightening that was for you. Please, just listen to my voice, and remind yourself that you're safe now. And that what happened was not your fault. There was nothing that you said or did that in anyway invited or deserved what happened!' And then it added, 'And that other officer sounds like a fucking prick!'

Shaun jerked his head up to look at The Tree and began to chuckle, startled by The Tree's emulation of his own language. A wave of relief seemed to spread through his body, as did a growing feeling of calm. He was indeed safe. And he wasn't to blame. But he had let his guard down, he knew that. And he regretted it. He was aware that he had feared that at some point something like this would happen. It didn't feel like a matter of if, it was more of a when. And now it had happened – mercifully he was relatively unharmed thanks to his eventual reflexes, and the fast response (he assumed fast because it was hard to tell in his foggy state) of his fellow officers. Sadly though, he knew that he had to go back there.

'Do you think you'll go back?' said The Tree, as if reading Shaun's mind.

'I'm afraid to. Part of me just wants to stay away. To call in sick. To not go back, pretend that whole fuck-up never happened.'

'I understand,' said The Tree. 'That man hurt you. That place is filled with hate and rage. Of course you would want to protect yourself from that. And perhaps you need some time.' The Tree paused and thought for a moment. 'What do you fear could happen if you do go back?'

'I'm afraid he will do as he said. That he will actually kill me. You can't know what that's like. It wasn't just what he said. It was the way that he said it. And I could feel it too. The other guys can be threatening and intimidating but there is something different about this guy … he really gets under my skin. I could literally feel and see in my mind what he wants to do to me. And its fucking terrifying. He is fucking terrifying!'

'You're right,' said The Tree. 'I can't fully know or understand what you've been through. Or what you fear. But I can feel your terror. And I can see how dangerous that place is. But what you've also shown me is the support and care of your colleagues … well, most of your colleagues. That there are things in place to keep you safe, if indeed you were to return. But it is entirely your choice not to.'

Shaun listened. Conflicting emotions stirred within him. He wanted to be kind to himself. But he also wanted to prove himself. To not let other people get the better of him. He had been doing that all through his life.

'If I may offer you something from what I have seen and heard over the years of my existence,' said The Tree compassionately.

'Sure ... please do,' said Shaun, his focus now latched onto The Tree.

'It is understandable to want to escape. Your body and mind has been designed to protect you from harm by avoiding real and possible threats. But what I've observed happening in people over the years is that sometimes you may reinforce the fear by perpetuating the fantasy of that fear through your avoidance. Your home, for example, may become a place of safety for you – as has this space here with me – but the longer you stay away from people or situations that might be a threat, you risk unintentionally robbing yourself of the opportunity to experience something different. I wonder what it would be like to, at some point, return to the prison and for the outcome to be different. For you to be safe. For you to feel in control. For you to make a choice? It may be that upon returning you decide to leave, and that would be your right. But it might also provide you with a unique opportunity to learn ... to grow.'

Shaun looked deep in thought but said nothing.

'I wish I could see the future,' continued The Tree. 'I can see many things but the future is not one of them, sadly. I wish I could foresee how things will be for you, but all I can do is listen, is guide, and help you to make meaning of your experiences ... and indeed your fears, so that you can feel empowered to do what feels right for you. To do anything but that risks disempowering you and taking away your ability to charter your own ship on this voyage of life that you are embarking on.'

The Tree fell silent, hoping to give space for its words to sink in. It felt such love for the young man before him. As well as a deep fear that it could not shake. As though there was something about Shaun and now The Tree's life that were to become inextricably linked. But this was just a feeling ... something that it could not quantify but felt in its very soul. It prayed to the elements for this young man to be safe and to find a way to protect himself by whatever means necessary. It also felt the familiar urge emanating from Shaun to escape. An urge that The Tree itself had become all too familiar with.

Shaun, now standing, turned away from the fire and walked towards The Tree, where he placed his hands on its trunk.

'You're right, I know you are. I need to face my demons, whatever that means. I don't want to lock myself up in a haunted house where everything outside of it feels dangerous. I will go back, but I will also take some time. I need to really think about what happened and what I can do differently. I know I wasn't to blame ... BUT I need to know that I have some kind of control, that I can take something from this. That it won't define me. Or destroy me! I have power. I have control. And I have choice!'

'Yes, you do,' agreed The Tree warmly. 'And you will always have a place of sanctuary and protection here with me. No matter what, I will always make sure you are safe whilst you are here. I promise!'

Warm tears stung Shaun's eyes in response to The Tree's kindness. Wiping his eyes quickly, he nodded his head, knowing that The Tree would sense the gratitude that he was struggling to express in words.

Taking a few deep breaths and centring himself, Shaun awkwardly hugged The Tree and attempted to act like nothing had happened.

'It's the summer solstice next week,' he said casually. 'How about me and some of my buddies come up here for a celebration? Y'know, something to take all of our minds off what has happened and to just embrace life ... I'll even bring something to help get the party started!'

With that, Shaun winked and grinned at The Tree, followed by a gasp. He winced in pain having briefly forgotten about the burn on his face.

'I will look forward to it!' said The Tree with a flourish of its branches. And then added mischievously, 'I may even bring something of my own to help keep the party going!'

Shaun's smiled widened. He waved goodbye to The Tree for now and set off down the hill and into the night, unsure of what the following days would bring.

VIII

The summer solstice arrived the following week. And so did Shaun and his friends. The warmth of the sun and the blue cloudless skies did not disappoint. The days were long and a hum of energy reverberated throughout the valley. There was a warm and gentle breeze. The animals, the flowers, the forest and the river all seemed to be existing in harmony with one another, so unspoilt was this particular summer.

The Tree was intrigued by the new visitors that Shaun had brought with him. Both men and women of different ages attended and were no doubt colleagues of Shaun's, hence the cacophony of disturbing images that they each unintentionally shared from their minds as they entered the stone circle. They seemed less adept at shielding themselves from their day-to-day experiences within the prison ... but also seemed less haunted than Shaun.

The Tree could feel a mixture of experience and cynicism emanating from the group – an almost nonchalant attitude to the men whom they detained, and an imperviousness to the things that they witnessed and heard.

Whilst Shaun's friends had found a way to shield themselves from the emotions associated with their work, the same could not be said for The Tree, who more keenly than ever felt like an open wound soaking in the unacknowledged fear and disturbance. It noticed that as time progressed, and perhaps because of the life force it had given to others throughout its own existence, its defences were becoming weaker. The Tree couldn't decide if its capacity to be so attuned to the suffering of the human soul was a blessing or a curse. But given the feelings that assaulted its own soul as the visitors arrived, The Tree longed for the sweet escape that Shaun had promised, if only to protect its own soul from contamination.

Shaun and his friends were loud and spirited from the moment they arrived. Musical instruments from tambourines to guitars, small drums and even a violin were played, much to the delight and merriment the group. Familiar songs from many eras were sung as well as those that were simply inspired by the mood, and the fast-growing consumption of alcohol. The laughter and singing was indeed contagious and The Tree felt its own soul begin to lift, despite the continued barrage of fragmented and unsettling scenes that it desperately tried to ignore in favour of the celebration and enjoyment that was taking place under its watchful gaze. Even Shaun seemed different, his rare smile catching The Tree off-guard. The serious expression and furrowed brow were absent, and were instead replaced by a giddy cheerfulness and loud deep laugh. He was keeping his head shaved as well as his stubbly facial hair, which again was a stark contrast to when he first visited The Tree.

The Tree found itself wondering about the myriad ways in which human beings cope with their environments. The vast and creative ways that they learn to tolerate the intolerable and adapt to inhospitable surroundings. Perhaps, it thought, Shaun was becoming like his colleagues. The women had a somewhat hardened look in their eyes as well as a steely indifference. The men seemed large, muscular, and almost as intimidating as the inmates if it weren't for the jovial singing, laughter and banter that The Tree could sense in their souls.

Shaun too was changing in shape. The Tree assumed that he too was mirroring his colleagues, and perhaps even the men who dwelt within the prison. If you can't beat them ... join them! came the phrase. Shaun looked more muscular than when he first visited The Tree and carried himself with a different air of confidence, which surprised The Tree after his previous encounter with Shaun. However, despite the growing bravado and changed image that The Tree beheld, it could still sense fear. It could still sense the anticipation of danger ... even if these feelings had been buried somewhere deep in Shaun's psyche. But either way, The Tree was relieved that Shaun was surviving. That he had been back to the prison and was exploring his own ways to survive. But deep down, The Tree hoped that he would one day be able to escape, lest he become as jaded as it felt Shaun's colleagues had become.

IX

As the afternoon became dusk, the raucous clan lit a carefully constructed bonfire in the centre of the stone circle. Despite its small size, the glow and heat that emanated from it lent itself beautifully to the warm summer evening and the tone of the group. As well as alcohol, various other substances were being consumed. Powders, small tablets, and of course the familiar wafts of intoxicating smoke that The Tree had come to associate with Shaun, and both of their respective needs to escape.

The Tree delighted in the heightened and altered states of conscious displayed by the different members of the group, as well as the curious and sometimes incoherent conversations that would manifest. The dancing and the singing became even more carefree, as the men removed their shirts and clumsily peacocked in from of their female friends, much to the enjoyment and wolf-whistles that could be heard echoing through the valley.

Semi-high itself, The Tree giggled to itself as it witnessed this bizarre but oddly seductive display. Until it saw Shaun's body. Whilst The Tree's suspicions had been confirmed, that his body had altered in a way that looked somewhat unnatural, it could not help noticing something else.

Faded scars on Shaun's arms, too pale for anyone to see but noticeable to The Tree irrespective of its heightened state of consciousness. Faded cuts and faded burn marks. These were not the only ghostly wounds on his body. Shaun's back also displayed scars. Scars inflicted by someone long ago from Shaun's past.

As Shaun circled and whirled around the fire, he sensed The Tree's focus on him. His smile faltered and a look of shame temporarily caused his face to crumple. An image of a figure holding a belt. Menacing, threatening. And then a feeling of fear. Of powerlessness. Of disconnection from body and mind.

And then then image was gone, accompanied by the rapid sideways shake of Shaun's head, and another deep inhalation of the sweet mind-befuddling smoke.

The Tree hungrily breathed the smoke in too. It wanted to erase the horrible image. It couldn't bear the thought of Shaun being brutalised in that way as a child, by someone he trusted … someone that he loved. But the smoke wasn't working. The Tree could still feel the fear. The gruesome truth. And also the hidden pain of Shaun's friends. The more intoxicated they became, the more of their memories and emotions they split off, the more The Tree could see.

The Tree felt desperate. It wanted to escape. It wanted to share in the blissful dissociation that it observed in the group of friends. And so it did as it promised to Shaun in their last meeting. It brought a little bit of its own magic to the party.

Turning its focus to one of its silver branches, The Tree felt a swell of searing heat transmit to the branch – a quarter of which dissolved into a sparkling silver dust which blew towards the bonfire with the speed of an angry swarm of bees.

The bonfire erupted with shimmering golden smoke as the silver dust made contact with the flames, which themselves transformed from the alluring oranges and yellows to enchanting shades of green.

The gold and green-coloured smoke enveloped the hilltop with a mushroom-shaped cloud before it dispersed into the atmosphere above. The effects, however, did not disappear so easily. The fire remained green and alive with its phosphorescent glow, hypnotising the group … including The Tree.

A look of blissful calm overcame each of the group who had ceased their dancing and were gazing upwards, swaying, and all sporting an inane smile which only widened as the effects of the golden smoke took hold.

Like the group of friends, The Tree felt a rush of electricity pulsing through its limbs and a warm glow tingling through its soul, starting in its roots and reaching all the way through its trunk and branches. It could even feel every detail of its leaves. Of the veins in each and every leaf, and the ridges of the bark which now moved and slithered as though its body were a canvas of brown lava.

The Tree felt itself smiling idiotically like its companions, companions whom The Tree was now convinced were its best friends, its soul-mates in this life and the beyond. And of course, its spiritual brothers and sisters known throughout time and throughout the galaxy. It felt like it had known them its entire life and the swell of love and compassion that it felt for all of them was blissfully overwhelming.

To further express its deep-felt love and appreciation for the group, The Tree swirled its branches, thanks to the newfound elasticity that it discovered it had, and left a dazzling trail of starlight in its midst, which further enchanted Shaun and his friends who now erupted in cheers and shouts for more.

The Tree, having discovered its newfound sense of confidence swished and swirled its branches even more and showered the group with stardust, as well as a cascade of fiery petals that it created from flowers once inspired by a young friend who had sadly died.

The awestruck friends fell into silence as the flaming petals seemed to be suspended in mid-air, their mouths gaping, eyes wide, and heartbeats racing. Pausing for dramatic effect, The Tree left them hovering for what felt like hours … and then let them fall, showering a delighted Shaun and his friends with richly scented petals, drowning them all in an ocean of seductive perfume.

The group roared in appreciation and picked up their instruments. The most melodic and beautiful music that The Tree had ever heard was played and serenaded its soul, which was now soaring. Shaun was singing, he sang the language of the universe, a language which The Tree was proud to say it knew, and was deeply touched and impressed by the talent of its marvellous best friend. Shaun's voice seemed to harmonise with the sky, the stars and was the colour of the moon.

The Tree too felt that it was the colour of the planets. It was entranced by the cold and isolated desolation that was Neptune, and thanks to the inviting serenade from Shaun, and the accompanying crescendo of musical instruments that accompanied it, The Tree knew that it could befriend the lonely and sad planet that was Neptune. It found its mind spiralling as it catapulted itself through the solar system and greeted the numerous celestial orbs that it had only heard of thanks to the stories regaled by its many visitors over the years. Never did it believe that it too could take occupancy in the sky, and perhaps become its own planet someday. A friend to all and a powerful reminder of love and hope for all those who occupied planet earth below …

Don't be so ridiculous. What is happening to you? A rational thought, suddenly plucked from nowhere. What is happening to me? thought The Tree.

It was back on earth. Firmly rooted in the depths of the hill and the valley. Shaun and his friends were uttering similar absurdities about the meaning of life and their connection to the fibres of their clothes, the animals roaming the forests, and the very water itself of the river below. Their silly songs were amplified by the golden smoke but were much less enchanting as The Tree regained some composure.

Shaun, having noticed something change within The Tree, whispered like a schoolboy in the ears of his giggling friends, who simultaneously blew into the green fire, sending another irregularly large waft of golden smoke in the direction of The Tree.

The colours were dazzling! Everything seemed to ignite despite the ever-darkening sky. The Tree could see a shimmering halo surrounding its outstretched branches – the leaves changing colour from emerald green to pink blossom, and autumnal shades of orange and scarlet. The valley seemed to come alive with sound as the nocturnal creatures sang their songs in an amplified symphony. Even the trees of the forests below on the surrounding mountains wanted to join the festivities, and seemed to grow faces. They smiled and waved their branches back at The Tree, a clear acknowledgement of their profound connection and love for The Tree, a love that The Tree reciprocated as it waved its own ever-morphing arms back in return.

The river below seemed to whisper to The Tree. It too longed to be part of the celebrations. The Tree's heightened senses beheld an aquatic performance like no other. The river seemed to take on a life of its own, flowing forwards and backwards, and creating beautiful funnels of water that whirled towards the sky and exploded like shattered glass, water droplets catching the moonlight and sparkling like stars in the night sky. Not yet finished with its display, the river water morphed into shapes. A giant octopus … humpback whales … a school of dolphins. Then galloping horses … roaring lions … and phoenix-like birds that glided over the valley like watery ghosts.

Not to be outdone, the moon also wanted to perform for The Tree and its friends. With a soft and cherubin face, the moon turned from silver to blue to purple and swelled in size.

The Tree, Shaun, and his friends were mesmerised as the purple moon seemed to hurtle towards them, its craters and strange little face becoming sharper in focus. As it did so, the sky changed from night into day – the sun had decided to join the moon, it would seem. Blazing like a fiery orb, it too grew in size but dimmed its shine turning from gold to blood red.

Both the sun and moon appeared to dance around each other, both shrinking and expanding in size intermittently. The sky was blue one moment, then pink. Then all manner of colours as the sun set and rose once more. The moon passed before the sun and plunged the valley into darkness, with only the corona of the sun remaining visible. Then it slowly glided away so that once more the valley was bathed in light.

The sun and moon bowed to each other, and waving goodbye, the sun set once more, leaving the moon to own the starlit summer solstice sky.

As the golden smoke continued to envelop the group, a heavenly white glow seemed to bathe the hilltop and bless The Tree and the souls of light that danced around its trunk and the fire. Their bodies seemed to have dissolved into translucent snow, leaving behind the essence of their very beings – a light so sharp that it pierced the soul and flooded The Tree with a rush of pure and uncontaminated love.

The Tree itself felt its own spirit shining … so unnecessary were the restraints of one's physical body. It longed to shed its bark, its branches and its trunk so it could join its ethereal family as they continued to duck, weave, sing, and dance to the melody of nature and the symphony of the cosmos. However, feeling trapped in the prison of its own beginnings, it decided to instead put on a show for its rapt audience. Fiery petals were but a thing of the past. The stuff of fantasy is what was called for.

Plucking the most fantastical beast from the minds of Shaun and his friends, a flurry of green leaves were shaken loose from The Tree, leaving its branches near bare. These leaves, however, did not fall, for such things as gravity were but a mere inconvenience to The Tree and one that it knew it could overcome by sheer will and cockiness.

The leaves that had been shed were suspended in the air and formed a ring around The Tree … if it was good enough for Saturn, it was good enough for The Tree and its friends, it mused to itself. The green ring circled and gathered speed as it swirled around The Tree. The effect was dizzying.

The leaves shot upwards towards the sky and a strange shape emerged. Firstly, an amorphous blob which then elongated. A body. Clawed arms and legs. A long crocodile-like snout. Wide, menacing eyes. A spikey and jagged tail that thrashed in the air. And two enormous bat-like wings.

Shaun and his friends gasped and burst into applause and whistles at the sight of the magnificent dragon!

Feeling inspired still, and determined to ward off the catalogue of images that threatened to smash into consciousness with the force of a water from a shattered dam, The Tree summoned its power and sent a roar of fire from its very own core. The fire exploded from the mouth of the writhing dragon-of-leaves that soared through the air above the group, and round and round the hilltop until, its energy spent, the dragon exploded – raining leaves and silver dust on to the ecstatic friends.

The Tree's energy was clearly spent and it felt itself coming back to reality. The light and colours of the valley calmed and settled, but also become somewhat dull and depressing. It felt a cold trickle throughout its branches and trunk … and a growing sense of despair. These feelings appeared to impact The Tree only. Shaun and his friends were now truly in the zone. The Tree heard Shaun gushing about his relationship with The Tree, a relationship that the others begged to be a part of and to cultivate themselves.

But The Tree felt sick. It felt the opposite of the love and warmth of earlier in the evening. It felt irritated. Impatient. And depressed. What was the point of all this?

The Tree now gazed at the group. This was far from magical. This was tragic! The Tree listened now more intently and rather than hearing profound wisdom being espoused, it instead heard the incoherent and absurd ramblings of a group of drug-addled humans.

And far from embodying sublime beings of light and creativity, it saw a group of shirtless fools, doe-eyed women behaving like schoolgirls, and stupid dancing that they should all be ashamed of. The Tree felt its own judgement towards the group, a feeling that was somewhat alien to The Tree. There was also a sense of sadness. Their faces, especially Shaun's, no longer looked angelic but were instead twisting and contorting as they gurned. Their eyes were wide, pupils dilated and blinking rapidly. Shaun's once smiling mouth was warped and chomping at nothing. Others had protruding tongues, their speech slurred and again uttering incoherent nonsense.

What have we done? thought The Tree sadly to itself

The Tree knew that they would all feel terrible when the effects of the magic smoke had worn off. But it also knew why they needed it. Because The Tree itself understood that it too needed something to help it escape from all that it had heard throughout its life so far, from all that it knew.

The Tree began to feel sympathy again for the group of prison guards. It felt compassion again for Shaun, for what he had experienced recently … but also for what he had experienced in the past. The Tree knew that people need to protect themselves in whatever way they can. To escape by whatever creative means they deem necessary. The Tree wished that things could be different. But it was also realistic.

The nature of the environment that they had all chosen to work in replayed something. It allowed them to face their past demons, their past aggressors, and to feel in control ... inasmuch as they ever could. It allowed them to face the monsters from their own past but this time to be the ones with the power – to be the ones in control. And so, The Tree left Shaun and his friends to their night of celebrations, which would last long into the morning.

The Tree tried to hold its love and understanding for Shaun and his friends through its own emerging sense of gloom and despair.

As the they all partied and rode the high from the gift that The Tree had given them, The Tree allowed itself to sleep. The last thing it remembered was Shaun's strong arms wrapped around its trunk as he embraced The Tree and huskily whispered something.

'I love you, man!' came Shaun's slurred but heartfelt expression of gratitude and care towards the ancient being that had been there in the aftermath of his trauma.

When The Tree awoke the following morning, Shaun and his friends had gone. But the lingering sorrow and desperation that The Tree had felt the night before, sadly, had not.

The Tree looked out over the valley and allowed itself to weep. It wept for nothing and for everything. And possibly all that was to come.

X

Over the coming months, The Tree continued to listen to and guide the people who came to visit. But its heart was not in it.

The silver branch that it partly used on that summer solstice evening still retained its power, and in small doses, The Tree realised that it could soothe itself with the branch's essence. Not enough to get so high that it lost control, but just enough to block out the pain and sorrow of what it heard, and to ward off the terrible feelings of dread that came when the effects of the silver branch had worn off.

One year later, on the summer solstice, the whole of that month was starkly different to the one that came the year before. An endless torrent of rain and storms assaulted the hilltop. Fewer visitors came, much to the relief of The Tree, who had used up the final piece of essence from that particular silver branch.

The Tree felt like a part of its soul had died!

Its mood was low and was reflected by the abysmal rain and heavy grey sky. The Tree had moments where it did not want to live. It saw no point in being in a world where so many people suffered needlessly. The Tree had fantasies of being chopped down and no longer having to bear the weight of the world's woes.

But at other times, it would feel a sudden surge of anger and a desire for vengeance towards those who had done harm to the kind souls that had shared their stories with it over the years.

The Tree didn't know what was happening to it. Why its mood was so changeable. Why it felt more irritable, and less compassionate. Why its thirst for vengeance was becoming so all-consuming …

As lightning tore through the sky, and crashes of thunder rumbled through the valley, an epiphany struck The Tree. Half of its life was spent! Since its birth, it had used its own essence six times to either save or enhance the lives of others. And in doing so, it had slowly depleted itself … without knowing it.

The Tree reflected on its sacrifice over the years: the creation of the sacred circle that offered safety and protection; the aids that enabled Luke to walk; the stargazing platform where two lonely teenagers found friendship and the orbs of communication it had given them; the enchanted apple that slowed the progression of Austin's virus; the liquid essence that had saved Jonathan; and then the silver essence that The Tree had needlessly wasted by getting high and trying to escape the growing pain its soul.

The Tree was able to remember with fondness the love it felt for the various people who had come into its life. And why, especially for the key figures who had touched its soul so profoundly, it had stepped out of its role as a guide and listener, and had instead acted with determination to intervene in their lives, and desperately try to save them.

As The Tree remembered these people, something familiar began to stir within. It was a feeling of compassion that seemed to have become a distant echo over the past year … but it was returning!

The Tree knew that it did not need to escape from the sadness, pain, or horror that its visitors shared with it. Nor did it have to drown in misery with them either. Its role was to listen, to care, to temporarily bear the weight of other people's woe, so that for a time they could feel less alone in their despair. It didn't have to hold it forever.

But The Tree realised something with sadness. The Tree now knew that it was halfway through its life.

It suspected that should the final silver branch fall, no matter what the circumstances, so too would The Tree's soul. For every silver branch it relinquished, the closer to death it would become ... and the less able it would be to hold the same love, hope, and compassion that it had felt for its visitors before.

But The Tree also knew that it had a choice. That perhaps it was not meant to live forever, and that what it offered to the world was precious. That it could give without sacrifice ... but when sacrifice was indeed necessary, it would give a part of itself willingly if it meant saving the soul of another.

With this realisation, the rain stopped for the first time throughout the whole month of June that year. The thunder ceased. And a gentle calm came over the valley. Whilst the sky remained dark, a faint slither of sunlight broke through the heavy cloud and illuminated The Tree. And for the first time since Shaun and his friends visited The Tree, it felt like it wanted to live again, to continue to make a difference, and to help others rediscover the value of life.

But The Tree also knew that it had changed. It was no longer in denial about the other parts of itself that had come to the surface – the shadow parts. There can be no light without the darkness, it reasoned, and it would embrace these growing facets of itself. But The Tree knew that it needed to hold these aspects of itself in its consciousness, lest they take control and enact the fiercest forms of revenge that deep down The Tree knew it was capable of. And perhaps even wanted!

PART TWO

CHAPTER SEVEN
July: Becoming

I

'Hide me!' came the desperate whisper. 'You can't let her find me … please, hide me!'

Sensing the young woman's terror, The Tree did as it was instructed. Softening its branches, The Tree morphed its shape into an igloo-like cage, camouflaged by the luscious green leaves of the wet summer so far.

It was still night when The Tree had been awoken to the desperate pleas of the woman, and hoped that the absence of light on the hilltop would further lend itself to the young woman's concealment. But concealment from what? it wondered. Or more specifically, From whom?

A shrill cry came from the edge of the hill as another woman came into view. Of similar age, and dressed strikingly similarly to The Tree's new charge, even down to the hairstyle (although much messier), a mad-looking wide-eyed woman scurried around the stone circle like a rabid animal.

'WHERE ARE YOU?' shrieked the mad thing. 'YOU ARE MINE! YOU CANNOT LEAVE ME … I WILL FIND YOU!'

And then in a hushed whisper, only audible to The Tree and its superior hearing, the mad thing said, 'If I can't have you … nobody will!'

The Tree could feel the curious mixture of hate and desire emanating from the woman. Its instinct right there and then was to swipe its powerful branches and knock the woman from the hilltop. But this of course was not The Tree's way. So instead, it remained true to itself, stayed still, and protected the young woman hiding in its cage-lake sanctuary.

After what seemed like hours, the frantic skulking ceased, and the woman gave up her frenzied search. Her dramatic howling sobs boomed from the edge of the stone circle, accompanied by tears, flailing arms, and a childlike collapse. She sat on the ground, her head in her hands and kept repeating the same phrase.

'How could you do this to me?'

The Tree felt very little compassion for this woman. In fact, what it did feel was irritation and disdain. Whoever this woman was, she endeared very little sympathy from The Tree. It did, however, wonder if this was a lingering effect from its misuses and sacrifice of its own silver branch over the past year ... but no! There was something disturbing about this woman. Something that The Tree neither liked nor trusted.

The young woman whom it was now protecting evoked something very different – care, curiosity, and compassion.

Tired of her own cries, the sobbing wretch eventually left the hilltop and disappeared, still wailing into the night but mercifully, her sorrow became less and less audible to The Tree and its charge.

The Tree sensed that the young woman whom it was protecting was now asleep, clearly exhausted from whatever ordeal she had endured, and finally feeling safe enough to rest. The Tree did not disturb her. It let her sleep, and returned to its own slumber so that it could feel fresh and revitalised the following day to hear the young woman's story.

II

The early morning sun rose over the valley, turning the sky a sinister blood red. The orange glow of its rays, however, signalled for The Tree to unfurl its branches, revealing the sleeping young woman within the protective cage. As The Tree morphed back into its commanding and statuesque shape, the young woman stirred. Eyes still closed, she gave a slow yawn, and stretched out her arms above her head.

The Tree recognised her. But who was she? It could not yet fathom the answer to this. But something about her was familiar, like a song from a distant memory where it could hear the tune but not recall the lyrics.

As the sun rose higher, the sky gave way to more comforting oranges and golds.

The young woman opened her eyes. Suddenly remembering where she was, and indeed why she was there, her serene and sleepy face dissolved into a look of panic. Her eyes, now wide, were darting back and forth as she surveyed the hilltop in the daylight. Jumping up, she asked The Tree imploringly, 'Please … is she gone? Am I safe?'

'Yes, my dear,' replied The Tree calmly. 'She is gone, but for how long, I cannot say.'

The young woman continued to survey her surroundings frantically. Her hair, long, curly, and beautiful shades of silver did not seem to match her youthful appearance. The Tree was curious. Why was she here?

The young woman sauntered to the edge of the stone circle, and then to the edge of the hilltop. Walking its perimeter, she hesitantly glanced over the edge, no doubt making sure that her pursuer was indeed gone. As she came to the edge closest to The Tree, the fragile earth beneath her seemed to crumble. She stumbled and fell forward.

With unfathomable speed and reflexes, The Tree caught her. A long lasso-like vine shot from its trunk and wrapped itself around her waist, pulling her back with a jerk to the safer and more steady ground at the base of The Tree.

Feeling a mixture of terror and relief, the young silver haired woman began to cry as she fell to her knees.

'Breathe … you are safe now,' reassured The Tree. 'I promise that no harm will come to you whilst you are in my presence.'

The young woman slowed her breathing, felt the solidity of the earth beneath her, and inhaled the refreshing scent of the grass and flowers that surrounded her and The Tree.

'Who was that woman? And what does she want with you?' asked The Tree kindly, inviting the young woman to share her story.

'SHE is someone I used to know. SHE thinks we are a couple … BUT WE ARE NOT!' she shouted angrily to the air. And then she added quietly, 'She is my stalker. She has been terrorising me for the last year, and I'm afraid she is going to kill me!'

The Tree felt a terror in its soul. It believed that this belonged to the young woman, but it knew some of the fear was its own. It had felt the woman's hatred as she skulked around The Tree. It had heard her threats, and it feared that the young woman's intuition about her own fate was true.

'Tell me,' said The Tree, 'how did this begin?'

And so came the familiar sensation of swirling in mist as the colours and sounds of the valley evaporated and The Tree was taken back to the beginning of the young woman's tale.

III

It was night-time.

Savage waves, the colour of oil and emeralds smashed against the seemingly redundant sailboats anchored in the dimly lit harbour. Even larger waves, like giant fists, slammed the cottages as they nestled themselves into the side of the enormous hill. The spray of frigid sea water left a distinctive salty taste on the lips of anyone who happened to be out this night.

One hundred and ninety-nine steps coiled their way around the hill that seemed to watch over and guard the harbour, leading up to a cemetery. The cemetery was near enough invisible as a ghostly fog clung with its spectral claws to the old, eroded headstones. But despite the fog, the foreboding castle-like structure of the derelict abbey remained back-lit and silhouetted against the supernatural mist, giving it a somewhat eerie phosphorescent tinge. Where a once magnificent stained-glass window hung, there was instead an enormous gaping space between the stone columns and arches, much like a frightened and contorted mouth howling into the night.

There was movement in the graveyard. A hunched woman with hair the colour of a raven scurried between the tombstones, breathing rapidly and praying to the mist to keep her hidden. Without the moon's friendly sliver light to guide her, she felt blind. Her hands reached to her mouth to suppress the gasp of pain when her body made contact with the cold hard headstones in the packed graveyard.

She could make out a bench in the very corner of the yard, an unforgiving stone wall on one side, and on the other a wrought-iron fence that separated her from the sheer drop, and the ferocious ocean below.

The sound of crashing waves, once a source of comfort to the pale-faced woman now seemed to only whisper her doom. She tucked herself behind the bench, pulling leaves and small branches from the hedges that surrounded her, foolishly hoping that this would be sufficient to hide her from the monster that stalked her.

CLAAANNNGGG!!!   DONNNNNGGG! CLAAANNNGGG!!! DONNNNNGGG!

The woman jumped at the sudden sound of the church bell. Her heart beat quickened. Who had done that? They must be close, she thought. The fear was growing ... as was her paralysis. Trembling, she brought her two freezing cold hands together and began to pray. But these words brought her no solace, even in this hallowed place of supposed sanctuary.

A heavy, rasping breath ... getting closer ....and closer. She could almost smell the stench of the creature's breath ... or was it the corpses of the graves clawing their way out of their coffins, determined to silence her forever? Don't be stupid, she said to herself. Just open your eyes, you're safe!

But this was a lie. A cloaked figure towered over her, eyes hollow and deadened, a faint trickle of blood coating his fanged teeth, spilling over his chin.

Arms outstretched and with a hideous roar, the vampire pounced like a panther, and sank its teeth deep into the pulsating neck of the terrified woman.

Her shriek pierced the night as a spray of blood, much like the spray of the sea below, squirted into the air and settled on the cold steely fence.

Applause and cheers erupted from the side of the graveyard and a bright electric light suddenly illuminated the scene.

Helping her to his feet, Count Dracula extended a hand to his fallen comrade, who, with a smile, accepted this and stood by the side of her colleague. Act One was over.

'Mina Murray' and 'The Count' gave a humble curtsey and a bow and then left the scene. Their adoring fans continued their rapturous applause, eagerly awaiting Act Two.

'Well, you were very popular this evening,' said The Count, dropping his Transylvanian accent and instead reverting to his own somewhat exaggerated 'Queen's English' voice. 'Especially with her ... did you see her? She's back ... AGAIN!'

'Of course, I saw her. This must be the tenth time she's been here. I mean Christ, I know we're good, but we're not that good!' the young woman said with a laugh.

'We've only done five performances, dear ... but who's counting,' said The Count. He then reached for the champagne. He'd been sure to request that it was in a bucket of ice waiting for them, and proceeded to pour two glasses.

'It wouldn't be so bad if she looked happy to be here,' the young woman continued, seemingly oblivious to her friend's remark. 'But she is just weird. Have you noticed? She just stares at me with this deadened expression. Even you playing a vampire look more alive than that ... that zombie!'

She laughed again, and removed the black wig that she'd been wearing for the play. And the hairnet. She shook her real hair free. Long, beautiful, curly red hair – hair the colour of fire.

Of course! The Tree knew that that it recognised the woman ... the red hair. The little red-haired girl. Luke's friend from all those years ago. But now all grown up!

The energy that she exuded was one of confidence and joy, but only in this memory. The curiously silver haired woman on the hilltop was far from confident. She was afraid, and a mere shadow of the woman she had clearly been only a year ago.

So relieved that it remembered her, The Tree refocused on the memory being shared, eager to discover what had befallen Elizabeth that had led her to this place of terror.

'Don't worry, sweetheart,' said The Count, laughing with her. 'I'm sure she just wants a kiss with the famous Mina Murray ... as they all do, darling, as they all do!' he added with a playful wink.

'Oh stop ... you sound like my wife. I swear she's convinced I'm going to run off with her. I mean she is rather pretty, I'm not going to lie ...' and with that she returned his wink and gave a mischievous smile. 'But seriously? I like my ladies to be safe ... and preferably sane!'

'Daaarling ... it is true ...' The Count replied in an exaggerated theatrical voice. 'One must never date the fans. They are far more trouble than they are worth. Even the smallest of dalliances – especially when one is visiting another town – will always come back to bite one on the arse. Trust me, dear, I know. Remember that fellow who had a thing for me ... AND puppets? Never again, I tell you. NEVER AGAIN!'

He mock-swooned and fainted.

Chuckling like naughty school children throughout the rest of the interval, they clinked glasses and enjoyed their ritual champagne toast … and indeed the rest of the bottle. They had both been with the theatre company for years, and loved performing the gothic tales. Performing Dracula at The Abbey was a particular highlight for Elizabeth and a role that she had coveted for some time. They toasted each other because they were quite literally 'killing it', as the reviewers had said in their praise for the production.

The Tree could feel the pride that Elizabeth had cultivated in her craft, and the hard work it had taken to get here – monotonous jobs to pay her way through university; minor acting roles in plays that weren't fit for purpose; hideous directors who thought they could say and do what they wanted to her. But she had a fire in her and was not afraid to stand her ground. This made her both popular with some, and deeply unpopular with others. And yet, here she was, playing one of her favourite characters in a beautiful location from the original novel itself.

As they downed the last of the fizz, Elizabeth positioned herself in front of the dressing room mirror and began to re-apply her make-up, tie her hair back up so that it was neatly concealed under the net, and then replaced the black wig. She was amazed at how different she looked … but she was pleased with what she saw. Again, a silent nod to all that she had worked towards to get here. And readying herself, she, 'Mina Murray', and 'The Count' prepared to go back out to their adoring fans.

However, in that moment, the woman in the crowd came in to Elizabeth's mind. Her face, that haunted and strange face, so full of longing. But also hate!

A flutter of fear passed through her accompanied by the sensation of being punched in the chest. It was only small, but it was something. Elizabeth felt uneasy, something which was rare. When she was on the stage, she owned it. This was her world and she could be anything and anyone that she wanted. I'm not afraid of anything! she told herself. But that wasn't true. Something about the woman in the crowd unnerved her.

Silly nonsense, she said to herself. And then shaking her head and taking a few long, slow, deep breaths, she once again became 'Mina Murray', left her dressing room, and emerged into the night, determined to not be distracted by any pretty (or strange) faces that may be lurking in the crowd.

As this part of the memory faded The Tree found itself observing the applause of the crowd once more as Elizabeth and her friend completed the final act of the play.

Strangely, but also to Elizabeth's relief, the woman in the crowd was not present during the final stage of the performance, and yet she found herself scanning the unfamiliar and adoring faces ... just in case.

Was she waiting? Was she hiding? Where was the woman in the crowd? But ultimately this didn't matter. Elizabeth knew she had performed brilliantly this night. Even the moon had made an atmospheric appearance by breaking through the fog and illuminating her pale face as she succumbed to Dracula's seduction.

Smiling and blowing kisses into the crowd, she turned to her friend and hugged him before stepping back and inviting the crowd to share their appreciation for his sinister performance.

As the crowd eventually dispersed, Elizabeth retreated from the bright lights, waved to the last straggle of fans, and made her way back to the dressing room.

'Daaarling, I'll see you at the pub,' came her friend's voice from behind her. 'I promise I'll be there before it closes this time, I just need to speak to Margo in props. My bloody cape is coming apart at the seams ... its unbefitting of The Count, you know!'

And with a swish of indignation, he marched off in the opposite direction.

Elizabeth chuckled to herself and wandered through the dark graveyard to the small caravan that had been set up in the carpark, basking in her own well-deserved triumph. Ahhh, she thought with a smile, my own private dressing room.

She opened the door and stepped inside. It was cold. She switched on the lights but was greeted by a pathetically feeble glow. Some of the bulbs must've blown. Typical, she thought to herself, and rolled her eyes. Still, all she needed to do was remove her make-up and change. It's not like I've got anyone here that I need to impress. She sighed and locked the door behind her.

Looking around the dim room, she gazed with fondness at her costumes, the cards wishing her well, and the array of flowers from her wife and friends.

And then Elizabeth saw it. The vase of roses. But the flowers weren't fresh. In fact, they were decaying. The once vibrant reds and pinks had turned a sinister darker shade. They almost appeared burnt in appearance. The ghastly flowers drooped sadly, desperately deprived of water.

There was a small white card amongst the rotten stems. Feeling her heartbeat quicken, Elizabeth approached her dressing mirror where the flowers had been so strategically placed. She picked up the small white card and unfolded it.

'My Mina ... True love never dies. And nor will my love for you ... ever!'

There was no signature. But it was written in red and an ugly childlike scrawl.

Elizabeth froze. The blood seemed to drain from her face. A cold wave of nausea rose within her. What is this? She dropped the card, which fluttered in slow motion to the floor.

The hideous flowers seemed to taunt her, blocking the view of her own reflection. NO, she thought firmly to herself, I have had fans before. I am the one in control. I won't be rattled! And with that, and regaining her composure, she swung her arm towards the offending foliage and sent the vase and its contents hurtling across the room.

The vase smashed – dead flowers scattering to the floor. But she did not care. This was her night. Her space. No one else's!

Slowing her breathing once more and composing herself, Elizabeth settled down in front of the mirror and tried to resume her task. Remove the make-up, get dressed, and get gone.

She released her hair from the wig and shook loose her fiery curls. She loved her hair. It was her thing ... something that people always commented on.

The stage make-up was always a hassle to remove. Elizabeth reached for the wipes and lotion that would do the trick. For once it came off easily, a blessing considering the poor lighting. Not much more to do. apply some eye-liner, find her earrings, and then ...

She gasped, her hands instinctively raising to protect her heart.

Someone was in the corner of the room. A woman lurking. Elizabeth could see her in the reflection of the mirror. Partially concealed in the shadows, but crouching in the darkness ...

Breathing heavily ...

Watching her!

Instinctively Elizbeth whirled around. She recognised her instantly. It was the woman from the crowd. Her hair was tied tightly in a knot on top of her head, her arms rigidly by her side as she slowly rose like a hideous wax-work dummy. Her eyes were no longer haunted, but burned with longing. With desire. And malice!

An unnatural smile spread across the woman's face. And then came the words in a flat whisper, like a hiss. 'I've been waiting for you!'

The woman from the crowd slithered forwards. Her face frozen in a grotesque mask-like grin.

The lights went out.

Elizabeth screamed!

BANG ... BANG ... BANG!

Elizabeth's friend was at the window, his fists hammering against the glass.

'OI ... YOU! GET THE FUCK AWAY FROM HER!'

Clearly startled, the woman from the crowd froze, a look of shock, then fear crept across her face as she spun around to face the window.

SMASH!

Shards of glass exploded into the caravan as a rock came crashing through the window, barely missing the woman, who was now frantically retreating from Elizabeth.

Seizing her opportunity, and breaking through the momentary paralysis, Elizabeth rushed forwards. Her body slammed into the woman from the crowd. They both fell to the ground.

Scurrying in the dark, and feeling the woman's hands grabbing hold of her body, Elizabeth thrashed and kicked until the woman released her vice-like grip.

Elizabeth leapt up and made for the door. A hand grabbed her ankle, but not for long. She twisted and then stamped her foot. A cry of pain pierced the darkness. But her ankle was free. And she was at the door. Releasing herself from her prison, she fell into the cool summer night, and into the arms of her friend ... and sobbed.

As Elizabeth cried into the fake-blood-stained shirt of her friend, she heard the sound of harried footsteps crunching and darting across the gravel car park. The woman from the crowd had escaped into the night. She was gone ... for now!

The Tree found itself gasping for air. It gratefully brought itself back to the hilltop which now, mercifully, was bathed in golden sunshine, and not the cold misty night that Elizabeth's cries still occupied in The Tree's mind. It looked downwards. Elizabeth was sat upright, her knees brought up to her chest, and both arms wrapped around them, leaving no part of her torso exposed. The Tree felt such sadness for her. She looked so different, and it was not just how she looked. Or her white hair, her frightened eyes, or how thin she was. It was also her energy. She seemed both drained of life, and colour. It was as though The Tree were viewing her in black and white.

'It's okay,' said The Tree. 'You are safe with me. look around you. This is proof that you're safe. And that she is not here. What you have been through sounds truly terrifying, and I'm so sorry for that ... but I won't let anything bad happen to you!'

'But she won't stop! And she didn't! What I've just told you, that was only the beginning!' came Elizabeth's frantic and desperate reply.

'A couple of days later I received a letter ... slipped under the door of my dressing room. It was the same childish writing in red ... Why always red?! She apologised and said she just wanted to meet me. That she was a HUGE fan. That she was concerned that the lights weren't all working in my dressing room and wanted to warn me "in case something bad happened". She went on about the lights going off being a coincidence, faulty power cables, or some such rubbish. And the flowers, those ugly dead flowers. She claimed that it must've been the heat that killed them! Can you believe it? Honestly, that evening it was so cold. Not warm. It was cold! She's a liar.'

'You poor thing. How horrible. How frightening! What did you do next?' came The Tree's concerned response.

'So I of course took all this to police and told them everything that had happened. And they did nothing! NOTHING! They shrugged and told me "This is the price of fame, love."'

Elizabeth shook her head in fury and disbelief. The Tree did the same with its branches.

'They told me that she is probably harmless and just a fan, that I should take it as a compliment and not get so spooked. They said that her alleged explanation sounded plausible and that I shouldn't worry about it. That she is probably just lonely and looking for a friend. And get this ... maybe I could just smile at her and sign an autograph if she approaches me again. Unbelievable! I was so frightened that night!'

'Of course you were,' replied The Tree compassionately. It was saddened and deeply alarmed by what it heard. 'She broke into your dressing room. She was lurking in a darkened corner. And she came at you without warning or consent. Of course you were terrified. What she did to you was wrong. And so was the response of the police!'

The Tree knew that the nature of the woman's behaviour, whilst frightening, could also be dismissed by others as just a misunderstanding. But The Tree had been alive long enough to recognise patterns. To trust what it felt. And it felt the malevolence of the woman who pursued Elizabeth. It felt it the night before when Elizabeth had come to The Tree seeking refuge. And it felt it as it observed Elizabeth's memories.

'The next few weeks were hell,' Elizabeth continued. 'I couldn't focus ... AT ALL! I stumbled with my lines, and that NEVER happens. Dracula had to keep whispering prompts at me. It was humiliating! I found myself scanning the crowd just in case she was there. Thankfully she wasn't, but I couldn't shift the feeling that she was out there. Watching me! And it wasn't just when I was acting, everywhere in that town felt weird.'

'How so?'

'Well, we were doing the play in this lovely little gothic town by the sea. It's one of my favourite places. But everywhere I went I saw her ... well, not always her, but anyone who even slightly looked like her made my heart stop. And I know it sounds like I'm being paranoid but there were times when she was actually there! I got off the bus and I swear she was sat on the back seats, her eyes bearing into my soul. My friend said that it's a small town and it's not impossible that this was a coincidence, and to be fair, yes, that's true. But then she was in my favourite the coffee shop. I've posted pics of me in there several times before. And there she was, just sipping a coffee. But she was there!'

'Even one night in a restaurant, my friend couldn't deny this one or put it down to coincidence! I'd not even finished my meal. She glided in like some Victorian phantom and actually smiled at me. It made me feel sick! And she sat – so brazenly – on the table next to us as though it was nothing! I made us leave immediately. I couldn't bear to be in the same space as that … that lunatic! But she followed us. She actually followed us because when I kissed my friend good night, there she was. In the distance under a streetlamp. Just watching us. I hate her! I really fucking hate her!'

The Tree was stunned. As Elizabeth spoke, it glimpsed fleeting memories. Memories of uncertainty and doubt, of cobbled paths, dim streetlamps, and misty dark alley ways – the fear and anticipation growing in Elizabeth. Could the woman be down there? Is she waiting for me?

The Tree saw Elizabeth walking the robust harbour walls that protruded out into the ocean. It could taste the refreshing salty air as the waves smashed into the bay, and the hauntingly beautiful atmosphere created by the dim lamps which bathed the promenade in a soft glow as nighttime fell. But it also saw Elizabeth there alone, squinting into the distance as another lone figure emerged from the fog. Not clear enough to make out, but slowly approaching her and then just stopping and standing eerily still. The Tree heard Elizabeth screaming into the night.

'WHAT DO YOU WANT FROM ME? WHAT … DO … YOU … WANT?!'

The Tree wept as Elizabeth collapsed onto the cold hard wood of a nearby bench, the distant figure remaining motionless and silent before retreating into the mist like some malevolent sea-witch, leaving Elizabeth alone once more.

Elizabeth's words brought The Tree out of her memories and back to the hilltop.

'I love … well, I used to love, the play. But she has spoilt it for me. Completely ruined it! The last night of any performance is always my favourite. I've always felt so proud of myself. And I'm not going to lie, I love the applause and the cheers. The play, and the story, means so much to so many people. It feels such an honour to bring it to life and do it justice. But I just didn't feel it this time. My final performance felt just like that, a performance. I wasn't living Mina. I wasn't being Mina. I was just terrified – and eager to get the damn thing done so we could leave.

'So, when the lights came on, I bowed, I curtsied, and I smiled. And then I saw her! She was dressed in costume. She looked exactly like me! It was so unnerving! Fans do this a lot. They come dressed up and really get into the spirit of the play. But this felt different, it was just creepy. Because she looks so dead – not like she's made herself look like the un-dead, but she actually looks dead. Like a soulless ghoul. And what I feel coming from her, it's so confusing. It's like I can feel her desire for me, but I can also feel her hatred. It's vile, its honestly so hateful. And so, we left that night. No party, no celebration, just a quick change of clothes and then we were on the road away from that town. And away from her, or so I thought!'

The Tree pondered on all that it had heard so far. It was deeply disturbed by the woman in the crowd's behaviour. It felt the fear and pain that consumed Elizabeth's heart and soul. It also knew that her tale was not over, that the events recounted were indeed only the beginning, and it feared how things had escalated ... and indeed what fate may yet befall his young friend.

It desperately wanted Elizabeth to stay, because whilst she was here, she would be safe. The Tree would do whatever it could to protect her from harm. It even pleaded with her to stay when she announced that she had to leave the hilltop, that she knew she couldn't stay here forever, and that she had to get back to the semblance of life that still remained. But, she promised that she would return and would continue her story.

Reluctantly, The Tree let her go, and waved its strong branches as Elizabeth made her way across the stone circle, and deep in thought made her way down the hill into the unknown.

The Tree's soul lamented over the black and white hologram that Elizabeth had become, a far cry from the spirited little red-haired girl that it had first met when she and Luke had visited The Tree. However, all was not lost. The Tree could sense that a fire still burned in Elizabeth, even it was deeply buried for the moment. The Tree would find a way to help nurture these embers so that she could reclaim her light and no longer feel like she had to hide from the world. Or from the woman! I will protect her, said The Tree to itself. And then added, by whatever means necessary!

IV

Over the following week, The Tree noticed that it did not quite feel itself – It felt agitated and on edge. The usually comforting sounds of animals visiting The Tree, especially at night, instead gave rise to apprehension and fear. The slightest crack of a twig or the rustling of branches evoked fantasies of danger, of people lurking in The Tree's branches hoping to tear its limbs from its trunk – or of wicked people seeking to burn it to the ground.

The animals that would normally seek refuge within The Tree's roots and trunk no longer felt welcomed by The Tree. Instead of seeking to offer comfort and shelter, it longed to dispel them from its presence and protect its precious insides, it feared that if they took hold, they would consume and destroy it from within. And The Tree thus had to protect itself lest something, or indeed someone, be able to decimate its soul and claim its very life for themselves.

The Tree couldn't explain its newfound sense of paranoia or the growing fear of its once peaceful and familiar surroundings. The harsh brightness of the sun and the cold glow of the moon all felt like an intrusion. The Tree felt convinced that both the sun and the moon were watching it, and were planning to harm it in some way. The howl of the wind felt like a deliberate attempt by nature to unnerve and rattle it. And the rain felt like it had been sent to torment and persecute The Tree, thus rendering it vulnerable and open to attack. And so, it found itself cowering. It wrapped its sagging branches tightly around itself, creating a makeshift cocoon that made it impenetrable … and safe.

At night it rocked itself into unconsciousness, hoping that the fear and torment would abate during its slumber. But this was not to be. Its dreams were haunted by faceless figures, people stalking The Tree, armed with axes and burning torches of fire, all seeking to destroy it. And when they pounced, The Tree could do nothing. It was paralysed with terror. It felt the heat of the flames consuming its trunk and the sharp blades of the axes hacking at its limbs … until it awoke with a start, shaking, disorientated, breathless and afraid.

V

It was a peaceful morning, and the valley was silent. The Tree, still wrapped tightly in its own cocoon, dozed in and out of consciousness. Its mind still swam with images of violence and threat to its very existence.

The silence was shattered by the sound of footsteps, and heavy breathing.

Instinctively, with the ferocity of a tightly wound spring that had been released, The Tree unfurled itself, its branches whipping outwards like the tentacles of a kraken.

'Bloody hell!' came a familiar voice, as Elizabeth – with equally honed reflexes – instinctively ducked as a one of The Tree's many branches swooshed violently over her head, nearly sending her flying. Catching her breath and staying still until The Tree had settled itself, Elizabeth spoke again.

'My God, you're worse than me. Are you okay?'

Feeling somewhat ashamed of its erratic response to her presence, The Tree gathered itself and took several long deep breaths and reconnected to the beauty of the valley, whilst reminding itself that it was safe, and not in the nightmarish dreams that had plagued it since Elizabeth's previous visit. Sensing its friend's concern, The Tree apologised and shared its feelings from the past week. To The Tree's surprise, a look of relief came over Elizabeth's face and she ran towards it, embracing its trunk in a wide and loving hug.

'Oh wow, so it's not just me! I thought I was going mad, or have been going mad. That is EXACTLY how I felt after we left that town. It was like she haunted me. My mind … my dreams … every empty street or dark room. Even when she wasn't there, I felt like she was with me. Inside of me somehow. You must be channelling something of what I felt!'

Of course, this made sense to The Tree, but it was astonished that it had not realised this itself. The emotions that it felt had been so powerful, so intense that it had started to really believe that it was truly under threat. For some reason it had not had the clarity of mind to realise that it was experiencing what Elizabeth had experienced. It too then felt a sense of relief, relief that it was safe. But then, it felt angry. Angry at the power of the woman from the crowd to make it – and indeed Elizabeth – feel this way. The Tree felt hatred towards her, and even more protective towards Elizabeth.

'I just wanted to say thank you,' said Elizabeth, now sitting on the soft grass of the stone circle and facing The Tree. 'Just speaking to you last week started to shift something for me. Don't get me wrong, it wasn't great remembering what had happened, but there was something reparative about being able to share it with you, and to feel safe, protected, and seen by you.'

Her eyes glistened with tears. So did The Tree's soul.

'I know this isn't over, but last week I felt less alone with it all. Plus, you hid me from her. You saw her. And felt her presence. I know I'm not going mad, because you saw her too. She really is after me!'

The Tree nodded. 'I do see her, and I feel her. I assure you that you are not going mad, nor is your fear of this woman a figment of your imagination. I have sensed her soul, and it is dark. It is angry. This woman is dangerous, and I will do everything in my power to protect you from her. But I must know more. Do you feel able to continue with your story?'

'I can, yes, but are you going to be okay?' she asked cautiously.

'Of course. You don't have to take care of me!' The Tree said gently with a reassuring smile, but it also flushed with shame as it feared that its own vulnerability was becoming more evident. Not just to itself but also to others. To compensate, somewhat excessively, The Tree made its trunk swell, and it stretched its leafy branches up towards the sky to demonstrate its strength and solidity.

'Please,' it said, 'continue with your story. I am listening.'

The familiar swirl of sounds and colours came as the valley dissolved and The Tree was deep in Elizabeth's memories again.

It saw two very tired looking young women at the breakfast table. A lovingly prepared spread of pastries, fruit, coffee and juice were placed between them as they sat on opposite sides, deep in conversation. Light was streaming through the large glass panels that made up the entirety of what once was a solid wall, but now gave views of the tall pine trees that populated the surrounding forest. They loved their home together. It was in peaceful location where only the sounds of nature could be heard. Other wooden cabins could be seen throughout the forest but were sufficiently far away for Elizabeth and her wife not to be disturbed.

Ping … ping … ping … PING … PING … PING!!!

It was the harsh and intrusive electronic chime of multiple notifications on Elizabeth's phone. Her wife took a long sip of coffee and then looked at Elizabeth with concern. Elizabeth stared down at the offending object as it continued to alert her to the 'likes' she was continuing to receive online. Her eyes were wide encased in dark puffy circles. She clearly hadn't slept that night.

'Wow!' said Jennifer, a touch of humour in her tone. 'So that's her, right? Well, I'll give her this, she's nothing if not persistent!'

'Do you think this is funny?' Elizabeth snapped. 'All night, all bloody night she's been doing this. Every picture … I mean EVERY SINGLE PICTURE that I have online she has liked. And not just the ones from my plays. She's somehow in my private account too. Pictures of our wedding, our holidays, our home! And she's not just selecting one or two … it is all of them! And then there are the comments – how beautiful I look, how wonderful the scenery looks, how she wishes she could have that view from her home, how she wants to visit wherever we have visited one day. It's relentless!'

'But how do you know it is her? I believe you and everything, but you've got tonnes of fans who follow you online. And they often like your pictures and comments. How can you be sure it's that woman?'

Elizabeth sighed, exasperated. 'Because I know. I can feel it,' came her weary reply. She too took a gulp of her coffee and angrily bit into one of the pastries.

'She calls herself "Lucy Harker". It's a nod to my character in the play. Not only is she positioning herself as my "best friend" but she's also wedded me by taking on Jonathan's surname in the play. It's just weird. She is obsessed!'

'Sweetheart, that really could just be a fan, surely?'

'NO IT COULD NOT!' bellowed Elizabeth, pastry crumbs spitting form her mouth.

'Every picture of me and you, or just you on your own, she comments with a skull emoji. You can't tell me that's not the behaviour of a jealous psycho! She hates you and envies me. I swear she wants to be me. Her profile picture is of … guess who? Of me. ME!!! And it's from that last night of the play. I know because I look like shit in it. I couldn't even do my make-up properly. And I look terrified. Who would have taken that? And who would think to even use that picture as their own profile picture? I'm telling you … it is her!'

Elizabeth's voice cracked and tears began to roll down her cheeks, so frustrated and exhausted was she.

'It's bad enough she ruined the performance for me,' Elizabeth continued through her sobs. 'And now she is following me everywhere. She did back in that town, and now online … she's even in my head!'

I mean, what's next? The bitch moves in next door? Are you going to believe me then, or just invite her in for a cup of fucking coffee?!' Elizabeth slammed her own mug down on the table.

The Tree could see the concern, love and care that Jennifer felt for her wife as she apologetically rushed from her side of the table to embrace her. Elizabeth gratefully collapsed into her wife's arms and wept.

'I'm sorry, honey. We will get through this, I promise. You have me, and I will not let that woman get anywhere near you ... or our life!'

'Thank you,' whispered Elizabeth. And for just a few fleeting seconds, she felt safe. The chorus of bird songs outside of their wooden cabin were a reminder of the life that she and her wife had worked so hard to create together. It was peaceful. It was idyllic. And it was theirs. And nothing could or would destroy that, she vowed to herself.

VI

The Tree observed from her memories that the following weeks were sadly no better for Elizabeth and Jennifer. Elizabeth's frustration and anger were clearly getting the better of her. She would increasingly snap at her wife, whose patience was also beginning to wane as she snapped back.

When the sickly-sweet messages continued online, both Elizabeth and Jennifer turned their anger towards the offending profile and would scream at their respective computers as they told the person, in no uncertain terms, to leave them alone. Elizabeth sought advice and changed her passwords, cancelled her accounts and set up new ones. But within days, the same profile, and the same messages, reappeared, leaving neither Elizabeth nor her wife in any doubt that she was being targeted.

And then came the phone calls. First just an unknown number that would ring off before it could be answered. But The Tree saw these escalate. Silent calls, then calls accompanied with heavy breathing. At other times a childlike crying, clearly a woman's cries. And then on Jennifer's phone too. But the calls she received had a different quality, more threatening. High-pitched squeals of electronic alarms, clearly designed to cause damage to her hearing. At other times it was the sound of glass being smashed. And then the call that prompted them to contact the police yet again.

'You don't deserve her ... she is mine!' came the sinister childlike whisper of the woman from the crowd.

The scene dissolved and The Tree found itself in a packed theatre. Luxuriously soft jade-coloured seats contained excited men and women in tuxedos and ball gowns. A plush red curtain hung over the stage, complete with gold trim as was common in the old-fashioned theatre décor that never failed to draw the crowds.

The Tree observed the backdrop of the stage, two huge golden masks laughing and crying, one signifying comedy and the other tragedy. It was an awards ceremony. Both Elizabeth and Jennifer were in the crowd – Elizabeth's unmistakeable fiery hair and emerald green dress making her stunningly visible amidst the safer clothing and colour choices that the rest of the crowd had made.

As The Tree honed in on Elizabeth, it felt her fear mixed with determination. She wasn't going to hide. This was, she hoped, her night. But the fear about what could happen, or more importantly who could be there, weighed heavily on her heart and mind.

As the auditorium lights dimmed, plunging the theatre into momentary darkness, Jennifer squeezed her wife's hand reassuringly and heard her sigh deeply.

'You've got this!' she whispered encouragingly into Elizabeth's ear, who turned to her wife and gave a weak but grateful smile.

The next thing The Tree heard was the roar of applause. It observed the spotlight weaving its way through the audience until it landed on Elizabeth.

She had won! Best Actress, and an additional award for her ongoing commitment and dedication to the craft of acting, in particular bringing back to life the gothic classics, which she and her colleagues performed in outdoor and eerily atmospheric environments only ('come rain or shine').

A look of shock was replaced by delight on Elizabeth's face as her wife adoringly kissed her on the cheek and ushered her out of her seat and towards the stage.

The Tree watched her tentatively make her way on to the stage, where she accepted her awards with dignity and grace, her heart pounding, and forcing a smile that would hopefully not betray the underlying feeling of panic that was growing inside of her.

In the glare of the lights and the silent anticipation of the crowd, Elizabeth was hit with the memory of a scene from one of her favourite novels. A young woman on stage smiling into the crowd … until a bucket of pig's blood was dumped onto her head, humiliating her, and leading to the violent decimation of her school bullies. But this was not Elizabeth. She was not at a high school prom. She was accepting her awards, celebrating the hard work and dedication she had shown to her craft. She had been wanting this all her life. And I deserve this, she reminded herself.

Mustering her strength and reaching deep into her soul for the confidence that she had once possessed, she took a deep breath and lifted the trophies that she held in each hand upwards, and beamed into the crowd. The roaring cheers and applause were deafening and reignited her confidence even further. Finding her voice, The Tree heard Elizabeth address the crowd.

'Thank you. You have no I idea how much this means to me. I feel so honoured to be here and to be—' She stopped and fell silent, the words catching in her throat.

A door at the back of the theatre swung open with a bang. Someone was in the doorway. Elizabeth could only make out their silhouette as the light from the lobby cast a malevolent looking shadow in front of the figure. Elizabeth's pulse quickened, as did her breathing. Her hands were no longer held aloft but were lowering to her sides, trembling.

The spotlight felt like it was blinding her. Instinctively she raised her arm to shield her face from the harsh light that now felt like razorblades on her retinas and reddening face.

The figure stood motionless in the doorway.

Why aren't they moving? thought Elizabeth, the familiar feeling of terror creeping through her body like spiders made of ice.

And then the spotlight found her. It weaved through the crowd again until it landed on the figure in the doorway.

Elizabeth gasped, as did the audience. The trophies fell from her hands and crashed onto the stage floor, shattering into pieces.

A woman with flame-red hair inched forwards. The spotlight followed her and revealed her dress. The exact same emerald green dress that Elizabeth was wearing.

It was like she was looking into a mirror, except the reflection was broken. Instead of a smile of pride, Elizabeth saw a familiar malevolent grin spread across the woman's face. And the same malevolent eyes that she first saw in her dressing room several months ago burning into her soul.

It was the woman from the crowd, and she was holding a knife.

It all happened so quickly.

A piercing shriek. The flash of the knife hovering above the intruder's wrists. A look of malevolent glee and burning hatred emanating from her.

Then Jennifer slamming into the woman, taking her by surprise.

Screams erupted from the crowd. People jumped to their feet. And security guards piled into the theatre auditorium. The knife was retrieved, having been released from her hands by the force of Jennifer's tackle. The woman was restrained and dragged from the theatre by the security officers and onsite police, and her fading screams could be heard echoing into the night.

'YOU OWE ME ... YOU ARE NOTHING WITHOUT ME! I DID THIS ... YOU ARE MINE ... YOU ARE MINE ... MINE!'

The last thing that The Tree saw was Elizabeths terrified face. Her eyes wide. Her mouth open. And the smashed trophy pieces at her feet. A single tear trickled down her ghostly pale face.

Elizabeth stayed still, paralysed with fear. The deep-red curtain came down. The lights went out.

The Tree stood frozen in horror as it witnessed the scene fade to black. It felt its heart rate quicken as it struggled to catch its breath. The Tree felt powerless and afraid. But its temporary paralysis was broken as Elizabeth's voice brought it back to the safety of the hilltop.

'They arrested Jennifer. Can you believe it? They actually arrested her for assault. Apparently, the knife that the crazy woman was holding was actually just a silver comb, or something stupid like that. And other than the weird stuff she was shouting, the police said that she hadn't done anything wrong. She was just a guest arriving late! They said nothing about the fact that she looked EXACTLY like me. They didn't even seem to care about all the other stuff that we told them about. "Circumstantial", that's what they said. Circumstantial! And the only person who behaved erratically ... was my wife!'

The Tree could feel its trunk and limbs starting to relax as it settled back into its surroundings thanks to the sound of Elizabeth's voice. But a new feeling was coiling around its insides. The Tree felt furious on behalf of Elizabeth and her wife. How could the police be so stupid? The Tree wondered indignantly to itself. Could they not see the pattern that was emerging? The danger that they were in?

'That sounded truly horrifying and terrifying for you,' said The Tree kindly, attempting to hide the tremor in its own voice. 'And I'm glad that Jennifer did what she did. She was trying to protect you. She recognised the threat, and she acted, which is more than anyone else seems to have done.'

'Thank you,' Elizabeth replied quietly. 'So I'm not going mad then? You believe me? You believe that it was that woman?'

'Of course I do. How could I not? After everything you've been through, everything you've shared with me, and everything I've seen since you came back her to visit me. I know it in my soul. That woman is a threat to you. And I can see what she has done to your soul. I see the erosion. And this makes me sad!'

Feeling the sincerity emanating from The Tree, Elizabeth allowed herself to sob. As she did so, The Tree extended its branches and softened them into an embrace. It was determined to keep her safe … and to give something back to her. Something of the life that she had been robbed of over the past year since the stalker had come into her life and tried to take and spoil what she owned.

The Tree sensed that the stalker wanted, no, needed, something from Elizabeth. It was as though she needed something from Elizabeth so that she could feel whole. There was both a longing and desire to be with Elizabeth, but also a deep-seated envy and hatred for all that she had, and a ferocious and unsatiable hunger to take it for herself, whilst defiling and contaminating Elizabeth's goodness in the process. It was as though the stalker wanted to actually be Elizabeth. This thought alarmed The Tree. It knew that if that were to be the case, then the stalker would stop at nothing to eliminate anything (or indeed anyone) that became a threat to her mission. The Tree feared, knowing what it did of such behaviours, that in order for the stalker to feel whole, she would have to take everything from Elizabeth. And perhaps even destroy her.

As if reading The Tree's mind, Elizabeth spoke through her tears. 'It's like that hateful woman took something from me. My enjoyment, my passion for what I do. Even the way I look! It's like she wants to become me or something. So I made myself look like this,' and she looked down sadly at her grey and scraggy hair, and her colourless clothes.

'Of course, that bitch now looks like this too, but good! At least we both look like shit! I hate her for what she is doing to me. I really hate her!'

Good, thought The Tree. A spark of anger. There was energy in anger ... there is fight!

'I don't know what I've done to myself.' Her tone was melancholy once more. 'I don't even recognise myself anymore. And I've still not told you all of it. I nearly lost my wife, I've lost my job, my reputation. I've even had to move! All I do is watch. And wait. Wait for her to be there ... in a café ... in the supermarket ... down every dark alley ... outside my window. Just standing there. Watching me. Waiting. She's like a spectre that haunts me. CHRIST! She even haunts my dreams.' She placed her heads in her hands and sighed deeply. 'I just wish I could make myself invisible!'

But that is exactly what you've done, thought The Tree to itself.

'Perhaps this has been your way of protecting yourself. By taking good things from yourself first, she is less able to take or spoil them. And if you fear that the spoiling is inevitable, then perhaps this is the only way that you feel able to be in control of it.'

'I think you're right. It's like if there is nothing left of me to have, maybe, just maybe, she will leave me alone. But it's like she can't stop, she wants all of me. She wants my image, she wants life. It feels like she wants to devour my soul. And I'm scared, scared that she won't stop until there is nothing left of me!'

Unable to suppress it any longer, Elizabeth allowed herself scream in frustration.

The Tree echoed her scream in solidarity, and then gently placed its branches around her in a comforting embrace again.

'Envy is a destructive thing. It consumes the person who covets, but it can destroy the person who is coveted. But I promise you this – she cannot have you, nor will she destroy you. I will protect you, and I will help you find yourself again.'

And with that, The Tree determinedly breathed into one of its remaining silver branches. And from this branch it willed fruit to grow. Berries of every colour of the rainbow grew, tinged with a sparkle of gold. The Tree lowered the branch so that berries were within Elizabeth's reach. And it urged her to eat.

At first, she seemed somewhat confused by the spectacle but then a spark of memory returned to her. Luke's magical crutches. And the fiery flower from The Tree when she was just a little girl. She remembered ... how could she have forgotten this? But she remembered. And trusting The Tree as she had all those years ago, she ate the berries that were offered.

A strange but comforting warmth began to ripple through her body. The warmth rose slowly upwards until she felt her face and the top of her head tingle. And then, something wonderful happened. The cold silvery grey of her hair began to change colour. Within seconds, any remnants of lank white hair had evaporated and were replaced with Elizabeth's beautiful fiery, curling locks, now full-bodied and framing her pale face. And her eyes, no longer did they appear as lifeless as the woman's who stalked her. But they too had returned to their original colour, vibrant green with flecks of hazel.

Elizabeth gasped as she touched her hair, tears forming in her eyes again. But not with sadness, with joy. With appreciation. With love.

'What, what is this?' she said looking up to The Tree.

'I'm giving back some of what she took. I may not be able to change what has happened, or what you have yet to tell me. But I can give back to you some of what has been stolen. She may look like you, but she cannot be you. And hopefully this is a reminder of who you are, of the young girl that I met all those years ago.'

And Elizabeth felt it. She felt that something had changed within her. It was slight but there was definitely something. A confidence. A fire. An energy that she had not felt for quite some time. It was a flicker of memory, memories of the past and the journey she had been on to get where she had in life. The struggles and the triumphs. They were hers, and now she felt determined. Determined to become the woman that she once was. She still felt fear, but she also felt courage. And she felt protected. She felt believed. And she felt loved. She would not let her stalker win, and she would get her life back ... no matter what it took!

The Tree beamed at the perceptible change that it witnessed taking hold.

'Come back and see me, and tell me the rest of your story,' said The Tree. 'Whatever it takes, and no matter how small it may seem, try to take back some of what has been taken from you. Your greatest shield against that woman's envy and hate is your enjoyment and appreciation for who you are and what you have. If you hide who are you then she will win ... her greed does not deserve to be satiated. But you deserve to be happy. You deserve to be loved, and you deserve to shine. She has taken enough. It is time for you to take your life back!'

Elizabeth stood up. She felt empowered by The Tree's words. She closed her eyes and allowed herself to bathe in the essence of The Tree's belief in her – in its encouragement. When she was here, she felt that The Tree reflected back the person that she used to be, and this energised her. She nodded towards The Tree and marched across the stone circle and out of sight, determined to rise from the ashes.

The Tree too felt briefly energised. It felt a sense of hope. But then it looked at its silver branch ... some of the essence still remained. It would save this as it anticipated that Elizabeth would need more – her journey of recovery was not yet complete. It knew that the sacrifice would take its toll on its own soul, but The Tree did not care. It had come to care very deeply for Elizabeth and its own soul could not rest until hers was healed.

VII

Over the following week, The Tree eyed the other trees in the valley with suspicion. It was unable to tell if they were friend or foe. It periodically changed its appearance. At times it was a weeping willow, and others a mighty oak. At other times a gentle blossom tree and then an autumnal wonder – its fiery leaves glowing in the summer sunlight. That will teach the other trees, it thought to itself. They won't be able to copy me now!

But then The Tree grew fearful. What if the other trees envied its ability to change? What if they sent animals or even the wildest of weather to attack and destroy it? What if the animals started to hate it and desired to steal its fruit for themselves? It felt so visible on the hill. So exposed ... so vulnerable! There is only one thing for it. I must make myself less attractive. Less colourful. Less desirable, then maybe I will feel safe, thought The Tree, its anxiety beginning to build. With that thought, The Tree shook loose the beautiful autumnal leaves, leaving its branches bare and exposed. It twisted itself into an ugly contortion of bark and branches, carefully concealing anything that may be perceived by the other inhabitants of the valley as extraordinary or desirable. For now, it would just become a gnarled old stump, and make itself small and unremarkable. This is the only way to stay safe, it reasoned with itself.

In the evenings, the various nocturnal beasts and the owls and bats who had once sought refuge and comfort from The Tree circled nervously, daring not to approach. When badgers or foxes braved the walk across the stone circle, they did so with hesitancy, and were soon met with a low and unfriendly growl from The Tree. The animals scattered, and the owls and bats took to the skies, hooting and screeching, in search of friendlier pastures. The Tree felt relieved but took no pleasure in scaring its fellow inhabitants. This was simply self-preservation. The Tree knew that if it were to protect itself, and indeed protect Elizabeth, it must do what was necessary, and that meant dimming its own shine so that the other wicked and covetous trees would leave it alone. The Tree giggled silently to itself – so smug did it feel about its own cleverness. And so, it allowed itself to fall into a deep and dreamless sleep until Elizabeth returned to the top of the hill to continue her story.

VIII

There was something both refreshing and reviving about the warm morning rain on a summer's day. The Tree woke from its deep sleep, relieved to be free of the nightmarish hauntings that had preoccupied its subconscious. It felt relieved to see that the other trees in the valley remained where they were, and had not marched upon it in the night and stripped it bare of its goodness and soul after all.

As the rain drops soaked its gnarled and twisted stump, The Tree felt a change within its heart. Why have I done this to myself? it thought, feeling the pain of its twisted limbs. The beautifully fresh scent of pine wafted through the valley, further intoxicating The Tree's senses and evoking a sense of clarity. It realised that its fellow trees were not the enemy – they of course did not wish to take from or destroy it. They were simply trees in the valley. Harmless and beautiful in their own right.

The Tree knew that what it felt was no different to the haunting trauma that its beloved Elizabeth continued to experience in the wake of her stalker's relentless pursuit. It could empathise deeply with her paranoia, her fear, and the subtle ways she had tried to protect herself from envy – these were now being utilised by The Tree itself. Again, it was befuddled as to how it had not recognised this, but then it remembered how powerful the processes of envy and stalking could be. It knew that envious people, and in particular stalkers, will split off the hated parts of themselves and force them into other people to be contained and identified with.

It also knew that perhaps Elizabeth's only means of tolerating the intolerable when talking with The Tree was to split off some of the pain and horror that she felt, and without knowing it, give this to The Tree to safely hold and contain until she was able to take it back. The Tree felt that it was its duty to do this for its friend, and now knowing the power of this, it could be forewarned and less impacted by the paranoid fantasies that had come to permeate its nightmares.

Further inspired and determined to mirror Elizabeth's courage, The Tree allowed itself to unfurl and breathe into the rain. It stretched its beautiful branches up towards the sky, and allowed them to swish and shake free the tension that it had been holding. As it did so, The Tree felt something lift within its soul, and a surge of energy ignited through its limbs. The healing drops of rain mixed with the burning energy within The Tree's body and succulent green leaves burst forth from its branches, restoring The Tree to its former glory. It felt like itself once more.

As the day wore on, the rain became a light drizzle, before once again giving way to blue cloudless skies. Butterflies and ladybirds circled The Tree, a sign that the creatures of nature had also felt a change in The Tree's demeanour, and felt safe to return to the hilltop.

The Tree basked in the sun, and felt a surge of joy as Elizabeth emerged from her climb and made her way towards The Tree. Her red hair shone with life, and her eyes continued to burn with the same fight that The Tree had witnessed at the end of their previous encounter.

Her clothes, however, still looked misshapen and dull, and her walk had lost the confident stride that The Tree thought had returned.

Elizabeth stopped at the edge of the stone circle, catching her breath. And then – to The Tree's delight – she strode forward with a fierce determination and sense of growing power. She had not lost this after all.

'I've been offered a part!' Elizabeth shouted joyfully to The Tree. 'Can you believe it? I didn't think I'd get offered any more roles. But I have … and it's one I've always wanted. Of course, it's from one of my favourite gothic novels!' she continued excitedly. 'I get to play a malevolent ghost. A woman dressed all in black … AND … ' she paused for dramatic effect.

'And …?' said The Tree, its curiosity peaked, and feeling equally as excited.

'And … they've asked me to also direct it. Me! I mean the role is great, but I don't have to do a great deal, but the chance to direct the play is amazing. They think I can bring a fresh take to a classic story!' Elizabeth beamed and settled herself on the warm damp grass, not caring if she got wet.

The Tree was overjoyed to see her emerging happiness. She was indeed reclaiming her life. 'You said that you feared you would never get offered another role again. Why was that?'

'Oh God, well, that's the part that I haven't told you yet,' she said with a sigh. 'It was AWFUL. That woman pretty much shattered my marriage and my career, or so I thought.'

As she spoke, The Tree could feel her energy diminish. It could feel her sadness and the weight of the devastation that the stalker had wreaked in Elizabeth's life.

'I'm here for you,' The Tree said. 'You can tell me.'

And with that, The Tree and Elizabeth were transported back into her recent memories.

IX

It was night-time. An angry Jennifer thrust her laptop in front of a confused and frightened-looking Elizabeth. The gentle sound of the swaying trees outside of their forest home could be heard in the background, but rather than providing the familiar hypnotic sound of comfort, the sway and swish of the branches felt intrusive and aggressive.

Jennifer continued to glare at her wife, her face reddening as her breathing increased.

'Go on,' she seethed. 'Open it ... I SAID OPEN IT!'

Terrified, Elizabeth did as she was instructed. The silver laptop hummed in front of her. Pulling it closer, she opened it so that the electronic screen was now visible to her. The screen was blank. She gingerly tapped one of the buttons so that the screen would come to life, and gasped. It was as though her heart and frozen in her chest. A sickening wave of nausea rose in her stomach and a sharp pain stabbed her chest.

'W-w-what is this?' she stammered, her voice barely audible.

'You fucking tell me!' demanded Jennifer. 'It's not bad enough that you are fucking around behind my back, but you let them take photographs? Recordings? ARE YOU STUPID?'

Tears formed in Elizabeth's wide eyes. 'But ... but that's not me! How could you even think that? I swear ... those pictures ... those videos ... that is not me. I would never do that to you. Never! Please, you have to believe me!' pleaded Elizabeth.

'Are you kidding me? Are you blind? Do you think I'm stupid? That I don't recognise my own wife, in bed with another woman!' she bellowed, causing Elizabeth to shrink back into her chair and tremble.

'I have been getting these all day. Every time I switch on my computer I've got an email ... and then another ... and another! And it's not just my emails. I've had colleagues coming up to me showing me this.' Jennifer reached for her phone, swiped and unlocked it and then thrust her phone towards Elizabeth so its screen was inches from her face.

It took Elizabeth's eyes a few moments to adjust to the bright glare of the screen through her tears. And then she saw the familiar logo. A logo for a website where adults share sexual content of themselves. And then she saw it. Her face. Her body. And then the bio. A bio explaining all the things she wanted people to do to her sexually. That she didn't care about their sex. Or how clean there were. Or how rough. That she would take anything ... that she would be at their complete mercy.

'I'm going to be sick,' mumbled Elizabeth. The queasiness rose in her stomach – she didn't make it to the bathroom.

Warm disgusting vomit erupted from her mouth and onto the kitchen floor next to where she sat. Jennifer jumped backwards, her phone falling from her hand, and the images and hideous bio disappearing from the screen.

Elizabeth began to sob. 'It's … not … me,' she whispered weakly. 'How can you even think I would do something like that? A sex site. Really? It's disgusting!'

'Well, if you've been fucking other women all this time then what the hell else are you capable of? Who are you? I feel I don't even know you anymore!'

'It is her,' Elizabeth whispered in exasperation. 'Don't you see? It's all her!'

'Oh for Christ's sake stop it. Not everything can be HER! Take some fucking responsibility for your actions! You have been careless. You have been caught, and you have humiliated me!'

With that, tears forming in her furious eyes, Jennifer threw her wine glass across the room. The glass smashed against the fireplace mantlepiece, red wine soaking and spattering the cream rug, like blood.

Elizabeth froze in terror. She had never seen the side of her wife before. Jennifer had stormed from the room leaving Elizabeth alone with phone, the open laptop and vile pool of sick at her feet. There were no more tears. The fear and confusion consumed her. How had this happened? How could this happen? Was this even possible?

That same night, Elizabeth and Jennifer slept in separate rooms, although The Tree could see that neither of them slept. The argument and the images swirled in both of their minds, haunting images that tormented them both. The Tree knew that Elizabeth was not responsible for what she was being accused of. It had heard about the uprising of certain technology in the modern world where images could be created, and even convincing videos could be crafted by an artificial intelligence that was alien to The Tree. It did, however, know that Elizabeth had fallen prey once more to the devious attempts of her stalker to attack and destroy that which she held most dear … her wife and their marriage.

Jennifer left early the next morning. A simple note was left on the kitchen table. She had taken the car and would be staying with a friend for a few days – she needed to have some space and clear her head.

Elizabeth held the note in her trembling hands, reading and re-reading the note but surprisingly feeling nothing. She was numb and in shock.

The Tree watched as the note fell from her hands and fluttered to the ground. She did not pick it up. Like a zombie in a trance, she walked back to her bedroom and pulled the covers over her head.

Over the next few days Elizabeth remained in bed. She was exhausted and had given up hope. She had heard nothing from Jennifer, despite the numerous calls Elizabeth made, the voice notes she left, and the text messages she sent. And then the phone calls came. From her parents, her father expressing his deep-seated disappointment that a daughter of his would flaunt herself so shamelessly over the internet. From her manager, expressing a growing concern that the new 'image' she had created was not in keeping with the values of the theatre company she worked for. And that it might be time for her to take a break from acting, just until this 'scandal' had blown over.

The early hours of the morning were the worst. A terrified Elizabeth could be seen dashing from window to door in home, frantically making sure that they were all locked. The slightest sound or movement outside caused her heart to thunder in her chest.

And the calls ... the sick and obscene calls that people would make to her. Disgusting filthy whispers, both men and women, sharing their fantasies of the sexual torture and violation of her. Rasping voices saying that they knew where she lived ... and describing in vivid grotesque details what they would do to her when they found her – in keeping with the invitation she had allegedly provided online to be sexually dominated and humiliated.

Clutching a kitchen knife, The Tree saw an almost animalistic and wild-looking Elizabeth scurrying through her home, hiding weapons within easy reach, and finally settling back in bed, the knife now safely under her pillow.

The Tree's heart broke at what it was witnessing. It had known of people who had been stalked in the past ... the visitors to The Tree had shared many such stories. But what alarmed The Tree was the evolution of such disturbing behaviours. No longer were they restricted to the sending of unwanted gifts, or the classic following, or lurking in the shadows, which in and of themselves could be truly frightening. The Tree saw that the rise of technology and its significant advancements meant that nowhere was safe for the victim. And perhaps no one could escape the jaws of this growing monster. That any image could be obtained and manipulated, often with great skill, cunning, and cruelty. And The Tree feared that every aspect of Elizabeth's life could be targeted, and indeed contaminated and spoilt through the relentless harassment by this disturbed soul. The consequences were ghastly. Elizabeth's reputation, her relationships, her livelihood were all being eroded, leaving her with nothing. Leaving her as an empty husk … alone … terrified … and destroyed.

A shrill and deafening noise pierced the silence of her sedative-induced slumber. Elizabeth leapt from her bed and instinctively grabbed the knife from under her pillow. Her arm raised, and the knife pointing forwards in parallel with her cheek, her eyes darted around the room for the source of the intrusion. Her eyes fell to the glowing mobile phone screen. She thought she'd put it on silent, but obviously not.

What time was it?

07:15.

Somewhat groggy and disorientated despite the adrenaline rush, Elizabeth gathered herself and inched towards the phone. No longer was this common household item a source of excitement and simple communication, it had become an aggressive intruder only bringing her terror, bad news, and hatred.

As she hesitantly reached for the phone she saw the caller ID. She was stunned. They hadn't spoken in weeks. And now she was calling. Why? Something must be wrong! The familiar feeling of nausea and terror rose in her like lava. Elizabeth answered the phone.

'Jennifer?'

No answer.

'Jennifer …?' She paused.

Nothing.

'Why aren't you speaking?' she yelled, her body tense and trembling. 'JENNIFER?!' she screamed, the panic in her now escalating.

Heavy breathing. A horrible rasping noise like chains being raked across shattered glass. And the giggle. The low, unmistakenly sickening giggle of a woman. Of her!

The phone line went dead.

PIIINNGGG!!! It was the familiar tone of a new message arriving.

Unable to control her trembling hands, the adrenalin surging through her body now, Elizabeth swiped to her message screen. It was a picture attachment. She opened it, her breath quickening.

What is it? The picture was grainy. It had been taken in the dark and was not clear on the tiny screen. Running to the living room, she grabbed her laptop and booted up. COME ON! She yelled frantically at the slothful whirring machine as an eternity seemed to pass.

Finally, the familiar message icons appeared at the bottom of the screen. She clicked on the one that was synced to her phone.

GOT IT, she thought triumphantly as the messages on her laptop pinged repeatedly, catching up with the data from her phone. And then she saw it. Full screen and in higher resolution. A person, their face bloodied and lifeless, slumped over the steering wheel. The shattered windows of the car suggested an accident – that something had smashed into the car, or the car had smashed into something. Elizabeth recognised the car instantly. And she recognised the dead woman at the wheel. It was her wife!

Elizabeth's anguished scream echoed through the silent house as she fell to her knees, the sorrow and rage ripping apart The Tree's soul too as the truth of what it beheld sank in.

PING!

Elizabeth's cries were stifled as another message came through. This time there was no attachment. No picture. Just eight chilling words: 'If I can't have you ... no one can!'

X

'Ladies ... ladies ... please, calm down!' said the flustered police officer, frantically searching his computer database for the case number assigned to the two glaring and formidable women in front of him.

'DO NOT call us "ladies" like that. AND DO NOT TELL US TO CALM DOWN!' yelled Elizabeth, her patience and tolerance had clearly reached breaking point.

'Darling ... I'm fine ... I'm fine!' came Jennifer's voice, reassuringly. 'You see me. I'm not dead. It was just an AI image!'

'Just an AI image? JUST AN AI IMAGE!' Elizabeth roared at her wife. 'I THOUGHT YOU WERE DEAD ... DEAD! I thought she had killed you!!! Do you have any idea how horrifying it was to see you looking like that? Your face all smashed up like that?!'

'Yes, Elizabeth, I know EXACTLY how it feels for someone to send me a fake image showing me my very worst fear!'

Elizabeth's face softened and she hugged her wife. 'I'm sorry,' she whispered.

'No, I'm sorry. I should have believed you. I'm sorry. But we need to get her. We can't let her divide us again.' And then turning to the blundering officer, she fixed her steely glare upon him and repeated very slowly, 'We need to get her!'

The Tree sighed with relief. Jennifer was alive. And she believed Elizabeth. The Tree knew that their love would keep Elizabeth from falling into the abyss of despair. So often it had seen and heard people losing hope, no longer believing in themselves and losing faith in their fellow human beings. And The Tree knew, with anger and contempt, that this is what the stalker wanted. It wanted to make her feel alone. Betrayed. Abandoned. And that would make her easier to destroy. But thankfully this was not the case for Elizabeth. People were listening. And they were willing to believe her and help. But The Tree also felt fear. It could see how the stalker's behaviours were escalating. That she needed to be stopped because, The Tree feared, she was capable of anything, and would do anything to get what she wanted, no matter the cost.

XI

'I can't get out of it, honey. I'm sorry! I'll only be gone for a week.' Even as Jennifer said this, she knew it was too long. She could see the fear creeping back into her wife's eyes.

'A week? A WEEK?! You said it was only for the weekend!' Elizabeth's fear gave way to anger. How can she leave me alone for a whole week, she thought to herself, her mind swimming with images of the hateful woman hurting Jennifer in some way. Or hurting her.

'I know, I know, I told them I needed to be back but they've insisted. I'm the only one with the knowledge and experience of this project to close the deal.'

She could see that this explanation made no difference. 'I'm sorry. I really am. I promise you I'll call you every night!' she added, hoping that this would help. From the look on Elizabeth's face, she could see that it did not.

'What if she comes here?' cried Elizabeth, her voice becoming shrill.

Trying to remain calm and defuse the situation, Jennifer replied in as calm and measured a tone as she could muster.

'Honey, she doesn't know where we live. And you have your alarm. The police are now properly involved, and you've been taking those classes!'

'Oh great, so my protection is a loud noise and police that will take twenty-five minutes to get here. By which time she'll have strangled me or something!'

Jennifer could feel herself losing patience. 'If she comes at you, just punch her in the fucking throat. Isn't that what they've been teaching you in your classes?' she retorted sharply.

The bluntness of her wife seemed to do something to the growing tension in the room. And despite the fear she felt, Elizabeth couldn't help but smirk. 'Well,' she said with a slight chuckle, 'I'm not quite sure that counts as reasonable force, but I get your point.'

Jennifer smiled too, a feeling of relief washing over her. 'Honestly, honey, do whatever it takes if you ever feel threatened. And that camera doorbell thing will be arriving sometime later this week. If anyone comes near our property we will know.'

The Tree could feel the care and tenderness between the two of them, and again, it felt relieved that Elizabeth was not alone. But as the scene changed, so did the atmosphere of the memories.

Over the week that Jennifer was absent, The Tree observed a pale and anxious Elizabeth dressed in oversized clothes, a baseball cap and sunglasses whenever she left the house. Every sound seemed to startle her. Every alleyway, every shop, every café ... all became a possible hiding place for her stalker. The Tree observed with sadness the way she gripped her personal alarm, no matter where she was. And the seeming readiness to defend herself should she encounter danger.

The Tree felt fury on her behalf. It wished it could have left the hilltop and been with her, like an enormous bodyguard ready to swing its powerful branches in defence of its friend.

When Elizabeth was safely back in her home, she would use the numerous bolts and locks that had been added to the doors and windows to keep her safe. The once beautiful glass wall that gave her such joy because of the spectacular view of the forest now filled her with dread. Before she could switch on any lights, she must first close all the blinds, just in case she was being watched. She did so ritualistically, peering out into the forest before sealing herself in her fortress, safe for the evening.

Outside amidst the pine trees, a figure lurked in the shadows. It watched as Elizabeth drew the curtains and smiled triumphantly. She had found her.

The following afternoon, after a particularly successful visit to the nearby town, Elizabeth gave herself permission to relax in the hot tub. The woodland home didn't have a garden – the garden being the forest itself – but the decking provided a beautiful spot for her to practice yoga to the chorus of the birds, the gentle breeze in the swaying trees, followed by some well-earned relaxation. There had been no instances of threat.

She had been practising self-defence, and a part of her – dare she allow it – was feeling significantly more at ease. After a particularly enjoyable half-hour of doing the sun salutations, Elizabeth eased into the hot tub, a glass of wine on the side, and her favourite classical music playing quietly in the background. As the warm bubbles enveloped her, and the sleepiness induced from the red wine kicked in, Elizabeth allowed herself to close her eyes, just for a few minutes, she told herself.

Elizabeth awoke with a start. How long have I been asleep? she thought.

Reaching for her phone next to the empty glass of wine, she saw the time. Two hours had passed. You idiot! It was dusk.

Looking around frantically, she saw that she had not locked the door. It was open, just slightly … but it was open. She was convinced that she had bolted it and placed the keys in her bag. Where is my bag?

Leaping out of the hot tub she searched for her small canvas bag, where she had safely placed her keys. It was exactly where had left it. And so were the keys.

A feeling of relief washed over her. But why was the door open? Surely, she wouldn't have been so careless.

Feeling uneasy, Elizabeth gathered her belongings and darted into the house, not caring that she had left a trail of water behind her, a trail which now followed her into the house. As was her ritual, she locked and bolted the door.

Looking around the kitchen area she noticed nothing out of the ordinary. Everything seemed to be where it should be. She moved into the open plan living room area and again surveyed the scene. Everything seemed normal. She breathed a deep sigh of relief.

Cautiously, and for no reason that was immediately obvious to her, Elizabeth reached for her personal alarm as she moved towards her bedroom – the beauty of living in a single storey home, she thought to herself – and opened the door.

It was just as she left it. Neat, tidy, everything in its place. But the closet door was ajar. She had left in a hurry that morning and she could see inside. Just clothes. Shoes and garments hung neatly on hangers. And white wooden slatted doors to allow the clothes to breathe. She slid the door closed and reminded herself that she was safe. Jennifer would be back in a couple of days. And everything was okay.

That evening, after finishing the bottle of wine and dozing off halfway through the chapter she was reading, Elizabeth engaged in her usual nightly ritual. She checked all of the windows and doors. They were secure. And so was she. She brushed her teeth – no need to remove make-up as she hadn't worn this for some time – so afraid was she of being seen, of being noticed, of being envied.

She looked at her reflection in the bathroom mirror, an expression of sadness forming. She looked older. She looked tired. She looked like a shadow of herself again.

'I can't keep living like this,' she said to herself quietly.

The Tree felt her pain. It longed for her to become the woman she had been.

Elizabeth turned off the light, left the warm bathroom and entered her bedroom. Dimming the lights, she undressed and snuggled into the warm and freshly laundered duvet. It smelled of lavender. She took her nightly sleeping pill, leaned over to her bedside table and took a sip of water, and switched off the lights completely. After practising her nightly meditations, Elizabeth drifted off into a dreamless sleep.

In the darkness of the closet, behind the wooden slats, a dark figured watched. She held up her phone and pushed record, the video capturing in vivid detail the unsuspecting Elizabeth sleeping soundly in her bed. The stalker's breathing quickened. She began to touch herself.

XII

Both Elizabeth and Jennifer stared horrified at the laptop monitor. What they saw sickened them. The woman had been in their house! Not just once, but several times. And not just when they were out. There were moments when one or both of them had been in the house and so had the stalker. Neither Elizabeth nor Jennifer knew exactly where, as the camera only showed the woman entering the house … with a key. A key she must have stolen and copied on the day that Elizabeth fell asleep in the hot tub, they guessed.

'I thought it was supposed to alert us when anyone approaches the door, not just record!' said Elizabeth.

'It is, it should,' replied Jennifer, confused. 'But it's not been set up properly. We've got the settings as record, not record AND alert! I'm so sorry. I should have been here to help you set it up!'

'But I installed it weeks ago. She's been doing this to us for weeks! She's found me. How the hell has she found me?!'

'I don't know, honey, but she obviously doesn't know that she's been recorded otherwise she wouldn't be coming through the front door.'

'I DON'T CARE WHICH DOOR SHE IS COMING THROUGH … I DON'T WANT HER COMING THROUGH ANY DOOR!' screamed Elizabeth, taking Jennifer by surprise. 'We have to leave. Don't you understand? We can't stay here any more. We have to leave. NOW!'

'I WILL NOT LET THAT BITCH DRIVE ME AWAY FROM MY OWN HOME. FROM OUR HOME!' bellowed Jennifer. 'When she comes back, and she will come back, I will be ready for her!'

'What the hell are you thinking of doing? She is dangerous. Don't you get that? She could kill you. She could kill me. We cannot engage with her. We have to just get away!'

'NO!' replied Jennifer defiantly. 'I will not be at the mercy of that woman. This ends now!'

'What are you going to do?' whispered Elizabeth, sounding both afraid and defeated.

'I'm going to wait for her. I'm going to follow her, and I'm going to do what is necessary!'

And so The Tree watched the two women hatch their plan. It saw them dressed up for date night and leaving the house in their car, only to park somewhere else in the forest. It watched as they crept back under the cover of darkness and waited in the shadows themselves until their phones alerted them to the unwanted presence.

As predicted by Jennifer, the same woman from the recordings was outside of their house. The stalker had returned.

Shivering in the bushes, Elizabeth and Jennifer watched the figure – dressed head to toe in black – trying to enter their home. A feeling of triumph overcame them. She couldn't get in. They had changed the locks. Like a desperate animal, they saw her frantically try the other door. And the windows. But to no avail. She could not get in.

Being careful to remain hidden, they watched the defeated woman back away from their property and disappear into the woods. They followed her, stalking her like the prey they had been to her.

As they crept through the woods, keeping her in sight, she stopped at one of the many similar looking wooden cabins that populated the forest. And to their dismay they saw her reach for a key, insert it into the door, and enter. She now lived in the same forest as them.

Anger boiling inside of Jennifer, she leapt from her hiding place, much to Elizabeth's terror, and ran towards the house. Elizabeth raced after her wife, fearful of what would happen next.

BANG ... BANG ... BANG ... BANG!

Jennifer's fist thundered on the wooden door to what she assumed was the stalker's home. The door opened a crack, but this was enough. Elizabeth saw her wife barge through the door and out of sight into the house.

Gasping for breath, Elizabeth found herself in the spot where she had seen Jennifer disappear into the house. Screams and crashes – the sound of furniture breaking – could be heard coming from inside. A surge of adrenaline erupted through her body ... the instinct to protect her wife overcoming any sense of fear. She pushed through the door and saw Jennifer and the woman wrestling on the living room floor.

Without hesitating Elizabeth reached for the nearest thing she could find. And with lighting speed ran towards the woman who had her wife pinned to the ground. Elizabeth smashed the lamp into the back of her stalker's head. The woman howled in pain and toppled off Jennifer and lay motionless on the floor, seemingly unconscious.

Elizabeth ran to comfort her wife but stopped dead. She could not believe what she was seeing. A cabinet had been smashed open – its door now hanging from its hinge. Elizabeth felt chilled to her soul, paralysed and unable to look away she saw what the cabinet contained. This was no ordinary cabinet. This was a shrine ... to Elizabeth.

Inside were candles. A bottle of the perfume that she liked to wear. And was that her underwear? Elizabeth felt sick. Then she saw the pictures, photographs of her in her plays. All of her plays! Tissues with what looked like stage make-up on.

Has she been through my bins?

Photos of her at the supermarket, in the street, in cafes. In her bed ... asleep!

And that horrible picture of Jennifer ... dead. And a picture of Elizabeth and Jennifer's wedding – how does she have that? But instead of her wife being the one to gaze lovingly at Elizabeth, the super-imposed image was of the stalker, smiling back at her like some malevolent and maniacal clown.

The room swirled and became hazy. Elizabeth collapsed. Her wife rushed to comfort her. As she did so, the woman lying deathly still seized her opportunity to run. Jennifer, more concerned about her wife, let her go.

The stalker escaped into the night.

XIII

Back on the hilltop, The Tree shuddered. It felt deeply disturbed by what Elizabeth had shared – no doubt an echo of her own feeling of disturbance in the aftermath of such traumatic events.

'And that's where we are up to,' said Elizabeth. 'The police searched her house and confiscated the items we found. They even discovered videos – videos she had taken of me whilst I was asleep. In my own house! Standing at the edge of my bed, just filming me ... and ... and masturbating!'

Sensing the pain from her trauma, The Tree held up its branches as if to stop her, and gently – as it had done so many times before – invited her to connect to where she was. It reminded her that she was safe. That she was with The Tree, and that no harm would befall her whilst she was here. This seemed to help. Elizabeth settled and was more able to regulate her growing sense of overwhelm as she came back to the present moment.

When The Tree felt it was appropriate to do so, it asked what happened next.

'They can't find her! We know who she is now but the police can't find her, not even for us to be able to issue a restraining order. Not that she would stick to it, I'm sure. The last time I saw her was when I came up here to see you again. I knew she was following me again, and I knew I had to get somewhere safe. That is why I came here to find you, but she followed me. So even being here isn't safe!'

'Trust me,' said The Tree firmly. 'You are safe. I cannot control what happens down there. But up here, I assure you, I have the power to protect you!'

Elizabeth did feel reassured. She trusted The Tree and felt its power, its strength. But she also knew that she felt contaminated. That her stalker had gotten inside her soul. The Tree knew this too. It knew that Elizabeth had been forced to hold the unwanted and hated parts of her stalker, which were continuing to erode her identity, even when the woman was absent. So, The Tree did what it could to help. It focused once again on the remaining essence of the silver branch that had produced the berries, and this time willed the essence to create something else. Where the berries had grown previously, large silver pinecones began to grow instead. Once formed, The Tree shook them loose so that they fell into a neat pile next to where Elizabeth sat.

Elizabeth looked down at the pile next to her. She was confused. 'What am I going do with these?' she asked, a touch of dismay in her tone. 'I need a baseball bat, or something. Am I going to throw these at her whilst you throw fiery flowers?' she said dismissively.

The Tree felt a pang of hurt at her remarks, but it knew that she was frustrated, and angry. And again, it recognised this as being a good sign, a sign that she had not been defeated. That there was still a fight left in her.

The Tree smiled kindly.

'No, my dear,' it said. 'She has made you believe things about yourself that are not true. She has tried to take anything and everything from your life that was precious and good. She has forced you to hold the parts of her that she cannot bear to hold, and you have become a vessel for these parts. Her self-hatred has latched itself to you and is trying to erode your soul. But I am going to help you to reclaim it, and disentangle what does not belong to you!'

With that, The Tree, still connected to the now glowing silver pinecones, focused its energy on them. One of cones began to levitate and hovered above Elizabeth's hands. Instinctively she opened them palms upwards as the cone slowly lowered itself into her hands. She looked back at The Tree, astonished.

'Now,' continued The Tree, 'I want you to keep hold of this. Close your eyes … and tell me something of the lies that she has left you believing about yourself … and then tell me the truth about yourself.'

Elizabeth did as she was instructed. Eyes closed, she felt the dark and sickening feeling of shame and inadequacy swimming around her soul like a hungry slippery eel.

'I am worthless and not good enough, and I am wrong to my core.' As Elizabeth said this, the cone in her hands changed from silver to a murky, oily black.

'And the truth?' asked The Tree.

'It's a lie! I AM good enough. I am not bad or wrong. SHE is inadequate!!! She is the one who is sick and wrong. Not me!!'

'Good,' said The Tree with a smile. 'Now stand up … and throw the cone as far as you can over the side of the hill … and scream!'

Doing as she was instructed, the dark and murky cone in her hand, Elizabeth walked to the edge of the hill the drop was most sheer, and hurled it away from her and into the empty space. She did not scream. She let out a deep and guttural roar!

As the cone sailed through the air, The Tree focused its energy on the flying cone.

BOOM!

The cone exploded like a mini supernova and bright shockwave pulsed outwards like the rings of Saturn, knocking Elizabeth off her feet. But as the shockwave hit her, she felt something. A warm and comforting feeling filled her body. She felt electrified, pulsing with energy, and colour seemed to return to her skin.

Grinning up at The Tree, Elizabeth got to her feet and ran back towards it. 'Again, I want to do it again!'

The Tree bowed and another cone floated up from the pile and into her hands.

'She made me feel hated, and made me believe that I deserved the pain that she's caused. She stole my confidence, and the way I look. But she can't have it, she can't have me, AND I DO NOT DESERVE WHAT SHE HAS PUT ME THROUGH!'

And with the same roar as before, Elizabeth ran towards the edge of the hill and hurled her cone into the abyss.

BOOOOOMMMMM!

Another golden explosion. This time the shockwave didn't knock Elizabeth down. Instead she stood firm, her arms outstretched, welcoming the glorious feeling as her soul was restored.

Again and again came the pinecone explosions as Elizabeth let go of the lies she had been told. The lies she had started to believe. And the toxic traits and emotions that her stalker had brutally forced into her.

As she collected the final silver cone, she allowed herself to feel the fear. The terror that had gripped her since the stalker had come into her life. She remembered how haunted she felt ... how nowhere had felt safe. How she had taken her own goodness away from herself so that it couldn't be spoilt by that woman. In a loud voice that boomed over the valley, Elizabeth shouted, 'YOU CANNOT HAVE ME! YOU CANNOT HAVE MY LIFE! I WILL NOT HIDE FROM YOU. AND I AM NOT AFRAID ANYMORE!'

And with tears streaming down her face, and her heart racing she propelled the final cone off the side of the hill with all of her might.

Boom ... BOOOOM ... BOOOOOOOOOOOOOOOMMMMMMMM!

The cone exploded like a multitude of fireworks, all the colours of the rainbow. This time the shockwave did knock Elizabeth down, but as she lay on the grass, laughter escaped from her mouth, the familiar warm tingling emanating trough her body. She felt magnificent. She felt confident. She felt powerful!

As the glow from the explosions faded, Elizabeth sat herself upright and smiled lovingly at The Tree. Tears formed in her beautiful green eyes.

'Thank you,' she said. And then again in a whisper, 'Thank you!'

Elizabeth began to cry. But not tears of sadness or fear, tears of relief. She didn't know what would happen next. The woman was still out there. But she was not afraid. She would fight. And she would get justice. And she would not hide away any more. She would live her life with enjoyment and appreciation for what she had. And no one ... NO ONE ... would ever take that from her again.

The Tree's own soul swelled with both pride and joy. It could see that Elizabeth was back. That she had let go of all that did not belong to her. And all that threatened to contaminate her soul. It could feel the hope that had returned for her, and for this it felt glad.

But it also felt the toll of its own sacrifice. A jarring pain flashed through its own trunk – albeit briefly – but present enough to know that something had changed. Its love for Elizabeth remained constant, but a stirring of fury pulsated in its heart. A fury that wanted not just to protect. But also wanted revenge, revenge on anyone who could hurt the people that it had come to love.

But this part frightened The Tree. It would need to be concealed, for now was not the time to indulge such a thing. It's concern right now was for its friend. And the life that it hoped she would allow herself to live.

As if partly reading The Tree's mind, Elizabeth approached The Tree and wrapped her arms around its trunk.

'I promise I will live my life. I won't let her or anyone else to take it from me. She doesn't have the power anymore. I do! And I will get justice. She won't get away with this. Nor will she ever be able to do this to anyone else!'

The Tree allowed its branches to soften once more as they returned Elizabeth's embrace until she was ready to leave. She could feel its love. Its care, but a part of her also sensed something else. She couldn't quite put words to the change. But she knew that something had changed within The Tree, that it had been impacted in some way. But that was not her concern right now. Her mission was to reclaim what had been stolen. And she would do so in honour of The Tree. And in honour of herself.

Elizabeth, now in full technicolour, crossed the stone circle, waved goodbye to The Tree, and made her way down the side of the hill – the hum of a song from her favourite musical echoed through the valley and into the dusk. The Tree smiled to itself and basked in the transformation of its young friend until the dusk gave way to the evening sky.

The Tree's brief moment of enjoyment was interrupted. It could feel the presence of another – someone lurking on the edge of the hilltop, just out of sight. The Tree's heart hardened and mirrored the malice emanating from this uninvited visitor.

She remained still. As did The Tree … both held their breath in anticipation.

'I know you are there,' said The Tree in a deep and menacing voice. 'Show yourself you wretched creature … NOW!'

A pale, ghostly, and colourless figure emerged from her hiding place. A true reflection of what she had forced Elizabeth to become, but not anymore. To The Tree, the stalker's soul was hideous, with hate and malevolence shining in her eyes. And that frightful maniacal grin … it disturbed The Tree even now!

As Elizabeth's stalker inched forward out of the shadows, The Tree felt a surge of energy as it drew upon the last few remaining drops of essence from the silver branch. A loud rumble followed by a shockwave came from The Tree's roots and reverberated through the hill. The ground shook violently and rocks began to crumble and tumble down the side of the hill.

Where the stalker now stood, there came the familiar sound of crumble of rocks on the fragile ledge. With a startled look upon her face, the ground disappeared beneath her, and she lost her footing on the edge of the chasm.

Time seemed to slow down. Her eyes became wide, as did her mouth, but no sound came from it. Her hands rose up into the air and spun like slothful windmills as she tried to regain her balance. The flash of the knife that she had been concealing in her hand fell to the ground.

The Tree knew that if it just extended one of its branches by only a few inches, the stumbling woman would be able to grasp hold and save herself from falling … and be saved from certain death.

The Tree did not move. The Tree simply watched, just as the woman had done with Elizabeth. The woman fell from the top of the hill, a scream releasing from her gasping lungs as she plunged into the darkness below … into the silence.

The Tree remained still.

The Tree remained silent.

The Tree felt nothing!

CHAPTER EIGHT
August: Survival

I

'It's my birthday today.'

The Tree awoke to the sound of the young woman's voice.

'It's my birthday today,' she said again. 'I've just turned eighteen!' she added cheerfully.

The Tree did not feel cheerful. The long August days had been unusually and unwelcomingly hot. The grass surrounding The Tree and the stone circle had turned a sad and parched yellowy brown, and The Tree itself found that its own leaves had begun to wilt.

The suffocating humidity of the days had left The Tree feeling groggy and lethargic, and certainly not in the mood to be awoken from its doze. However, so as not to be rude, The Tree offered a quick flourish of its branches in the hopes that this would satiate the uninvited guest and allow it to return to its slumber. Sadly, it did not. Instead, it encouraged the young woman further.

'I'm leaving at the weekend,' she continued.

The Tree now noticed the hint of an accent. It recognised this as being Chinese in its origin, but it could not be certain. The pretty young woman – enthusiastic and wide-eyed – looked up at The Tree expectantly and stroked her long silky black hair.

'Yes, I'm moving away ... finally. I can't wait to leave. It's been a long time coming. I must get away from here. The countryside is nice, but I need to be by the sea. I'm going away to study. Did I tell you that?'

Go away ... shoo! thought The Tree irritably. I just want some peace and quiet!

'And it's my birthday! What a curious place this is. So high up. It reminds me of home. I don't think there will be views like this where I'm going. I'm going away to study. Isn't that interesting! I'm going to be a—'

Oh will this torment never end? The Tree thought impatiently to itself.

The Tree caught itself and felt ashamed. The young woman wasn't doing anything wrong. She merely wanted to share something that was important to her, and after all, it was The Tree's role to listen.

'Congratulations, my dear,' said The Tree wearily. 'And happy birthday!'

The young woman grinned, clearly satisfied by the interaction. 'Oh good,' she replied. 'You can talk. How strange!' But she did not appear perturbed by this, just simply excited and relieved to have someone to speak to.

'I've been wanting to come here for a while. Ever since they found that woman last summer. Did you know her? Did she fall from up here?'

The Tree bristled instantly at the mention of that woman.

Irritated by the young woman's impertinent questions, The Tree said nothing but offered a non-committal grumbling sound instead. It did not want to think about the events of last year. Nor did it wish to discuss these with the silly girl now smiling inanely at it.

'Oh yes, I thought so. You must see everything from up here. Can you see my boarding school? It's right over there somewhere.' She gestured absentmindedly behind her but in no particular direction before resuming her questions, rarely waiting for an answer.

'I live in a boarding school. Well, I did, but not after next weekend. Did I tell you that I'm going to study to be a—'

The Tree felt like it was being fired at with a machine gun of curiosity. If it had eyes, it would have rolled them.

'Have you been here long? Do many people come up to see you? I wonder what happened to that woman. I bet many people have fallen from here. The edge does look rather steep! I won't go near it, just in case. I don't want to fall because I'm going to university soon. So are my best friends. We leave next weekend. Did I tell you that?'

The Tree sighed. It felt exhausted by her questions, but also found something strangely endearing about her enthusiasm. It could tell that its rest was now over for the day, so persistent was the young woman's desire to speak with The Tree.

So as not to do her a disservice, The Tree stretched its branches and willed the water deep in the valley to permeate the hill and feed its roots. It felt the cool and delicious sensation of the water as it hydrated its trunk, and spread into its wilting leaves, giving them a fresh and more enlivened appearance. The Tree gulped in the sweet summer air, and despite its heaviness from the humidity, The Tree felt satiated and connected with its surroundings once more.

'Yes, my dear, you did indeed tell me this,' said The Tree more patiently, now that it was more fully awake.

Wanting to further demonstrate kindness towards the young woman, The Tree willed beautiful blossom – the colour of peach and rose – to intersperse with its healthier looking leaves, and sent a surge of water and energy to the parched grass within the stone circle, sufficiently quenching the drought. The grass outside of the stone circle remained the colour of hay but inside it became a rich and luscious green once more.

'Oh! That's lovely!' the young woman said in awe, and in what felt like genuine appreciation.

'Thank you,' said The Tree, warming to her even more. 'But you have not yet told me your name.'

'Oh!' she said with surprise. 'I thought you'd know. I'm Mei. I live at the school, you know, the one over there, the one that looks like a castle. We don't have buildings like that in Hong Kong. That's where I'm from. Did you know that? I've lived at the school since I was eleven.'

'Have you now,' replied The Tree, trying to sound interested. It could tell that her answers would always be like this. 'How nice. Do you—'

Mei interrupted The Tree before it had chance to finish its sentence. 'Well, it's not really. It's not that nice, although it sort of is. Sometimes nice, but not always. My friends are nice but some of the other girls are awful. They've not always been kind to me, or my friends. They come from money. We don't ... there's a sort of hierarchy there. I mean, we have money, of course, but not as much as them. They're a bunch of bitches to be honest!'

Mei's face remained neutral. Her statement was simply one of fact. But The Tree chuckled, caught a little off-guard by the refreshingly honest and matter-of-fact way that she spoke.

'And some of the teachers are weird!' she continued. 'The men are worse. They stare at the students. They think we don't notice ... but we do! Have you noticed men can be like that in this country? I don't like it. An old man tried to touch me when I was a little girl in Hong Kong.'

The Tree found itself harden. It was all too familiar with the way that people will try (and often succeed) in violating the boundaries and bodies of others, especially when they are vulnerable. It felt a protective surge swell within its trunk in anticipation what Mei would share next.

'But he didn't get very far. He tried to lift up my dress so I slapped his old haggard face. He then tried to grab me again, so I screamed. I screamed right in his face, and I slapped him again. I was only a little girl. I knew he was wrong, and I wasn't going to let him get close to me, or hurt me. It's the same here. People have always leered at me, so I confront them. I simply say in a very loud voice What are you staring at? Or You should be ashamed of yourself! They often turn red. And so they should. It's odd how people think it's okay to behave that way, don't you think?'

Mei looked very pleased with herself, a look of defiance and justice set in her expression. She was clearly someone who had learnt how to protect herself. But with a sad heart, The Tree sensed that the reason for this was because, so often, Mei had been left on her own to cope. She had learnt to survive simply because she had to. There was no one there to protect her.

'Don't you think?' she repeated again.

The Tree did think, and chuckled to itself again. Not because of how people had behaved towards Mei, but because of her responses. The Tree was starting to really like her. She had spirit. She had grit, and she reminded The Tree a little bit of its red-haired friend.

Mei seemed to know how to protect herself and The Tree could tell that she would not stand for anything – she recognised what was wrong and was not afraid to say so. The Tree respected her and knew that she would be a force to be reckoned with. It wanted to nurture this within her and make sure that she never lost what seemed to come so naturally to her.

'Good for you!' said The Tree. 'You're right. It's not okay for people to treat you that way. I'm pleased you slapped that man! You also said something about the teachers at your school, something about the way they look at you?'

'Hmmm, yes, them!' Mei rolled her eyes and tossed her hair. 'There is something strange about that place! Me and the girls, you know them, Sarah and Gemma, Lisa and Sal, Gill and Helen – my girls.'

The Tree smiled to itself again at Mei's assumption of what it knew about, and indeed who The Tree knew, and did not know. It could feel that this group of girls were like sisters to Mei, and that they were fiercely protective of each other.

'We all feel that there something wrong with the place. An atmosphere of ... of ... Oh I can't think of the word! It just feels ...' Her eyebrows knotted together in frustration as she tried to think.

Unsavoury ... dangerous ... predatory, thought The Tree, a feeling of concern spreading through its body.

'It holds a secret. It's like if the walls could speak, they would share unspeakable things. Things that have gone on for years, but things no one is allowed to speak of. The teachers give each other these creepy knowing looks, well, some of them do. And they act suspiciously! Thank God for Gary, the caretaker. We all love Gary the Caretaker! He's always there with his broom. Even when he's not sweeping anything up.' She laughed.

The Tree chuckled again at the way the caretakers name and occupation had become fused together.

'And who, may I ask, is Gary the Caretaker,' asked The Tree, fully anticipating a long and convoluted answer.

'Oh, he's our favourite,' she beamed. 'He's in his fifties, we think. And he's from the north. I sometimes can't understand him because of his accent. It's quite charming really. But he's very friendly, and earthy some would say. He is always around, watching ... oh, but not in a creepy way,' she said quickly, sensing the growing concern from The Tree.

'He doesn't speak much, but his face says it all! I don't think he likes the teachers. He often just appears, just at the right time, and gives the teachers, mostly the men, the most withering of looks.' She giggled to herself and screwed her face up in an attempt to mimic Gary the Caretaker's face.

'I think all the teachers are terrified of him, but we love him. He feels like a really pure soul, a bit like you! And my girls, my girls are pure souls too, of course!'

The Tree was flattered, and continued to marvel at the unashamedly honest way in which Mei spoke. A part of it did, however, feel suspicious of the man she was speaking about. After all, The Tree knew that sometimes people will disguise their true intentions through the mask of kindness when in fact they are weaving a web of deceit designed to exploit and hurt the very people they claim to care for. It hoped that this was not the case here, so The Tree allowed itself to briefly scan Mei's memories so it could experience what Mei had of this allegedly friendly man.

The view of the valley and hilltop quickly faded and gave way to a girls' locker room. From Mei's perspective, The Tree saw the door to the locker room slowly open … just by a few feet. And stood there, peering in, was a man in crisp shirt and tweed jacket. He looked young and was adjusting his grubby spectacles, which had begun to slide down his nose. He wore a lanyard and name badge, suggesting that he was staff. The Tree then heard a loud clearing of a man's throat, and saw the startled teacher jumping backwards whilst stammering a ludicrously convoluted reason for his being there. The last thing The Tree saw was the stern and withering look of the ruddy-faced grey-haired man holding a broom. The Tree deduced that this was Gary the Caretaker. As the door closed, The Tree heard the unmistakeable northern accent uttering some kind of threat towards the cowering teacher who scuttled off down the corridor like a frightened mouse. The Tree smiled to itself and was satisfied that Gary was indeed a trustworthy soul. In fact, like Mei, The Tree knew that it liked him very much.

The Tree's consciousness returned to the hilltop where it could hear Mei in full flow, speaking rapidly about something or other again

'—is what she said. Can you believe it? I couldn't! And I keep having these strange dreams. I bet you have interesting dreams living up here. My dreams just feel weird. I've had them since I came to live at the school when I moved from Hong Kong. Did I tell you that that's where I'm from?'

Without waiting for a response, she continued in her characteristic rapid manner.

'So, in the dream there's this cat. A beautiful black cat with silky fur. But she keeps meowing. I think she's lonely. But no one comes. She's been abandoned. I find her in this old rickety haunted house. It looks like its falling down. She meows and meows but won't let me near her. I can feel that she needs to be looked after, and that she wants this too. But she is scared, so she swipes her paws at me. She's not very old. Who would leave such a vulnerable creature all on their own?'

'I have this dream a lot. It's pretty much the same but the cat now lets me look after her. But she hisses at the shadows. There is something always in the shadows. I can't see what it is ... but she can. Her back arches and her fur stands on end as she hisses. She always leaps in front of me as though to protect me ... but from what? I can never make out what is hiding in the shadows.'

The Tree took a deep breath. It could tell that this was going to be a long day, but it sensed that there was more than meets the eye with this young woman, and her story. It sensed that the young woman was more vulnerable than she seemed, and the collapsing building that she spoke of in her dream may indeed be a representation of her own collapsing defences, perhaps she was much more exposed than she realised.

The Tree knew that dreams can be a window into the soul of a person. They can hide forgotten truths that the person themselves may not yet be ready to see or remember. It knew that aspects of the dream can be a manifestation of the different parts of the dreamer, including the parts that feel too frightening or forbidden to recognise. But it also knew that truths and instincts can be cloaked in the symbols of the dream.

Mei's dream both saddened and alarmed The Tree. It could sense Mei's loneliness and the unmistaken grief that accompanied the feeling of betrayal when one feels abandoned by one's family, but perhaps this was too much for Mei to consciously know, so perhaps she had to project these feelings onto the image of the silky black cat instead.

But The Tree could also sense a threat, a threat that on some level Mei knew was there, but did not quite have the words for yet. The Tree had its suspicions, but it was determined to give Mei the space that she needed to make sense of what she had experienced, and indeed why she had come to The Tree.

'Mei,' said The Tree softly, interrupting her flow, 'I sense that you have come to see me for a reason. What brings you here now, apart from the woman who died last year? If I may, I think there is something bothering you. Actually, I think there is something frightening you.'

Mei's eyes started to glisten with tears and her mouth trembled. 'I think something bad is going to happen to me!' she said in a soft whisper. 'My girls, they've all left the school for the summer. None of us are coming back. But I am the only student left in the school until this weekend. I have no choice but to stay because I've got nowhere else to go until then.'

'You're in the school completely on your own?' said The Tree, its concern growing.

'No, that is the problem. It's just me and some of the other teachers. And of course, the headmaster.'

Mei shuddered when she mentioned the headmaster, and The Tree felt a chill in its heart. What was it about this person in particular that evokes such a response in us both? thought The Tree.

'What about Gary the Caretaker? When does he leave the school?'

At this question, Mei burst into tears.

'They fired him. Last week, the headmaster fired him. They've been trying to do so for ages … I think because he sees everything. And knows so much – he's been there for years. And I think he may have reported some of the other teachers in the past, not that anything was done about it. But at least he tried. He's always been around when it's felt like something bad could happen, and thankfully, because he's always been there, nothing has. But now he's gone. And so have my girls – Sarah, Gemma, Lisa, Sal, Gill and Helen. My sisters have gone. I'm alone, again. I'm alone in that school … with him!'

The Tree could see how frightened Mei looked, and the threat that she believed she faced. With growing concern, The Tree braced itself.

'Please, Mei, I fear that we don't have much time. Tell me your story. I will help you!'

Mei nodded through her tears. And once again, a fog clouded The Tree's mind and took it away from the sweltering valley and back into Mei's memories.

II

The Tree found itself in a cable-car beholding a steep and jagged mountainside as it ascended higher and higher towards the monastery perched majestically at its peak. A befuddled wide-eyed ten-year-old girl stared up at her mother, ignoring the beautiful scenery as it whizzed by outside of the cable car windows.

'But I don't want to leave here. This is my favourite place to come. I won't leave here!'

The young girl's mother looked impatient and agitated, having anticipated this response.

'You have no choice. We go where your father's work takes us. You either come with us and make new friends, or we send you to a different school where you will live. These are your options!'

The little girl appeared not to have heard her mother. Or if she had, she was choosing to ignore her words. Instead, she turned away defiantly and stared out of the window. Her heart leapt and her eyes widened in excitement, apparently distracted by what she saw.

'There it is!' she cried and pointed excitedly out of the window.

As the cable-car continued its ascent, the enormous stone buddha came into view. A stunning statue that was only accessible by the hundreds of steps that led from the monastery and even higher up towards the mountains peak. Mei had seen this many times before, and had climbed the steps so she could rub the enormous buddha's belly for luck. But it never failed to amaze her. This was her favourite place to be, even when tourists flooded the place. But early mornings were her favourite because it was quiet and peaceful – she could imagine that she and the buddha were speaking with each other secretly. And this was lovely.

'You have seen it before, you silly girl!' her mother said sharply. 'Now answer my question, what do you want to do? Come with your father and I, or go to another school? Answer me this instant!'

A defiant Mei continued to ignore her mother, so enthralled was she by the beauty of the distant statue, and the sense of peace she felt every time she saw it. But something in her soul saddened. Her mother had brought her here deliberately. She knew in her heart that her mother had already made the decision for her, and that this was to be the last time she would come to the gigantic buddha. It would be the last time that she would race up the hundreds of stone steps, only to collapse exhausted at the foot of the statue. Never again would she walk through the lush green forest, following the famous Wisdom Path, or emerge on the mountainside where the white ornate columns rose into the sky, engraved with beautiful Chinese calligraphy from the Heart Sutra.

Mei loved the feel of the cold mountain air and the sight of the other hulking mountains and peaks that populated the valley, shrouded by swathes of fog. This was her home, and she loved it. On a clear day she could see all the way out to the glistening waters of the bay, and the myriad boats carrying tourists that would skate across the calm waters.

Mei did not want to leave. Nor will I, she thought angrily, making a secret pact with herself.

'MEI!' yelled her mother, before roughly turning her daughter's head so that she was forced to face her instead – and not the stunning scenery outside. Holding the sides of Mei's face firmly, she coldly demanded an answer. 'What … will … you … choose?'

Determined not to cry, Mei hardened her expression and held her mother's harsh and piercing gaze. She could not bear to be around this woman any longer. Her cruel words. Her violent slaps and outbursts. Her distinct indifference to Mei's hopes and dreams. Mei felt like an inconvenience to her mother. Her father was barely present, and even when he was, he too seemed cold and aloof to his daughter's presence. A part of her hated them, but also loved them and needed them. They were all that she knew. But she felt that her fate was sealed. And so, she replied with as much anger and defiance as she could muster.

'I choose the school … that way you can both be free of me. And I can be free of you!'

Mei forcefully pulled her face out of her mother's grip, tossed her hair, and turned back to cable car window, the ancient monastery now coming into sight. They were ready to disembark.

'Very well,' came her mother's steely voice, her eyes narrowing. But then with a slight smirk creeping on her lips, she added, 'You have made your choice. There will be no going back on this, no matter how much you cry in the end!' She turned from her daughter and said nothing further to her for the rest of the day.

III

A sleek black limousine pulled up outside of the cast iron railings that surrounded the school. A stunning sandstone building that looked like a castle – the central tower rising into the sky as the sunlight reflected off of its dazzling stained-glassed windows.

Mei was enthralled by the perfectly manicured lawn, the array of bright and colourful flowers that had been so carefully planted in the borders, and the perfectly sculpted trees and topiary that gave the gardens extra character. As did what appeared to be some form of war memorial. A stone statue of a man ... a solider, frozen in motion pointing ahead of him, seemingly running into danger.

Is that what I'm doing ... heading into danger? Thought the eleven-year old Mei.

'Oh, isn't this just perfect!' cried Mei's mother clapping her hands together in delight. Her father looked bored and uninterested, not bothering to suppress his yawn. He looked up at the school briefly, and then down at his expensive watch. Time was getting on.

Hmmm, yes, it is perfect, thought Mei. A little too perfect! And it was. The more she looked around, the more artificial the school looked. Yes, it was both grand and beautiful, as were the grounds. But something about it didn't feel right. It felt as though the school was trying too hard – too hard to be perfect. Too hard to prove to the world that it was a good place. But it looked so ... so ... Mei couldn't think of the word. And then it came to her. Unnatural. Mei felt herself shudder.

'The brighter the shine, the deeper the grime,' she said out loud, without thinking.

Her mother turned sharply towards her and scowled.

'You chose this. Remember?! We offered to take you with us, but you chose this!'

Mei could have sworn that she heard her mother mutter something like 'You ungrateful little brat,' under her breath. But her mother was no longer looking at her and instead peered through the railings in adoration again – waffling on about the wonders of the British boarding school system. Her mother seemed not just elated by the spectacle that was the castle-like school, but also at the prospect that she would be rid of her daughter for at least seven years.,

Mei looked at the hateful woman who raised her, and even though a part of her felt glad that she too would finally be rid of her, the crushing feeling of abandonment and grief still engulfed her soul. Tears formed in her eyes, but no, she would not permit herself to cry and prove her mother right. Instead, Mei took a deep breath, stood up straight and turned to her mother, and forced a smile.

'You are right, Mother, of course. This place is perfect. And I did indeed choose this. I think I will be very happy here!' she lied.

Her mother's smile widened but she did not turn to look at her daughter. Her father tapped his watch impatiently and beckoned for them to follow him through the imposing gates and into the grounds.

This was really happening. She was going in, and they were going away. In that moment, Mei's heart broke.

'What a curious smell,' Mei's mother said as they were led through the enormous arched wooden doors and into the echoing school. 'What is that? It smells a little like our monastery back in Hong Kong ... how comforting! Mei, dear, what does it smell like to you?'

'The stench of secrets,' she said suspiciously under her breath.

'WHAT?!' hissed her mother, her eyes narrowing in the familiar characteristic fashion.

'Nothing,' Mei said feebly. 'It just smells ancient.'

Her mother was no longer listening. She was eagerly dashing towards the headmaster, who was making his approach down the grand central staircase to greet them. Mei thought he looked like a tall lean snake, slithering down the staircase – his smile wide, teeth flashing, and eyes unblinking. He dressed like an old professor but with neatly combed hair, and a sharp and somewhat angular face, but also a certain charm and finesse that clearly seduced her mother. But not

Mei! She looked over at her father – another yawn and the continued expression of boredom and indifference.

The two men sharply contrasted. Not just because her father was Chinese but also in the energy they gave off. Both were powerful but one was cold, the other slippery. Her father didn't even seem to notice his wife giggling like a giddy schoolgirl as she spoke with the headmaster. Or perhaps he just simply did not care … about either of them.

The snakelike man slithered over to Mei and put his hands on her shoulder, that horrible grin spreading even more widely across his face. His eyes seemed to pierce her soul, and his hands felt disgustingly clammy.

The headmaster squeezed her shoulder a little more firmly than felt comfortable – but of course, neither of her parents noticed.

'Well now,' he said, his voice as slick as oil. 'Aren't you a pretty little thing!' The horrible leering smile grew even wider, revealing yellowing teeth and a foulness of breath that Mei could smell as his face inched closer to hers.

'Yes, a very pretty little thing indeed. You'll be right at home here. In fact, you can be my special little helper, if you like. Each year I select only the most well-behaved girls to be my special helpers. You aren't a naughty girl … are you, Mei?'

'Oh no, of course not!' said the stupid mother in her churlishly giddy voice.

'She is a very good girl and of course she would love to be your special little helper. Ask her to do anything and she will of course do as you say. Won't you, dear?!'

The last part sounded more like a threat than a question.

Mei looked into the cool and icy grey eyes of the man's leering face and then up at her mother. One final desperate plea from her own eyes, hoping that her mother would be astute enough to read the signs and muster some semblance of maternal instinct. But there was nothing. Her mother's face looked back at Mei menacingly, willing her daughter to obey whatever the headmaster demanded, without question.

Mei's father was looking at his watch again, his foot tapping impatiently on the immaculately clean stone floor.

Mei's heart sank. She had lost them. And now she was at the mercy of this strange and sinister old man. Despite her best efforts, the tears she had been fending off slid down her cheeks.

'Oh dear, now then,' said the headmaster, pulling an exaggeratedly sad face. It looked like the mask of tragedy that accompanied the mask of comedy. She'd seen these above the red curtains of so many theatres. His face sickened her.

'Don't be sad, darling. We will all take care of you here. We have excellent staff and facilities for all of you young girls. Before long you'll barely remember where you've come from, so happy and immersed you'll be in your new life!'

Again, there came the exaggerated smile of reassurance as he turned towards Mei's mother – who of course nodded approvingly.

'We have the nicest nurses and the kindest teachers, and the female staff will always be available if you need them. As will the men. But of course, not at night. At night it is only the female staff who are permitted in the girl's dormitory wing. Obviously!' He turned from Mei and towards her mother again, this time wearing a mask of sincerity.

Mei's mother mirrored his look of faux-sincerity and nodded along with him.

The headmaster then turned his back to her and gave Mei a long and hard stare, all emotion and expression seeming to disappear from his face. He licked his lips like a hungry wolf. And then, in a most uncharacteristic fashion, he knelt down before her, winked, and extended his arms outwards as if to embrace the now trembling and frozen eleven-year-old.

"SCUSE ME!' came a loud and somewhat brash voice.

A ruddy-faced man with a broom pushed between the headmaster and Mei, preventing the curiously timed hug from taking place, much to Mei's relief. The headmaster stumbled back from his kneeling position and glared at the caretaker. To Mei's astonishment, the caretaker glared back and gripped his broom even more tightly … so much so Mei could see his knuckles turning white.

The headmaster stood up and the two men were now face to face. It was clear that they did not like each other at all.

'Gary!' said the headmaster crisply. 'There is nothing for you to clean up here. Please be gone. I will request your services later in one of the other parts of the school. As I said, there is no filth to sweep up here!'

'Oh?' replied Gary the Caretaker, a slight smirk appearing at the edges of his mouth. 'I'm not so sure!'

He looked the headmaster up and down disapprovingly. His body then seemed to grow in size and stature as he squared up to the now furious looking headmaster.

A heavy silence fell between them for what felt like several minutes – neither of them breaking eye contact. Each one willing the other to die, Mei thought.

The headmaster relented. He cleared his throat and then backed away from Mei and the caretaker sheepishly.

Gary turned to the little girl, and with a friendly smile and a wink said, 'All right, lass?'

I am now, she thought to herself. Mei smiled and winked back at the kind and friendly man. She didn't reply to his greeting but in her heart, she felt relief, and for the first time in a long time, she felt safe.

Smiling back at her, Gary the Caretaker resumed his sweeping up of absolutely nothing at all, and made his way out of the entrance hall, but not before throwing a final and undisguised scowl in the direction of the unnerved headmaster, and, Mei suspected, at the two adults abandoning their child in a school that clearly was not safe for children.

As The Tree witnessed the memories that Mei was sharing, an overwhelming swell of compassion, care, and desire to protect her surged through it. Any hints of agitation or irritation that it felt when Mei first interrupted its sleep had completely evaporated, especially now having witnessed the unkind and dismissive way in which her parents had treated her ... and the unsavoury predatory energy that emanated from the headmaster. It felt even more determined in the present to help the eighteen-year-old girl. By whatever means necessary!

The Tree was astonished that such a young child could be left in a place without her parents, without anyone to really understand or soothe her fear or distress. It was saddened to know that in order to survive, so many children will find ways to deny what they really think and feel, a desperate attempt to make the intolerable tolerable. It knew that children can be made to feel ashamed of their emotions in such environment as these, and that punishment and shame could come from both those in authority but also from one's peers when one does not conform.

Already, The Tree could sense the messages that Mei had internalised about her worth and that the very people whom she relied upon for her survival were also the sources of her greatest terror and discomfort. Thankfully, The Tree saw that she was discerning with her trust, and less easily hoodwinked than her mother. It was glad that she had found 'her girls', an unending source of love and support for her.

But The Tree felt angry towards Mei's parents – anger towards their indifference and their apparent naivety to the danger that they were placing their child in under the guise of the eleven-year-old child having made 'a choice'. As far as The Tree understood, the poor child had no choice but to choose the lesser of two evils, but it was unsure whether or not the school really was the lesser of two evils. Or if Mei had been abandoned in a new form of hell. Either way, she had needed her parents to protect her. But they had not. They had betrayed her. And Mei, a mere child, had been left to fend off of the wolves ... alone!

IV

In another memory, The Tree watched with fondness as Mei and her group of girls laughed together in the school courtyard whilst eating their lunch. She had formed a solid friendship group and seemed less frightened and alone in comparison with the day that she arrived.

It was a sunny day, which made the school gardens look even more beautiful, but still alarmingly perfect. The group of girls hushed when five fellow students could be seen walking from the main school doors towards the available table in the courtyard. Hushed whispers were exchanged between Mei and her friends as they glanced over at the 'The Elles', so named because of the first letters of their names.

Lucy, Lydia, Lisa, Lilly, and Lexi walked like they owned the school and treated everyone else as though they were their subordinates, a particularly cruel quintet of girls who seemed to have targeted Mei for no reason other than her kindness and her intelligence. The Tree did not like these girls and was astonished that five people could emit such hostility, envy, and cruelty for ones so young.

The Tree observed with curiosity the manner in which they smugly dismissed and criticised everyone outside of their small quintet, and the shocking ways in which the teachers seemed to praise and endorse these behaviours. The Tree could tell that the five girls were extremely wealthy from the clothes and jewellery they wore, but also the sense of entitlement and superiority that seemed to ooze from their souls.

From its years of existence, and from all the tales it had heard throughout its life, The Tree knew that the sad and uncomfortable truth is that children can be cruel. It knew that there are many reasons why but this does not detract from the fact that the harmful behaviours that some children and young people can act out can cause deep pain, fear, and snuff out the light of another person's happiness.

Over the years of its life, and especially when recalling the stories of Sergio and Christoph, The Tree had seen that bullying can leave children feeling depressed, lonely, frightened, confused, hated, worthless, and ashamed – feelings that can and often are carried with the child throughout their life. The Tree looked on with sadness, hoping that the same fate would not befall Mei, or indeed the other vulnerable girls who had been left in this school. But its own soul ached as it observed Mei's memories. A tremble in its very own core had now become a furious rumble – it knew it had less patience and less understanding for cruelty. And the desire to protect now burned as fiercely as the sun.

As The Tree watched Mei traverse her school experience, it realised that it wasn't just the teachers that she had to be wary of. The students also seemed to be equally infected by the strange secrets and wickedness that the building contained. The school environment was saturated with envy and spoiling ... and not just between the students.

Students envied the power and authority that they themselves lacked but perceived the teachers to have, and as such would construct elaborate schemes to disrupt lessons and evoke feelings of despair and inadequacy in the teachers. Teachers would envy the opportunities and popularity of certain students and would take secret pleasure in the public ways in which they could humiliate them in front of their peers, thereby reclaiming a sense of power and triumph to satiate their own latent insecurities.

The Tree observed with despondency how students with neurodivergence were bullied by the students with behavioural problems – the girls found it unfair that 'those kids' got all the support from teachers because of their struggles, whereas they themselves were ignored or excluded. These angry girls received much less compassion and support from teachers and were deemed 'problematic' or 'unruly' ... and therefore not worth the investment or consideration from the teachers, despite their own internal struggles.

The Tree was dismayed at the rampant bigotry that played out in the secluded school. It saw how the girls who were exploring their sexuality or those who were even 'out and proud' would be tormented by their peers. It also saw the shame and denial in those who were questioning their own identity – these feelings being deeply frightening and forbidden, so much so that this part would need to be denied, split off, and even projected onto others so that the hated part of self could be attacked and destroyed.

The homophobic students found ways to torment the lesbian and bi students during and after their classes, especially when these activities were perceived to give the girls a sense of achieving and enjoyment. Spaces that once felt safe and a source of joy would quickly become spoilt and associated with fear. The girls who were perhaps in denial about their own latent sexual curiosity seemed to deny these forbidden parts of self – parts of self that would inevitably result in violence, rejection, and shame from their volatile or heavily religious parents.

In one such scene, The Tree saw the conflict within one of 'The Elles' (Lydia) as she caught herself glancing at Mei's friend Gemma – one of the openly lesbian students – in the shower and feeling desire, but also shame about these feelings. These were quickly defended against with denial and anger but also projection. Lydia accused Gemma of staring at her, and vehemently requested that Gemma not be allowed in the changing rooms with the other girls ... for their safety, of course. The teachers unquestioningly obliged. Gemma was also given detention for a month for no good reason at all.

Mei defended her friend both against the teachers but also when other girls would physically attack Gemma at night, but also openly in the oppressive and empty corridors during the day. The Tree sadly knew that the aggression towards Gemma was born from envy, because of how free she must feel to be so open and happy at school. But The Tree also witnessed Lydia's resentment – that Gemma could be herself and be loved by her friends unconditionally, whereas she herself could not. The Tree saw that this evoked a sense of grief. Lydia would never have what Mei and her friends had, so she cruelly sought to take it from them.

Again, The Tree watched as the athletically gifted girls shamed and humiliated the academically gifted students in the common room or demonstrated physical 'superiority' by behaving in an aggressive and threatening manner. But equally, The Tree observed the assertive and academically gifted girls like Sal and Helen, who created subtle ways to deface the school sports trophy cabinet and humiliate their peers in academic competitions and other contexts of aptitude.

The Tree witnessed with sorrow how the seemingly 'popular' girls who felt obliged to conform and maintain a sense of homogeneity would envy and bully the girls like Sarah and Gill who appeared more alternative, confident, and proud in their appearance. They were less conforming to school and societal expectations, and as such, they felt freer. The Tree knew that those who are perceived to be without envy will sadly become the targets of attack by those who are consumed by it.

'The Elles' were perceived by Mei and her friends as envious because of their own secret wishes to explore the parts of themselves that they feared would never be accepted by their own 'stuck-up' group. But in turn, Mei and her friends found ways to mock their bullies and find ways to degrade and diminish the perceived power and influence that these allegedly 'popular' girls had, whilst they themselves secretly longed to fit in. The Tree knew that everyone carries their own demons, and everyone simply wants to be loved and accepted for who they are.

From The Tree's ever-growing insight and learning, it could tell that the students who were unhappy at home would hate and envy the students who were happy in school. The students who struggled financially would loath and covet the perceived privilege of the wealthier students, sometimes resorting to vandalism and theft of their property both at school and in the dormitory. The wealthy girl whose family was cold, distant and unavailable envied the love and care that their less financially comfortable peers enjoyed. And in some cases, they would concoct cruel ways to ostracise these girls – turning their own group against them so that they too could experience loneliness and abandonment that they themselves knew all too well.

The Tree watched with powerless anger as 'The Elles' would mock Mei in class whenever she spoke out. They would place their fingers to the corners of their eyes and stretch them horizontally whilst speaking in a nonsensical and mocking Chinese accent, much to the delight of the other laughing girls in the class. The teacher did nothing except smirk in her silence.

Mei's girls did not laugh and would gather in solidarity with their friend, but the impact on Mei was evident. She raised her hand less. She spoke out less. She did whatever it took to not draw attention to herself and to hide her shine, a trick that she had learnt from living with her mother for the first eleven years of her life.

However, The Tree did find itself smiling triumphantly when one lunchtime, 'The Elles' engaged in their typically horrendous and racist behaviour towards another girl, which finally roused such anger in Mei – an anger that, again, she knew from her mother. She yanked the girl's hair and then slapped her face so hard that they both fell to the ground. For the rest of that afternoon 'the smug bitches', as Mei had called them, were a little less smug. After all, it was difficult to be superior when one had a red-raw handprint on one's face for the remainder of the day, and a tuft of hair missing.

These wars continued throughout the girls' adolescence. No one seemed to be safe. The Tree lamented the demise of these girls who were fighting for their survival but turned on each other like a pack of animals. The Tree saw that the school corridors, the courtyard and even the dormitories became a frenzied feeding ground – the perfect storm where students could harass, torment, and abuse each other. But no parents, or any adult, would ever come to the rescue of these children. They were alone.

One of 'The Elles' (Lilly) had become the recipient of unwanted sexual attention from a boy in the neighbouring school, and subsequently found herself at the centre of the online rumour mill.

This particular 'Elle' also envied her pretty, quiet, and less visible friend Lisa, who had a seemingly 'perfect' reputation and was definitely the kinder of the quintet. As such, Lilly found herself becoming an aggressor towards her friend, proving that no one in the school was safe – not even if you were part of the in-crowd. The Tree knew that she had targeted Lisa to deflect the unwanted focus from herself, and to be rid of the feelings of shame and fear that she had been left carrying because of the original rumours created about her.

The Tree was enraged as it witnessed the photographs in the locker room distributed by the spiteful Lilly in secret, and the cruel and sexualised slurs about Lisa that found their way on to her social media account and on the bathroom walls. This of course then fuelled rumours about the 'perfect' (now not so perfect) student Lisa. And thanks to the wickedness of her alleged friend, Lisa's reputation was both tarnished and in tatters. She was now an outcast, feeling ashamed, defiled, and as objectified as her cruel friend had been made to feel ... except Lisa was now the scapegoat.

All hope was not lost for this group of struggling teenage girls though. The Tree observed with love and pride how Mei extended the hand of friendship to Lisa, who was quickly absorbed into their group. The Tree marvelled how Mei's kindness, and indeed the kindness of her group, seemed to nourish the soul of the ex-'Elle', prompting her to apologise for her past behaviours and actively make attempts at reparation, not just to Mei and her friends, but also towards the other girls in the school whom her previous group had tormented.

The Tree had faith once more that with the right people and the right environment, anyone can change. The Tree knew that it is not important for people to be perfect as such a state does not exist. Nor do they have to get it right all the time. But what can be both healing and nourishing is the capacity to recognise when a mistake has been made, to take ownership of the harm that has been caused (irrespective of the intention), and to actively make attempts to learn and grow from the experience – to ultimately do something different next time.

The Tree knew that Lisa was not a bad person, but she had been surrounded by unkind people, and sadly she had adapted in the only way she knew how to survive. Tragically, this was the case with so many of the girls who attended that particular school ... kill or be killed!

What a deeply sad and tragic tale, thought The Tree to itself.

V

'And that was just day-to-day life,' said Mei, bringing The Tree's consciousness back to the sweltering heat of the hilltop.

She looked up at The Tree, wide-eyed and expectant, waiting to make sure it was fully back with her. And then she continued.

'I know it looks bad, and yes, to be fair it was, but at least it was out in the open. Every day felt like a battle, but at least it was a battle that we knew, and could sometimes win. 'The Elles' could be bitches, but to be fair, so were we at times. I think that place does something to you. It makes you mean. But I think we had to all be mean so we could survive.'

The Tree nodded. It understood perfectly.

'The hardest battles, and I think the most unnerving, came from the threats that we couldn't see. We could feel it, all my girls could feel it. Even the girls we hated could feel it. In some ways it was these threats that brought us all together. Even if only for a short time! But there was an underlying fear that something, or someone, could get us. And sometimes it did. So many girls over the last seven years have left, or just disappeared without any warning or contact afterwards. It's horrible!'

'Disappeared?' said The Tree, a sickening chill spreading through its trunk.

How could children disappear from a school ... and no one notice? The Tree thought to itself, feeling deeply alarmed.

'So there has always been talk amongst the older girls – mostly whispers – when one of the teachers seems to take a particular interest in a student. And then they would disappear.'

'What do you think?' the older girls would whisper after class. 'Pregnant at seventeen ... or never to be heard from again?' This would often be accompanied by giggling from the older girls ...

'But I wasn't laughing. No, I was not! I wanted to know what they meant, but of course they never told me. They were of course faaaaar to busy and important to be bothering with a first year like me.' She rolled her eyes in the air and then tossed her hair. 'It wasn't until we got older that me and the girls – Sarah and Gemma and ...'

'Yes, yes,' The Tree said a little impatiently. But then catching itself added more kindly, 'Your girls. The ones whom you regard as sisters. Yes, I know them now.'

Mei beamed. 'Yes!' she said with a giggle. 'My family of girls!'

'Anyway,' she continued, 'so the girls and I noticed that Amanda – she was head girl – started to change. It was so strange but also quite subtle, it was a gradual change, sort of like an erosion to her soul.'

'Like a drop of water on a rock,' said The Tree. 'At first the water makes no impact and on its own it looks unlikely that it ever will, but when the drops are constant over time, they leave a deep and painful hole.'

'Yes, that's it!' she exclaimed. 'By the end of the year it was like there was nothing left of her. Like all of her personally had been lost. She even looked different – more pale, more fragile, definitely more vulnerable. She was always quite bossy. Assertive and confident – you knew where you stood with her. She had quite a hard edge at times, but not nasty, not like 'The Elles'. But she seemed nice. She was older than us so we never saw her in class but it was during break time and in the evenings. She became more withdrawn. She stopped taking care of herself. Even in our uniforms she still managed to look glamorous, but not that year. She just looked worn down.'

The Tree caught fleeting images of Amanda, stumbling over her words in class – other girls laughing at her and whispering that she must be 'on something'. It saw her feeble attempts at order and control as she attempted to maintain her head girl duties, only to be ignored or ridiculed. It saw her woozy expression and fainting fits in the corridors but also the trembling at night – outright panic attacks when the lights were tuned out. It saw her sleep-walking down cold dimly lit stone corridors, and the mornings of endless vomiting even before she had had breakfast.

What on earth has befallen this poor girl? thought The Tree.

'And then she disappeared! We all knew, of course, that she would be leaving for university after the summer break. And she was of course predicted the highest grades, but no one heard from her again. Not any of the girls who left the same year as she (allegedly) did. Nor any of the younger girls who were her friends. It's like she just vanished. The teachers knew nothing. Well, they said that they didn't know anything and that we were all getting ourselves "whipped up into a frenzy about nothing". What they did say was that she had problems – absent parents, something about drug use and the "apple not falling too far from the tree". But it all felt suspicious. It just felt like lies. But for there to be nothing?! No one ever saw or heard from her again after that summer … It just didn't make sense!'

Mei looked tense and exhaled deeply, blowing some errant strands of hair from her face – hair which she then tossed again. 'You believe me … don't you?'

'Of course, I believe you,' said The Tree earnestly. 'From the moment you have spoken to me about that place I felt that there was something wrong. You are not imagining things, my dear. I can assure you!'

'Oh thank you,' she said and wrapped her arms around The Tree. 'I knew you would understand. That's good, because there is more. It wasn't just Amanda! We saw similar things happen to other girls. Every year. And always girls who were in their final year. After Amanda, I remember Beth. She was pretty, blonde and again one of the more intelligent girls, but she also had a thing for bad boys from the other school. People say that one of the guys got her hooked on drugs which is why she started to look strung out all the time. But we (me and the girls) think that's a lie. Sure, she liked to party, we all did when we got the chance, and especially when we got to her age, but I remember hearing the whispers about her. She was also a prime target. Her parents were separated and never kept in contact with her, And certainly not with each other. It's like we've all got similar stories. Dumped here and forgotten about.'

Easy prey, thought The Tree cynically.

'Everyone knew that Beth spent her Friday nights in the library. And she would always come back to the dorms looking victorious. But in that final year, there was talk of her coming back to the darkened dorm room later and later. Sometimes her clothes would be torn. Other times she had bruises. Some of the girls said they saw these things in the locker room. Other times they said she came back mumbling incoherently. And of course, there were the night terrors, apparently the girls would be woken up to her screams convinced someone was in the room with them. There wasn't, but something seemed to be haunting that girl's sleep. Some people reported it but again, the same tale was told: "mixing with the wrong crowd"; "pressure of academic perfection getting to her"; "a troubled childhood" et cetera, et cetera! And then she disappeared, just before graduation. The teachers stood up in assembly and said something about ill-health and her parents returning to collect her in the night, checking her into some clinic. But of course, that was a lie. Her parents were never present in her life throughout the entirety of her schooling. And they certainly didn't sound like the type to band together to stage an intervention!'

The Tree was deeply troubled. It could hear that a pattern was emerging. That lonely, vulnerable and isolated girls seemed to be going missing, and no one was protecting them. The Tree tried to remain hopeful but from its time on the earth so far it knew that the people who have wickedness in their hearts will strategically position themselves in environments where they can prey on the weak and vulnerable. The Tree knew the subtle ways in which these people can groom and coerce children into a false sense of safety whilst slowly and systematically eroding their souls for their own sadistic pleasure.

The Tree felt fiercely protective towards Mei, and indeed all the girls in this school. It knew that so many schools can be a sanctuary for children, especially when their home lives were frightening, but this school was not a sanctuary. It was a prison. And a breeding ground for something deeply dark and sinister.

Mei was staring up at The Tree again in that same sweet, wide-eyed and expectant way.

'Did you hear what I said?'

The Tree hadn't. It was lost in thought and concerned for Mei's safety.

Apologetically The Tree bowed and admitted its fears. It knew that there may be a part of Mei that was too afraid to see the truth of her circumstances. That her defences had been so carefully cultivated to tolerate the intolerable that she could not see the possible horror that was happening all around her ... and could still happen to her.

222

'Trust me, I know!' she said, reading The Tree's mind. 'Especially when they got to Natalie. To be fair we hated her, she was a typical mean girl. Popular, opinionated, had the whole school under her spell. She was even crueller than 'The Elles' but one of the most gifted musicians the school had ever seen. That's why she got away with everything, until her final year when she was clearly … um, what's the word? Oh yes … "selected". She was selected. And gosh, did she fall hard! Under normal circumstances I would've been happy to see that bitch fall from grace, but this was just horrible. They humiliated her. The teachers taunted her in class when she couldn't perform. They even encouraged the other students who started it. People laughed and booed her off stage during recitals. Sometimes she could barely even hold her violin. The crash of it on the stage was sickening. So were the roars of laughter.'

The Tree winced in horror at the cruelty of these people. A reflection on what can happen when children are abandoned, and in some cases left to find for themselves, thought The Tree sadly to itself.

'And then there was the pregnancy. I mean they never admitted to it, but we could all tell. I mean, we're not idiots! One day she was pregnant – and obviously showing – and then she wasn't. Her body returned to its normal size, but she looked like a ghost. And then just before the end of term she went missing. But she didn't disappear. One of the girls found her in the forest. She had taken an overdose and was found in the morning … dead. It was horrible! There was a funeral, but of course no relatives. Another abandoned girl! She took her secrets, and the secrets of this school, to her grave!'

Mei fell silent, the disturbing memory swimming in her mind.

The Tree too was silent, contemplating all that it had heard. It was not convinced that Natalie had done this to herself, but if she had done so, the sadness and desperation of this final act chilled The Tree to its core.

What must that poor girl have been left holding that meant she had no other choice but to take her own life, if indeed she had done so. And where were her family? Where were her friends? How could such a devastating tragedy even happen?

The Tree was outraged.

'And that brings me finally to Patsy, our beloved Patsy. She was my friend. Well, she was everyone's friend but she was always a good friend to me. Especially when my parents died …'

The Tree's branches tensed. 'Your parents … they are dead?' whispered The Tree, shocked by the matter-of-fact way in which Mei had shared this information.

'Yes,' she replied with the same emotional detachment. 'He died of a heart attack, which is ironic considering I didn't think he even had one.'

The Tree tried to suppress a giggle at her dark humour. She too smiled fleetingly and then became serious again.

'And she … that woman … she found a new and very rich husband. They were married within a couple of months, and I haven't heard from her since. She may be dead. Or she may not be … but she is dead to me!'

'I'm so sorry,' said The Tree sadly. 'I am sorry for who they were … I'm sorry for the appalling way that they treated you. And I'm sorry that they will never be the parents you needed them to be. And if I may, I can honestly say that they did not deserve you. You deserved better!'

Mei stared up at The Tree and tried to keep her expression passive. Her eyes betrayed her feelings, though. Tears formed, which she attempted to conceal with a flick of her hair and by turning her head away.

'Thank you,' she whispered. 'I know!'

Mei cleared her throat and shook her arms, trying to disperse the mounting emotion that she and tried so hard to suppress.

'So, as I was saying,' her voice trembling a little. 'Patsy was kind to me. She had lost both of her parents in childhood and had been raised by her grandparents. They died whilst she was at school here. So, she knew … she knew how it felt and helped me to make sense of why I felt so conflicted. How I could love and hate my parents simultaneously. And why I would blame myself for their actions, all because I needed them to be good. I hoped they would be good. But if they were good, I started to believe that maybe I was the bad one. I know now that I'm not. Patsy helped me to see this. She taught me to paint, and we would sit for hours just painting, and singing, and talking, or sometime just being with each other in silence. But she was solid, and wise, and unthinkably kind. I never felt alone when I was with her. I always felt safe.'

The Tree softened its branches and gently placed them around Mei as her shoulders began to shake, and tears flooded from her eyes amidst the silent sobs.

'But then it happened to her. It started with the dreams. Dreams that terrified her. Of people in masks, of a sense of threat lurking in the shadows. Of dark dungeon-like rooms. And missing time, she told me that she was sleepwalking and would find herself in strange and unfamiliar parts of the school. She told me of how she couldn't concentrate enough to paint, that her mind felt fuzzy all the time. And even her speech. She would come to class slurring in the mornings. And at night, we couldn't find her. She would always turn up sooner or later but when she did, she seemed drunk and confused. Oh God, it was so horrible.'

'I felt like she was trying to tell me something in those last few months, but I could barely understand her. She could barely think, let alone tell me what was happening. She made me go to the school nurse with her. She felt like something wasn't right ... down there. Patsy could barely focus, but I could. I saw the look in that nurse's eyes when she said everything was fine. But that look told me something different. I knew she was lying. And I told her so. I was given detention for a week and banned from speaking to Patsy again. They said I was envious of her and trying to corrupt her. That I was filling her head with "lies from my own sick fantasies", they said!'

'In Patsy's final few weeks of exams, her beautiful clothes and her artwork was shredded or defaced. Again, the teacher blamed her ... blamed the stress ... blamed other students. But it felt like someone was tormenting her, and not one of the students. Me and the girls said that the teachers were playing with her mind, which is sick, I know! She barely graduated, but such a spectacle was made of her when she collected her certificate. It was as though the teachers wanted us to see her. They made us all wave goodbye to her on the final day of term, this poor shell of a girl that they carted off in a stupidly pretentious limousine. As one of the teachers drove her away, they said that her new life by the coast would "bring her back to the old Patsy – that a fresh start would be just what she needed, just the tonic", or some such rubbish. And of course, none of us ever saw or heard from her again. For all we know they tipped her off the edge of a cliff of the stupid coastal town she was allegedly going to.'

The air seemed thick and still. Tension hummed in the air. The Tree felt like it was holding its breath. It noticed that Mei was doing the same ... and so too was the valley.

Mei's body was eerily still, except her hands were now trembling. The Tree could feel its heart rate quickening, as was Mei's. She moved her lips to speak but before she could do so, The Tree's heart sank with sorrow and despair. It knew what Mei was going to say.

The whole valley seemed immobilised. Not a single tree stirred. No leaves fell. No birds sang. No bees buzzed. Just a heavy and foreboding silence.

'I'm next,' she whispered. 'I've been sleep-walking .... My memory is all fuzzy. And the dreams. I've been having... the dreams!'

VI

The Tree felt sick in its soul. It could see the growing terror that overcame this poor orphaned girl. As it peered into her mind, it caught fragmented scenes. Incoherent narratives of strange and fractured situations. The Tree saw leering faces in the dark. It saw hands groping in the night-time. It saw Mei, confused and disorientated, wandering the school halls at night, alone and bewildered. It saw the headmaster's face throughout the years ... and the close eye that he seemed to keep on Mei throughout her life. It saw the arm that we would place around her shoulders when she was sad and the way he pulled her close – a little too close – to him in the guise of comfort. It read the invitations for private tutorials with the headmaster, because only he had 'the knowledge and skill to better Mei's education'.

And throughout the years, The Tree glimpsed with relief Gary the Caretaker. His well-timed and by no means accidental presence irritating the headmaster, and indeed many of the other teachers when they appeared to be engaging in less than salubrious behaviours towards the girls.

The Tree saw the caretaker being reprimanded and threatened behind semi-closed doors but also the indignant and sturdy response of the man who whispered threats under his breath, causing the headmaster to cower. It saw a triumphant Gary when the police questioned the headmaster, only to see the dismay and disappointment in his, and indeed the students' faces, as smiling police officers left the building amidst handshakes with the staff, and disdainful looks at the caretaker and the students.

Desperately trying not to, The Tree witnessed more recent memories. The caretaker being marched off the premises, much to the distress of Mei and her friends. It saw the smug and victorious exchanges between the teachers having rid themselves of the pest that seemed to thwart their every move. It watched Mei tearfully say goodbye to her girls as they left for summer break and either travel back home or to the location of the prospective university.

The Tree felt alone. It felt frightened. It felt dread. Mei was alone, with them, and anything could happen. And no one would be around to save her.

'I've not eaten for days,' Mei said suddenly.

And The Tree could now see this. From its grumpy morning haze, and the incessant barrage of questions before it had truly come back to itself, The Tree hadn't noticed just how thin the young woman was. It hadn't seen the truth of what this young woman had been holding, but The Tree knew that people can hide their truths. Both from others but also from themselves. The Tree could now see the true Mei before him – a brave but equally frightened girl who had been abandoned, who was alone, and who was desperately in need of help. The Tree could now see beyond the words of this young woman's narrative, and instead could feel her pain, her desperation, and ultimately, her need to survive.

'I think that's how they do it. In the food? They must be putting something in the food. Or in the drinks. That's why I'm not eating, and why I had to get away. They must've done that with the other girls. And now they are doing it to me ...'

Her voice trailed off.

'I came to you for help, because I heard that the dead woman they found last year was stalking someone. An actress, or something. I wondered ... actually, no, I hoped that maybe you had something to do with that, that maybe you had protected the actress. And maybe ...' she paused, her wide eyes beginning to glisten again. 'Maybe you could protect me?'

The Tree's heart broke. It would do anything for the kind sweet soul staring hopefully at it. No matter what it took, The Tree knew in its soul that it had to do something, it had to intervene. It could not ... no, it would not stand by and do nothing.

A part of The Tree felt conflicted though. Its role thus far had not been to act with vengeance. Last year was indeed an anomaly, but it justified its actions (or inaction) when it came to not saving Elizabeth's stalker as being a service to the wider world, but most importantly, it cared deeply for its beloved red-haired actress.

In the short time of knowing her, The Tree had come to care for Mei. The Tree knew that it could not just let fate take its course. It feared that Mei's fate would be similar, if not worse, than the missing girl's ... so it decided that it would act. And if necessary, it would act with force!

'I need to tell you about my dreams!'

Mei's voice sounded urgent and broke the concentration of The Tree, bringing it back to the desperate young woman on the grass – her narrative becoming even faster than normal.

'They don't feel like ordinary dreams. There is something, wrong. When I wake up everything is foggy still, just like in the dreams. It's like I'm seeing everything through a veil. Strange figures, maybe in robes, but there's definitely more than one person there. I feel afraid but then I'm sleepy. Sometimes I feel nice in the dream ... you know, aroused?'

She had the last part quietly and a faint blush came to her cheeks.

'It's okay,' replied The Tree kindly and gently. 'There is nothing to feel ashamed about. Bodies will respond in all sorts of ways, irrespective of dreams, fantasies, or events in real life, it is an automatic response that you are not in control of!'

Mei nodded gratefully and continued. 'Okay then, if I'm being completely honest, it sometimes feels euphoric, like the feeling of pleasure is magnified. How on earth is my brain able to do that? And then when I finally wake up, I feel groggy. Sometimes I'm in a different place, and I have no idea how I got there.' She began to cry. 'And then there are the bruises,' she continued through her sobs.

'What bruises?' asked The Tree tentatively. Alarmed – and with its own pulse quickening – The Tree knew where this was going. And again, its heart sank. It anticipated the location of these bruises. And there they were. Mei pulled back the sleeves of her shirt to reveal faded pale purple and yellow rings around both of her wrists. And then she pulled the sleeve back further revealing her elbow and forearm.

Just as The Tree feared, there was an injection wound on the site of her brachial artery where yet another ugly bruise had formed. Whoever had done this was clearly getting careless and was no longer concerned about stealth.

The Tree wept silently in its soul. It knew that Mei was being drugged. And that her dreams were not dreams after all but fractured fragments of memory from some form of drug-induced horror. It did not know how much of the truth Mei knew, nor how much of the truth she could handle. The Tree felt conflicted and was cautious not to terrify the young woman further, nor place thoughts or memories in her mind based on assumption rather than fact. However, what was clear was that she was suffering from something that had been done to her – whatever that something may be – and that she was not responsible for it. The Tree knew what these people were doing to her, and it disgusted The Tree. It made it feel rageful – vengeful, even. And so, it harkened back to its original thought. It silent vowed again to protect Mei. By whatever means necessary!

'Do you think it's a dream?' asked Mei, her voice sounding fragile and childlike.

The Tree could feel itself wilting. It could not bring itself to speak. So instead, it slowly shook its powerful branches gently from side to side.

Mei's face crumpled but through her tears she gathered herself and looked resolute.

'I didn't think so,' she whispered. 'But I don't have proper memories. Everything seems weird and hazy.'

'Perhaps that is necessary,' said The Tree softly. 'We don't always need to remember to be able to heal. If your mind is protecting you, let it do so for now.'

The Tree knew that memories will only return as and when it is safe to do so. That Mei's psyche was trying to spare her the pain of recalling the abuse that she – and no doubt the other girls in the school – had been subjected to. If and when the time was right, she would be able to process these memories, if indeed they returned. But for now, The Tree knew that its priority was Mei's safety –

helping her to survive the remaining days in that hateful school. Remembering the details of what had happened to her was not going to help her right now. But empowering her to find the strength to fight and escape was.

'Never again!' said Mei. 'I hate my parents for leaving me here. I hate the teachers for what they have done to me, and I hate them even more for what they have done to all those other girls!' The tears stopped and her face hardened. 'NEVER AGAIN!!!' she screamed.

The Tree mirrored its young charge. It pulled itself upwards – stretching its branches into the now cooler air. It mustered a loud rumble from its soul in solidarity for Mei and felt a surge of power rising, and channelling into one of its silver branches.

The Tree knew what it must do.

As if echoing The Tree's fury, a deep rumble of thunder echoed across the valley and dark heavy storm clouds began to form over the hilltop. Mei could feel the power of the electrical charge in the air, and small strands of her hair began to separate and lift, now crackling with the hum of electricity that filled the air. Her breathing became faster, as did The Tree's.

With another roar that broke free from The Tree's soul, there came a ferocious thunderclap and a blinding flash of lightning. The pink and purple particles of light ripped through the dramatic plum-coloured sky and struck The Tree in a dazzling flash. The air broke, and with it came the refreshing deluge of rain that the long hot day had begged for. A cool sweetness filled the air, and as the rain fell, Mei sheltered under the canopy of branches.

With a final roar, The Tree twisted its now fully charged and crackling silver branch, severing it from its mighty trunk. The glowing rod fell into Mei's outstretched arms, humming with power and electricity. She looked down at it in amazement, her eyes mirroring back the faint traces of lightning that now pulsed through the branch like tiny glowing veins. As Mei looked down, she knew that in her hands she held a mighty weapon … the gift of protection from The Tree.

Mei started to thank The Tree but she could see that something was wrong. She dropped the branch and put both her hand on The Tree's trunk. She could barely feel its soul. And it had stopped speaking to her. The Tree was still.

Hours passed. The rain began to ease into a fine drizzle and the dark clouds soon gave way to dusky orange sunlight and a golden sky laced with shades of lilac and rose. The powerful summer sun was starting to set, and Mei knew that she would have to begin her journey back to the school. Alone. But for the first time in a long while, she did not feel afraid. She was armed. And dangerous, she thought to herself. They should be afraid of me!

'They will be,' came the rasping whisper of The Tree, reading her mind as it slowly came back into consciousness. 'They will be!' The Tree said again, more firmly. 'The branch will come to life at the moment you need it most. But only then will I be able to connect to it! So please,' implored The Tree, 'do not let it out of your sight!'

Mei said nothing but nodded obediently. Mei gathered herself, and preparing to leave she rolled the sleaves of her top back down to cover her bruised wrists, but then thought better of it. She would not hide what they had done to her. No! She would leave this place armed with the gift from The Tree – a powerful weapon – and she would do whatever it took to survive.

'I'll come back,' she called to The Tree, as she made her way across the stone circle towards the edge of the hill.

I hope so, thought The Tree desperately.

The Tree bid her farewell and whispered a final 'Happy birthday!' under its breath, but this felt hollow and pointless given everything it knew of Mei's past, and indeed, the uncertain future that lay ahead of her.

The Tree felt uneasy – it feared that this would be the last time that the girl would ever brave the hill and seek refuge under its branches.

Sadly, The Tree was right.

VII

The Tree endured a deeply unpleasant week. Not only did the suffocating heat return after the small storm, but the mugginess added to its agitation ... and its fear for Mei's safety. It still felt connected to the silver weapon that it had fashioned for Mei and knew that it had not been used as yet. But this only added to The Tree's concern.

What if Mei had lost it? What if someone had taken it from her? What if she was hurt?!

The Tree felt helpless and powerless. It longed to uproot itself from the hilltop and cross the valley to the castle-like school where it knew it could protect Mei. But The Tree also knew that it had to trust in Mei and her ability to keep herself safe as she had already done so throughout her life. But this did not stop it from worrying. The Tree acknowledged the curse of caring and that with its concern and love for the young woman also came terror, paranoia, and uncertainty.

It was on the Friday night of that week that The Tree was jolted awake. Something was happening at the school ... The Tree could feel it! It sensed fear. It sensed desperation. It sensed a predatory hunger. And it sensed anger.

Transporting a part off its consciousness into the silver weapon, which it prayed was still in Mei's possession, The Tree found itself in Mei's hands in the darkened dormitory of the school.

The headmaster's shark eyes looked huge and black, as though he were possessed by an ancient demon. He leered at Mei with a disgusting hunger that only fuelled The Tree's fury but also Mei's fear.

She swung her arms desperately with the silver weapon as he inched closer to her, the putrid stench of his breath causing Mei to gag and cough. The man was not deterred by the weapon ... in fact, her fear and feeble flailing seemed to arouse him even more.

Mei backed away until she felt the cold brick wall behind her. A haunting and unfriendly moon cast long shadows of the dormitory beds across the room as it shone through the high stain-glassed window. The headmaster crossed through the light – his face seeming to distort like a grinning salivating monster that longed to devour her.

The Tree could feel Mei's paralysis ... and heard her terrified inner monologue.

Why can't I move? Why can't I fight? Why can't I run?

But The Tree knew from its life so far that when faced with a threat that one cannot escape from, a person's body and mind will shut down as it prepares for imminent (and what it perceives to be inevitable) death. And so, poor Mei stood motionless – frozen in fear.

The Tree desperately drew upon the very core of its soul and willed the energy of the silver branch to not just enhance the weapon but for the energy to also surge into Mei herself. The branch glowed white, and Mei felt the warmth of the object permeate her skin, causing her body to tingle. It was as though a fire erupted within her heart and spread through the rest of her body. And as it did so, she felt her fear melt away – replaced by a feeling of fury.

The disturbed and degenerate headmaster before her seemed to cower and stumble backwards as he witnessed the change come over his prey. Wide-eyed and backing away his face fell, and his body trembled with the same terror that he had induced in his victim.

Seizing her opportunity, Mei regained her own sense of balance and strength and leapt forward with the glowing weapon raised above her head. With a single and powerful swing, she cracked the silver branch into the headmaster's chest. A flash and sparks of lightning erupted from the branch as it made contact – a scorch-like scar burning into the man's skin.

The blow, so powerful, sent the fiend hurtling across the room. His body slammed into the opposite wall, and crumpling to the ground like a fragile wooden puppet. The bloodied welt on his chest was now fully exposed, and a trickle of blood oozed down the side of his face as his skull impacted the unforgiving stone wall.

The Tree felt Mei's relief but also her growing terror as her fight response gave way to the impulse to run. The Tree felt her fingers release their grip on the silver weapon. It fell to the ground. The last thing The Tree saw was Mei racing from the room. The headmaster lay unconscious like a bloodied rag doll next to the beautiful arched wooden door.

Back on the hilltop, The Tree's consciousness returned to its surroundings. It could no longer sense Mei.

Where was she? Was she safe? What had happened?

A feeling of helplessness returned to The Tree. Yet again, it felt powerless and drowning in uncertainty. But all it could do was pray that Mei had somehow escaped. It knew that her plan was to leave that weekend, that some semblance of sanctuary would be afforded to her, if only she could escape from that place. But would that be enough? What about the other girls who returned to the school in the autumn?

The Tree knew that places like this school can become infected ... infected with the wickedness of the deeds committed by its inhabitants. The Tree had heard so many tales throughout its life, of schools, of houses, of prisons, of hotels, all where bad things had happened, and where evil things continued to happen long after the original tragedy. It was as though a trace of evil was left behind and acted as a beacon to other monsters to come and contaminate the heart and soul of these buildings further through continued acts of unspeakable cruelty.

As the night wore on, The Tree fell into a nightmarish sleep, consumed by shadowy figures lurking in the darkness of castle walls. And as it had dreamt before, The Tree felt fear – fear that people were coming to the hilltop to tear it limb from limb, and scatter its broken branches into an enormous roaring bonfire.

The last thing that The Tree saw before drifting into complete unconsciousness was the leering faces of a dozen nameless abusers, their distorted faces melting like wax in the glow of a curiously blue fire. The Tree screamed! It was met with the sound of malevolent laughter. And then nothing but a chilling, empty silence ...

VIII

The Tree awoke to the sound of sirens fading into the distance, and the familiar smell of tobacco smoke billowing around its leaves.

'Alright, lad!' came a gruff but friendly northern voice. The Tree recognised it instantly ... it was Gary the Caretaker, puffing on a cigarette.

'I don't imagine you've slept well,' he said. 'But don't worry, the lass is safe. She packed her bags as planned and she's gone. She sent me here to tell you.'

Gone? The Tree's soul jumped with joy and a cool feeling of relief washed through its trunk and branches. Mei is okay! But then its mind returned to the sound of sirens, sirens that could no longer be heard.

'Oh, don't worry about them,' said Gary the Caretaker, as if reading The Tree's mind. 'They've taken away those dirty bastards to be locked up. And good bloody riddance. Except one ... he's ... he's ... let's just say he's going somewhere else. And good bloody riddance to that too!'

234

The caretaker, seemingly comfortable leaning up against The Tree, continued to take deep drags from his cigarette and exhaled the sweet smoke into the air around them both.

'I don't understand,' said The Tree, still confused from its nightmarish sleep. 'Mei said that they asked you to leave. They had escorted you and all of your belongings from the premises!'

'Yes, lad. And so they did. Forgot to take me spare set of keys though didn't they, bloody idiots!' he added with a wink. 'It's funny what you know when you've worked somewhere as long as I have, and amazing what you find in a damp old cellar if you just know where to look!'

The Tree noticed that the ruddy-faced man had brought with him a cardboard box. The Tree saw that it was full of files. Something about the box disturbed The Tree. It could see that it contained records ... but records of what it could not say. All it knew was that it felt uneasy.

'Names, photos, even descriptions of what they did to them poor lasses. For years ... and years! Things have always been reported of course, but of course nothing gets done. Amazing what money can do, ay lad? That's why I stayed. I figured someone had to keep watch. Someone had to do something!' He took another deep inhalation of smoke and then exhaled.

The Tree didn't need to hear the details of what the caretaker had read, or even seen. The Tree knew. It could feel it in the soul of the vile headmaster that Mei had defended herself against. It saw it in her memories, and felt it saturating the very walls of the place that should've been a place of refuge and sanctuary.

The Tree knew that this place, like so many others, had exploited the vulnerability of the sad, lonely and abandoned boys and girls who had been left there. Of course, The Tree reasoned that not all places and not all people would commit such acts of violation and betrayal ... but The Tree was no longer naïve to the reality of horrors that adults can perpetuate towards children, especially those who are alone and voiceless. The Tree felt sorrow returning to its soul.

'So, I came back and found the files. And gave copies to the police. They couldn't deny it this time. And then there was the body, some poor lass called Patricia, although I think the girls called her Patsy. Poor girl's remains were found buried in one of the lower levels of the cellar. I didn't even know it existed. But someone had obviously gotten lazy! And so all those who were implicated were taking away ... except one!'

'Except one?' repeated The Tree, unsure what was coming next.

'Yep. One couldn't go with them,' he said calmly, and took another drag on his cigarette.

'And why not?'

'Because lad, the fella is dead! Fell from the girl's dormitory window didn't he! Everyone knows that the men aren't allowed up there, but there he was. They found him sprawled on the grass and surrounded by glass. Surprisingly (or perhaps not) this didn't seem to elicit much sympathy.'

'He fell ... or was he pushed?' asked The Tree cautiously. But it knew the answer.

'I've worked there for many years, lad, you can't fall through a window with glass as thick as that!'

The Tree gasped as a feeling of fear and trepidation began to creep through its body. That was not part of the plan! It wanted to protect Mei, not drive her to murder.

Could Mei have done that? it wondered to itself. Could she really have killed him?

The Tree mustered the courage to ask that very question.

Mid-inhalation, Gary the Caretaker coughed and spluttered. 'Gosh, lad, nooo! Of course not! You think a sweet lass is capable of that? No, lad, that dear girl was safely on her way when all this happened.'

If The Tree had eyes, it would have narrowed them suspiciously.

'So, if it wasn't Mei,' said The Tree hesitantly, 'how did he fall?'

The caretaker said nothing and took another long drag of his cigarette – a small, almost imperceptible twitch, and the subtle curling of his mouth.

The Tree also said nothing. They both sat in silence. No further words needed to be spoken.

'Right!' Gary the Caretaker said abruptly. 'I best be off.'

And with that he climbed to his feet and nodded down at the box of files. 'Thought you might like to keep that, just in case you're in any doubt!'

The Tree looked at the box with disgust. It was in no doubt whatsoever.

Hesitantly, small roots broke through the earth and wrapped themselves around the box like tentacles. The Tree didn't see images or words – instead it felt the truth. The nameless dread and terror of a long history of victims. And the salacious and unsatiated appetites of the predators who tormented them. The Tree felt a mixture of horror and revulsion as it ripped the contents of the box apart and dragged their remains deep into the earth, where it would be shielded from the echoes of images and feelings that the box's contents emitted.

As Gary the Caretaker, reached the edge of the hilltop, he stopped, lit another cigarette and turned his head ever so slightly to address The Tree one last time.

'You know,' he said. 'Accidents happen, don't they?! People sometimes fall, don't they?! And old nasty buildings sometimes catch fire, don't they!'

And then he added darkly, 'And we both know that places like that will repeat history … unless somebody has the courage to do something to stop it! Catch my drift, lad?'

There was a moment of silence. And a powerful communication pulsed between them like electricity. The Tree understood completely.

IX

Back in the girl's dormitory of the now entirely empty castle-like school, the discarded silver weapon began to glow for the final time. Sparks crackled and the vein-like electricity spread through the branch. With a burst of power, and low grumbling roar, a cleansing and supernaturally powerful fire ignited within the weapon and tore through the empty school.

But so too did a roar of pain flash and rip through The Tree's soul, far away on the hilltop – another piece of its life being sacrificed in service of others.

Old curtains, lavish paintings, and ancient wooden furniture were consumed by the inferno. The ornate and delicate stained glass windows blasted outwards. The headmaster's study – dripping with sin and deceit – imploded. The furnace, an object that offered no warmth but instead had disposed of the school's most insidious secrets, was now nothing more than a pile of ash. And the once beautiful but foreboding fortress, home to so many dark and terrible uncovered secrets, swelled with the heat and finally exploded over the once pristine and manicured lawns – the horrors and gruesome history of the school was reduced to nothing but rubble, shattered glass, and a swelling hurricane of black smoke.

Back on the hilltop, an echoing boom ricocheted across the valley, and a dark mushroom cloud could be seen far off in the distance where the school once stood.

Patiently waiting for the cloud to dissipate into the atmosphere, Gary the Caretaker, took a long and final drag of his cigarette whilst surveying the horizon. A small smile crept across his lips and he turned ever so slightly towards The Tree again, and gave a subtle but respectful nod in its direction.

'Well done, lad,' he said quietly. 'Well done!'

And with that he left the hilltop and strolled down into the valley, accompanied by a cheerful and tuneless whistling.

The Tree surveyed the horizon and a small and triumphant smile crept through its soul. It could tell, without any shadow of doubt, that today was going to be a most beautiful summer's day. Mei was safe. A predator was dead. And the school was gone – justice had finally been served.

Yes, The Tree knew that it was going to be a beautiful day. But what The Tree did not know, was that its act of retribution against the school had not just cleansed it of the evil that had lurked and spread there for many years. No. It had also destroyed the last remnants of evidence that could have revealed the stories of so many of the missing girls (and the boys from the neighbouring school) who had disappeared over the years.

Sadly, The Tree would come to know a painful truth, that some secrets are so well hidden that they are never brought into the light, leaving those who are left behind in the darkness to be lost in the abyss of confusion and melancholy – always fearing the worst, and sometimes being right to do so.

But for now, the legacy of abuse this particular school had been exposed. And a new generation of children were safe, thanks to The Tree … and of course Gary the Caretaker.

CHAPTER NINE
September: Desperation

I

I t was a mild and blustery September morning. The sky was a mixture of pale ash and charcoal grey in colour. A strong wind hurtled through the valley tossing the green and yellowing leaves as they had begun to fall from their branches. The swirl and crackle of the fallen leaves was comforting for The Tree. The days were still warm, but both the dawn and the dusk gave way to a chill – a reminder that the autumn months were approaching. Occasional rays of sunlight would split through the rapidly rolling clouds causing random columns of light to beam down into the valley like spotlights. Visitors at this time of year often remarked at the serenity induced by this phenomenon, and likened the curious display as being a sign of their God blessing the landscape. The river below shimmered in this light, and the subtle shades of green had started to give way to golds and browns spreading over the tree covered hills as nature began its beautiful decay.

A murder of crows, as black as coal, had found refuge within the stone circle and upon the branches of The Tree. Their aggressive caws echoed through the valley, the only sound that could be heard in the stillness of that September morning once the wind had died. The presence of these crows unnerved The Tree. There was a shadow of foreboding that it felt within its soul.

Perched on the various stones surrounding The Tree, the crows seemed to be watching. Waiting, their beady eyes calculating their next move. A particularly large specimen spread its wings like a jagged cape and skulked through the circle before its audience, displaying its might and power to the others and cawing loudly. This crow seemed like an army general – aggressively barking orders at his soldiers, preparing them for an unknown battled ahead.

The Tree felt uneasy.

There was movement on the hill. A heavy panting accompanied the sharp crack of a broken twig and a stranger emerged over the hill's summit. As he approached, the crows scattered into the sky with a collective battle cry of caws leaving the stone circle and the branches of The Tree empty, and ready to welcome the unfamiliar guest.

As the man emerged from his climb, he stopped at the edge of the stone circle to catch his breath. His posture was stooped. His eyes turned downwards, and as he eventually crossed the circle towards The Tree, it noticed the slow and sluggish gait of the man, as though he were dragging heavy boulders shackled to his ankles. There was a hollowness to the man's eyes and cheeks, and he emanated the greatest sense of sorrow that The Tree had ever felt.

The wave of sorrow that hit The Tree was such that it wanted to recoil, to reject the man and banish him from its presence, lest the melancholy act like a contagion that would bring The Tree down into the depths of desperation and despair alongside the man. However, despite the ever-growing jadedness of its own mood, this was not The Tree's way. And so, as it did for all of those who came to the hilltop seeking support and refuge, The Tree opened its branches wide, ready to hear the man's tragic story and embrace whatever he needed.

Most people who visit The Tree would stand on the edge of the hillside and admire the breathtaking views of the valley. They would sometimes climb The Tree to acquire a better view. They would try and glimpse the ruins of an old castle-like school that and burned to the ground the year before. They would admire The Tree because of its stature and size, or explore with curiosity the formation of the stone circle and wonder how it came to be. The man did none of these things. Instead, he walked slowly around The Tree, occasionally touching its trunk with the palms of his hands and then stopping to look up at the canopy of leaves, as they cast a soft emerald glow upon his face, the faint rays of sunlight creating such a dazzling illusion.

240

The man would then move towards the edge of the hill where the descent was most sheer, and rather than looking out to the horizon, he spent several long minutes gazing downwards at the jagged rocks and the unwelcoming chasm below.

Something about the man's demeanour disturbed The Tree. He did not appear to notice the valley's beauty and The Tree could sense that something weighed heavily on the man's soul. After minutes that felt like hours, the man broke his statuesque stillness and moved back from the edge of the hill and leaned his back against The Tree's strong and supportive trunk, before finally lowering himself down on to the grass with a heavy and defeated sigh.

'What troubles you, my friend?' asked The Tree softly.

The man let out another heavy sigh and without looking up just slowly shook his head from side to side. The Tree stayed silent. It knew that sometimes people just need a quiet space to form their thoughts, for sometimes they do not have the words to describe the enormity of what they feel. But The Tree could sense the man's pain. His despair. His desperation. The man felt without hope.

Whilst The Tree had encountered similar feelings before, there was something different about this man. There was an eerie resignation that surrounded him, which permeated The Tree's soul. This man had given up!

After several moments had passed, the man slowly lifted his head and spoke.

'My name is Joshua.' And then added flatly, 'And I have come here to die.'

Fine misty rain started to sweep over the hill and surrounding valley. As it did so, Joshua began his story.

The Tree listened.

II

'My mother was depressed. From the moment I was born there was an air of sorrow that surrounded her. She told me when I was small that I was a difficult birth and that she couldn't connect with me. That she had named me Joshua because it means "God is Salvation" – she was hoping God would save me. Or maybe save her from me. Apparently, I cried all the time, which made her angry. She would often leave me in a room alone to cry until I was silent. My dad was often away visiting family in Jamaica. He wasn't around to help. My mother felt lonely and overwhelmed – she didn't know how to soothe me when I cried. She struggled to even calm herself, so what hope did I have?

'My father came back when my mother started to speak of strange things. She spoke of demons being in the house and that I might be possessed, that something had stolen my soul and replaced it with something else. She became convinced that our neighbours were in on this and were conspiring against her, that they were part of a cult that swapped the souls of children. She became more and more confused and refused to hold me, apparently, scared that she too would become possessed. The neighbours would hear my cries as well as her rantings, and eventually called the police. Soon after she was hospitalised.'

'The doctors said it was an illness of the mind. Something that can happen in the aftermath of birth, where people can become depressed but also confused. They lose their grasp on reality until they are treated. Medication temporarily alleviated her symptoms but in later years when these stopped working, they administered electricity to their brain in the hopes that this would lift her mood and end her psychosis. I don't know exactly how long she was in hospital for but I'm told it was several months that I was separated from her. My father "took care of me" until she was better.'

The Tree listened silently. It tried to imagine the confusing and terrifying world that this baby had been born into. It imagined the terror of isolation when the baby was left alone, and the way he must have learnt to shut down his needs and feelings because of the fear that help and sustenance would not come, falling into an abyss-like void that he must have felt when needing to be held. But no strong or comforting embraces came to help him feel his own skin, or know his own existence.

The Tree felt enormous pity and compassion for the struggles of the mother. For her nightmarish fear as she lost her grip on reality. And the frightening and unpredictable world that the baby was absorbed into. The Tree knew that people don't always have a narrative for the feelings and sensations that they experience in their early years. Nor do they have memories in the same way that they create as they become older. But it knew that memories are formed nonetheless. They are memories without words and that they are recalled in the form of strange and unnameable sensations that can feel like a haunting spirit that has not yet been laid to rest.

'School was hard and so was home. I didn't fit in at primary school. All of the other children were white. They were confused that my mother had light skin, my dad had dark skin and my skin colour didn't match either of them. Even I sometimes felt confused. I didn't know where I belonged – not within my family, and certainly not within my school. Some children would laugh and make cruel jokes. Others looked at me as though I was from another planet. They didn't always include me in their games and would whisper about me when I would speak in class. No one ever hurt me with their fists, but their words could cut deep.'

'At home, my mother's moods were erratic. She was unpredictable and frightening, especially when she was angry. I learnt how to gauge her mood and made myself good and quiet. I hoped this would make her less angry, but it was worse when she was depressed. Her eyes would become lifeless, her voice was flat, and her face was blank. She would sometimes sit in silence looking out of the window and wouldn't respond to me. She looked like she was a statue made of wax. When I couldn't reach her this scared me. It was like the soul had left her body and what was left was just a hollow shell of a body.'

Joshua stopped. The Tree felt a heaviness as though carrying a boulder in its soul. The man's voice became barely a whisper as he continued, and an eerie sense of foreboding seemed to surround them both.

'When I was ten years old, I came home to a silent house. My father was away ... again! Mother was nowhere to be found. I remember climbing the stairs and walking to her bedroom to see if she was asleep. She sometimes would take to her bed in the afternoons when overwhelmed. But not that day!'

'The door to my bedroom was open but she was not in there. The only other room was the bathroom. And the door to this room was closed. I knocked once. Twice. And then called for my mother ... but there was no reply. I pushed open the door but don't remember much from then onwards. I remember seeing her in the bathtub and then everything went foggy.' He paused, tears filling his eyes.

'I knew that she was dead and that she had taken her own life. I remember there being a spatter of blood on the bathroom floor. Time seemed to slow down, and then nothing. The next thing I can remember was the sound of sirens – flashing blue and red lights – and a kind paramedic handing me a hot chocolate as they put their arm around me, and pulled me into their warm body for a hug. I don't remember crying but I do remember the woman's gentle voice and the sadness in her eyes as she kept glancing at me when she thought I wasn't looking.'

Joshua felt numb, and so did The Tree. His voice remained flat and somewhat detached as he described the harrowing events of that day when he was ten years old.

A wooziness overcame The Tree as it tried to imagine the horrific scene, but something seemed to block it. It was as though a thick opaque veil had cocooned its mind, preventing any further imagery from breaking through. The Tree wondered if this was part of the man's defences – a powerful protective process that he had used to shield himself from the shocking scene that he had beheld all alone.

Joshua continued his story with the same dull and flattened affect.

'After that, the other children at school were silent. I could feel them watching me. Pitying me. It made me angry. I would shout and lash out, but I didn't get into trouble. The teachers were kind and sympathetic. But after a while the other children avoided me completely. I can remember feeling utterly and desperately alone.'

'I felt the same at home. My father was of course back in the house but his mood was sombre, or angry. He was always working so when I did see him, he would be tired and irritable. I wasn't allowed to speak about my mother because this made him sad, or furious. And, if I came home from secondary school having been in yet another fight, he would be livid. If I wasn't doing well at school he was disappointed, and frequently told me so. I didn't feel like I could do anything right. On those days he would bellow at me. He would scream in my face and tell me that I was waste of space. Once he even said that he wished I had been the one to die, and not my mother. But then he would break down in tears and hug me, apologising through his sobs.'

'On other days, the fire of his anger could not be extinguished, no matter what I did or what I said. On those days he beat me with a belt – something his father used to do to him. Apparently, it would "make me into a man". It got to a point where I no longer felt the pain. I no longer pleaded with him. I no longer cried. I just took the beating in silence. I had learnt how to disconnect from my feelings and from my body. I became a ghost. And I learnt to feel nothing. I trained myself to become dead inside. Even when he would lead me up to his wardrobe and ask me to choose the belt that he would beat me with, I did so obediently and without question. The sooner it was over, the sooner we could carry on with our day, or night. The beatings could come whenever. I just accepted that this was my life.'

The Tree's numbness had shifted and was now replaced with compassion, and sorrow (and a growing anger) on behalf of the man, the child, and the teenager, alone in a world where parents were either absent or the source of terror, pain, and loss. The Tree was no stranger to such tales from its years of existence – the impact of hearing such stories had not lessened either. The Tree longed to bring the man's mother back to life, to protect him from his abusive father in the past. To give him the safety, the care and the love that he had desperately needed but had been deprived of so early on in his life.

The Tree could see that the man was getting soaked by the rain which had increased in its assault – the pathetic fallacy to match the dismal, despairing, and sombre mood of the man and his story. The Tree drew its branches and remaining leaves into a tight leafy canopy to shield the man from the onslaught of rain, hoping to give some temporary reprieve to the man's discomfort. If it did so, the impact was not visible. The man's facial expression remained impassive, and his eyes hollow and blank. It was as though such trivial things as precipitation would have no bearing on a man who had already suffered in such bleak and terrible ways.

Joshua did not notice that he was no longer being battered by the elements and simply continued with his story.

'The first time I tried to kill myself was when I was eighteen years old. It was the anniversary of my mother's death. I didn't have the courage to slit my wrists so I lay in the bath and drank my dad's booze and took a bunch of tablets I'd gathered. I don't know what they were.

Nor did I care. I hoped to pass out and slip under the water and then it would all be over. But it wasn't. I was pulled into consciousness by my father, who found me. After feeling his fists pound on my chest to expel the water in my lungs, I gasped for breath and then vomited. He didn't call an ambulance. Nor did I go to hospital. The swollen face and black eye that he gave me for being "a selfish little bastard" would have raised too many questions.'

The Tree was aghast. Who was this man? How could he behave this way to his own son? His own flesh and blood?

'Shortly afterwards I moved out. I got a job in an office. It was boring, unskilled, and low paid, but I didn't care. I was away from my father and able to go through the motions without anyone asking questions. I didn't have to think. Or feel. I could just exist day to day. Even though I was still alive, I had succeeded in killing off something that day when I was in the bathtub. I lived in a constant state of purgatory, biding my time until I could try again.'

'The second time I tried to kill myself I was twenty-one. I found myself on the roof of a multistorey car park. The location was perfect. Not only did it have height, but its location was also on the edge of a ravine. The city itself having been built upon numerous caves meaning the drop was even more sheer. High on whatever drugs I could get my hands on, I stood on the edge, looking down into the precipice, swaying in the wind, longing for it to take the decision from me and cast me into the abyss.'

'People had gathered below and were watching. Some of them recording with their mobile phones. Others were jeering and laughing. Some screamed for me to "JUMP!" because then there would be "one less" to worry about. They threw racial slurs at me. Some even threw bottles at me as I balanced on the edge of the building. Their feeble attempts to knock me off were ineffective … they were too far away from me. But the message was clear. They wanted me dead. I wanted to be dead. The world clearly wanted me dead. So, what was the point of living?'

'"JUST DO IT … JUMP!" came the cries from below, an echo of the voice in my head. I remember closing my eyes. Their echoing laughter seeming to fade away. I was feeling woozy and nauseous from the cocktail of drugs, and the dizzying height of the ledge where I balanced. I felt like I was walking on a tightrope, not caring whether I made it to the other side or hurtled into the chasm below.'

'Goodbye' I thought, and then bringing that hateful image of my mother in the bathtub to mind, I whispered into the hollow air 'I'll be with you soon.' I leaned forward and felt my world spin. I was beginning to fall. But I did not. Someone grabbed me roughly from behind, yanked me back from the edge, both of us collapsing on the hard concrete floor of the car park. Someone had saved me ... and I was devastated!'

Joshua gave a snort of mirth, and shook his head and repeated. 'Saved me ... huh ... from what? From myself? From the people who enjoyed watching a man on the edge? From the world? I did not feel saved. I felt doomed to live out my existence in this hateful world with no escape. What the fuck was I saved for?!' he added angrily.

The Tree swelled with compassion for Joshua, and its focus was drawn back to the crowd of onlookers, and the gang of people laughing and jeering, willing the man to his death. They laughed? It thought it itself. They told him to jump? They filmed him?

The Tree was momentarily blinded by fury, disgust, and disbelief. A shudder rippled through The Tree's soul alongside a sense of desperate anguish. What was happening to the people of this world? Where was the kindness and compassion towards another human being who was in pain – for someone who was suffering? Who had given up hope? Through its fury, The Tree silently wept for the man before him. For the child that he had been. And the love and care he had not received.

The Tree's attention was pulled back to the present moment. The man was continuing with his story but not in words but with a flood of memories and feelings split off from himself, but deeply felt by The Tree. The images flooded its mind ...

A cold and clinical psychiatric ward. The sounds of other patients shouting obscure and nonsensical sentences. The strange and acrid smell of psychosis, a mixture of sour perspiration, incontinence ... physical and psychological decay. The Tree felt the gloom of the ward and the contagion of desperation which lingered sombrely in the atmosphere – blank faces. Deadened eyes. Indistinguishable mumblings.

The Tree could feel that the man had lost hope. He had surrendered to the bleakness of his environment. He took the injections that the staff gave him. At first, he fought them, ignoring their reassurances that the injections would help – they would help him to feel calm. And they did, but not before he tried to fight them. After a while he gave up fighting. He accepted their words. He accepted the medication. He accepted the locked doors that held him prisoner on the dismal ward.

However, there was a room that sharply contrasted with the dark and oppressive corridors of the ward. The man would take refuge in this large room with soft furnishings, tables with old-fashioned games on top of them, a selection of random and curious books, and a rectangular window that reached from floor to ceiling – a window with a view of manicured land. Green grass. Rolling hills. And a vast expanse of sky. The Tree could feel the man's comfort as he would gaze outwards, unsure if he would ever be part of the world again. Or even want to be part of it. The Tree sensed his ambivalence and the strange safety that the ward had come to represent. Was this his prison or was this his sanctuary? It had become an escape from the pressures and dread of the outside world.

The cascade of memories continued …

Many of the dreamy memories lingered on the view from the large window but The Tree caught a glimpse of a young woman. A young woman whose eyes were kind. Soft dark skin, a cloud of black hair that framed her elegant face, and a gentle compassionate smile. Joshua tried to withdraw from this image – a deep emotional pain and sadness being felt by both The Tree and the man.

'Who is she?' asked The Tree.

'Her name is Carrie-Anne,' replied Joshua. 'She is my wife!'

III

'Tell me,' implored The Tree. It sensed a change in the man as the image of his wife lingered – a mixture of sadness but also a deep and unwavering love.

'Back then I barely knew her,' Joshua continued. 'I was confused and surprised when she sat next to me one day in the garden room.

That's what we used to call it – because of the view. To be honest I actually didn't recognise her at first. But when she spoke, I remembered her from the office where I worked. I didn't know what she did but I remember seeing her around. She would always smile and say hello every morning, without fail. And her smile always seemed so warm. So, kind. So genuine. I was embarrassed because I sometimes didn't reply. Or could only manage a weak smile in response. But even so, she would still persist. Every day!'

A look of regret passed over his face, accompanied by fantasies of missed opportunities.

'She came to visit every week. She said she had heard that I was unwell. Unwell!' he repeated and then scoffed.

'Yes, I am unwell. Why do people find it so difficult to just say what they mean? To speak the truth? I knew she was trying to be kind … it can't have been easy for her visiting someone she hardly knew in a place that was so devoid of life and hope. But just like she did in the office, she persisted with an unwavering kindness. She would bring me books to read, keen for me to share her love for particular authors who wrote about witches and vampires. Carrie-Anne loves the supernatural. She would bake cakes and other snacks for me, and would stare keenly at me with her large beautiful eyes, anticipating my response, hoping I would like them. And I did – but not as much as I liked her. I enjoyed her company. I enjoyed her smile. I enjoyed the walks in the hospital gardens that I was eventually allowed to take with her. I can hear the sound of her laughter as we talked. And the warmth of her arms when I cried. She gave me a reason to live. And faith that a life beyond all that I had known could be possible.'

Joshua paused. A wistful look upon his face and a stirring of some forgotten emotion that had been banished as he had journeyed to The Tree.

The Tree could feel the love that the man felt for his wife and the tenderness of their beginnings. It saw memories of their wedding day and the bittersweet emotion that accompanied it – the profound misery that accompanied the absence of his mother, and the bitterness and resentment that accompanied his father's absence. One unable to attend, the other choosing not to.

The wedding was humble with a handful of treasured guests but the safety, the love, and the care that the man felt when his wife said her vows, and when he said his in response, rippled through the church, and was felt by all those who attended long into the night as they sang, danced, and got drunk on cheap wine.

The Tree could feel the man's conflict, a constant battle between the pain of his past, and the hope for a better future – but also the fear that this would not come to pass. A darkness lingered in the man, and was felt by The Tree in its own soul, a pull towards life but an equally strong pull towards death ... and uncertainty of which force would be the strongest in the end.

Joshua continued.

'I remember the love my wife showed our son when he was born, especially after there were complications. Not with my son – he was fine, bless him. But with Carrie-Anne. She bled a lot during the birth, but the doctors managed to stop it. We didn't have much money and our flat was small but her love for our little boy was unwavering. We were young parents but we made ends meet with what little money we had. She held him and sang to him when he cried. She rocked him to sleep when he was tired. She nourished his hunger without irritation. And when he cried, she went to him. She couldn't bear to leave him alone and in distress. It warmed my heart to see this, but also fuelled my grief – grief because of what I needed as a baby and for what my mother could not give me.'

'I continued to work and Carrie-Anne looked after our son. He seemed happy and content when he was with her. I love him very much, but sometimes I would get angry. I felt impatient when he cried. I felt irritated by his endless needs. I felt exhausted by his energy when I was tired from work. I even felt jealous of the relationship he had with my wife, and I feel ashamed of that. I never hurt him. But sometimes I thought about it. I remembered how my father would hit me and I imagined doing the same to my son. But I didn't. I would die before I ever hurt him like that. But I'm scared that I'll be like my father. Or my mother. Or both.'

The Tree listened intently, drawing upon its wisdom and experiences of human beings over the many years of its existence. It could feel the love that the man felt for his family but also his fear of repeating the past. The Tree knew that for everyone who is born, a blueprint of life and relationships becomes imprinted on them, a story that has been told and passed down over generations. People know only what they've experienced and don't always realise that the blueprint can change, that they themselves can change it. Joshua was afraid of being like his own parents, but The Tree saw that already the man was breaking the cycle. His fear of being like his father had taken him to a crossroads – a crossroads where he could follow a familiar path, or choose a different one by actively not repeating his father's behaviours.

The Tree saw that the man was so close to breaking the cycle that he experienced with his father, but feared that he was dangerously close to repeating the same blueprint that had been written by his mother.

The Tree was confused. Why could the man not see that the dark parts of himself that he feared could be understood if only they were brought into the light? That to purge himself of these hated parts of himself does not mean destroying himself in the process. The Tree knew that all of these parts can co-exist, that the haunted books of one's past can be integrated into the internal library of one's soul, where the stories can be revisited, but not relived or repeated.

'Sometimes I would just leave the house. I'd leave Carrie-Anne and my son together because I knew he was safe with her. I'd drive for hours along dark winding roads. I'd sometimes turn off the headlights … willing death to come to me on the treacherous country roads. Sometimes I would close my eyes, a fleeting moment of suspension where my life would hang in the balance. Images of swerving off the road and crashing into a tree were frequent. Sometimes the thoughts came to me even when Carrie-Anne and my son were in the car. What if I did that, and killed them both? There is something inside of me that takes over. I can't control it. And I don't care if I die. But not them … never them!'

The Tree knew that people have fantasies all of the time, and sometimes these fantasies can create relief – a series of options to counteract feeling trapped in their lives. These are often harmless and vanish as quickly as they form. But in the case of Joshua, The Tree feared that these were not just fantasies, they were plans. Plans that he sought to execute.

The Tree felt that this is a man on the edge – a man who truly believed that he had nothing left to lose and all too much to gain by ending his own life. He had convinced himself that his life was worthless, and his absence would bring some form of contentment to his family. The Tree felt befuddled by the distortion in the man's thinking but felt that the man truly believed that his death would solve everyone's problems. He could no longer see the irony of this.

'One month ago,' Joshua continued, 'Carrie-Anne told me she was pregnant again. And two days later, I lost my job. They can get younger people doing what I do for half the salary so they shook my hand and sent me on my way. I haven't told my wife. And I don't know what I'm going to do. I've spent weeks trying to find someone to hire me but there is nothing. My mental health history looks bad, as do my absences. I have no qualifications, so who is going to hire me now?'

Joshua sighed deeply and placed his head in his hands.

'Sometimes I just sit in the cemetery that's on the outskirts of the city centre. I drink and contemplate death surrounded by headstones and the buried corpses of all those who have come before me. It's quite peaceful. I listen to the birds, the rustling wind in the trees, and for a few moments lose myself in alcohol and the sounds of nature. But when the drink is gone, I remember why I'm there. I remember that I am useless. And that I can't do anything. I can't even take care of my family. Not whilst I am alive, but if I die, they get everything. The company I worked for made us take out an insurance policy. And if I die, my family gets money. They can live a better life without me and all the misery that I bring and the legacy of my family.' And then, he added sadly, 'I'm worth more dead than I am alive!'

And sadly, in his heart, Joshua truly believed this.

The Tree could feel that the man's mind had become so warped and invested in the belief that he was bad – a burden, and dangerous – that he could now justify eradicating his existence from the world so that he could make it a better place. He could not see the harm he would do to his family by repeating what he himself had experienced as a child. His desire was purely to save his family from threat and unhappiness. And in his heart, the man truly believed that what he was planning to do was for the best for everyone. It wasn't suicide. It was self-sacrifice. He was saving his family.

Joshua stopped talking. The synopsis of his life had been shared. The rain, even heavier now, thundered around them. Despite this, there was a chilling silence.

Joshua seemed to stand up in slow motion and in strange a trance-like state walked over to the bag that he had been carrying. He opened it and removed something. The Tree could not tell what this was, but Joshua held it close to his chest as he approached The Tree again and began walking around it whilst looking upwards.

The Tree felt Joshua climbing its trunk and then something tightening on one of its strongest branches … a silver branch.

A rope had been wrapped around it.

Still in a trance, eyes blank and his face without emotion or expression, Joshua looped the end of the rope to form a hoop, which remained in place because of the intricate knots and loops that he proceeded to tie. It was clear that this was not the first time the rope had been tied in this fashion. The noose, a grotesque instrument of death, swayed ominously in the wind and rain.

The Tree was paralysed – an unsettling deadness overcoming it. The Tree knew what Joshua was planning but felt powerless to act. It knew that that no words of comfort or reassurance could change this man's mind or heart. It felt hopeless. Despairing. Desperate.

The acceptance and welcoming of death that The Tree sensed within Joshua was contagious – it felt numb as though it were lost in a fog.

Suddenly, a loud chorus of cawing catapulted The Tree from its stupefied state. The crows had returned and were in a frenzy. Alert once more, it surveyed the macabre scene as the crows surrounded The Tree, each one perched on the stones that circled it. But Joshua was nowhere to be seen.

And then it felt Joshua's body climbing The Tree's hulking trunk once more. He had reached the branch where the noose was tied. He placed the hoop of the rope over his head and tightened it around his neck.

He closed his eyes.

And in an unnervingly calm voice, Joshua simply said, 'Goodbye.'

He stepped off the branch.

253

IV

The howl of the wind echoed the howl inside of The Tree as it saw Joshua fall in slow motion.

The rope became taught. And the weight of the body strained The Tree's branch as gravity pulled it downwards. Joshua had chosen this branch because it was the strongest. It would not break despite the weight of man's body that it now supported.

A sickening choking sound could be heard as Joshua's body twisted, contorted, and grasped – his face turning from red to an ugly shade of purple, and his eyes wide and bulging.

The Tree was desperate, and mustering all of its strength and energy, it did the only thing that it could. A heat like fire surged from its very roots and spread through its body. Like rivers of lava, it willed the fiery sensation through its veins towards the very branch where Joshua hung. And with a silent roar, and pain like electricity, The Tree ripped its own silver limb from its body – another tear in its increasingly fragile soul.

Joshua's body fell and lay still and crumpled on the ground.

'Please,' implored The Tree with desperation, not knowing to whom it was praying. 'Please!' it begged again.

The crows were silent. The downpour of rain had ceased. The wind vanished. The air was still. The world held its breath with anticipation.

A loud gasp erupted from Joshua. His eyes now wide with shock. Desperately clawing at the rope around his neck, Joshua began to breathe. He loosened the rope and a healthy colour began to return to his face.

'Breathe,' said The Tree softly. 'Breathe, my friend,' it repeated with the same feeling of desperation and longing.

Joshua breathed.

Emerging from the initial state of shock, he looked around him, at the large and heavy broken branch by his side, the unravelled rope, and the audience of birds that surrounded them.

And then he screamed – a scream like nothing The Tree had ever heard before. A scream of sorrow, of anguish and of misery.

Joshua's deep voice bellowed through the valley causing the crows to scatter and take flight once more. And then placing his face in his hands, he sobbed.

'I can't even get this right,' he uttered between his gasps. 'I'm useless! Everyone would be better off without me!'

Joshua continued to weep. 'If I could just get this one thing right my family would be free of the burden that I've become. They would have money because of my life insurance policy. My son, and my unborn child could be set for life. And at least one of them would never know me, or have to suffer my depression or my anger like I had to suffer both of my parents when I was a kid!'

Joshua's voice faded as he became deep in thought.

The Tree felt confused. Could the man not see that in an attempt to break the cycle of violence and sorrow that he had experienced, he was still perpetuating the cycle of pain and grief, and the legacy of death?

With compassion, The Tree responded softly. 'But aren't you repeating what your mother did to you? By trying to extinguish the parts of both of your parents that you have been left holding, repeating, and hating, you are killing off the parts of you that can be different. You are killing of the parts that can choose to break the cycle – not through death, but through life! Your family legacy does not have to be one of violence and death. Instead your legacy can be one of transformation, the desire to be different from your parents and to make the choice to do something differently. To be different!'

Joshua looked agitated and leaned against the strong thick trunk of The Tree and contemplated what he was hearing, searching for arguments to counteract The Tree's words.

'But I've caused so much pain already,' he said despondently. 'And I will again, I'm sure!'

'Pain and suffering are inevitable,' replied The Tree. 'But it is what you learn from these that can enable healing in our souls. In life you will make mistakes, but you can also grow from them. The process of repair can be transformative for everyone involved if these mistakes and their impact are acknowledged. In causing death to yourself, there is no working through, just endless pain for all of those left behind. Unanswered questions, and a legacy of anger, confusion and sorrow … as you yourself know all too well!'

The Tree paused, allowing its words to penetrate the soul of the man. The Tree knew that when we are in the eye of a storm, we are not always able to see the world clearly. The Tree knew that if it could help Joshua see that if his life could have meaning – if even the slightest amount of change were possible – then this could ignite the tiny part of him that did want to live. The part that did have hope for a different life. A part that would make a different choice, and break the tragic legacy that he had inherited. The Tree desperately hoped to bring the man to the safety of the shore, where together they could look out to sea at the storm in which he had been lost for so long. Where he could see more clearly that something could settle and change, that calmer waters could be possible for him and the new family that he had created.

The Tree continued.

'The world is not a perfect place. And nor are the people in it. But we do not have to be perfect – we can simply strive to be good enough. It is your imperfections that will give courage and resilience to your children and help them to accept these parts within themselves.'

'I know that people have been cruel to you. They have not shown you the kindness that you needed and deserved. You have tried to survive this world in the best way that you knew how, and now you're tired. Tired of fighting – of struggling to survive. But there can be goodness and beauty in the world too. There can be love and kindness. There can be hope, and all of these aspects I see and feel within your soul!'

Joshua was moved by The Tree's words. He could feel The Tree's compassion and its hope for him to live.

'But what if it's too late? What if it's too late for me to see the beauty?' he asked as something started to shift within his soul.

The Tree replied simply, 'It is only too late if you choose to die!'

And then The Tree did something … it asked the wind for help. A part of Joshua that wanted to live had ignited, even if it was only a small flicker of light. The Tree wanted to show him that there was still beauty in the world, even if he couldn't see it. And so, the wind blew harder, causing a flurry of leaves to swirl around The Tree. The heavy clouds that had occupied the sky and caused the deluge of rain to soak the hill parted for a few moments, allowing a single ray of light to break through and shone upon The Tree and Joshua.

Joshua squinted and shielded his eyes at the brightness of the sunlight, a sharp contrast to the gloom that had engulfed him earlier that day. As the warm sunlight split through the clouds, it caught the remaining droplets of mist that hovered in the sky, and in doing so created the most wonderful arc of colours to spread across the sky. A symbol of splendour … and hope.

Joshua gasped, entranced by nature's spectacle.

An unusually large descent of green woodpeckers could be seen on the horizon flying towards The Tree. Their gentle hypnotic weaving calmed something in Joshua's body, his heart rate slowing down, and a delicate calm spreading through his body and mind.

The birds gently settled on the surrounding stone circle and amongst the fallen golden leaves at the foot of The Tree. These curious green birds with their heavy bodies, yellow rump, and curious red heads did not appear daunted by the man or his enormous sturdy companion who was now swaying gently with the remaining breeze. The largest of them hopped towards Joshua, its wings spread wide – a vivid contrast to the menacing black crows that had occupied the space earlier.

As the woodpecker approached Joshua, he held out his hand slowly and instinctively. The woodpecker stopped and stared at him, its head moving slightly upwards and downwards as if surveying the man in front of him. And deeming him to be safe and worthy, it fluttered its wings and landed safely on the man's outstretched arm.

Joshua was unsure about what he believed. His mind felt muddled. I should be dead, he thought to himself, but yet again something had intervened, meaning that this was not so. He was alive! And as he beheld his surroundings, he could see a world that was teeming with life and beauty around him. He was able to see the beauty in the decay of leaves as the colours of autumn began to sweep through the valley. He could feel the ray of warm golden sun that seemed to shine only on him and The Tree. He beheld the colourful birds that surrounded him and heard the sound of life in the valley, and the comforting white noise of the rushing river below.

Joshua remembered his wife and son. He thought of his unborn child. He thought of his parents and wondered if their lives could have been different. He thought about the people who had shown him cruelty … but also the people who had shown him kindness. He thought about The Tree, and silently gave thanks to it.

He was still unsure about his life and indeed his future, but something small and imperceptible had shifted. He looked down at the green woodpecker now sitting contentedly in the palm of his hands and with a gentle lift of his arm, he tossed it into the air, where it took flight. Its companions took flight too with a raucous flapping of wings and squawks – the cloud of jade and red birds disappearing into the distance.

Joshua slowly rose to his feet and gently placed the palm of his hand against The Tree's rough bark. He closed his eyes and with a deep breath silently thanked The Tree again. He then looked down at the large broken branch, the noose still attached. He started to bend down to retrieve it but then paused. His hand frozen in mid-air, his arm reaching towards it … his hand locked in a frozen grasp.

Why? he asked himself. What for?

Joshua closed his hand and retracted his arm and turned away from the fallen silver branch. He said nothing more but smiled weakly at The Tree … and then bowed respectfully.

The Tree bowed back.

Silently, Joshua made his way across the stone circle – the light of the sun still shining like a spotlight on The Tree and stone circle – and began his descent down the hill and back to whatever life awaited him.

As the tormented and tragic man disappeared from sight, the clouds continued to roll, and the ray of sun that had pierced the gloom of the hilltop began to fade. The light drizzle had returned and the arc of colours vanished from the sky – a low rumble of thunder could be heard in the distance and the rain became heavier.

Whatever hope the man had left with did not remain with The Tree. The Tree felt a strange hollowness inside its own broken soul. And a spark of something else…

The feelings of despair were not alien to The Tree. It had heard and felt so many stories of sadness and sorrow, trauma and tragedy. As people left the stone circle, they took something of The Tree's vitality but sometimes left with it their own desperation and woe.

The Tree thought about the man's life and hoped that something would change. It hoped that its own act of sacrifice would help the man, but it no longer felt certain that the beauty of the world was enough to save people from themselves.

Indeed, The Tree thought about the man's story, the cruelty and spite that people had shown him. Their lack of care, compassion, and kindness. The Tree remembered similar stories from the past ... the injustices, the violence, the abuse. And something small but powerful ignited in the depths of The Tree's soul.

As the rumbles of thunder grew louder and ever closer, a different feeling started to awaken within The Tree, quite different to the love and empathy that it had felt before. This feeling was like a small knot, twisting like a fist being pummelled into its heart. It was a familiar feeling that was beginning to slowly burn like white-hot fire.

It was not just injustice that it felt. It was not just fury. The feeling was rage! And a shadowy and deeply buried part of The Tree started to emerge ...

The Tree wanted to act!

The Tree wanted revenge.

The Tree wanted to destroy!

CHAPTER TEN
October: The Reaping

I

O ver the many years of its existence, The Tree had come to love the autumn months most of all. October was held in particularly high regard because of the numerous celebrations that would take place over the decades under the blanket of orange, gold, and scarlet leaves populating its canopy of branches. The bonfires, the singing, the small and delicate candles that people would surround the stone circle with, all gave the hilltop an aura of wonderment and enchantment.

The Tree used to adore how the valley looked in the month of October. During the day, the sky would be covered with a heavy but comforting dark blanket of rolling cloud. A fine mist would nourish The Tree upon its hilltop and produce the most intoxicating scent from the surrounding grass and trees. The shades of green that typified the surrounding mountainous hills and forests now gave way to the stunning colours of autumn, which were exquisitely mirrored in The Tree's own appearance. It felt calmed by the gentle rumble of thunder in the sky, the soothing sound of the river below in the valley, and the small boulders being tossed and rolled in its ever moving current, winding its way around the base of The Tree's hill, and far off into the distance between the interlocking mountains.

On days such as these, The Tree bathed in the harmony of its surroundings – all birds, animals, and natural elements felt in balance with one another, which made The Tree's soul sing. Even the night-time storms provided it with spectacular lightshows as flashes of lightning forked and slashed through the sky, illuminating the valley with vivid electric blue, shades of purple, and dazzling white light. On less dramatic evenings, the howling wind would part the clouds, revealing a haunting celestial orb that glowed brightly amidst a blanket of stars – bathing The Tree in a cold but beautiful light. The surrounding dew and mist of the valley shimmered and sparkled with emerald hues, giving the valley a spectral and somewhat supernatural vibe.

Whilst the beauty of nature and The Tree's surroundings did not change, The Tree noticed that the energy of the valley had sadly done so as the decades passed. As the twentieth century had come to an end, and as the third decade of the new millennium began, The Tree noticed that the playful and spirted nature of its visitors became less and less. No longer did people come to The Tree and its stone circle at Halloween to celebrate nature and the veil between worlds being at its thinnest. Instead, a darker and more disturbing energy seemed to envelop those in attendance, causing The Tree's soul to shudder with confusion, and slowly wilt with despair ... and an ever-growing sense of fear and foreboding.

The people who visited The Tree began to share their experiences, but these were not ones of hope and healing. Instead, they were disturbing tales of violence, cruelty, and wickedness. The Tree knew that its power invited all who crossed the stone circle to be able to share their truths and the deepest and sometimes forbidden fears, desires, and confessions of their hearts. The Tree also knew that its role was to listen, to guide, to offer faith, and help people to make meaning. But sometimes, its only role was to be with people in their misery and sorrow so that for those few moments at least, they did not feel so alone.

Whilst The Tree had lived long enough to know that life and people are a combination of goodness, badness, and everything that comes in between, it found itself becoming increasingly concerned for the humanity that it had come to love, but found itself increasingly losing faith in. The Tree noticed that people were becoming less kind, less empathetic, so driven were they by anger, hatred, and greed. And their capacity to learn from their mistakes was dwindling – as was their compassion for their fellow human beings. Sadly, The Tree noticed, their capacity and desire to cause pain and suffering to others was also mounting.

And so, what would happen in this month of October in the early part of the twenty-first century would leave The Tree forever changed in ways that it could not have foreseen. Because whilst The Tree was both reflective and self-aware, it had not recognised the slow erosion that had been taking place – out of its awareness, from years of exposure to the growing toxicity of humanity's cruelty. Silently, The Tree sat with a growing sense of hatred and rage for all of the injustices it had beheld, and all those that it was powerless to prevent or change. After its encounter with Joshua, and having heard his story – and indeed all the stories from the second half of its life – the fury within The Tree was growing.

II

On the first day of this particular October, The Tree's fate was sealed, for this was the day that it met The Gang!

The day began deceptively well. A crispness in the air. A sky of azure blue with sporadic whisps of white, and a low golden sun providing moments of warmth and comfort to the valley and all its inhabitants. The Tree was dozing in and out of consciousness until it found itself startled into a state of alertness. The smell of tobacco, stale alcohol, and cheap acidic-smelling perfume was carried by the gentle breeze from the river's stepping stones up to the top of the hill. The sound of grunting laughter and a high-pitched cackle shattered the peace of the valley, like someone smashing glass against the rocks.

Four shadow-like figures emerged having climbed the steep hill, and undeterred by the incline or rough terrain, continued forwards towards the stone circle. The Tree had the delight of experiencing a range of diverse and wonderful people throughout its long life, but there was something mismatched about this particular group, and something ill-fitting about their presence in such a place of beauty.

Masks … why were they wearing masks? And not the masks that The Tree had been accustomed to seeing people wear in the aftermath of the mysterious virus that had taken hold some years ago. These were different. Filthy … grotesque … horrifying. Gruesome cloths interwoven with plastics and rubber to create grinning skulls, peculiarly blank but haunted expressions, sack cloth with crudely cut slits for the eyes and mouth, and a children's mask depicting a clown – so obscene it looked on the face of this hulking adult. As they entered the stone circle, they carelessly tossed their masks aside, revealing their hideous faces.

A sharp pain was felt by The Tree as a glass bottle exploded on its trunk, hurled by the female member of the group as she yelled a string of obscenities at the small fox that had been resting at the foot of The Tree, just narrowly escaping the shards of glass and alcohol raining down on it from the woman's poorly-aimed throw.

Alerted by the danger associated with such a sound, and the chilling energy that this group seemed to emit, the remaining wildlife that had been taking refuge amongst The Tree's branches and roots stealthily retreated from sight without a sound.

The Tree was alone as all four members of The Gang came into view – but a curious shadow was cast upon all four of their unmasked faces. The Gang seemed to emit a powerful odour. Whilst initially masked by the cigarette smoke and alcohol, The Tree sensed something else. It was a dank and rotten smell. Not one that could be associated with unwashed clothes or bodies, but something deeper. A stagnation and toxicity of the soul – the stench of pure evil.

The youngest member of the group – a man The Tree perceived to be in his mid-twenties – prowled around The Tree, and seemed to take great pleasure in kicking and stomping on the many carved pumpkins that previous visitors had left as a tribute to the season of harvest, their curious carved faces distorting and disintegrating as the young man's foot plunged into their faces. When his energy was spent, and the joy at his own destruction had clearly waned, he sat beneath The Tree and began to aimlessly stab and carve into its trunk using a large and jagged hunting knife.

As the knife scraped The Tree's hardened bark, it detected something else – the feel and scent of blood. The Tree knew this not to be animal blood, and it knew that the blood was fresh. Something (or someone) had been made to suffer very recently. There was both an eagerness and untamed fury that The Tree beheld in this young man's eyes, and a ferocious frenzied energy that swirled in the young man's heart like a ticking time-bomb, its release no doubt threatening to be as unpredictable and uncontained as the young man was.

The woman, in her thirties, The Tree estimated, looked cruel. Her sharp narrow features accompanied by hollow cheeks and haunted eyes were a manifestation of the emptiness that was within – a complete absence of conscience or empathy. From her bruised knuckles and sharp bloodied fingernails, The Tree beheld her weapon of choice, and the animal-like savagery that she inflicted on her victims. The Tree felt the triumph that emanated from her when her victims pleaded for mercy – mercy that she never granted.

The lieutenant, the largest and most alarming looking gang member, caused a shiver to reverberate through The Tree's entire trunk and branches. Whilst an ugliness emanated from the man's soul, very rarely had The Tree witnessed someone whose very appearance mirrored their innermost cruel fantasies. The man's hulking shape embodied a sense of threat and violence, but it was his face that evoked both fear and revulsion in The Tree. It reminded it of the moon – a cratered surface impacted over the years by meteors and space debris. The lieutenant's face was just as marked. Scars were visible across the man's face and exposed skin. Battle wounds no doubt. His skin resembled a canvas that had been slashed but also gave the frightening appearance of a body that had been pieced and sewn together, a grotesque monster known only in gothic novels. His eyes, whilst small, had seen atrocities – both those that he had committed and all that he had witnessed throughout his life. All that he had been forced to witness, and all that he had been complicit in. The lieutenant had earned his stripes through acts of physical and sexual violence, the age, gender and circumstances being irrelevant to the lieutenant. He did as was ordered, and revelled in the power that this gave him.

And finally, there was the leader of The Gang. In appearance The Tree beheld him to be unremarkable, apart from a visible scar on his face. He possessed pale almost ashen-looking skin. Greasy hair. Average height. And a shapeless physique which did not appear to exude any strength or sense of foreboding. The Tree imagined that this person could slip through life unnoticed and almost invisible. All except for the trail of destruction and terror that this man left in his wake. The leader's teeth were rotten, and his mouth produced a familiar rank stench.

The Tree could not understand its own feelings. Despite the leader's somewhat bland appearance, his presence caused the greatest apprehension and dread within The Tree. The man removed the dark glasses that shielded his eyes from the sun and then smiled at his subordinates. The smile was not one of care and warmth, but a warped and wicked grin that The Tree had seen in the jack-o-lanterns that visitors used to bring to The Tree on Halloween night. It longed for the time before the visitors to The Tree had grown darker and more sinister. The leader's smile looked like a jagged slash across his face and was accompanied by large eyes. The blackest eyes. And then The Tree understood...the eyes of a man without a soul.

The Tree knew what it was facing. In the other gang members, and indeed even within some of the worst of its visitors, The Tree bore witness to the souls of people who were cruel, spiteful, vengeful, and vicious. But within the leader's soul there was something different – something lacking. What emanated from the man was an absence, and a coldness, like iron. An abyss that swallowed and engulfed light. A chasm that suffocated hope and breathed life in to hate, into suffering, and a sadistic malice that knew no bounds.

The Tree found itself shrinking within itself – wanting desperately to escape this man and the contagious hollowness that he swam in. The Tree felt desperately afraid of this man ... and all those that he seemingly had the power to influence.

III

Day after day, week after week in this particular month of October, The Gang made their way across the river, traversing the stepping stones, and braving the climb of the hill until they reached The Tree. With every visit, The Tree felt its sense of hope fade. Its leaves became dull and fell from its branches, leaving The Tree looking most menacing and skeletal, a shadow of the beautiful and powerfully ancient being that it had once known itself to be.

The valley remained silent and deadened, a graveyard of nature where no life seemed to breathe. It was as though a silent warning had been sent across the valley, and anything that possessed a soul or beauty knew that it must seek refuge … lest it too become contaminated by this apocalyptic foursome. The only sound was the rasping breath, like chains on gravel, that came from The Gang, and their vulgar shrieks of triumph and confessions of the devastation that they wreaked in the lives of their victims.

The Tree felt painfully alone – its terror growing with every encounter. The Tree knew that the level of disturbance that it beheld was not typical – The Gang represented the perfect storm of ingredients that had gone wrong in the human psyche and soul. The Tree knew that in order to protect oneself from and deny the hated, fearful, and vulnerable parts of self, humans will force others to feel these emotions instead, so they themselves don't have to. The Tree also knew that the need for power and expressions of power can also manifest in different ways but when thrown into the toxic mix, such that it witnessed within The Gang, a seething cauldron of hatred and violence can emerge.

The Gang bragged and shared stories of their respective initiations into a world of crime and violence – the vengeance and lessons that they had been taught, and in turn had taught others. Lessons of brutality, sexual and physical violation, and for some, the torture, humiliation, and eventual taking of life. As these stories were recounted, the air within the stone circle thickened and seemed to squeeze any semblance of joy, life, and light from the world at the top of the hill.

The Gang leader recalled and bragged about his experiences of childhood and scoffed at the other children whom he had tormented. He spoke in detail of the hateful and cruel attacks that he had incited – others acting on his behalf, so terrified were they of being met with the same fate if they did not appease his wishes. Memories of the various small animals that he had sought out and tortured – an image of which came to the man's mind which The Tree caught a faint glimpse of. He saw the man hurling stones at dogs, rabbits, birds, and cats, and sadly often making contact.

The Tree convulsed with a sense of disgust and dismay as The Gang leader's behaviours escalated to even more frightening levels when he encountered other small or helpless creatures throughout his life – many of them not surviving the torture, which in some ways was a blessing, thought The Tree. The man was devoid of a soul. The Tree saw this from the way The Gang leader had sought out animals as a child to hurt and humiliate. Behaviours which had extended beyond parks, fields and gardens, and found their way into school as his fellow pupils were met with a similar fate to the poor defenceless creatures that he had preyed upon.

A more recent flurry of images were captured by The Tree of two beautiful (and somewhat familiar) ginger cats, one resembling a small but robust little lion with bright green eyes, and the other, a slightly thinner and regal looking creature complete with little white paws and a soft white chest resembling a waistcoat and striking hazel-coloured eyes. Both narrowly escaped the man's violence and cruelty as he emerged from the bowels of the prison he had been released from in the past, vowing under his breath to find the poor little beasts and skin them alive should they cross his path again. From what The Tree had glimpsed into the man's sickened soul, his malicious and sadistic fantasy had not yet come to pass.

From experience The Tree knew that no person is ever really truly all good or all bad ... but as it searched The Gang leader's memories and heart, it could find no trace of love or compassion, no conscience or care for another living being. And this disgusted The Tree, and a fiery hatred burned within its own soul towards this wretched man.

Eager to prove their worth, the remaining gang members shared their stories of grotesque torture and humiliation of others. They laughed with sickening glee as they recounted an incident of chasing and beating a middle-aged couple in the middle of a small town on a busy shopping day, kicking them to the ground and continuing the assault like a pack of wild animals. They triumphantly recalled the terror in the faces of the couple, as well as their pleas for help to the shocked and paralysed bystanders. They smugly described eluding the police as they arrived on the scene, and then unashamedly returning to the scene once the police had left and terrorising the traumatised couple further, adding to their sense that nowhere would be safe and help would only ever be fleeting. They basked in their power to incite others to join in their rampage, including the destruction of various shop windows, and upending café tables as a once peaceful afternoon was destroyed.

The more they spoke, the more The Tree's heart sank, until a contagious thirst for justice and vengeance began to swelled amongst The Tree's gnarled and glowing roots. They must be stopped!

IV

As the month of October continued, The Gang returned to The Tree and violated the sanctuary of its circle, continuing to recount to both The Tree and each other their brutal stories of abuse and torture of all those who were unfortunate enough to come into contact with them. As the days progressed, the stories became more extreme and disturbed. The Tree sensed that their insatiable hunger to induce suffering in others was building, but towards what, it could not yet fathom. No group, irrespective of race, gender, sexual orientation, age, or belief was safe from this despicable quartet.

Over time, The Tree learnt to tune into the sound of the wind, the scent of the valley, the ever changing and enchanting colours of the sky as the sun made its way across the heavens – dipping in and out of the voluminous clouds that often hung in the heavy October skies. This became its only solace, as it was ever increasingly exposed to the abhorrent tales told by The Gang who contaminated the sanctity of The Tree's protective circle.

The Tree could not bear to stray into the hearts and minds of these monsters whose sadistic pleasure outweighed the fear and sadness that they induced in their fragile victims. The sickening details of their tales made The Tree's soul lurch with disgust, often inducing a strange haziness and disconnect from what it was hearing. The Tree began to realise that its need to connect with the beauty of its surroundings and also to numb itself to the impact of The Gang's words was its only defence as it stood tall, strong but paralysed in their presence. It longed for their visits to end. Indeed, The Tree found itself hoping that perhaps their very lives would come to an "unfortunate" end.

V

The light of the day began to evaporate on 31 October – All Hallows' Eve. As the setting sun cast long shadows through the valley, the air became chill as the golden rays faded behind the surrounding hills and mountains. A sense of trepidation and foreboding had taken hold. Unlike the days and nights where this day in particular had brought much merriment and celebration, mystery and charm to The Tree, and indeed the valley, the feelings now within The Tree were ones of dread and anticipation.

The Tree sensed danger – something was wrong. In the distance it heard the cawing of crows and marvelled at their hypnotic dance through the valley, a cloud of black mist rising, falling, and undulating through the sky.

The Tree's brief sense of wonderment and peace was brutally obliterated by the unmistakeable taunting voices that echoed through the valley. The Tree knew with deep sadness that The Gang had returned. And this time they were not alone … they had fresh prey, and an insatiable thirst for blood.

As they came into view, the light faded from the valley and dusk approached. The Tree heard the familiar laughter of The Gang – dragging a man with them who looked barely conscious. His face was swollen, bloody, and bruised, making him unrecognisable. The Gang roughly threw him to the ground a few metres from the edge of the stone circle and proceeded to kick the man mercilessly – his cries of pain splintering the peace and sanctity of the valley.

The Tree could not imagine what reasons could have befallen such a fate upon the man, but The Tree also knew that it no longer understood the intentions of humankind. With the passing of so many Octobers, and exposure to this particular gang, it knew that no reason could possibly justify this brutal assault, but nor could it prevent such an atrocity from continuing. The violence was happening outside of The Tree's sphere of influence, and as such it was rendered frozen in both fear and horror – ever the observer, and ever the witness to the demise of the human beings who now visited.

The Tree's soul stirred with a growing sense of self-loathing – for its weakness, for its lack of power. And ultimately, the shame it felt for wanting to disconnect from the scene unfolding before it … to lose consciousness itself and deny the truth of the cruelty that was so normal in the world these days. To just let the poor man die…and even for The Tree's own suffering to end.

A fierce orange light stunned The Tree out of its ruminations, as did the smell of burning. The Gang's leader had entered the circle and using a bottle of liquid (the smell of which repulsed The Tree), and some old logs and branches created a small bonfire. This time, the flames did not offer a comforting glow. Nor did they produce a sense of warmth. Instead, the flames licked at the air like daggers, the crackling of the wood and dry leaves sounding like bones being broken.

A deep shadow was cast upon the face of The Gang's leader, his eyes flickering with an unnatural spark, his pupils dilated and black, giving him a look of something monstrous, and even demonic. A look that The Tree had seen before.

Gesturing and grunting to his subordinates, they hauled their victim into the circle and laid him down next to the fire. The Gang leader walked up The Tree, and in a vulgar act of disrespect proceeded to defile its strong and beautiful trunk with a torrent of his own urine. The Tree recoiled in its soul, wishing to strike the man down. But this was not its way. It was nothing like the foul being before it. The Tree was noble. The Tree was wise. The Tree was kind. But then a sudden wave of pain accompanied the sickening crack of one of its branches – The Gang leader tore free one of its lower branches and walked back to where his underlings looked to him with anticipation and glee. They awaited their instructions.

The captive lay on the ground, bruised and panting, his breathing becoming shallower. His face swollen and bloodied. His broken ribs causing screams of pain to split through his body. But no screams would come from his mouth. His mind had shut down, in the same way that The Tree's had longed to do upon beholding the savage attack.

'YOU!' the leader barked aggressively at the youngest gang member. 'Tie this to the tree! NOW!'

The Tree saw him hand a familiar object to the young gang member. It was an item that it had once seen a visitor tie to its branches in an attempt to end his own life. The Tree knew that this was not the intention of the leader, to end his own life. But felt in its soul that the rope was meant to be the sickening finale for the captive whom they had dragged into the circle.

The young gang member gingerly took the noose from his boss's hand and looked down at it with dismay, knowing all too well what its purpose was. Terrified of disobeying orders, he secured the rope to the strongest branch he could find, the bottom loop of the noose resembling an open mouth of a scream as it swayed menacingly in the breeze.

As the youngest member returned, the leader held up the branch that he had torn from The Tree earlier. Pulling off the remaining leaves and smaller stalks, the branch resembled a rough wooden pole.

'It's time we teach him one last lesson!' the leader said and then smiled cruelly. 'Who wants the honour? Who wants to make the piggy squeal?'

Eager to please and show his dedication to The Gang, the hulking lieutenant with scars on his face (like Frankenstein's creation) grabbed the wooden stick from the leader and raised it ready to beat the captive again.

'NO!!!' bellowed the leader as he grabbed the man's arm mid-swing.

'He knows that lesson. You know the other lesson that he needs to learn …' The leader turned his attention to his lieutenant and the youngest member as he said this and gave them a strange repulsive grin that The Tree could not decipher. The leader nodded down to the captive, and made another strange gesture with his hand. The Gang members clearly understood and after exchanging brief but somewhat alarmed glances, they did as they were instructed.

The younger gang member held the captive face down, whilst the lieutenant roughly pulled their victim's jeans and underwear down so they were scrunched around his ankles – a sadistic grin spreading across the lieutenant's face as he did so.

The Tree's soul lurched in disgust and abhorrence. It had listened to the tales of these four people for long enough to know what this meant … and what would happen next. Its mind went back to one of their stories of a violation that that they and committed in a men's bathroom once – leaving a man brutalised, naked, weeping, and for dead. The Tree felt immobilised – horrified and dismayed at the cruelty of these men and those who had sculpted their wickedness into being. But The Tree could not will itself out of its terrified and traumatised paralysis.

Voicing the very thing that The Tree feared, the leader triumphantly turned back to the youngest member and in a sickening rasp ordered him to defile their captive. The woman clapped her hands maniacally and screamed with delight before looking down at the captive and spitting on his now motionless body. She goaded the younger one – an energy of pure malice and spite emanating from her

271

malignant soul. And if he doesn't have the guts to do it, I will gladly prove my allegiance, she thought to herself.

The Tree could not fathom what could have corrupted such a soul that meant they would take such glee in something so brutal – so cruel. As it tried to comprehend this horror, time seemed to slow down, sounds became distorted and for a moment everything seemed hazy. The Tree did not know if these feelings were its own or the survival responses of the dying captive. But suddenly, these curious sensations gave way to the growing sparks of fury that were building, as was the untamed hate for these despicable people which surged through The Tree's trunk, branches and soul. A darkness began to consume it – a darkness as deep and heavy as the black vacuum of space. And just as powerful...just as destructive!

The Tree's attention was quickly brought back to the grotesque scene as the gang surrounded and moved in on their captive, a terrible and sinister aura emanating from them all. It heard the sound of another belt being unbuckled, and The Tree observed the leader unashamedly unbuckling his own trousers and pulling down his underwear, exposing his aggressive sadism and arousal before saying to each of them, 'And when you're finished, I will show you all how it's really done! And I will be the one to string him up like the filthy squealing pig that he is!'

Not looking up and starting to shake with a mixture of excitement and fear, the younger member began to advance on the captive as the soulless eyes of the leader remained fixed and unblinking on the group, daring any of them to be foolish enough to defy him.

Something in The Tree's soul snapped.

As The Tree had done so many times before, it drew upon the sacred power of its tenth silver branch …

A flood of raw fury and strength erupted from the core of the earth and coursed through the now shaking limbs of The Tree, the essence of the liquid silver taking hold and emboldening The Tree with the ultimate power to protect … and destroy.

A roar tore free from The Tree's soul and shattered its momentary paralysis. A cascade of images and memories of all those who had come before flooded The Tree's mind – people who had been hurt by those they trusted or those they did not know. People who had been targeted ... and others who were simply victims of circumstance.

Summoning its strength, The Tree sent a surge of energy that electrified its limbs and roots, and burst upwards in a terrifying display of fury.

The night sky split open as lightning sliced through the darkness, a deafening crack and rumble of thunder ricocheting through the valley.

The Gang stood momentarily stunned and released their grip on their captive, the leader hastily pulling up his trousers to hide his own limp shame and fear at the strange scene that was beginning to unfold. The Gang turned their attention towards The Tree, whose branches and body were now twisting, swaying and contorting violently amidst the rising wind.

The flash from the lightning cast an eerie and foreboding shadow of The Tree as it appeared to swell in size and ferocity. The youngest of the gang released his hold on the wooden weapon and with a terrified look frozen on his face attempted to flee from The Tree. He made it out of the circle and as far as the edge of the hill but stopped at the side where the drop was sheer and vertical – a wall of jagged rock tore down the side of the hill to the now ferociously unsettled river below.

With a sudden and sharp swish of its branches, The Tree lashed out at its first victim. The whip-like motion made a cracking sound as the vine-like branch made contact with the youngest one's chest – the force of which sent him reeling into the air. The Tree watched in slow motion, and with growing satisfaction as the young one's body seemed to levitate in the air – remaining suspended and twisted against the backdrop of the darkening sky – before plummeting over the edge of the hill. His body crashed upon the jagged rocks, and tumbled down the side of the hill, his neck twisting and finally breaking as his now torn and lifeless body reached the remorseless valley floor.

Seeing this alarming display of power and rage, the woman no longer clapped her hands or screamed for the defilement of their captive. Her focus shifted from the planned humiliation to her own terror and desire to survive. Knowing that she was next, the woman attempted to flee. But the surge of energy that The Tree had sent to its branches was now pulsing through its roots.

The Tree's rage intensified as the earth beneath trembled. Gnarled roots began to snake their way out of the damp fresh earth, causing the ground within the stone circle to become a treacherous terrain of shackles that threatened to anchor its victims into the bedrock of the hill.

As the woman fled from the motionless captive, her foot caught in one of the emergent roots, which tightened like a vice around her ankle. The ankle snapped. The swift movement was replaced by slow motion as The Tree observed the woman's expression shift from fear to confusion ... and then stunned realisation as her body twisted and fell. The last thing she remembered before she died was the smell and richness of the damp earth before her skull cracked on one of the circle's many stones. A spray of red liquid stained her hair, and spattered the once chalk-white rocks of the sacred circle - her face immortally frozen in shock as the light drained from her cruel and haunted eyes.

The Tree's thirst for vengeance swelled at the horror that was playing out in the once peaceful stone circle. It experienced a momentary shift within itself – a glimmer of past conscience that had been locked away as the night's events had unfolded. But these doubts were quickly locked away once more and replaced by a growing sense of righteousness as The Tree's ruminations were interrupted by the anguished scream of the lieutenant as he beheld the fate of two of his fallen comrades. He leapt away from the captive and his leader, who was now looking from The Tree to the last member of his gang. He understood the enfolding danger that he faced.

Ignoring the look from his leader that threatened vengeance and violence for his cowardice and betrayal, the lieutenant chose to save himself. He took flight from the circle, leaping over the gnarled roots and narrowly avoiding the whip-like branches now thrashing from The Tree. The lieutenant breathlessly and triumphantly raced down the side of the hill – occasionally slipping and falling on the damp grass that carpeted this side of the hill, but triumphant that he had escaped.

The Tree's rage was not to be quenched and as such it sent forth commands to the elements. The wind wailed and rose with the force and intensity of a hurricane. Rain and sleet pelted the fleeing lieutenant with a shower of icy bullets. The fierce river now bubbled and seethed – the rocks it contained smashing against themselves as the force and speed of the current intensified, and a slick layer of slime and algae coated the familiar stepping stones that had safely allowed those in the past to seek The Tree's wisdom. This time the stones would serve a different purpose.

The lieutenant reached the edge of the river and stopped. Panting and attempting to catch his breath, his reeling mind tried make sense of what was happening. From high above on the hill he could hear screams of fury and pain and beheld an orange glow which seemed to reflect off the swirling clouds above, and shimmer through the rain like a cascade of fiery droplets.

A feeling of dismay wrenched the lieutenant's heart as he beheld the river's raging current and the barely visible stepping stones that he and his comrades had crossed on their numerous journeys to and from The Tree. He knew that time was running out – the stepping stones were harder to find as the storm and elements assaulted him and the valley. Knowing that it was now or never, he waded into the water and hurriedly attempted to traverse the stones to the safety of the other side.

The Tree's focus was momentarily drawn from the scene in front of it on the hilltop, and instead redirected itself to the river far below. It communed with the once tranquil waters to intensify their journey through the valley and to claim the soul of the fleeing man. The river roared and rushed in silent agreement, bringing rocks and debris hurtling down the river's winding procession through the valley, knocking the legs out from underneath the lieutenant as he reached the halfway point across the river. He cried out in pain as his feet slipped on the slime coated stepping stones, and the river's cargo of rocks and branches slammed into his shins. A further cry erupted as his back slammed on to the stepping stones. He slipped and fell.

A flood of water surged into his open mouth, filling his lungs as he gasped for air. The lieutenant's hands clawed at the sky and then to the side, desperate to grasp something that could save his life. But the river was now in control and would not give up its prey. It swelled and deepened, and pulled the flailing man into its cold and tragic depths, dragging him along the riverbed. The man's silent screams gurgled in the water – his lungs burning with pain as they filled with the water, slime and debris that was hurtling through the river's body. He could feel his flaccid body being tossed as though it were a rag doll, his limbs twisting and contorting. The final image that burned into his soul was the hulking and monstrous silhouette of The Tree against the backdrop of the sinister sky, before an invisible pressure crushed his chest. The life that he had abused so terribly was expelled from his body and extinguished. The lieutenant was dead … and the river smiled.

Back on the hill, the final battle of vengeance was taking place. The Gang leader was no stranger to threat or violence, nor was the cowardice displayed by his inferiors an option for a leader such as he.

The leader stared defiantly at The Tree as he began to smirk. The Tree towered in front of him swaying menacingly in the storm.

The rain stopped. The thunder ceased. And an eerie calm seemed to hang over the man and The Tree. The valley held its breath in anticipation. Both the man and The Tree stood still – time seemed to stop.

Minutes felt like hours as both The Tree and the leader surveyed each other with silent disdain.

Seizing his moment, the leader's face contorted with fury, and with a guttural roar he charged The Tree, wrenching another one of its lower branches that was still dry and leafy. He twisted. The leader's fury matched that of The Tree's as he continued to wrench and tear at the limb until it was ripped from The Tree's body. With a triumphant yell he retreated backwards – mockingly and aggressively waving the stolen branch at The Tree like some grotesque trophy. He proceeded to hold the tips of the branch over the small bonfire, which continued to cast the unnatural and disturbing glow on the silent captive, who remained still and lifeless but was alive and breathing...but only just.

The branch crackled. It began to smoke, and then the sparks became hot and foreboding flames, igniting the remaining leaves on the stolen limb. The leader's sinister smile returned and spread unnaturally across his face. His free hand reached inside of his jacket pocket and withdrew a small bottle of clear rancid-smelling liquid. With a sound more like a cackle than a laugh, he held his new weapons above his head and began his second approach towards The Tree.

The Tree howled in pain – the clear liquid drenched its trunk and ignited. The heat of flames engulfed The Tree like an inferno tearing through the branches. The beautiful autumnal colours dissolved as violent and merciless flames tore through The Tree's branches, scorching its once beautiful body and bark. It was an oddly and tragically beautiful spectacle … The Tree now dancing in an inferno of fire, its powerful limbs and form whipping the air violently against the backdrop of the night sky, whilst uttering the most blood-curdling of screams.

Something about the raw untamed flames fuelled The Tree's rage rather than defeated it – a power and energy stronger than the sun was coursing through The Tree's soul, intensifying its desire for justice and vengeance. The leader's smug and triumphant smile faltered as The Tree's gargantuan form began to viciously sway, causing a storm of fiery leaves and embers to rain down upon him, searing his flesh – the smoke stinging his soulless black eyes.

The hateful man's stubborn defiance was his downfall as he raged at The Tree, until The Tree outstretched its burning branches towards The Gang leader, tightening around his body, and drawing him closer to its flaming trunk. Smoke from the burning bark seeped into his lungs, causing him to cough and splutter. A slippery tentacle-like vine wrapped itself around the man's throat and began to squeeze, his eyes now bulging with fear and hatred, whilst fiery tears rained down from the burning canopy above in a harrowing apocalyptic scene.

The Tree held the repugnant atrocity in its grip and searched within the man's soul for any sign of goodness or humanity, but a grim kaleidoscope of visons permeated The Tree's own soul – memories of what the man had disclosed but also the secrets that were locked in the void …

The Tree lamented for the women and men that the gang leader had raped for vengeance, for pleasure, and for power …

For the broken faceless man he would have surely raped and killed tonight …

For the nameless sons and daughters he had beaten and abandoned …

For the old man he had kicked and punched, and left for dead – all for the sake of a piece of jewellery …

For the children he'd forced to smuggle drugs into dangerous places, and the subsequent abuse they suffered …

The drugs he himself had sold to addicts, despite seeing their pain and vulnerability …

For the child who was never born because of the savage assault he had made on its pregnant mother …

277

For the many women he had terrorised and stalked ...

For the children and animals he had bullied, tormented, and tortured in his youth without care or conscience ...

For all those people whom he had harmed ...

And for lives that had been senselessly extinguished for the sole purpose of greed, power, and sadistic pleasure ...

The abyss that was the man's soul was dark and cruel, and without remorse or conscience. He was a terrible symbol of all the trauma that The Tree had come to know in the world because of the stories shared by the thousands who had trusted in The Tree, seeking compassion and sanctuary as they had.

As The Tree looked back on the face of its captive, it saw the sickening jack-o-lantern grin slice across the man's face, no doubt the last thing his victims had seen as they pleaded for mercy before they met their demise.

Time stopped once more.

The Tree's soul raged.

The Tree's soul wept.

The Tree's soul howled at the injustices that it had come to know.

And The Tree's soul was breaking!

It could feel the hate gushing through its limbs, its trunk, its roots, and its heart. The Tree felt infected by years and years of knowing the truth of the pain and horror that existed in the world. The Tree could not find forgiveness for The Gang leader, nor the trail of fear he had caused, and would inevitably continue to perpetuate if he lived.

And The Tree knew that it could not forgive itself for what would happen next. A wheel of vengeance and justice had been set in motion that it was powerless to resist. Ultimately it knew that it had come too far...and there was no turning back.

Through its tears of fury, pain, sorrow, and despair, The Tree crushed The Gang leader even more tightly and brought its flaming branches into the terrifying embraced. Screams erupted from the man. His writhing body ignited, his skin sizzled and melted, and the flames that he had forced upon The Tree finally engulfed his wicked soul.

Screams echoed through the valley, causing the birds, the owls, and bats to screech, and the wolves, the foxes, and the wind to howl. The Tree's screams joined the terrifying symphony as the man's flesh burned in its flaming embrace, leaving nothing but a charred and unrecognisable husk within The Tree's flaming arms.

With a final glimpse into the murderous soul of its victim, The Tree saw the wickedness that would never have been tamed, the hunger for power and violence that would never be satiated, and a soul so black that no redemption was possible.

The Tree's own soul roared!

And shattering like glass, The Tree tore the blackened and smoking body apart – dragging its charred remains into the bowels of the earth, to live forever entwined and strangled amongst The Tree's coiled and tormented roots.

VI

Heavy rain enveloped the valley like a fog. The torrential downpour cleansed and purified the valley of the murderous scene that had befallen The Tree and the valley on that fateful October night. The large and continuous drops of water quenched the flames that had torn through The Tree's branches as well as the fierce rage and vengeance that had erupted from within.

The rain created an unusually beautiful fresh and crisp aroma, which emanated from the grass and surrounding forests, mixed with the lingering scent of burnt wood.

The last remnants of smoke could be seen swirling into the sky from the top of the hill, where The Tree, now charred from the fire, towered above the valley, its vein-like and leafless branches reaching into the sky like inverted and blackened lightning. It was a monstrous silhouette against the deep grey and purple sky.

Evidence of the tragedy that had befallen the hill and valley were washed away by the fresh rain … but the poisonous remnants seeped deep into the earth where no beauty would flourish for several years thereafter.

The Tree's lower branches had warped and created a domed mesh of hardened vines that resembled a cage. Inside the cage was a lifeless body.

The Tree wept and noticing the bruises around the man's neck, feared that he had not survived his injuries from the previous night and thus, The Tree lovingly cradled him in its arms as the dawn greeted that first morning in November, before the rain had come.

The Tree's soul ached and was shattered. But it had no more tears to weep. Its consciousness was fading. The Tree's soul was sick and dying. The despair and hopelessness gave way to a desire for death. But in a final desperate act of hope, The Tree willed the blackened branches that held its charge to spread wide one last time as tiny white flowers of jasmine grew in seconds on its fragile limbs.

With a shudder and a swish, a flurry of jasmine scented petals fell like snow on to the body in a mournful act of love and sorrow, accompanied by The Tree's heavy tears, falling on to the man's bruised and battered body. Droplets fell on the man's bloodied and swollen face, The Tree willing its tears to bring some healing to the poor shattered creature in its arms, and as it did so, the man's features began to return.

But this act of compassion and generosity used too much of The Tree's already depleted energy. Its consciousnesses began to fade. But before its vision dissolved, The Tree witnessed the blood on the man's face evaporate, and the swelling reduce, revealing the once handsome and tormented face of his troubled friend … and for just a split-second, the events of the previous night made sense.

The Tree roared with fury. It screamed in pain. And it wept with grief.

Beholding its lifeless friend cradled in its arms was too much for The Tree to bear.

A dark wave emanated from its blackened trunk. It pulsed through its branches and its roots – permeating the entire hill which held it aloft, and the air that surrounded it. The once beautiful colours that characterised the valley, and the myriad sounds of wildlife and hope that had once been carried on the wind – enchanting so many visitors over the years – began to fade and disappear…

The valley fell silent.

The Tree's soul collapsed.

The world faded to black.

CHAPTER ELEVEN
November: Forgiveness

I

Since the harrowing events of that October night, an amorphous fog clung to the top of the hill, shrouding The Tree in a ghostly cocoon. Passers-by were oblivious to the possibility that anything existed on top of the hill. And for now, that was what exactly The Tree wanted, and needed.

No birds sang. No flowers bloomed. No bees buzzed. The woodland animals left for more colourful and life-enriched pastures. Even the river had become a sluggish shadow of its former self, a gurgling swamp of stagnation rather than the shimmering beauty that had once enchanted its visitors. The once glistening waters, crystal clear and teeming with life, had become a viscous swamp of decay – a dank and rotten smell emanating from its depths, utterly devoid of motion or transparency as it concealed the bodies of those who had been unfortunate enough to cross The Tree.

The sky remained a dull sepia colour, completely devoid of life, and seemed to mirror the temperament of The Tree as it slipped deeper into a torturous abyss of self-contempt and despondency, its life hovering in the balance. It was a bleak and dismal scene.

The heavy silence in the valley was deafening.

The guilt and dismay at its own vengeance and the unspeakable acts of violence had rendered The Tree (and its surroundings) profoundly changed. A feeling of melancholy hung in the air and infected all those who entered the valley, inducing within them a feeling of such sadness and anguish that they were compelled to turn away and return to their happier lives quickly, without really knowing why.

The last thread of consciousness began to fade, and The Tree's soul fell quiet. It had no idea how much time had passed, nor what had befallen the broken body that it had so lovingly cradled. It desperately tried to push away the horrifying images of wolves savaging the remains, dragging his entrails away in their salivating mouths, or the wretched crows pecking out his lifeless eyes.

The Tree silently prayed that some form of ceremony had been performed, and that the body had been committed to the earth with the peace and dignity it deserved. But The Tree did not know. The world was a hateful place, and so were all those in it. It no longer believed in any semblance of goodness in humanity and simply accepted that its dear friend had probably been dragged away by the lowest of the low, and his organs harvested to be sold to the scum of this planet.

The Tree felt tired. Tired of life. Tired of helping. Tired of caring.

It wept for the people it had helped, but also for all those whom its compassion would never touch. It also feared that it had nothing left to give, that its love and power was spent – power that The Tree no longer believed it deserved to be in possession of.

Barely able to stay conscious, and wanting nothing more than to fade from the world, The Tree allowed itself to lapse into a dreamless sleep, hoping and praying to whatever Gods existed that it would stay asleep, and perhaps never wake up.

II

Offensive and penetrating crackles, booms and bangs shattered the silence of the valley, accompanied by aggressive music without melody. The desolate and bleak landscape was temporarily illuminated by flashes of colour – poor imitations of the colours that once bloomed so naturally and beautifully on the slopes of the mountainous hills. Instead, these were the man-made flashes and explosions of fireworks.

Crowds had gathered around the burnt and blackened Tree, oblivious to its distorted appearance and suffering – these visitors had no reverie for nature but had simply found a viewpoint that was high enough to observe the annual spectacle, and a space far enough from the cities where they could drink, get high, and inevitably fight and destroy their surroundings.

It was Bonfire Night, and the visitors were already raucous.

The Tree stirred amidst the irritating 'ooohs' and 'aaaaahs' of the ludicrous insects that it now beheld trespassing on its land, its fragile consciousness being brought back into the present by the sickening smells of alcohol, tobacco, bodily fluids, and human beings.

Their mobile devices glowed as they sought to capture the artificial beauty in the sky that they were all so proud of, focusing more on the screens of their phones than on the actual wonders of the night. There was no peaceful and curious seeking of answers to their existence. No searching for the beauty of the constellations in the sky, or the tranquil hum of nature that gives birth to life. No ... The Tree saw these people with their greed and their ignorance taking ridiculously posed pictures of themselves, and no doubt uploading a vapid commentary on the banal day and night they assumed others would find so interesting.

The Tree had no patience for these people. No compassion. And certainly no love.

The Tree observed with contempt the party taking place in its presence and its own misery deepened. It heard indistinct chatter about facile topics. But it also gleaned conversations ... excited exchanges between people longing to find bodies that they could take 'selfies' with, as this site had become renowned for the discovery of mutilated corpses.

From what The Tree understood, a year must have passed since the events of Halloween night. And this once hallowed and sacred site had become a tourist trap. A place where people relished in the discovery and pursuit of the violent and the gruesome. But also, a site where people looked for 'treasure'.

The Tree heard whispers, rumours being shared of silver treasure that could be harvested. And even more fantastical stories about a magical tree with the power to perform miracles. The Tree could feel their hunger, their greed, their desire to steal from it. But it laughed ironically.

Good luck, you hateful parasites, it thought to itself. There is nothing left of me but misery, self-loathing and desolation ... and you can gladly have this!

Booming music now replaced the offensive bangs and crackles of the fireworks, and an aggressive form of merriment began on the hill. Slurred jeers and laughter. Reckless abandon with no sense of morality – drinking and dancing, fucking and fighting – with little care or consideration for anyone else who was in their presence.

People were fighting about whose views on anything and everything (politics, religion, class, sexuality, gender, and race) were right, and the complete inability to hear what the other was saying, both so convinced of their view being correct and therefore the other being wrong.

The Tree observed the complete inability of the hilltop inhabitants to sit with curiosity, to be open to the otherness of the other. Instead, it saw their respective determination to annihilate the other, to eviscerate the possibility of free-thought, or free-feeling, or even the possibility that there was a much broader spectrum that existed between the poles of good or bad, right or wrong, hero or villain.

The Tree saw how these heated arguments became explosive, no doubt fuelled by the intoxicating substances being pumped into their bodies. It observed the extreme ways in which both sides would act out verbally and physically to prove their point, making them no better than the other whose beliefs and opinions they sought to destroy.

Glass bottles being smashed on each other's faces, sticks of burning fire being pulled from the bonfire and used as weapons. Man against man. Woman against woman. Groups setting upon each other like packs of hungry wolves.

It sickened The Tree to behold, but it could muster no strength to fight. Let them kill each other, it thought. Sooner or later that's what they do any way.

Reluctantly, and with the little power it had left, The Tree peeked into the souls of the crowd that were in the process of trashing the once beautiful hilltop with their empty cans and bottles, with their packets of processed food wrapped in plastic, with their urine and vomit, and with the blood from their fighting. And what it saw in their souls confirmed its worst fears. It saw masked teenagers bearing weapons, terrorising and killing each other in the streets and in schools. It saw parents too preoccupied with their own quest for social media popularity and toxic relationships (which seemed to repeat over and over again), to focus on the needs of their crying and frightened children.

The Tree saw violent altercations between adults of all genders, race and classes, so filled with hatred and contempt for the world that this spilled out onto each other. It saw people fighting for change but fighting anything that represented difference. It saw the hunger to consume, to have more, to be more, and the absence of appreciation for what one has – for the simpler things in life.

There was a growing preoccupation with self and materialism. The Tree saw the dwindling of care and compassion for one's fellow human beings. Cities and populations ravaged by war and genocide. Families starving whilst others bathed in lavish decadence.

The Tree wept for it all.

Most tragically for The Tree, it saw the ways that these people had violated its beloved planet. How oceans, forests, lakes, and mountains were being desecrated. How the creatures that dwelt in these places were being systematically poisoned and destroyed. How human greed was beginning to tarnish everything that was once beautiful and soulful. And for this The Tree howled amidst its sobs ...

It wept for the animals. It wept for the trees. It wept for the rivers and sea. It wept for the planet surrounded by a field of metallic debris that obscured the once turquoise and emerald magnificence of earth, even from outer space. It saw the desire to colonise new worlds – new planets even – without care or concern for the world that would be left behind.

The Tree knew that the planet would thrive without human beings. But also, that history has a horrible tendency to repeat itself and that no doubt wherever they went, the same patterns and fate would befall the new planet, just as it had on Earth.

The Tree allowed itself a fantasy. It imagined apocalyptic scenes where the once proud glass and metallic skyscrapers were empty and wrapped in the tendrils of trees and plant life – strong and powerful branches tearing down these monuments to a fallen humanity and reclaiming the land once more with a carpet of mesmerising flowered meadows and woodland.

It imagined the man-made canals and rivers bursting their banks, creating tranquil lagoons and gushing, powerful rivers – crystal clear and free from the grease and slick oil that had killed so much plant and fish life.

It saw skies free from pollution and debris, enchanting whisps of cloud and exotic coloured birds soaring through the air rather than jet-streams of commercial sky-vehicles.

In its fantasy, The Tree swam with the schools of fish in azure waters, danced playfully with dolphins, rode the backs of the majestic humpback whales, and marvelled at the extraterrestrial wonder that were the octopi and squid as they navigated the unspoilt depths of the oceans.

No creatures were hunted for sport. No creatures died because of rubbish or pollution. The air was clean ... and the only sounds that could be heard were the roar of the wind and the rain, the chorus of beasts and birds, and the tranquil ebb and flow of natural life on this planet. A planet without human life. A planet of peace and sublime beauty.

Heartbreakingly, The Tree had lost all perspective.

It was falling into the very trap that it witnessed in those who were violating its landscape. It had fallen into the mindset that prevented it from seeing balance in the world – the good, as well as the bad, in human beings. It had forgotten that struggle and strife are necessary for learning and growth to be achieved. That it had heard so many stories of tragedy and triumph that proved that there could be healing and growth, even within the most shattered of souls.

But sadly, The Tree was now the one whose soul was shattered. It longed for nature's beauty but had forgotten the beauty that can be the human soul in all of its fallibility. Whilst it could acquire glimpses of the world, it only knew what it saw, and this was by no means a true representation of everything, or indeed everyone. Everything it perceived now was distorted through the lens of trauma and pain ... and also its own shame and guilt. It had started to project the very things that it hated about itself on to the world that it inhabited, so unthinkable was it for The Tree to believe that it was becoming the very thing that it had come to loathe in others.

The sound of retching woke The Tree from its lamentations.

A group of young women were holding each other's hair as they spewed forth the excessive food and alcohol consumed throughout the evening's celebrations and deposited it in sticky puddles on the deadened grass carpet beneath them. Simultaneously The Tree felt the warmth of something running down its once majestic trunk – a group of young men had encircled The Tree and were relieving their bladders before the journey home, slurring and shouting without shame or conscience.

Even the two men who had clambered amongst The Tree's fragile branches, sexually pleasuring each other, gave no thought to those who might see them or be showered by the sticky mass expelled from their loins in this moment of uncensored passion.

The Tree felt used. It felt abused and disgusted. It had no fight left. And when these last stragglers – pitiful remnants of selfishness and excess – announced 'WE'VE FOUND IT!' The Tree's heart sank even further into the pits of the living hell that it existed in.

Concealing their modesty, the two men in The Tree called down to the remaining urinators and vomiters to come closer. They had discovered a small but definitely visible silver branch.

'The rumours are true!' they slurred and shouted triumphantly.

A chorus of gruff and giddy cheers erupted form the group, their eyes growing wide and hungry as they too beheld the dazzling shimmering branch. And like a frenzied bunch of termites, they scaled The Tree – greedy goblins tearing and trampling its branches in order to reach their prize.

The Tree could feel its burnt and fragile branches cracking and falling under their weight and then of course came the pain. The ferocious pain as several hands wrapped themselves around its eleventh silver limb and began to twist, and wrench, and kick and bite – anything so that they could tear this glittering gift from The Tree's trunk.

The Tree had neither the power nor the will to stop them. It knew that they would succeed in their violation. And in some way, it did not care. It knew they would take the branch and no doubt use it to abuse its precious planet further, or simply turn it into some form of ugly decoration that they would photograph on their bodies ... or sell to the highest bidder.

But at last, the searing pain that spread through its branches, through its trunk and through its soul abated. The scavengers had torn the wretched branch free.

The group fought over who would take it.

The Tree smirked at their greed – knowing they would no doubt fight to the death so that only one of them could emerge victorious. As they pushed at each other and pulled at the branch, it broke into pieces, giving all an equal claim to their treasure. Cheering, and forgetting their fickle feud, they made their way across the stone circle and to the edge of the hill, whilst greedily clutching their treasure and cautiously eying their comrades with suspicion and envy.

They began their descent, leaving behind a heartbreaking scene – rubbish, desecration, and complete lack of care for the ground that they had partied on. They had enjoyed their night, they had trashed the site, and they were satisfied with what they had taken. They got what they had come for.

But The Tree would not give them the satisfaction. A familiar but somewhat diluted fury rumbled within it. It would rather sacrifice more of its life than have others misuse its power. And so, still connected to the divided silver limb, it sent a final surge of life and energy into their bounty.

The stolen pieces branch glowed white-hot, scorching and scarring the hands of the petty thieves, as they screamed and dropped to the ground in pain and confusion. And in an unremarkable spectacle of sacrifice, the broken silver pieces of branch simply lay on the grass of the hilltop and dissolved into nothing – much to the howls of frustration of the thieves. Despite the feeble display of power, an explosively painful wound shredded The Tree's already dwindling soul, causing the inevitable acceleration of its trajectory towards oblivion.

However, something else curious and unexpected did happened in that moment. Something that had not happened before …

As the branches disintegrated at the feet of the now arguing and disappointed thieves, back on the hilltop two spectral whisps seeped from the wound where the branch had been so carelessly and cruelly torn from The Tree.

These two ethereal and spectral phantasms swam through the cool November air like smoke and settled on two of the larger rocks on the edge of the hilltop, and slowly began to take shape.

III

Two ghostly beings the colour of jade sat opposite one another.

The hazy sepia night sky had begun to clear. A gentle breeze removed the last shades of smoke from the fireworks, revealing a dazzling half-moon and a sky full of unobscured stars. The embers of the deadened bonfire ignited again, and within seconds enormous flames curled and roared in the centre of the stone circle between The Tree and the two spirits, creating an atmosphere of safety, comfort, and warmth.

The Spirit of The Tree (the manifestation of its broken soul) looked bemused and befuddled. It resembled a man wearing a hooded cloak of moss and leaves, and his features remained remarkably tree like. Appearing younger than his years with a short beard of leaves, and a complexion of bark he stared at the alarming spectre in front of him. It was a familiar and ferocious looking face. A face etched with brutal and jagged scars ... but oddly seeming to appear at peace.

The gentle smile that The Scarred Spectre gave to the Spirit of The Tree was actually very kind, and not at all in keeping with the menacing face or stature that it originally perceived.

'Where am I?' said the Spirit of The Tree, clearly still confused and disorientated. 'And who are you?' he added suspiciously.

'You are on a once sacred hilltop,' came the Scarred Spectre's reply. 'And I am the man who was killed here!'

'Oh!' replied the Spirit of The Tree uneasily. 'That is sad! I'm sorry for you,' he continued innocently. 'And may I ask ... who am I?'

'You, my dear fellow, are the one who murdered me!'

The Spirit of The Tree looked alarmed and made to speak but the Scarred Spectre raised his hand patiently to silence the befuddled being in front of it.

'Fear not. I had it coming. It needed to happen, not just so I could be stopped, but so you could be here now. This was the only way!'

'The only way for what?' asked the now shivering and fragile Spirit of The Tree.

'The only way to remember who you are ... and why you are here!"

The Spirit of the Tree seemed afraid. 'But I don't know who I am. I don't know where I am. I don't know why I am! And I don't know you! Please,' he implored. 'Help me! Help me find out who I am, and what I have done!'

The Scarred Spectre nodded and under the cold starry night sky began to tell its fellow phantasm a story that would shine the light of truth through its hazy amnesia, not just about the Spirit of The Tree and its reason for being ... but also on the very nature of the darkness within.

IV

'I can see that you don't remember. I look different to the man whom you killed, and there is a reason for this. But we will get to that in time. But for now, you need to know one thing ... I needed to die. And you needed to be the one to kill me. Do you know why? Do you know what I planned on doing to that young man – your friend? I was going to humiliate him. I was going to parade his naked body around your precious hilltop and smear dirt and filth in his face. I was going to make the others violate him – with whatever instrument they could find. And then I was going to violate him. And when he begged for mercy I was going to slit his throat and toss his ravaged body from the hilltop so that it shattered on the rocks below. That is what I was going to do ... and that is what you saved him from!'

A hideous smile spread across the Scarred Spectre's face, much to the horror and dismay of the Spirit of The Tree.

Who was this evil loathsome being? It thought to itself.

'All in good time ... all in good time,' The Spectre replied, reading The Spirit's thoughts.

'You don't have to say anything just yet. Everything will become clear about who I am, and yes, who you are! But for now ... simply listen to me!'

The Spirit did as it was instructed. It felt fragile and vulnerable. It was disorientated but felt tethered to this place, and this horrifying and wretched creature in front of him. A painful stirring was felt in his soul, as well as fleeting fragments of memory too abstract and incorporeal to make sense of on his own just yet.

The Spectre continued his story. 'I should never have been born. But when I was, it was into a perfect storm of chaos. It turned out my daddy didn't like competition for my mummy ... he didn't like it all. They were both junkies. He was violent, and she was cruel. When he failed to kill me in her womb, he tried again just after I was born, leaving me in the bath to drown. My mother barely noticed. She was high again the moment she was released from the hospital. And he was just as violent as before ... towards her ... and towards me.'

'They left me to cry. A hungry and helpless little baby, drowning in my own excrement because they were too strung out to change my nappy. When I cried, they screamed at me. When I was sick, they shouted at me. When I shit myself, they punished me. They never held me with kindness or showed me love. They didn't protect me from each other, or keep me safe from their buddies, their buddies who would get drunk and smash up the place ... who would have sex with my mother for money whilst my father watched. They would get high together. They would fight each other, and when I got older, they of course started on me. I became just as valuable to sell and use. They abused and violated me, as I would come to do to others. They exploited me sexually. They exploited me financially – making me fight other children in dark dirty basements, and betting on me to win, by whatever means necessary. And my parents did nothing, except take the money or beat me if I lost.'

'My father gave me my first scar. In a moment of rare lucidity my mother screamed at my father. She said his face was as ugly as his soul. She goaded him by saying that her "beautiful baby boy" could not have possibly have come from him. She smashed a glass in his face. Through his howls and blood he smashed up the kitchen – tore it apart like a wild beast. And then he turned his attention to me. With the broken glass that my mother had shattered on his rageful and contorted face, he gave me this scar on my face. I was four years old. This was the first of many, some of which I added to myself. They became a tribal marking, a rite of passage. Something to make me look as frightening and grotesque as the monsters who raised me!'

'The teachers at school tried to report the bruises and cigarette burns on my body, but I was terrified I would be taken away. The monsters were all that I knew, all that I had. And if the police, or anyone, were to get involved, they'd just beat me harder. So, I stayed quiet. I stayed savvy. I hid my injuries but I punished the other kids.

Especially the happy ones, always the happy ones whose lives seemed perfect. I would threaten and intimidate them. I'd humiliate them. I'd beat the shit out of them. I would make them feel as inadequate and worthless as I felt, and I would enjoy It. I laughed when they cried. I spat when they begged. I fucked harder when they were in pain – girls or boys, I didn't care. All I knew was hatred and ruin, power and powerlessness. I vowed that I would never feel powerless again so I became just like the people who made me once feel afraid. And I made everyone else hold the terror and shame that I vowed I would never feel again!'

'The two coffins in that sad pitiful graveyard were a woeful sight. No one came to mourn or pay their respects. Why would they?! It was just me and a social worker. A fifteen-year-old boy needed support when his parents died, apparently. I didn't cry. I felt nothing except contempt. She died on a cocktail of drugs and with my father's fist pummelling her head. The pathetic prick of a man tried to overdose afterwards, but failed. So instead, he went to a bar, messed with the wrong people, and got a knife in his throat and was found gagging on his own blood. I found her, and was then taken by the police to identify him.'

'Soon after I went into care. I quickly learnt what it took to be top-dog. It was like animals in the wild. Find the biggest threat, the alpha, and then take him down by whatever means I could. I owned him. And I owned the other kids – my parents had taught me everything I needed to know. They and their friends had schooled me well. But a boy needs a family. So, the other lads became mine. A gang of broken lost boys, united in our hatred of the world and hidden self-loathing. We were the people that society forgot – the exiles. We were feared, and rightly so. We were cruel, and sowed seeds of desolation and terror wherever we went.'

The Spirit of The Tree listened patiently but felt even more confused.

'But why would you do that?' asked the Spirit of The Tree. 'You knew how it felt to be frightened. To be tormented. To be betrayed in the worst ways possible by the very people who should have loved and protected you. How could you make a choice to repeat that? How could you behave that way in good conscience?'

'Ahh, well there you have it,' replied The Spectre. 'It was all we knew. The frightened parts of all of us had to be destroyed. Our vulnerability had to be forced into others. We could only do that by becoming the very things that we feared, and knew. And as for conscience, we had none. A conscience can only be born when the conditions are right. My beginnings in the womb were traumatic, flooded with chemicals from stress and fear. I was infected with the noxious chemicals my mother consumed during her pregnancy. I was neglected as a child – no soothing, no love, no being held and rocked to sleep. The only touch I had was violent, or violating. The only words I heard and internalised were ones of hate. I only saw horror! And so that became my world, both inside and out.'

'My parents abandoned me, not just in their death but through their neglect,' The Spectre continued. 'Bodies that were physically present but rarely emotionally. I had a father from a long line of violent men. Men who would beat their children into submission. They praised toughness, and punished weakness. You may not remember yet but you have seen into my soul. You have seen what I have done. And I have told you the conditions in which I was forced to live. How exactly are those conditions facilitating of a conscience? How can a body, a brain, a soul possibly thrive when it is forced to live in the depths of the dankest of swamps. No. I had no conscience. I had no ability to master my emotions. I had no reason to inhibit my violence. It was only violence that I saw. Only violence that I knew. Only violence that could keep me safe. And only through violence could I be free of my own fear ... my own weakness!'

The Spirit of The Tree gazed upon the hateful phantom before it. Astonished by its justifications for cruelty, but also finding remnants of sympathy for the poor wretched being. It knew that the infant that The Spectre once was did not have a fair chance of life. That the environment that he was raised in was cancerous, and that the young boy had been infected by the wrath and toxicity that spewed from his parents. The Spirit wondered to itself if this boy's life could have been different if he had been met with love, compassion, tenderness? Could this have reversed at least some of the harm caused by his parents? Could his brain have evolved into something less primal and more compassionate?

The Spirit of The Tree did not know. But it did know that it felt conflicted. It wanted to forgive The Spectre in front of it for being fallible. For being human. But it also hated and wanted to punish The Spectre for the actions that were utterly unforgiveable.

Can one find forgiveness for a person whilst not forgiving their behaviours? And what does forgiveness mean? The Spirit of The Tree knew that we can find love and compassion for the wounded parts of another person's soul. That we can seek to understand the terrible journey they have been on to arrive at the point of no return. It can hold in mind the vulnerability and fragility of a child who is exposed to untold horrors. And it can feel love for that part.

But simultaneously, it can loathe the actions of that person. It can accept that the other has made a choice, a choice to cause pain and suffering to others. Sometimes intentionally, sometimes not. But for an action to be forgiven, the one causing the pain must demonstrate remorse – a desire to learn and grow from the experience. And ultimately to seek reparation and not continue on the same dark path.

There must be redemption, the Spirit of The Tree reasoned. As it mused upon this, a flash of memory struck.

Lightning … fury … mangled bodies … the intensity of flames … and a jack-o-lantern grin of a man before his body was torn apart.

The events of Halloween night came crashing into The Spirit's consciousness, and the same devastation that shredded its soul that night returned, as did the gravity of the crimes it had committed … and the consequences to its very sense of self.

How can I justify what I did? How can I forgive myself? The Spirit of the Tree thought sadly.

The Spirit of The Tree felt shame. It felt guilt. It did not doubt that it had acted to protect the beaten and tortured man. But in doing so it had become the very thing that it was repelled by. It had become everything that it hated. And for that, the Spirit of The Tree hated itself.

But that is a good thing, the Spirit of The Tree thought to itself. I feel guilt because I am with conscience. I feel pain because I know that I caused pain to others. I acted with vengeance because of care for another, not because it gave me pleasure. I acted to save, not to humiliate. But … I did act to punish. And in doing so, I have destroyed a part of my soul.

Both The Spirit and The Spectre sat in silence.

Neither were affected by the cool winter air. The moon hovering above continued to give them both a wistful supernatural shimmer, as both figures were illuminated on the hilltop, their particles swirling like silver dust. The Spirit of The Tree surveyed The Spectre with the jagged scar and fierce eyes. And in return was eyed up and down by The Spectre. A secret was held between them – a hidden truth that was yet to come to light.

The Spirit of The Tree looked back at its burnt and broken trunk, and the single, barely visible silver branch that remained – the last remnants of its life-force. Its once mighty body now reflected the pain and sorrow that resided within its soul. And for this, it felt inconsolable.

At last, the Spirit of The Tree spoke. 'I am sorry for what I did to you, but I am not sorry for the reason. I may not deserve forgiveness, but I did the world a favour by defeating you – murdering you! I can forgive the child in you for being raised in the depths of hell by those monsters, but I cannot and will not forgive you for the choices that you have made!'

'I don't need your forgiveness,' whispered The Spectre calmly. 'Nor have you defeated me. You assume that you have defeated me, but we are two sides of the same coin, you and I. And you have not yet grasped the bigger picture ...'

'What bigger picture?' demanded the Spirit of The Tree impatiently, a sense of strength and power beginning to return to its voice.

'We are linked, you and I ... and always have been. From the very beginning of your life, I have been there.'

'We are nothing! And I am nothing like you!' retorted the Spirit of The Tree, a growing indignation rising as it felt something changing in the energy of the being before it.

'We are nothing alike!'

'You cannot exist without me and I cannot exist without you,' The Spectre continued in his eerily measured tone. 'Think back across your life. For every visitor that has shared their story ... I have been there!'

'That it is impossible,' growled the Spirit of The Tree. 'I have been around for centuries! And you ... you have been in existence for half a century at best!'

'You misunderstand,' said The Spectre, with a coolness in its voice. 'We are timeless, you and I, but so too are my kind. We are infinite and cannot be defeated. We prey on the fractured souls of the weak, the desolate, and the wounded. We whisper in their ears, corrupt their hearts, and wrap our tentacles around their souls until they suffocate.'

'You owe your very existence to me!' the Scarred Spectre continued. 'It was I who made the crowd stand paralysed as they let their fellow men and women be tortured on this hilltop because of their feeble-minded fears and superstitions. I was the fire that burnt the healers and witches of the nearby villages, as they were condemned to death on this hilltop. Their ashes – thanks to me – fed the very earth that your hungry roots now draw food from.'

'I was the infection that killed the small child buried on this hill that gave birth to your soul, whilst the families lost faith in their Gods and became lost in their grief.'

'It was I who ate away at the hopes and dreams of the little boy on crutches and forced those who cared about him to watch and suffer as he did.'

'It was I who whispered in the ears of teenagers and incited them to target and humiliate those who are lonely, those who are different … those who are lost.'

'It was I who relished in the demise and decay of the rejected, the hopeful, and optimistic. I salivated over the young American's desperation for sex and drugs and provided the means that would bring about his ruin. I was the virus that coursed through his blood … and the blood of so many men like him.'

'I was in the hearts and minds of the gang who set fire to a seemingly quiet quayside of boats, and I urged them to bring ruin and destruction, to spoil and decimate everything that symbolised what others have and ultimately what they themselves lacked!'

'You already know me in the form I took in that fortress of misery and rage, and you did nothing to protect your so-called friend. Instead, you got high. You fuelled his addiction and lost yourself in your own drug-addled haze, leaving him and yourself even more vulnerable and exposed.'

'I am the drive for love and hate that exists in the stalker … and the desire to consume and destroy all that is loving and good. I am the fear that people feel when left all alone in the darkness.'

'I am the perversion that seeks to control and dominate – to destroy and sexually exploit. I am the rage that violates the innocent and thrives in secrecy. I am the contamination that fuels indifference and inaction that allows the innocent, the vulnerable, and the abandoned to be exploited and destroyed.'

'I was there when a fragile young man stood on the edge of a precipice … and I called for him to jump. I am the inciter of misery and sadism and the pack mentality that laughs at suffering. I am the camera that documents pain and horror, rather than the phone that calls for help.'

'I am many…and collectively, We are famine. We are disease. We are the ravages of war. We are torture and suffering. We are betrayal. We are the erosion to the soul of this planet, and all those who dwell upon it. We are death and destruction. And as you know all too well, I am the gang who rapes. Who maims. Who kills. I am the absence of conscience and I spread like disease! I infect the good, the kind, the righteous. And my greatest triumph of all, I have infected you!'

The Spirit of The Tree was aghast. This being had indeed been there throughout its entire life, and not just in the stories that it shared. But also in the memories that the Spirit of The Tree was slowly beginning to recall. But as it did so, a further realisation came. This was not just a single entity. This being had existed in many forms from the dawn of time. It had risen in the actions of cruel dictators. In genocide and mass murder. Through cults and abuse within families. It was the one who caused the loyal to betray those whom they follow. It goaded people into the betrayal of those whom they loved. It was active in the natural disasters that eradicated beauty and life. It was in the man-made atrocities which contaminated the soul of the planet. It was in the weapons of violence and the explosions of bombs. And it was in the laws and behaviours of the powerful who governed through oppression, through hate, through fear.

The Spirit of The Tree rose to its feet and bellowed at The Spectre, its form glowing brighter with the emerging rage that it felt.

'You are a disgrace! You are an abomination of nature! You are nothing! … And you do not have power over me!'

'You naïve fool,' laughed The Spectre. 'You don't even know who I am. You can't even remember who you are, and I have destroyed you!'

The Scarred Spectre rose to its feet but despite its measure voice, its energy was darkening. It could see the terrible truth as it dawned on the Spirit of The Tree. But it could also sense that the Spirit of Tree was recalling something else.

The Tree was getting closer to knowing its own truth – that if the Scarred Spectre was indeed many, as it had proclaimed, then so too was the Spirit of The Tree, and in that moment, the Scarred Spectre smiled.

V

As the rage within the Spirit of The Tree rose, so too did its power. A righteous anger illuminated its translucent ghostly form and infiltrated the sky, the earth, and the soul of the universe itself. A rush of euphoria was accompanied by waves of realisation and truth, and the powerful pull of particles, as the essence of the Spirit of the Tree was drawn back into its burnt trunk and branches.

The Tree could now feel its fiery vitality weaving through the bark, through every limb, both strong and broken, and it could feel its strong and sturdy trunk as its soul took hold of its body once more. The Tree felt a warm and comforting glow emanating from its very being as it stood mighty upon the hilltop, towering over the darkened spectre in the stone circle.

The Tree searched its soul and in doing so, a flood of memories came cascading into its consciousness. It saw the myriad faces of the people whom it had come to care for and protect throughout its lifetime and a flash of truth and realisation came to it like a thunderbolt.

'I have wisdom. I feel compassion. I give meaning. And I can forgive myself for the mistakes I have made!' The Tree whispered to itself.

But The Tree also knew that it had fallen from grace. It knew that it could no longer trust itself with human beings. It no longer believed that it could be immune to the melancholy, the pain, and the suffering that it saw and heard from the people who shared their stories. It knew that that it could not be trusted to not just act from a place of care but also from a place of destruction and vengeance – so great was its love for the people who trusted in it. And so strong was its desire to protect!

And so, The Tree made a choice in that moment. As it surveyed the desolate landscape – partly because of its own actions, and partly because of humanity's demise – The Tree chose to dedicate its remaining years in the service of the valley. It could forgive itself for its fallibility. For its desire to help, but it could not forgive its actions in the past and therefore it resolved to only use its power (its gift) for the restoration of the valley, and the beauty and harmony of nature.

And so year after year, it vowed to itself, that with whatever life it had left in its remaining silver limb, day by day and piece by piece of its soul, it would try to restore the valley back to its former glory. And maybe in the process it would discover its true nature. Perhaps it would discover who it really was. And perhaps it would find redemption, and maybe even peace.

The Spectre observed The Tree with curiosity. It could see how it wrestled with itself and its own conscience. It could see its need to repair the damage it had caused, and to be transformed in the process. The Spectre could see how close it was to the truth, but how The Tree continued to miss the bigger picture. It needed The Tree to understand the truth, because its own existence depended on it.

And so, The Spectre spoke up again, not to taunt or torment but to bring clarity. And it knew that there was only one way for The Tree to find peace. For it to reach the clarity it needed without the conflict of its fall from grace holding it back … The Tree needed to be forgiven.

The Scarred Spectre glided towards The Tree and placed its ghostly hands against The Tree's burnt and blackened body.

'You had to fall from grace,' it said, with an unusual kindness in its tone. 'You have prized yourself on being a saviour, a paragon of goodness, but the bigger picture that you are missing is the very message that you've shared with others over the years of your existence. You know the nature of duality, of the concept of yin and yang. And yet you fail to apply this to yourself. You have become so lost in your pride and desire to do "good" that you have forbidden yourself the necessity of being "bad". You know better than anyone that one cannot exist without the other. I needed to die … and you had to be the one to kill me. This had to happen so that we – you and I – could stand in this very spot so that you could discover the truth. But for that to happen you must first hear and feel what I have to say!'

The Tree stirred, interrupted from its fantasy of redemption. It had heard The Spectre's words, but only as a distant echo. But then three words came from The Spectre's mouth – not just from its mouth, from its soul. This being without conscience, this being who had brought death and destruction and terror to all those who crossed its path, this being who seemed to revel in hate, for once, said and felt something that at last The Tree could relate to.

The Tree felt compassion emanating from this being. It felt The Spectre's understanding. It heard the words. But most importantly … The Tree could feel them.

'I forgive you!' said The Spectre.

As The Spectre uttered these words, something happened within The Tree's soul. It was as though the shattered pieces began to weave together into an ethereal glowing orb. It spread from the heart of The Tree, reaching up through its branches, and deep into the earth through its roots.

And then came the familiar hazy feeling as its mind began to cloud, and the cold and barren landscape of the valley receded into darkness, replaced by the dawning of a long-forgotten truth.

The Tree could feel the essence of the other beings like itself that had existed throughout time. They were all connected through memory, like an enormous golden web of tendrils that traversed time and space.

As The Tree glided through time, it witnessed the beings that opposed the darkness. It saw the thunderstorms that quenched the parched earth but also how lightning caused the forest fires. It saw how the fires cleansed the forests, making room for new life, but also felt the sorrow for all that did not survive. It saw the bees, the butterflies and the array of colourful flowers, and their short but productive lives come to an end amidst the beauty that they had created. It saw the animals that thrived and soared in nature and the circle of life as their death nourished the earth and the other living beings – both animal and human – who inhabited it.

The Tree saw beings like itself in the souls of the leaders throughout time, known by many different names – both religious, spiritual and political – who rose in power and presence to offer faith, love, compassion, wisdom and guidance to many, only to later be sacrificed and betrayed. But their messages of love remained in the hearts of those who believed.

The Tree wept at the small acts of kindness that proved that beings such as The Tree were everywhere. They danced in the aurora borealis, much to the awe of human beings, the birds of the sky, the beasts of the land, and the creatures of the deep oceans. They manifested in colourful arcs in the sky as light refracted through tiny water droplets. They were manifest in hulking majesty of tornadoes as they swirled and weaved through the landscape, sparing many but sometimes claiming the lives and homes in a cruel act of destruction. But The Tree could recognise that this was not an act of cruelty itself – it simply just was.

The Tree felt the silent presence of beings such as itself in the wise words of teachers. In the tenderness and touch from those in the caring professions. In the courage and support shown by friends in the face of adversity and bullying. In the fierce protectiveness of parents towards their children, both human and animal alike.

The Tree could see that beings such as itself were many. That they existed in the many marvels and spectacles of nature. In the life that inhabited the planet, and sometimes only once in a single kind word or gesture. But no matter how fleeting, and no matter how tragic the circumstances, ancient beings of kindness existed and they eased those moments of suffering where a soul was on the brink of being shattered. In those moments, the lonely and wounded could feel less alone … even if only for a moment.

And so, The Tree understood what The Spectre had said – that they existed in harmony, that one could not exist without the other, and then another truth revealed itself. It was the truth of impermanence.

The Tree knew that duality was necessary. That peace follows conflict. Death accompanies life. And so, the cycle of constant change and impermanence continues. It knew that there could be no light without the dark. It was even coming to understand the wise musings of a particular philosopher and also a renowned psychoanalyst, both of whom it had come to know of from its life of listening – that in order to have branches that reached upwards to heaven, it must have roots that are strong enough to reach into the depths of hell.

And the painful truth was that The Tree had to fall. Not just fall from grace – it understood the necessity of this fall for its own learning and evolution – but also that its own life was not infinite. It had now witnessed the many beings such as itself. Sometimes they lived for years. Others for decades, others for just a second or two, and others for centuries. But irrespective of their lifespan, one thing was inevitable. The being, whether one of shadow or one of light, must (and will) come to an end.

Death is inevitable, and so was the suffering, the pain, the melancholy, and the desolation that accompanied this.

A part of The Tree hated this and fought this truth bitterly. A part of it wanted to deny it, to summon the last of its power and destroy The Scarred Spectre once for all.

'You cannot destroy me,' said The Spectre in a calm but somewhat weary voice. 'Because wherever you are, I too will be. And the same will be so for all of our respective beings, both young and ancient. I am inevitable. And I will always come back. And we will always die so that life can begin again. This is the cycle of impermanence and inevitability!'

And at last, the truth of who this spectral being was settled in The Tree's heart, its mind, and its soul. 'I finally know who you are,' The Tree said with a sad resignation. 'You are Despair!'

The Scarred Spectre nodded and smiled grimly. And then addressed The Tree one last time.

'Yes … and thus I trust that you now finally know who you are!'

'Of course I do!' whispered The Tree.

The Spectre nodded, and then bowed to the The Tree.

'Until we meet again!'

And with these parting words, The Spectre dissolved into the darkness, returning to the burning depths of the hilltop hidden amongst The Tree's roots, never truly vanquished and always lurking in the shadows.

Relieved that it was alone once more, The Tree gazed out towards the horizon with reverence, at the glorious constellations in the sky, towards the ever-present mountainous hills, and the forgiving forests in the distance.

The Tree sighed with relief. It connected to its soul and in doing so, felt the soul of the planet. It connected to the other ancient beings such as itself, and again caught glimmers of their existence. Of lyrics and melodies that moved people to tears. Of performances by actors that brought literature to life and both joy and laughter to the crowds. Of paintings and sculptures that evoked intrigue and debate. Of the warm colours of the sunrise and the cool majestic beauty of the moon.

The Tree remembered the loving expression of two handsome ginger cats and the love they evoked in their owners. It saw a child fall down and cry only to be hugged and comforted by a friend. It saw crowds of people massing together and taking to the streets in protest against injustice and cruelty towards the vulnerable and persecuted. It saw the splendid architecture that human beings had created, and the subsequent awe as people beheld pyramid structures orientated to the constellations and cardinal directions of the planet. The Tree felt itself in the glacial waters flowing over the mountaintops in the form of roaring waterfalls. It was in the stories woven through time through literature that inspired, that created meaning, that gave an escape, and brought peace and comfort to the lost, the lonely, the despairing, and the afraid. And, of course, it was in the feeling and expression of love.

With these visions, a sense of power, joy, and true realisation returned to The Tree's soul. And with a deep booming resonance, its voice echoed across the valley into the silence and emptiness of the night.

'I finally know who I am,' it said triumphantly to The Spectre lurking within the dark burning embers of its roots. 'You may be Despair. But I am Hope!'

CHAPTER TWELVE
December: Healing

I

The dreams began on the winter solstice of that same year. People all over the world woke with a feeling of recollection, and a growing sense of sadness. A powerful and vivid image haunted their subconscious – an enormous, majestic tree, branches full and lush with leaves, purple blossom, and an array of colourful birds swooping and orbiting it like a planet. It rose from the hilltop like a mighty warrior, its branches reaching into the dramatic plum-coloured sky, with a single silver limb semi-hidden amongst its foliage, shining and pulsing despite the surrounding gloom.

And the image of its roots – thick and serpent-like coiling deep into the fiery soul of the earth itself. The hilltop and surrounding valley appeared sombre and bleak, once stunning and enchanting, but now a mere shadow of what was.

But The Tree breathed ...

The Tree had life ...

And the dreamers felt its soul ... barely. They could feel that its life was fading.

When the dreamers awoke, the image lingered. Uncertain of what it meant, they went about their daily lives – taking their children to school, going to work, worrying about the myriad stresses and challenges that life delivers. But even in their daily meetings, or when shopping for groceries, or when engaging in conversations with friends, the image returned. And so did the fleeting feeling

– a pull towards something, a mysterious place where a powerful tree resided.

***

Another year passed. And on the same mystical night of the winter solstice, another dream came.

Dreamers all over the world once again beheld The Tree. Whilst still statuesque, The Tree appeared smaller. No peach or lilac or fiery blossoms decorated it branches, but the leaves however, remained vibrant. The sky had taken on a powder blue appearance, streaked with trails of white from the flying vehicles that flew overhead – creating a hypnotic, albeit unnatural, spectacle as they painted the sky.

A stone circle, once covered in moss and filth, was now exposed. Clean and sturdy rocks protruded from the earth in a circular formation at the foot of The Tree. And bluebells, unusual for this time of year, carpeted the hilltop, inviting the return of wildlife that had long since deserted this part of the world. The silver limb remained in its pulsing beauty ... but like The Tree itself, it seemed smaller.

The dreamers felt a sense of hope and wonderment as they beheld the scene, but the sadness and longing that they felt did not abate. It haunted them as they shopped for Christmas gifts. It lurked in the mind as they sang carols with their loved ones. It permeated their souls as they gave their prayers of gratitude.

***

Another year passed.

The world had become a darker place. Wars raged in different parts of the planet and humanity was despondent – the majority of people suffering poverty, uncertainty, and a growing sense of threat to their security and privacy.

But again, on the winter solstice, a new dream echoed loudly in the subconscious of people all around the world. A Tree appeared in the throes of autumn, despite the wintery landscape that surrounded it. It was shedding its golden brown leaves, the setting sun catching them as they fell, giving the illusion of the mighty tree raining fire upon the hilltop. The more the fiery leaves fell like tears of lava, the single waning silver branch was revealed – its glow and its pulse more diminished than in the previous dreams.

Despite the autumnal scene presented by the haunting image of The Tree, the surrounding valley seemed to be teeming with life. Unspoilt by human beings, technology, or pollution, the valley was returning to the sacred space that it had once been. A river of clean glacial water ebbed and flowed through the valley, and with it sprang new life – otters, and carp played wistfully in the cool river and glided without concern through the rippling water as dazzling sunlight sparkled on its surface.

Fields of poppies nestled into the base of the sloping mountains, and what seemed like an army of pine trees stood proud and tall, protecting their steep slopes. The dreamers observed the curtain of rain as it swept through the valley, further nourishing the earth and sacred circle where The Tree stood proud … but its fragility was evident.

As powerful winds tossed the falling leaves further from its trunk and carried them across the valley, a feeling of joy and peace could be felt emanating from this ancient being as it surveyed the return of nature's beauty, but at a growing cost to itself as the silver branch grew ever shorter.

The dreamers woke feeling confused by the spectacle, of something so pure and picturesque accompanied by a feeling of grief and decay. They felt longing and hope … but also the creeping feeling of fear.

***

Another year passed. And so too came another dream. But this time the dreamers did not just behold The Tree, now entirely bare and exposed in the swirling snow that eventually settled on its naked branches. The Tree had grown even smaller, its branches having shrunk and curled as though desperately hoping to coil around its exposed and feeble trunk, to protect itself from the onslaught of the elements. And whilst the hilltop remained quiet, the blanket of snow absorbing all sound, the surrounding valley continued to thrive. The crystalline waters of the river were not just restricted to the winding valley floor anymore but now spewed forth from the peaks of the mountains in glorious waterfalls whose rush and roar now resonated throughout the entire valley.

Deer and foxes, rabbits and donkeys, birds and insects all existed in harmony with one another, curiously shielded from the elements and able to thrive no matter the season or weather. And again, no trace of humankind could be found. The valley seemed to glow with an otherworldly hum as the energy and power of nature surged through the surrounding forests, igniting a chorus of wonder and jubilance from the creatures who inhabited it. Even the dramatically contrasting figure of the gnarled and shrunken tree added to its beauty. But for the dreamers it conveyed a message that had long been felt ... but not entirely believed.

The Tree was dying ...

And they were being summoned!

Unlike with the other dreams, a personal and unique memory fused with the scene that they observed. People from all around the world not only saw The Tree as it is ... they also remembered The Tree as it was. The first, and perhaps only time that they had met The Tree. And with this came the memories. Memories of their own tears, hopelessness, sadness, and despair. Memories of the wise and gentle words of the ancient being who consoled them. Memories of the spirit who offered them compassion and gave them hope, inviting them to cherish their lives and value the lives of others. And helping them find healing and growth from their trauma, and to rebuild and reclaim the shattered fragments of their lives...and indeed their shattered souls.

Yes, the message was clear to the dreamers. The Tree was dying, and they were being called to save its soul.

II

A sombre yet beautiful song wove through the restored landscape of the valley. A primeval and timeless melody of lamentation and reflection known only to the spirits of nature, and the creatures who found life in its presence. The Tree's soul was dying. But its song blessed the valley, inviting a charge of glistening energy to pulse through the river and waterfalls, the forests and trees that lined the jagged mountains and hills, and the stone circle upon The Tree's hilltop.

The Tree communed with the spirits of fire and a bonfire sprang to life in the stone circle's centre, bathing its blackened and burnt trunk in a soft and comforting orange glow. As the song resonated from its soul, it beheld its own form. A mere shadow of its former magnificence – gnarled and shrunken with barely any branches left. And its last silver limb, just a foot in length, continued to glow and pulse as it nourished and nurtured the valley back to its former splendour.

The Tree felt no regret. In restoring the valley, it knew that it had atoned for its actions. It understood who and what it was, and whilst not yet completely at peace, a growing sense of acceptance and understanding of its life had settled within its heart.

It was a crisp winter's night in the last month of the year, and also the longest and darkest night of the year thus far. A light flurry of snow sprinkled the hilltop. Tiny crystalline snowflakes created a magical sparkle on the rocks of the stone circle, and The Tree's scorched and tender trunk.

A slight but biting breeze carried The Tree's song with it … a song that found its ways into the hearts and souls of the people in nearby towns and cities as they too shared their own songs of festive joy and the arrival of a child - another being of hope and faith from the past – a gift from their own God. The Tree now understood the mythology of this being, as it too knew its own. And thus, it lent its own delicate chorus to the rising and rejoicing voices of hope and faith all around the world.

The fine wispy clouds that had deposited the snow were beginning to dissolve, giving way to the familiar constellations of the cosmos and a waning crescent moon in the night sky. The moon's cold but gentle glow caused The Tree to sparkle, the frost and snow still clinging to its form like mystical silver amour. The hooting and screeching of owls echoed through the valley, accompanied by the hum of fireflies, their tiny glowing bodies swarming towards The Tree and encircling the hilltop like the rings of a celestial planet. The luminous creatures ducked and weaved whilst still maintaining their circular orbit, much to The Tree's wonderment and delight.

Tears formed in its soul as The Tree wept at the simplicity and serenity of this spectacle, and felt a growing sense of calm envelop its entire being. And then, something even more wonderful happened ...

Deep in the valley, a pageant of lights could be seen. Tiny flickering candles being held lovingly by the procession of cloaked and hooded figures as they followed the river to the base of The Tree's hill. And with their soft and tiny fires, there came their own song, a song as ancient as its own that the spoke to the soul of the world. Its hum and soft melancholic melody resounded through the trees on the valley floor, and was carried both in the glacial river water and by the curious flock of red-breasted robins that had now joined the hundreds of people as they began their ascent towards the stone circle. Even the bees with their tiny furry bodies swarmed the valley and joined the procession – not particularly enjoying the cold night and breaking from their usual ritual – but nevertheless wishing to be part of the sacred ritual of reverie that was taking place.

Much like in the beginning of The Tree's life, the cloaked and hooded figures – shielding themselves from the elements – climbed the hill and emerged on the edge of the stone circle. One by one they placed their candles on the top of each stone, which curiously seemed immune to the frost or wind once within the circle, and continued to burn ever brightly. The bonfire continued to crackle and roar at its centre and gave the visitors welcome respite from the chill of the night, and invited warmth and care to be shown towards each other as they gathered round The Tree and circle. They lowered the hoods of their robes and revealed themselves.

As more and more visitors came, The Tree felt its soul lift with joy. The Tree knew each and every one of the visitors. It remembered the stories that they had so courageously shared. And it delighted in their lives and the continued glimpses of their stories and the conclusion that each one had reached.

The Tree laughed and sobbed as more visitors placed their candles tenderly on its remaining branches, and expressed their gratitude for the kindness that The Tree had once shown them. They thanked it for the careful way that it had listened. And for the wisdom and guidance it had imparted. Some shared further tales of sorrow at the ways that their lives had changed, and not always for the better, but also how the lessons they had taken from The Tree had continued to give them the strength to find meaning in their experiences, and ultimately, not to lose hope.

They shared stories of births and deaths, of the risks they had taken to find happiness and love, the losses that accompanied these choices, but also the settling of their souls as they gave themselves permission to listen to what makes their heart sing, and the risks they took in order to give these dreams a chance to be fed and to flourish.

The Tree felt blessed. It watched as the visitors shared their stories with each other, embraced each other through their tears, and in turn embraced The Tree – its love and compassion for these courageous beings growing with every greeting.

More visitors came. And more visitors left, but not before leaving some form of offering for The Tree as another token of their appreciation: lovingly grown flowers and vegetables, small but beautiful pieces of art, inspirational books filled with stories and poetry, hand-woven blankets of cherished children both alive and no longer here, and soft cloth animals representative of all those that were so common to the valley and the stone circle. And simple stones and sticks carved with beautifully ornate runes and symbols of the old nature religions, and photos of loved ones and stunning places of natural beauty that had been visited and explored thanks to the encouragement of The Tree.

The scene was indeed humbling. The Tree knew that its own life had made a difference in the lives of these people, and certainly the end chapters of its own life would not define its entire existence. It was humbled and in awe of the ways the visitors had continued to learn and grow. How their lives were not perfect (far from it), but how they endured and survived even in the face of continued adversity and struggle.

One by one the crowd dwindled, and the cloaked figures waved their final farewells and began their descent back into the valley, leaving behind just a small group of people.

There was something different about this particular group who lingered – they were gathered around the fire, their hoods still covering their faces. Not only was there a sense of familiarity and love, the feeling went even deeper. The Tree could feel its own essence in this group. It felt connected to them in a way that it had not with the others.

310

'Please,' implored The Tree gently. 'I can feel my life is waning. Show yourselves.'

And in the flickering candlelight and continued roar of the bonfire, each of the figures turned to face The Tree.

It recognised most of their souls instantly and a surge of pure love burned in its soul, emitting a beautiful glow. The tiny silver branch ignited causing a shimmer of light to shoot skywards. The beam of light split through the night sky releasing radiant waves of colour. The aurora borealis, set free and in motion, danced through the sky above the hilltop, illuminating the valley and the crowd below in exquisite shades of turquoise and rose, gold, fuchsia, and emerald as it weaved and undulated to the returning symphony of The Tree's ancient song.

III

The first of the company to come forward and lower their hoods were two giggling young women – the pair had been chatting with each other incessantly. Whilst The Tree did not know them, it recognised their souls instantly. One with hair the colour of sand, and skin as white as milk. The other with an unmistakeable Latin beauty, and long raven-black hair. The mixture of Spanish and Swiss German was exchanged between them, both leaving The Tree in no doubt as to who their fathers were. Now speaking in perfect English, but still retaining her lovely accent, Sergio's daughter embraced The Tree. Christoph's daughter, mirroring her friend, quickly did the same. With tears in their eyes and whisperings of thanks to The Tree, it beheld what had become of the two young men it had come to love so many years ago ...

As the wintery valley dissolved, The Tree was transported to the valley of waterfalls in Switzerland where Christoph and his wife, in full beekeeper clothing, tended so lovingly to the rows of beehives on their farm. Smoke puffer in hand and carefully inspecting the frames of the hives, they spoke with rapid enthusiasm about the honey that these marvellous creatures created. They spoke of the wax for the candles that Christoph's wife would fashion, and the medicinal concoctions that Christoph himself would create from the golden nectar, as well as the jars of honey that would be sold by the thousands.

The Tree saw their quaint and humble wooden chalet, surrounded by bell-wearing cows, nestled into the mountainside. This picturesque view was accompanied by the breathtaking majesty of the Swiss valley and the wispy waterfalls cascading from the mountain tops, wistfully billowing into the valley below. Their life was happy, but certainly not without its struggles and uncertainty. But The Tree could see that Christoph had indeed kept his promise to himself, and pursued his dreams. And what made it even more wonderful was that his dear friend was there to share it with him every step of the way.

The silver orbs that The Tree had given the young men to share had performed their task perfectly. Never to have a lonely day in their lives again, the silver orbs had kept the two young men connected ever since they had left The Tree and returned to their respective countries. Passionate conversations, laughter (and of course the occasional argument) were shared by the two young men as they grew into adults, their minds and souls connected by the magic of the silver branch.

The Tree saw its dear Sergio in the scorching hot Mexican sun as he excavated and uncovered new and exciting chambers and structures of his adored Teotihuacan pyramids, such was the renowned archaeologist that he had become. It saw him kissing his wife goodbye as he set out into the humid Mexican nights and regaled enthusiastically about the planets and constellations to wide-eyed students as they peered through telescopes on the dark and deserted Avenue of the Dead.

The Tree saw with delight that every six months both Christoph and Sergio would cross the oceans and spend time with each other in their respective countries, an act of friendship and love that would extend to their own daughters – curiously both born on the same day of the year, who of course became fierce friends. They too would never spend a lonely day in their lives, thanks to the true, precious, and unbreakable friendship of their fathers, and the power of the two silver orbs that the girls had inherited ... and used often.

As the scenes dissolved and The Tree returned to the crisp air of the hilltop, it saw both young women holding a gift for The Tree in their open palms.

'Mi padre found this rock in one of the hidden chambers of the pyramid,' Sergio's daughter said with a kind and delightful smile. 'He carved it himself and told me to bring it you, that you needed it, and you would know why it is important!'

In her hands she held an exquisitely carved and small obsidian replica of the Pyramid of the Moon, which she presented to The Tree before lovingly placing it on the ground in front of it. She bowed respectfully.

Christoph's daughter, mirroring her friend's smile, held a jar of golden honey, its powerful and intoxicating scent enlivening the soul of The Tree. She too placed this offering next to her friend's.

'Mein vater told me to tell you thank you and to give you this. He said you helped him find his way, but he also said you healed his loneliness. That you had given him the greatest gift of friendship with Sergio, and he hopes that you will accept his gift in return. A token of the love and labour of our farm.'

The Tree could indeed feel the love – love emanating from the well-blossomed friendship in its midst ... and also from the two men, separated by oceans, but forever in each other's hearts and minds.

Despite its fragile and decrepit appearance, The Tree respectfully bowed to the two young women without even trying to hide the tears of joy that streamed down its bark. They too reciprocated and embraced The Tree one final time before rejoining the others around the bonfire – their incessant chattering and laughter resuming and echoing through the valley.

***

'Howdy partner!' came the cheerful, cheeky and familiar voice of Austin over the crackling noise of the bonfire, his handsome face bathed in the glow of the flames as he too removed his hood and cloak to reveal his characteristic plaid shirt, jeans and cowboy boots.

The Tree's soul leapt with joy to see the happy and healthy man that Austin had become. Despite his healthy appearance, The Tree could sense that the years since their last meeting had not always been kind. It sensed that Austin, whilst smiling and relieved to be reunited with The Tree, had experienced deep and profound loss, and continued daily struggles that required him to always be mindful of how he looked after his body. But as Austin ran towards it, The Tree opened its remaining arms to embrace this wonderful soul, a soul who had finally found his sense of worth and an ability to finally be kind to himself.

'I'm still alive, buddy,' whispered Austin. 'It was close at times but the pills worked ... I survived!' And then added sadly, 'But not all of us did. You probably know that, right? I lost so many friends ... and boyfriends. I dunno why I survived though?'

He shook his head, and wiped tears from his eyes.

'I don't know if it was the fruit you gave me. Y'know ... that apple? But I think it did something, helped me to stay alive, just long enough for the treatments to change, to get better. And they are. Seriously, man, they are soooo much better! No one dies from this shit anymore, but there are other threats. You probably know it too.' Austin blushed, his eyes downcast before he continued.

'I got hooked on some other stuff, bad stuff that takes you out for days. BUT ... I am clean now. I've gotten help. I've met guys who have helped me. Some of them have fallen though, and I've had to end my friendship with them. I've gotta take care of myself, y'know? You taught me that! I know I'm worth more than the shit I put in my body, and I know now that I don't deserve to die no more, and neither did my friends!'

The Tree smiled but also nodded solemnly. It knew of the threat that Austin spoke of and had seen the pain these drugs still caused, and how they continued to ravage Austin's community. But it sensed a power in Austin, a determination, a strength. He is, and always was, a fighter ... and ultimately a survivor.

'And hey,' Austin continued enthusiastically. 'It's not just me anymore!' With a triumphant grin, he held up his left hand to show The Tree the platinum band on his finger – his wedding ring.

'You know that guy I met? Just before I left you? The one I was gonna go study with?'

The Tree nodded eagerly. It did indeed remember the man whom Austin spoke of and the connection they seemed to have formed.

'Well it's not him!' he laughed. 'He actually turned out to be a bit of an asshole. He fucked around on me. To be fair, so did I ... but he broke the rules and didn't show me the respect that you taught me to have for myself. So, he was gone! There were other guys too ... some were right, others were wrong. Others were right but it was just the wrong time. But anyway, I went back to Oklahoma ... not to see my parents! Hell, I don't even know if they are dead or alive. Well, they're as dead to me as they told me I was to them. But anyway ... I went back to Oklahoma and I went to my sister's grave. Out of respect, y'know? And outta some weird curiosity, I guess.'

The Tree felt proud of its American friend and the journey he had been on. But it could also see, and knew from his life, that some wounds never truly heal. The pain of betrayal and rejection by his parents still stung Austin's heart ... as did his grief for the sister he never knew. After all, how could it not? But The Tree did as it had always done ... it listened with love and compassion, and hoped that Austin could feel The Tree's unwavering care and acceptance of him.

'And right there in the cemetery, of all places, I met this guy. He had the kindest smile. He saw me laying flowers on my sister's grave and he just looked at me with such kindness that my heart melted ... I burst into tears. And then I felt his hand on my shoulder. He didn't say anything, he just looked at me with the same kindness you always did, and so I hugged him. I don't know what came over me, but I just hugged him. And the strangest thing was that he hugged me back. We didn't say anything. We just hugged, and I cried!'

'And to be honest, the rest is history. We went for coffee at this diner, he told me about his parents who had died. I told him about my sister, and those people who were never my parents,' he added bitterly.

'And I told him everything. About my past, about my struggles, about my diagnosis. And he was cool, y'know? He just placed his hand on mine and he smiled kindly, such a beautiful smile! And so, we dated. He treats me like a king, and guess what? I finally believe that I'm worth it! So, after a while we moved in with each other. Sure, we've had our ups and downs but hey, who doesn't right? And I asked him to marry me six years ago. And he said yes!'

'And where is this wonderful man now?' asked The Tree, mirroring Austin's joy and feeling intrigued, but also painfully aware of its own fatigue and waning energy.

'Oh, he's back in Naw'luhns ... taking care of our daughter!' he added with a grin. 'She's five years old, man? Can you believe it? And she's awesome. Apart from my husband, I don't think I've ever loved anyone so much in my entire life! I would do anything for her! So that's why we set up The Retreat back in Naw'luhns, good old Louisiana. It's still not the most progressive of places BUT there is something about that apple you gave me! I planted it in our backyard and now we have an orchard. Its damn huge, man, and it's always in bloom! What the fuck? The apples are always delicious too ... and the space somehow just feels safe. So, we opened it up, to guys like me and their friends and family. We've created this community where people can heal and find peace ... where no one has to feel alone with their diagnosis, or feel abandoned. We've created this community where everyone has worth and is respected. It's fuckun' awesome! My fella teaches yoga, and I love it. And so does my daughter. She's got a talent, even at age five. Some kinda musical prodigy maybe. And all the guests, they love her, and they love him. And so do I!'

The Tree's soul swelled with pride as it gazed on the content and loving face of Austin. It knew how far into the shadows Austin had fallen in the past and did not underestimate for a second the battles that he had fought, and the battles that he would continue to face. But what it knew for certain was this: Austin was loved, Austin was healthy and safe, and most importantly, Austin had found a love for himself that enabled him to show others the same care and compassion that he believed he was worthy of.

Austin now looked serious, and the tone of his voice changed. He held out a silver apple, slightly bigger than normal size and placed this with the honey and obsidian pyramid.

'I get the sense that you might need this. It's from my orchard but I think it's a part of you too. I don't know what it means, or even what it does, but you once gave me a gift when I needed it the most, and it's my turn to return the favour!'

With tears in his eyes, he wrapped his arms around The Tree.

'I love you, man. Please don't die! We need you ... we all still need you!' he whispered.

Wiping his eyes, he walked away from The Tree and back towards the fire, only turning back occasionally – an imploring and desperate look in his eyes.

The Tree wanted to offer something ... some semblance or reassurance. But as its energy waned, so too did its ability to offer the comfort that it knew its dear friends needed. But a warmth filled The Tree's heart as it reflected on Austin's life, as well as a heaviness.

The Tree closed its eyes and rested.

***

The gentle purring of two cats awoke The Tree from its brief slumber. But these were not ordinary cats, these two ginger beauties were curiously larger than your common house cat, and despite their age, seemed both youthful and exceptionally healthy.

As The Tree shook off its grogginess, it of course recognised its feline friends who were nuzzling at its base and rubbing their tiger-like heads affectionately against its bark. It also sensed traces of its own essence in these playful boys, and a flash of memory came of the two kittens eagerly drinking from its silver sap in order to save their beloved Jonathan. As this memory came, The Tree searched eagerly amongst the remaining robed and hooded visitors for any sign of Jonathan and Mary ... but there was none. The Tree's soul sank as it feared the worst – that the couple, once so grateful and full of life, had finally succumb to time or tragedy.

'Grandma and Grandpa send their love!' came a teenage girl's voice from the gatherers around the bonfire. Her older brother then chimed in.

'And they're sorry they couldn't come here themselves. They're getting on a bit and Grandpa's just had a new hip. There's no way he was going to make the climb,' said Sebastian with a shrug and a smile.

'Plus,' Lulu added, 'they have to look after the farm. I bet you didn't know that we've got one of those did you? Or maybe you did. Grandma and Grandpa said that you know EVERYTHING! We love it. Grandma and Grandpa opened a sanctuary for donkeys! Grandma inherited some money, not long after the pandemic. So, Grandpa used his skills – you know how he loves to build things – to create a beautiful paddock for all of these donkeys that they've rescued. I love them so much, and Grandma and Grandpa of course!'

The Tree gazed at the two blonde-haired, blue-eyed siblings and marvelled at the kind and affectionate way they fussed their two uncles' majestic cats and the incredible human beings they had become.

It remembered so fondly how they danced at their uncles' wedding right here on the hilltop. It recalled with joy the tender and sweet speech given by the bashful nephew, and the applause that followed. And it thought of Jonathan and Mary, how their lives had changed but how they had still found a way to give back and bring care and compassion into the lives of others.

'We're going to inherit it one day, Grandma and Grandpa said so,' said Sebastian excitedly. 'Of course, I might be a professional footballer by then, and maybe Lulu will be an actress or something. But we'll always make time for the donkeys. We ask visitors to take them for walks. There's a forest of blue bells on the edge of the field that people can take the donkeys for a walk in. Grandpa then teaches people how to care for them, to clean and comb them, and to just give them love. Then grandma comes out with her baking as a reward for people's kindness. It's great! People seem to love it, even the adults do!'

The Tree's soul soared. It could just imagine Jonathan and Mary recounting the day's events to each other, and of course expressing their gratitude for the blessings of each day. Even now it could sense the strength of their love, and how even with their change of fortune, their humility and kindness had not waned.

'And are they well?' asked The Tree, desperate to know that its favourite couple were okay, that their time was not yet at an end.

Both teenagers nodded and grinned. The two ginger cats purred in accompaniment.

'Oh yes,' the siblings said in unison. 'They are very well, and very happy, and very grateful,' concluded Sebastian with a laugh.

'Grandpa sometimes gets a little confused,' added Lulu. 'And Grandma gets more tired … but no, they are fine. And it's nice for us to look after them now. They've always been so kind to us. And fun. It's nice for us to be able to do nice things for them too!'

Again, The Tree pictured the peaceful scene of the elderly couple with their arms around each other, sitting on the open porch of the home on the edge of the donkey fields. Content. Happy. At peace. And grateful … grateful for their life. Appreciative of the lessons they had learnt from their struggles. And thankful to still have each other.

The Tree had a sneaking suspicion that when it was eventually the time for one of them to walk into the light, it would not be long before the other followed. The Tree knew that when a love is a strong as Jonathan and Mary's, a broken heart can bring death quicker than any other affliction. But it hoped that this time would not be yet, that their children, their grandchildren, the cats, and of course the donkeys would still have many more years of love and joy with these two incredible human beings.

The siblings approached The Tree and lay their gifts at its trunk. Lulu gently placed an assortment of baked goods in a familiar wicker hamper near to its roots, whilst her brother tied a scarf of his favourite football team around The Tree's body, and laid a small carved wooden donkey next to the hamper. They too hugged The Tree affectionately, joined by their handsome feline companions, and whispered their own prayers of gratitude to The Tree, who smiled kindly in response, so blessed it felt to have met this charming little family and to have shared in all that they had endured.

***

As Sebastian and Lulu returned to the fireside, a young woman came forth who was completely unknown to The Tree. She couldn't have been any older than eighteen, and she appeared somewhat hesitant and timid as she lowered her hood and approached The Tree. In her hands she clutched two objects. A small jade statue of a wise and enlightened buddha perched upon a jade mountain top. And a small set of metal scales, that The Tree recognised instantly as being The Scales of Justice.

'Welcome, my dear,' said The Tree kindly, emanating warmth and safety to put the young woman at ease. 'And who might you be? You have not visited me before.'

'Um, Hi. Ummm, my name is Paige. I've been sent here by my boss ... well, not my boss exactly but I am her assistant. Well, first I was a client but now I'm her assistant. Umm, does that make sense?'

The Tree chuckled to itself – the familiar way in which Paige spoke reminded The Tree of a young woman it had come to know for only a day, several years ago. And it suspected that this was the boss that Paige spoke of.

'Tell me,' said The Tree fondly. 'How is Mei?'

Paige smiled, and a look of relief seemed to overcome her body. 'Oh wow, she said you'd guess. She said that you knew everything. And she wanted me to tell you that she had a dream, or THE dream. I'm not sure which, she speaks very fast, have you noticed? I just about understood what she was saying. Something about a dream and you needing her. Or needing something from her, reassurance that she was okay? Or that she was doing good in the world. Or was it that you had helped her? Oh gosh, it's all a bit muddled now. I'm sorry. But anyway …, she sent me here because she said that you are in need. And that you kept her safe! She wanted me to tell you that she keeps people safe too, and then she asked me to ask you to guess how she does this.'

The Tree chuckled again. Mei had not changed. She was still a delight. Beaming with pride at what it suspected, The Tree answered the young woman's question.

'Well, I assume her studies trained her to work in the justice system, hence the scales you hold in your hand. And my guess would be that she is a lawyer, and a rather successful one at that, hence why she has you!'

Paige blushed but nodded. 'Well, she shouldn't really have an assistant, but she demanded it of her own boss. After she took on my case, she could see that I was struggling, that I had nowhere to go. And no one to support me … after my … umm, my– my ordeal.'

The young woman fell silent and looked downwards. A look of shame crept across her face. For a fleeting moment The Tree caught a glimpse of what the group of vicious men had done to her … but this was quickly locked away and replaced with the memory of how Mei had fought the case. The Tree saw the power and strength behind her arguments. Her rapid and obviously impossible to interrupt speeches. And the victorious cheers in the courtroom as the accused men were brought to justice, and incarcerated. The Tree saw Mei hugging the young woman who now stood before it, and the look of triumph and resolution in Mei's eyes, her growing determination to protect both men and women who had experienced similar to what she herself had escaped from in the past.

'Mei gave me the strength to fight. She fought for me and showed me how to protect myself. And she gave me a job so that I could help her to help others. Despite how much she talks, she was vague about her own experiences, but what she did say was that something dark had followed her throughout her school life. And that it was thanks to "a nice tree" that she survived. I thought she was speaking in riddles, but when she saw my confusion she shared something more. She told me about the dream. And that she had to come back here, but also that she couldn't because one of her clients needed her in court. She wouldn't abandon them! So instead, she sent me. She wanted me to see for myself the being who gave her the strength to fight … and to survive!'

The Tree felt deeply moved. And its soul soared knowing that Mei was at large in the world – that she had indeed escaped as it had hoped. And that she was engaging in a crusade of justice (Paige no doubt being one of many that she had helped already). The Tree felt relief in its heart to know that people like the abusers from Mei's school would be tried and brought to justice under the law … and not through acts of revenge or violence.

Awkwardly, Paige gave The Tree a hug and whispered to The Tree, 'We will keep fighting, I promise!' and then scurried back to the bonfire with the others.

***

Paige had barely made it back before two other robed figures bounded forwards – well, one was dragged by the other, their hands clamped firmly together. One of their hoods fell back … a serious but attractive face was revealed. The woman eyed The Tree suspiciously, as if not quite sure what to make of it and let go of her wife's hand.

'Oh come on, it's alright,' came the familiar voice. And again, The Tree's heart leapt. It was of course Elizabeth and her strong and dependable wife, Jennifer.

Elizabeth shook her hair loose dramatically as she lowered her hood, the stunning fiery hair of hers having not changed a bit. She wore a single plait amidst the cloud of natural curls and her green eyes continued to flash with the same hope and excitement that it had seen in their last meeting together. Leaving her stunned wife staring in awe at the fragile and broken tree, a tree that looked quite different to how it was once described, she ran forwards and embraced her ancient friend. But her smile faltered and tears formed in her eyes as she did so.

'I'm so sorry,' she wept. 'I should have come sooner. I meant to come back but everything became so hazy after that night. Until the dreams, they haunted me. And I couldn't quite put the pieces together again, until the most recent one. I remembered everything, and I could feel your pain. And it broke my heart. So, we came, and so did everyone, I see!' She gazed at the remaining people at the fire and smiled gratefully.

'You're not alone,' she continued. 'We have all come back to save you. And to tell you that we are okay. That I am okay, that you helped me to become myself again … and not just me. I've carried you with me, even though I didn't know it. But you inspired me to not hide any more, to allow myself to be seen and to not be afraid to be who I am. Let me show you. You can still do that can't you? See into my world?'

'Of course!' The Tree said, but its strength was fading – it could hear the uncertainty in its own voice.

Focusing as it used to, the valley and Elizabeth swirled and dissolved, and once again The Tree was able to glimpse her life beyond what it already knew.

As the scene unfurled The Tree saw the travelling theatre company in all of its gothic splendour. Swirling black capes and lace costumes, and dramatic natural backdrops – woodland lakes, mysterious standing stones, old castle ruins. They lent themselves perfectly to the curious and creepy vision that Elizabeth brought to life from her favourite novels. She and her colleagues brought the characters and terror to life under the moonlight and the bleak shrouded moorlands. The Tree rejoiced with the cheering crowd and shuddered at the haunting dialogues and tension filled scenes as ghosts, and witches, vampires, and ghouls stalked their prey, much to the wide-eyed horror and delight of the audience.

The Tree observed the kind and gentle way that Elizabeth comforted her student actors and emboldened them to become their characters, and allow themselves to truly shine. It witnessed their expressions of gratitude as they found their voices, and indeed a family within the circle of actors, a group of outcasts who had come to find kindness and acceptance amongst each other. It saw how Elizabeth shared her own story of becoming and gave strength to the fragile, the lost, and the vulnerable as she empowered them to reconnect to the forgotten and hidden parts of themselves.

But it also saw those dark and uncertain moments. Moments where her own confidence would shake – the darkened alleyways, the quiet and foggy nighttime streets, the unexplained sound outside of the window. The Tree could see that like with all wounds, whilst partially healed, a scar will always remain. And so it was for Elizabeth. Every day was a fight, a fight that she was determined to win, but a fight nonetheless, so haunted was she by her own experiences of torment.

And there had been others. Others who sought to take her goodness for themselves. But The Tree could see Elizabeth's determination, her enjoyment, and gratitude for her wife and the life they had created being a shield against the hateful, the envious, and the disturbed people who hungered to take good things from her. And with every fight, Elizabeth emerged victorious. She won more awards, and used her fame and her money for good. The Tree saw how she and Jennifer established a foundation for those in the arts who had been stalked and abandoned. They created a safe haven where men and women alike could feel seen, heard, and safe from the cruel and twisted pursuit of those who sought to cause them harm. It gave them hope and a family of fellow actors and artists, a family that would love and accept and protect them unconditionally.

The Tree beamed at the powerful couple who stood before it. It felt proud of all that Elizabeth and Jennifer had accomplished, how their care for each other had further strengthened their bond and made them an unstoppable force to be reckoned with. But it also saw the pain they carried and the moments where hope was dim. But, no matter how distant hope became, it was always there, alongside the determination to survive and to truly become oneself. The Tree knew that these two women could have hidden in fear, that withdrawing from the world would have made them feel safe … temporarily. But what it saw was their courage to shine a light into the darkness of their past and to face the demons that they encountered head-on, rather than being paralysed in terror, or left watching and waiting in fear.

Back on the frosty hilltop, Elizabeth took a small ceremonial blade from her satchel, and carefully raised it in the hair. With her free hand she lifted the single plait of hair from her head and used the knife to cut it free. It seemed to glow with the same fire as the night when The Tree had facilitated her return. She placed it tenderly to her lips to kiss it before laying this at the foot of The Tree with the other offerings that had been brought.

'You gave me back my life,' she whispered. 'You reminded me of who I am, and I want you to know that I see you. I see the wonderful and ancient spirit that you are. I see that you are Hope, because that is what you gave back to me. Hope never dies, and I beg you, please, stay with us. Please don't go. I need you, we all still need you!'

With a final squeeze and tear-filled eyes, Elizabeth backed away from The Tree and held her wife's hand once more.

Jennifer – still not quite sure what to make of this curious burnt being in front of her – gave The Tree a respectful and grateful nod, reached out her free hand to awkwardly pat The Tree, like one might do a new puppy. The Tree chuckled to itself and gave a subtle bow to her in return.

'Thank you for your strength,' whispered The Tree. 'And for protecting each other!'

Jennifer nodded firmly and sent her own thought to The Tree. 'I know what you did, and how you protected my wife. Thank you for giving her back to me, and for giving her back to herself!'

A moment of mutual appreciation and respect passed between them both. Then led by Elizabeth, they returned to the bonfire, exchanging a mutual hand squeeze, whilst desperately trying to hide the waves of their emerging grief.

***

Four more figures remained cloaked and hooded around the bonfire. Three of them now stepped forwards, clearly a loving parent by the way he held his arms protectively around his two sons. As their faces were revealed, The Tree could see that they were brothers with what The Tree guessed as being five years difference in their ages. Both boys had dark skin and somewhat haunted and sad eyes. The Tree had seen this look of sorrow and desperation before. The ten-year-old now moved to put his arm around his younger brother, who had begun to shiver, and then looked up at his father who finally lowered his hood. The faded but still visible rope burn could be seen on his neck. It was Joshua.

The Tree greeted its old friend with both joy and relief. Joshua had not completed what he set out to do on that bleak September day. The man who stood before The Tree still appeared haunted, but after everything he had been through, was it any wonder? The Tree swelled with compassion knowing that he had had another healthy son, who no doubt was loved as much as the first.

'Welcome back, my dear friend ... I am glad that you are safe. And I am grateful that you came! How have you been?'

Joshua's serious expression broke and a smile spread across his face, so unaccustomed was he to these simple expressions of kindness and gratitude. The Tree noticed how his face, always so troubled, completely transformed when he smiled. He led his sons towards The Tree, urging them not to be afraid. Cautiously they approached and placed their cold hands against its trunk, which now swelled with heat in order to keep them warm. Joshua did the same. And as he did so, the familiar waves of colour and emotion came as The Tree beheld the conclusion to Joshua's story.

The Tree saw his return to his wife after that day ... and that something had changed profoundly within him. That he had held a semblance of hope which had ignited a drive to live – to be there for his wife, his son, and his unborn child. With love and pride, The Tree saw Joshua commencing his training as a psychiatric nurse, so determined was he to offer the same compassion and care to those whose fragile minds had fractured – a bid, no doubt, to save these troubled souls because he could not save his mother. But The Tree also felt that Joshua knew that saving his mother was an impossibility, and that no child should ever be placed in the unfair and impossible position of trying to do so. But he knew that he could save himself. And he could support the desperate and the troubled – after all, he knew what it meant to carry the wounds of despair and depression.

The Tree observed the way in which he interacted with patients. The patience, the kindness, and the tenderness that he showed. The patient way in which he listened – so careful and validating, compassionate and empathic. It marvelled at the gentle challenges that he offered, and the strong and robust containment that he offered to those who felt they were lost in the abyss. Joshua had found his way out of his own darkness and became the light that guided others out of theirs.

But The Tree also saw that his life was not without further loss or trauma. As it tuned into the souls of Joshua's sons, new images emerged – a funeral held on an ironically beautiful day. Their mother, taken way before her time. A complication during the birth of their second son due to unexplained blood loss that could not be stopped. And a split-second choice being made by the doctors to save the child ... but the cost was Joshua's wife. The Tree wept silently as he saw the stoic man at the graveside, cradling his eerily silent newborn son with one arm, the other wrapped tightly around his eldest son's shaking shoulders.

As The Tree bore witness to this scene, it wondered how Joshua had found the strength to survive. But then it saw how he looked at his two sons, and the answer to this question was clear. Love. His love for his two boys, and the love he felt for his wife were the driving force behind his determination to survive. His sons' very survival now depended solely on him, and The Tree could see from the determined look in Joshua's glistening eyes that he would not leave his children fatherless.

The painful scene of the funeral dissolved and gave way to a graduation ceremony. The Tree saw Joshua's now nine-year-old son clapping and cheering for his father as he accepted his degree from the university, now a qualified psychiatric nurse. It also saw a kind woman with long curly hair and glasses, her arm around him and Joshua's three-year old. The woman also cheered, a look of love, tenderness, and admiration in her eyes. The Tree did not know who she was but it felt her love for Joshua and his sons. And it felt their love towards her in return.

The scene gave way to a wedding. Joshua kissed his new bride – his two sons standing proudly with him as he made his vows. The Tree felt the happiness of the day but also the tinge of sadness for those who had passed. It swelled with love towards Joshua's sons, who made an emotional tribute, despite their age, to their new mother whilst their father and his bride spoke fondly (and with sadness) of the wife and best friend whom they had both lost so tragically.

'Thank you for saving my life,' came Joshua's voice, bringing The Tree back to the hilltop. 'If I had died that night my children would have had no one, and even now the thought of that terrifies me. You showed me that there was a reason to live, even if I couldn't see it myself. But I do see it now. I see it every time I look at my boys. Every time I look at my wife. Every time I remember Carrie-Anne. And every day when I listen to my patients. There are so many reasons to live, even when life is hard. I now know that we can't escape from suffering. But we can learn to push through it, to survive it. And I know we become stronger because of it!'

The Tree nodded in agreement. It had no words. So sad it felt for the losses in Joshua's life but also the relief that he had found reasons to live. It could sense his wounded soul, but also the compassion and learning that had come from his suffering, and the beautiful and genuine way in which he drew upon this to care for those in crisis.

Joshua's youngest son laid a photograph of the mother that he never knew with the other gifts bestowed upon The Tree. And whilst he had not known his mother, he knew of her sacrifice and the stories of her kindness.

The eldest son then spoke. 'Our mother was a good soul. Maybe she can guide you where you need to go. And if you see her,' his eyes now brimming with tears, 'tell her that we miss her and that we think of her every day. That we all love her!'

Joshua bent to his knees and hugged his son, drawing them both close. The Tree too joined their embrace and agreed to the little boy's request.

Wiping their eyes, Joshua and his sons bowed to The Tree and rejoined those who remained around the bonfire. After hearing Joshua's story, they too came forward and extended their embrace towards the trio ... a scene that warmed The Tree's heart.

Kindness and care had not been forgotten by humanity after all ...

***

One figure remained and now approached The Tree.

The Tree could feel its own heart quicken as it began to tremble. *Who was this?*

In their hand they carried a book – the author's name strategically covered by the bearer's hand. But what The Tree did glimpse was the ominous front cover, a foreboding building with barred windows, surrounded by a tall fortress-like wall, topped with barbed wire, and encased by mist. Just this image stirred up a feeling of apprehension in The Tree for reasons that it could not fathom.

The figure bowed to The Tree and finally lowered their hood.

The Tree gasped.

Time seemed to stand still.

The Tree gazed at the man standing before it, who gazed back and said nothing. A swell of emotion churned within The Tree's soul as shock gave way to relief ... and a surge of love burst from The Tree's heart as the truth finally dawned on it.

'You are alive!' The Tree whispered in disbelief, tears forming in its soul. 'Blessed be ... you survived!'

Thank you for saving my life, came the silent message from the man, a look of pure gratitude and gentleness upon his faintly scarred but unmistakeable face.

The Tree's soul broke as it finally allowed itself to fully embrace the truth and the waves of emotion that overcame it. Shaun was alive! By some miracle, the young prison guard had survived the brutal attack on that fateful Halloween night.

But why was he not speaking? thought The Tree, feeling both puzzled and uneasy.

As if reading The Tree's mind, Shaun came forward and laid his hands on The Tree. Before it entered into Shaun's inner world, The Tree noticed how different Shaun looked. His body shape had changed – whilst still athletically fit, The Tree noticed that the hulking man that he was becoming during his early days of the prison seemed to have given way to a much less threatening demeanour. His head remained shaved, and his face remained stubbled – no doubt to hide the scars that were still evident from the ferocity of the assault. But The Tree felt a greater sense of peace emanating from him, a peace that was distinctly absent when the young man first came to The Tree in a bid to escape the horrors of both his internal and external world.

As the hilltop scene dissolved one last time, The Tree was taken back to the aftermath of Halloween night.

It heard the loud hypnotic whir of the helicopter's blades, accompanied the shouts of paramedics and police as the bodies were recovered from the valley. It heard the triumphant shouts of random hikers as they discovered 'a guy still breathing' wrapped safely in the cage-like mesh of The Tree's branches. It saw the fragile and beaten body being lifted onto a stretcher, and into the sky as the medical team in the helicopter began their life-saving procedures.

The Tree saw the moments in the hospital where the sombre-faced doctor told Shaun that with deep regret, he would never speak again – so damaged and crushed were his vocal cords from the violence of the assault. And it saw him return to the cold and dismal one-bedroom flat – a place where the electricity ran out, where drug users would hide in the secluded courtyard to shoot-up, and where mould grew in the shower. A cold and damp hideaway where Shaun tended to his own wounds and cocooned himself, so fearful was he of further violence from the world.

When the compensation money eventually came through, something in Shaun's soul settled. He would never have to return to the prison again. The authorities who owned and ran the prison took full responsibility for the premature release of the inmate – and their failure to take seriously the threats that had been made repeatedly against their now fallen comrade.

The Tree saw how fearful Shaun was – how every sound, any sudden movement, all sent him into a place of collapse. But the money he had received gave him space. It gave him freedom. And it gave him time, time to heal, and ways in which he could find his words again, even though his voice was lost.

The Tree saw that Shaun had found a new way to escape, very different to the substances of old that had so consumed his life. And so, Shaun travelled. He explored the ancient Colosseum and Forum Romana in Italy. He wandered the streets of Rome absorbing the beauty of the ancient sites, and lost himself in aromatic delicacies of Italian cuisine. He found awe and wonderment in the unearthly pyramids of Teotihuacan. He found peace in the Colorado Rocky Mountain National Parks. He found freedom in the streets of San Francisco as he lost himself in the Japanese botanical gardens, and sailed across the bay towards the Golden Gate Bridge, and beyond the island prison of Alcatraz.

Shaun found solace in the forests and rivers of his own home country, and the serenity these places induced – unspoilt oases that were a far cry from the imposing and claustrophobic prison walls. He roamed the dark and alien world of Iceland and fell in love with the dangerous magnificence of the landscape, of volcanoes threatening to erupt, of enormous roaring waterfalls that could sweep him away into icy oblivion, and the silent and haunting ice fields where the aurora danced through the sky without care or fear.

He found peace and enlightenment as he travelled the landscape of China, visiting temples and giant Buddhas on hills, whilst contemplating his life as he walked the ancient Great Wall. He allowed his fear and dread to seep away as the warm Hawaiian oceans cleansed and bathed his fragile soul, and returned confidence to himself, basking amongst the palm trees, white sandy beaches, and tropical forests

But most of all he found his words in the valleys of Switzerland, a place that he would come to hold in his heart as the place where he would write, surrounded by the powerful waterfalls, majestic mountains, glacial lakes, and comforting riverside walks at night. It was a place where his fear truly began to dissipate. He was alone … but he was content.

The Tree saw Shaun's journey as he reconnected to his soul and found the words to express these on paper. How he would write of his experiences whilst weaving these into works of fiction. How he would heal his wounds, and in doing so, begin a journey of healing the wounded souls of others. And so began Shaun's journey as a writer.

The Tree beheld with pride the day his debut novel was published, the excitement in which the mute young man tore open the large cardboard box containing several hardback copies of his beloved work of art. He surveyed them with a mixture of relief and sorrow, that in order to find his voice, he had to first endure so much pain. But he had survived. He had escaped. He had lost his voice, but had found it again through his stories.

And it was this debut work of fiction that The Tree now realised was clutched lovingly and proudly in its dear friend's hands as he returned to the hilltop.

As Shaun lay down his book with the other gifts, a tender moment passed between them. So much had happened, and so much had changed. But The Tree felt that now and forever, both Shaun and itself would be connected. Shaun leaned casually against The Tree and with a wink lit up a cigarette – not the same type of intoxicating cigarette as before, but the memories of those days flooded them both, a reminder of those euphoric feelings from the past (but without the dreaded comedown that had followed).

Together they watched the other visitors as they mingled around the fire, sharing their own further stories of triumph and healing, as well as their experiences of The Tree. It was a beautiful sight to behold.

And Shaun was alive!

For what seemed like hours, the two fragile beings leaned against one another, so transformed they were by the courage and strength of the other. The Tree could feel that Shaun's mind and his soul were both finally at peace.

As The Tree turned its gaze towards these remarkable people gathered around the fire, it knew what was left for it to do. The valley had been sufficiently restored and thus, only a small fragment of its final silver limb remained. The Tree's life was close to its end. And there was only one thing left to do.

You can do this! Came the thought from Shaun, as he looked encouragingly at his dying friend. *I know what you are planning to do!* And with that, he put out his cigarette, wrapped his arms around The Tree, the tears stinging his eyes.

I don't want to let you go. But I know I have to … I know it's time!

The Tree's soul wept.

I will never forget you and what you did for me!

Shaun bid his friend farewell. He bowed to The Tree and returned to the circle, surrounded by the still burning candles that flickered in the cool night air.

Through its tears, The Tree wanted to give a final gift to its triumphant friends. It wanted the magic of its ancient soul to be carried with the survivors so that its legacy would not be lost, so that it would continue. They would know what to do if they simply listened to their hearts, and like the valley, this final parting gift could restore some semblance of harmony back into the world and be used in a manner that would honour The Tree.

Summoning all of its strength, the familiar pain tore through The Tree's broken body, and the remnants of the final silver branch began to crack and loosen from The Tree's trunk.

The Tree's final silver branch fell.

IV

The fallen branch transformed into sparkling silver slices of wood – no bigger or thicker than a coin – one for each of the remaining visitors to take away.

The visitors ceased their conversations and watched in silence as the spectacle unfolded, and one by one they took a piece of silver.

As these gifts were gathered and safely stored by each person, a dazzling spectacle occurred. The waves of electrically charged colour and splendour continued to weave and undulate through the sky, bathing the inhabitants of the hilltop in an ethereal glow. But now, particles of sparkling dust rained down onto The Tree and the crowd who gathered around it, seeming to be revitalised by its enriching life-force.

Like the hundreds of candles left by the procession of people, The Tree began to glow – the light it emanated becoming so bright that the visitors shielded their eyes. But once the light faded, they beheld something wonderous. They were able to see The Tree in all its magnificence … its triumph … its majestic glory … and its stunning beauty that had changed with the seasons and at the whim and will of the mood of those who had came to love this ancient being. Their eyes wide, and with their mouths open in shock, the remaining crowd cheered and expressed their jubilation.

The exultant crowd shouted and jumped for joy, sobbing and cheering in their embraces, so relieved were they to see the return of their beloved tree. But in their joy and excitement, they could not see the truth, so desperate were they to believe that The Tree was not dying, that it could be saved by their love. And indeed, that they could be the ones to save it, as they themselves had once been saved.

The Tree willed its last drops of life force to dazzle and soothe – to emblazon in the minds and souls of its loved ones that hope was not lost, and that healing does indeed occur even when lost in the depths of despair.

And so, the visitors – having shared their stories once more, and left their precious gifts for The Tree – expressed their final sentiments of gratitude to the dazzling being before them, satisfied that their gifts and their pilgrimage had indeed saved the soul of their beloved protector.

And one by one, following a respectful bow from each of them, they made their way through the stone circle for the very last time, and wandered down the hillside through the frosty night and into the darkened valley. Even the two abnormally large and tiger-like ginger cats stopped at the edge of the hilltop and turned to offer a final acknowledgement to The Tree for the continued life that its silver sap had given them. The two regal felines nodded respectfully at The Tree with tears glistening in the huge green and hazel eyes.

The Tree bowed respectfully towards them, swished its renewed branches in return, and bid them a silent farewell, but not before their impeccable eyesight caught sight of the true image of The Tree behind the illusion that it had created.

V

As the cats and the last of the visitors disappeared from the hilltop, the breathtaking image of The Tree began to falter and flicker. The illusion that had enchanted all those whom had come to share their stories of healing and love with The Tree could not be sustained any longer.

The Tree's life was waning. And so too was its power. It felt weak. Its magic was spent.

The Tree felt alone, but its soul felt cleansed. The valley had returned. And so had the people it loved. They were safe ... and they had survived. And they would continue to heal and grow. The Tree had also atoned for its own fall from grace, and had finally found forgiveness within its heart.

But what am I to do now?

In the distance, amidst the sparkling frost, The Tree felt a presence. A lone spirit was shimmering and hovering on the edge of the hilltop.

'You don't have to do that anymore,' came the quiet child's voice, a kind and courageous voice that The Tree recognised instantly.

And then another sound. The soft tinkle of a bell and a gentle and comforting bleat. Alongside the lone childlike figure, another presence could be felt, the ghostly spectre of a sweet and friendly goat.

Tears welled in its heart and wept from the cracks of its blackened and fragile bark. The flickering illusion of The Tree finally faded, revealing the truth of its small, withered and decaying body.

Under the glorious and luminous arcs of the aurora dancing through the sky, the small spirit came closer – the familiar sound of crutches crunching on the frosty ground.

The Tree felt its heart lift as it greeted its old friends, and its soul filled with both love and the painful ache of grief.

Luke's spirit smiled kindly up at The Tree, tears forming in his large brown saucer-like eyes as he laid his hands on The Tree's ravaged trunk. Aussie, his faithful companion, nestled and rubbed his head affectionately against the bark.

'You've been through so much,' said Luke, his gentle voice much older and wiser than his years.

'But it's okay now. I am here. And you can let go. They sent me because they know that you are afraid. That you feel alone, but I am here. And we've come to take you home, if you let us.'

'My dear friend,' said The Tree through its silent sobs. 'I have missed you deeply, and I am so thankful that you are here.'

'I never left,' the Luke said softly. 'I have been waiting for this day. I have been waiting for you!'

'You never left? But why? You must have felt so alone!' replied The Tree, its heart breaking. 'I heard your mother's song, and I hoped you were at peace.'

'I am. I have been. And I have been with Aussie … They of course let me keep him with me whilst I waited!' Luke gazed lovingly at his bleating best friend. 'They told me that this was my destiny, that I had to be the one to help you. That only I could help you to finally let go.'

'Who are they?" asked The Tree, puzzled and growing fearful.

Luke simply smiled and remained silent.

The Tree knew … They were ancient beings, such as itself.

'But I can't let go,' said The Tree, with a hint of desperation in its voice. 'There is still so much I could do, I know that now. I know that all that I gave was not in vain. I know now who I am … and what I am! I now have faith in what we can do, and faith in humanity. I know all of that now!'

The spirit of Luke smiled sadly and nodded.

'Indeed, you do, but there will be others. There are always others! And you have done all that you can. You have fulfilled your destiny as it was meant to be in this life. But you must now trust that those whom you have helped will continue to heal, to learn, to grow, on their own! And trust that through their healing, others too will be transformed!'

The Tree searched its soul and knew this to be true. It had seen and heard throughout its life how a single drop can cause a cascade of ripples to affect the surrounding water. It knew that by making a difference to just one person, the lives of others can also be given meaning, and will be given hope.

Aussie bleated and nodded in agreement.

'But I can help them. I can keep helping them! I've done it before!' pleaded The Tree.

Luke calmly placed his hand on The Tree, and it felt its soul settle.

'Of course,' said Luke patiently. 'But that is no longer your role. You have inspired. You have given compassion. You have protected. You have enabled them to make meaning, to find the words for their suffering and pain, and most importantly, you have given them hope. But as you know, you are not infinite. None of us are! And you have earned your time to rest, to finally know the peace that you have afforded others.'

The Tree remained silent. It knew that Luke spoke the truth. And it allowed itself to search its own soul and accept a truth of its own.

'I'm afraid. I don't want to die!' whispered The Tree, its voice quivering.

'I know,' said Luke tenderly, and embraced The Tree. 'I was afraid too, but it was you who helped me to feel less alone in the world. It was your kindness, your presence, and your strength that gave me the courage to fight, but also to let go. That was your gift to me. And now in return, this is my gift to you.'

Luke's chid-like spirit smiled warmly at its friend and wrapped its ghostly arms around The Tree, in one final embrace of love and gratitude. Aussie nestled in too.

'The others are waiting for you,' he whispered to The Tree. He pulled back and extended his small arm, letting the sliver crutches fall to the ground and dissolve into the earth.

'Take my hand,' Luke said. 'You are not alone … it is time!'

In that moment, a feeling of both peace and clarity overcame The Tree. It no longer felt afraid because it was not alone, but it also remembered the truth that could only be recalled at the end. The truth was that its own death was inevitable, and this was so for all beings like itself.

The Tree knew that for the people that it loved and cared for to truly appreciate life – and the lives they would create for themselves – they must come to know the impermanence of existence.

The Tree knew that it must die. It must die so that others could live. It must die so that they could marvel in the beauty of all that life has to offer – the joy, the sorrow, the tragedy and the triumphs – but only if they have the courage to take the risk to embrace life and all that it has to offer. And of course, they must be willing to lose it.

With both sadness and peace in its heart, The Tree was ready to be released from its own life.

The Tree's burnt and blackened bark turn pale, and slowly it began to crumble like ash until there was nothing left of the magnificent tree that once was, its ashes being absorbed into the earth, along with the gifts of love brought by the visitors.

And out of the dust that remained, the childlike Spirit of The Tree stood – his skin a translucent bark, and his hair and clothes made of glowing leaves. The Spirit of The Tree reached out and took Luke's hand, who smiled lovingly at his new companion and then back towards Aussie, his old one.

The valley fell silent but for the howl of the wind, and from the animals, and the surrounding trees ... and the soft distant weeping of the visitors as they crossed the river,

Under the dazzling array of stars and constellations, surrounded by the glow of a hundred candles – and feeling the love, gratitude and hope of the people whom The Tree had helped and had come to care for – The Tree felt a sense of peace finally return to its soul.

The wise but frightened Spirit of The Tree held Luke's hand tightly, and with their eyes fixed firmly on the horizon, the three spirits rose together from the earth and faded into the dancing emerald and turquoise splendour that weaved so elegantly through the starlit sky.

So it was, on that beautiful winter solstice in the year 2030, The Tree's life of triumph and tragedy came to an end, and on that night in particular, without entirely knowing why, the whole world shone a little less bright because of it...but had been changed forever!

EPILOGUE

Darkness.

Echoes of The Tree's soul stirred ...

A strange and curious sensation could be felt. Its consciousness splitting, followed by a twinge of awareness. How long this would last, it could not be certain. But there were glimpses of something. Something wonderful ...

Its consciousness briefly found itself in the silver wooden ring of a lawyer from Hong Kong, gifted to her by a grateful assistant. And it heard the powerful words of her arguments that brought perpetrators of brutality to justice in a court of law ...

It felt itself in the sturdy wooden gate that opened to greet its visitors. It heard the sounds of braying donkeys in the distance and the laughter of children who looked just like Luke as they played with the docile animals, and walked them carefully through fields of flowers under the supervision of two siblings, siblings who continued their grandparents' legacy of kindness and gratitude ...

It found itself in the robust wooden structure of the comfortable armchair as a courageous man, once on the edge of life himself, offered words of compassion and hope, but also listened with care and respect to the vulnerable souls who too found themselves losing faith in life, giving them a space to be heard and to feel held ...

It felt its essence in the hundreds of wooden beehives so carefully constructed in the valley of waterfalls, where a beekeeper lovingly tended to his bees, facilitating new life, and always sparing a jar of honey for his best friend whenever he visited ...

It found itself in the wooden legs of a tripod that supported an enormous telescope. And it heard the passion and enthusiasm of the archaeologist and stargazer who shared his knowledge and wonders of the cosmos and constellations with the enrapt students that attended his nighttime classes amidst the breathtaking structures of the Mexican pyramids ...

It awoke to the sound of haunting violin music as it found itself in the wood of the musical instrument – a violin played lovingly by the daughter of The Retreat's leader. And it observed the tear-filled eyes of the tranquil men who gathered in a circle of an ever-blooming apple orchard, surrounded by love and validation, finally connecting to their own sense of worth ...

It heard the sound of laughter, sobs, and roars of applause from an audience, and found itself in the wooden boards of a theatre stage – a necessary part of a travelling theatre company that brought gothic tales to life and shared messages of acceptance and uniqueness. A place for both the audience and performers to shine without fear or shame, and truly become who they were always meant to be ...

It found itself in the writing desk of a silent man who gazed out at the lakes and mountains from his woodland cabin, writing stories that would heal and inspire his readers ...

And before The Tree's spirit faded back into the soul of universe, it found itself in the pages of a book ... a book written by a once tortured and tormented soul. A book about a wise and ancient tree whose spirit, compassion, and fall from grace would forever touch the lives of all those who it met. And all those who would read its story ...

Somewhere beneath a dark and heavy sky and amidst a picturesque valley, a stirring occurred deep within the earth of a mountainous hilltop. A silver apple, long since buried, began to hum with electricity until a pulse of energy was released like a shockwave, spreading throughout the hill and surrounding forests.

A sprinkling of rain fell from the sky accompanied by the rumble of thunder. And the sound of birds could be heard returning to the surrounding trees. A warm and gentle wind blew through the valley, bringing with it the scent of jasmine and a colony of colourful dancing butterflies and bees. Something was stirring in the ether ...

The silver apple, hidden within the earth – infused with gifts from the past – cracked open, and a single shoot burst forth from its core. The small but sturdy green shoot broke through the earth with all its strength.

As if to greet it, a thin shaft of sunlight split through the cloud illuminating the little plant, and the unmistakeable presence of the twelve tiny silver limbs that glinted and sparkled as they reached skywards.

Where there was once tragedy and triumph, hope and despair... new life would flourish again!

About the Author

R.D.K. Marjoram is the pen name of Ryan Bennett-Clarke, a psychotherapist and clinical supervisor with over two decades of experience exploring the depths of the human mind. Born and raised in Suffolk, Ryan moved to Nottingham in 1999 to study and has called it home ever since. A lifelong devotee of ghost stories, horror, and all things mysterious, he blends psychological insight with a passion for the strange and the spiritual to create fiction that lingers long after the final page. He lives with his husband and two beloved cats, and when he isn't writing, he can often be found reading by candlelight, wandering historic ruins, exploring forests and mountains, or dreaming up tales designed to both inspire and sometimes chill the souls of his readers.

www.ingramcontent.com/pod-product-compliance
Ingram Content Group UK Ltd.
Pitfield, Milton Keynes, MK11 3LW, UK
UKHW041124171025
464044UK00002B/81

9 781789 635713